Praise for
Deanie Francis Mills
and *Ordeal*

"*Ordeal* is a searing thriller as current as tomorrow's headlines and as tragically real as the aftermath of a terrorist attack. [This] book elevates Deanie Francis Mills to stand beside the top authors of suspense fiction. . . . She captures the horror of a woman confronted with a violent, forbidden past all too well. She is just as deft in her portrayal of that same woman's fierce struggle to save her new family. Gripping and compelling reading."
—Ann Rule

"Rarely do such fine writing and such a compelling story come together in a single novel. With characters so real we feel that we already know them, this gut-punching tale about the past returning to haunt the present—and one woman's journey into her past—holds us in its relentless grip from page one. We hit the last page regretting only that our harrowing journey through Deanie Francis Mills's w⎯⎯⎯⎯ ⎯⎯⎯⎯⎯⎯⎯⎯⎯⎯ ⎯⎯⎯⎯⎯ ⎯⎯aver

"*Ordeal* is pure k⎯⎯⎯⎯⎯⎯⎯⎯⎯⎯⎯⎯⎯⎯⎯⎯se and far too real f⎯⎯⎯⎯⎯⎯⎯⎯⎯⎯⎯⎯⎯⎯⎯hite

"*Ordeal* is as good ⎯⎯ ⎯⎯⎯⎯⎯⎯ ge⎯⎯ ⎯⎯⎯⎯ Olsen

continued on next page . . .

More Praise for
Ordeal

"A gripping, always unpredictable page-turner . . .
Mills writes with authority and confidence . . .
fraught with suspense."—*Lubbock Avalanche-Journal*

"Adds an arresting new dimension to the concept
of mother love."   —*Kirkus Reviews*

"A taut hardcover debut . . . a fast-moving plot,
infusions of Cherokee culture and vivid
characters help drive the action as Mills explores
the sordid reality behind the Oklahoma bombing
headlines."   —*Publishers Weekly*

"Mills's characters are vivid and her plot is all too
believable. This book places her in the same high
caliber as Ridley Pearson."
        —*Lake Worth Herald and Coastal Observer*

"*Ordeal* is all too believable in today's world of
violence and anti-government sentiment. That,
coupled with Mills's superb storytelling skills,
makes this one novel you won't want to put down."
                    —*Gazette Telegraph*

"This novel is swift and unpredictable."
                    —*Bookman News*

Praise for Deanie Francis Mills and Her Other Novels

"A spine-tingling tale of suspense full of startling twists and surprising developments."—Judith Kelman

"Mills knows how to take you down labyrinthine pathways to surprising revelations. . . . Satisfying."
—Billie Sue Mosiman, Edgar Award–nominated author of *Night Cruise*

"Deanie Francis Mills brings suspense and terror directly into the heart of every parent. . . . If this chiller doesn't keep you on the edge of your chair, not much will!"   —John Saul

"Mills writes the kind of book that Alfred Hitchcock loved to film. She's very, very good."
—Ed Gorman, *Mystery Scene*

TORCH

Deanie Francis Mills

A SIGNET BOOK

SIGNET
Published by New American Library, a division of
Penguin Putnam Inc., 375 Hudson Street,
New York, New York 10014, U.S.A.
Penguin Books Ltd, 27 Wrights Lane,
London W8 5TZ, England
Penguin Books Australia Ltd, Ringwood,
Victoria, Australia
Penguin Books Canada Ltd, 10 Alcorn Avenue,
Toronto, Ontario, Canada M4V 3B2
Penguin Books (N.Z.) Ltd, 182–190 Wairau Road,
Auckland 10, New Zealand

Penguin Books Ltd, Registered Offices:
Harmondsworth, Middlesex, England

First published by Signet, an imprint of New American Library,
a division of Penguin Putnam Inc.

First Printing, October 1999
10 9 8 7 6 5 4 3 2 1

 REGISTERED TRADEMARK—MARCA REGISTRADA

Printed in the United States of America

PUBLISHER'S NOTE
This is a work of fiction. Names, characters, places, and incidents either are
the product of the author's imagination or are used fictitiously, and any resem-
blance to actual persons, living or dead, events, or locales is entirely
coincidental.

For Kent,
who after twenty-five years
can still light my fire

All. . . . Then all afire with me. . . .
Hell is empty,
And all the devils are here.
William Shakespeare
The Tempest
Act I, Scene ii

torch: term used by fire investigators
when referring to an arsonist.

PART I

Smoldering Combustion

. . . and Time, a maniac scattering dust
And Life, a Fury slinging flame.

Alfred, Lord Tennyson
In Memorium, A.H.H. (1833–1850)

Chapter One

It was the deadness that consumed him.

As he went about his days, it nibbled at the numbness that was his soul, chewed at the emptiness that was his life, devoured the quiet desperation that was his personality, sucked at his existence until parts of him began to vanish into the void, taking him further and further outside himself.

To cope, he created a false self. This false self functioned in the real world. It made endearing remarks to the wife for whom he felt no love, since after all, he felt nothing, ever. It parented the son who was a constant source of disappointment to him, because there was no life there that he could steal; his son, his adopted son, was too much like himself for him to live through the boy vicariously. The false self counseled the patients who came to him suffering pain he envied, for the lifelessness that ate away at him daily left only unfeeling behind, only deadness.

His colleagues found him aloof. His wife thought he was depressed. His patients mistook his silence for thoughtfulness. His son returned his indifference with disinterest.

Nobody knew he was, in effect, a zombie. The walking dead.

Deadness was the only truth of his life. Everything else was a lie.

From time to time, he considered going into therapy

himself. He could select an analyst who did not know him. But he knew what would happen. He would be stamped with an inaccurate label and put on trendy medication that would not help. There was no magic pill for deadness.

The deadness was a stillness at the core of him, a malignant black hole that encroached, bit by evil bit, throughout his being.

Sometimes he lay awake at night and wondered what would happen if his existence were entirely swallowed up by the deadness. Just the thought of it would leave him drenched in a cold sweat, unable to breathe, suffocated by the black terror of it.

Fear, then. He could still feel fear.

What was left of his true self, which had not been consumed by the nothingness, still struggled to find something, somewhere that would make him feel alive again, that would have the strength to fight back the deadness.

And then one day, quite by accident, as he was stoking the fire in the fireplace, a stray spark drifted innocent as a firefly and landed without ceremony on the soft afghan his wife threw over her feet when she rested them on the hassock while sitting in front of the fireplace. The afghan had been left in a heap on the hassock, and the spark settled comfortably within the depths of one fluffy fold.

A tiny wisp of smoke spiraled up.

As he watched, transfixed, the smoke increased in density, and then suddenly, a minute flame—no bigger than that of a tiny birthday candle—sprung forth from the afghan.

It winked at him.

The white afghan curled blackly into the flame, and the fire grew.

He felt a stirring in his loins.

As the afghan began to disappear into the blaze, he felt the warmth of the fire against his face, its intensity and hot power and life, igniting within him an answering spark. His heart pounded with the sizzle and surge of the flames, and he laughed aloud.

The fire looked at him, and he gazed back into it with something akin to adoration. In that moment, he lost all sense of time.

When the smoke detector began its high-pitched squeal, his whole body jerked. Then his wife rushed into the room and screamed his name.

Almost without thought, he leapt to his feet, grabbed the fire extinguisher from its place in a nearby corner of the room, fumbled with it for a few timeless moments, then directed its powerful spray toward the afghan and the hassock, which was now burning as well.

Acrid smoke choked the room.

His wife stumbled, coughing, toward the sliding glass door that led to the patio, and opened it wide.

The flames did not want to die.

Sadly he pummeled them until the fire extinguisher was empty. Smoke poured from the burned-out top of the hassock, while the afghan lay in a miserable mess of melted and singed nylon. It reeked of foul fumes that caught in his throat.

The smoke detector continued to shriek.

"What happened?" yelled his wife, but he ignored her. Hoisting the hassock into his arms, he carried it quickly out onto the patio. He had to hurry, because it was surprisingly hot, and he didn't want to get burned. Once outside, he doused the hassock thoroughly with water from the garden hose. Through the still-opened patio door, he could see his wife open all the windows in the room, then stand on top of a chair in order to reach the smoke detector and disconnect it.

Absently he reminded himself to reconnect it later.

He could feel the blood coursing throughout his body with each surge and thrust of his heart.

For one brief, exalted moment, when he'd gazed into the flames and seen them looking back at him, he'd felt himself ignite with the fire of life in all its passion and glory.

A phoenix, rising from the flames of his own dead self.

But the exhultation had been all too brief, snuffed out by his wife's scream. Now all that was left was the sodden ash of his own cold, dead soul.

As he felt the flush fade from his skin, leaving him clammy and cool, his analytic mind attempted to explain the thrill, the rush he'd felt with the fire.

He thought of his dad, a strapping, lusty firefighter with the Fire Department of New York, who often took his only son with him on the fire truck to stamp out blazes in the south Bronx. That had been exciting, no doubt about it. His own name, Keegan, was a Gaelic name that meant "son of fire" or "little fiery one."

Then his dad had walked out on the family when Keegan was only twelve, and there had been no more fires. Only his alcoholic mother and her booze-heightened moods of hilarity, followed by violent rages and dramatic suicide attempts. Keegan never blamed his dad for leaving. He only envied him his courage.

The boy Keegan had survived by withdrawing into himself, so deeply into himself, in fact, that at some point along the way he got lost.

By the time his mother had died, when Keegan was eighteen, leaving behind a paltry life insurance policy that managed to pay for her burial expenses and a few years of college for Keegan, he'd felt nothing at all.

When the hassock was completely waterlogged, Keegan turned off the hose and rewound it. Putting out the fire had not been the source of Keegan's elation.

Setting it had been.

Watching it come to life.

Seeing it consume everything around it like an insatiable monster.

Gazing into its eye and discovering his own reflection in it.

The hassock had become a sepulcher for the fire. As Keegan stood staring at it, the deadness came gnawing back into him, licking at the aliveness he had felt for that one fervid, fiery moment, diminishing it, releasing as it did so a sinister, smoky tendril of an idea into his parched mind.

It occurred to him that, technically, he had not actually set the fire. It had been an accident. He smiled to himself. Talk about a Freudian slip!

He could set another fire, though, one that would not leave any witnesses who would scream at him to put it out.

Just the idea alone sent a welcome hot flush throughout his body, a tingle not unlike sexual arousal.

Cold thoughts intruded, scattering goose bumps over his flesh. What if he got caught? He could lose everything he had built for himself through the years—his position at the university, his practice, his family and home. If he went to jail, he would lose everything.

The deadness spoke to him. It said, *What does it matter? It means nothing to you anyway.*

A sick thrill of excitement and fear sizzled through his stomach. The warmth came flooding back.

He would set another fire.

"Yes, Mrs. Rodriguez. I was aware that you were divorced from Juan," said Jillian Ross in her best butter-smooth soothing tones, the telephone receiver held cocked against her shoulder, fingertips poised over the computer keyboard. "But I'm doing a profile of Mr. Rodgriguez for the *Dallas Mirror*, and I usually try to speak to as many friends and relatives of a subject as I can, in order to get a fully rounded picture."

The answering voice was suspicious. "I never heard of the *Dallas Mirror*. What's that?"

"It's an alternative weekly newspaper," said Jillian. "We specialize in investigative reporting. We're not owned by local businesspeople, but are part of a nationwide chain, so we aren't afraid to tackle controversial issues."

"Well, I can tell you that somebody damn well better start investigating that son of a bitch Juan. You know he's planning to run for the city council in the fall, don't you?"

"Yes, I was aware of that," said Jillian patiently.

"Being the first Latino school superintendent in Dallas wasn't enough for him. Suddenly an Anglo wife is no longer useful to him. And now he's gone and moved into Little Mexico. What the hell is that all about?" Her voice was harsh and scornful, and Jillian could hear her lighting a cigarette and taking a drag.

"My hunch is that, by moving into a fifty-year-old housing project in one of the worst neighborhoods in Dallas," said Jillian calmly, "he will present a sympathetic, blue-collar image to the Hispanic voting block."

The ex-wife of Juan Rodriguez made an unflattering, derisive snort into the phone. "He's such a damn phony," she said. "Ask him where he sleeps at night. If he says he sleeps at Little Mexico, he's an even bigger liar than I thought."

"Oh?" prompted Jillian. "Where does he sleep?"

"In a swanky apartment complex over in Prestonwood," answered Nancy Rodriguez, referring to an upscale north Dallas neighborhood.

Jillian's fingers flew over the keyboard.

"And ask him who built those apartments."

"Who?" responded Jillian innocently.

"What is that noise? Are you writing down what I say?"

"Don't worry about it," said Jillian. "This is a crowded newspaper office. Lots of reporters working on lots of stories."

"I don't give a shit anyway. Juan's construction business built those apartments. It's the same business

that built that new magnet school in south Dallas that
Juan rammed through the school board and then the
bond election. I'm not saying that they didn't need
that school, you understand. But nobody knew that
Juan's company had the inside track on the bids and
that he got very, very rich off that contract."

Jillian smelled blood. This was her second confir-
mation of the rumor. "What construction business?"
she said in her best confused voice. "I wasn't aware
that Juan Rodriguez had any ties to any construction
businesses."

"It's a dummy corporation. Not in his name."

"Do you have proof of this, Mrs. Rodriguez?"
prompted Jillian.

*"Who do you think kept the son of a bitch's books
all those years? I know how to operate a copy machine, too."*

Jillian's heart started to pound and her palms to
sweat—a sure sign she was on a trail that was growing
hotter by the minute. God, she loved her job.

Miles Tennyson, her editor, materialized at the corner of her desk and drew his finger across his throat.
He looked extremely agitated, but then, Miles was always agitated.

"Mrs. Rodriguez? Would you be willing to share
this information with me? This is something that I
think the voters would find very interesting."

"No shit."

"Could I come by your house some time tomorrow
and meet with you?"

"Could you come after I get off work?"

"Of course. Any time at your convenience."

"If you come after the kids are in bed, I can give
you all the time you need. Say, nine o'clock?"

Jillian agreed, wrote down the address on a piece
of scribbled-on scratch paper, and hung up. Miles was
already headed for his office. She followed him and
shut the door. If Miles wanted to talk to her in his
office, then it was serious. "What's up?"

"We're being sued," he said miserably. "We meaning you and the paper. Again." He scrounged in his desk for some aspirin, dropped them on the floor, and hunched down beneath his desk to grapple for them.

"Relax, Miles," said Jillian with a smile. "We've been through this before. Which story is it this time?"

From beneath his desk, he mumbled, "Abraham Artemis." He bumped his head on the underside of the desk and cursed.

"Oh, yeah. For that story when we said he was using his position as the new Black Panther president to bring in more listeners for his radio talk show, and that he was really a power-hungry, rabble-rousing, opportunistic phony who was only trying to stir up racial unrest in order to cover up his own criminal record so he could run for mayor? That story?"

With a glare at Jillian, Miles threw the aspirin down the back of his throat and gulped from a diet Coke can. "*We* didn't say it, Jillian. *You* said it. You. It's always you getting us sued."

"And I said absolutely not one thing that was not backed up by solid facts and sound sources. Legal checked it out, Miles, remember? Let them handle it."

He heaved a mighty sigh and put his head in his hands. Miles Tennyson was almost too good-looking to be real, with a near-perfect body, black hair, and electric blue eyes that would make any woman swoon—to no avail, of course, since he was gay. Jillian adored him and considered it yet one more extraordinarily lucky aspect of her life that she had him as an editor. Many was the night they'd sat up together in the empty *Mirror* offices until dawn, sweating over every word in one of her stories, trimming down the over-researched details, sharpening, honing, laboring and laughing with the hilarity of the punch-drunk while slurping bad coffee to stay awake.

Miles was biting his nails again. It was his only bad habit, and Jillian found it endearing. "It'll be all right, really," she said. "To prove libel, you have to prove malice, and there was nothing malicious about that story. It was all true."

"Do you know how much sleep I've lost because of you?" he demanded. "Do you have any idea how I lie awake the night before one of your pieces comes out, sweating and fretting that we'll get sued again? Jesus."

"You need a new boyfriend," teased Jillian with a wicked grin. "Somebody to help you release all that pent-up tension."

"You have a dirty little mind."

"Yeah, I know. Isn't it great?"

He sighed again. "So how's the Rodriguez story coming along?"

"Terrific." She filled him in on the conversation with the ex-wife and added, "He's having this big Cinco de Mayo rally in Little Mexico tonight. I'm going down there to check out the scene. It could get rowdy, especially if Artemis shows up to challenge him." Jillian was referring to the growing tension in the city between Hispanic and black factions, particularly in the schools. Hispanics had replaced blacks as the dominant minority in the city, their numbers growing all the time, and they wanted their fair share of the pie that blacks had wrested from the Anglos in years of angry confrontations, not just in picketed demonstrations, but at City Hall as well, where council people had been known to take swings at each other and council meetings erupt into chaos.

Some black city council members had been obnoxiously vocal throughout the eighties and early nineties, with much resulting unrest in the city, and city government had tended to overreact in response, making just about every major decision based on racial equality, even when race was not the issue. Consequently, tensions between blacks and whites were beginning to ease as blacks increased in number in city jobs, school administrative positions, police, and so on. But as the Hispanics gained in population, their resentment at

being ignored while blacks were placated began to
grow. Now they were trying some of the same tactics
against the blacks that the blacks had used against the
white power structure.

"You're going to Little Mexico?" asked Miles
doubtfully. "Take somebody with you."

"I am," said Jillian. "I'm taking Randi. She's going
to be my photographer."

"I'm not *talking* about a photographer, Jillian. I'm
talking about some kind of goddamned bodyguard.
Jesus."

"We'll be fine," she said.

Miles rubbed his forehead. "Look, I know you're
an independent gal. I admire that in you. But this is
a goddamned tenement slum we're talking about here.
Even the cops don't go there without bulletproof
vests, okay? Why don't you take your big, beefy boyfriend? He could look after you."

"I don't need looking after, Miles. And Derek has
a new opening tonight."

"They're opening *another* Power Play gym? How
many does that make?"

"Four. And he's in negotiations to do an
infomercial."

Miles groaned. "God, that's all we need. Some other
buffed-up toothy guy proclaiming the evils of fat."

Jillian grinned. "Like you've ever had a problem in
that area."

"Hey, I work out."

"Well, then, I rest my case." With a grin she glanced
at her watch. "I've gotta go pick up Randi. We're
going to swing by the new gym and wish Derek luck
on our way to Little Mexico."

"Yeah, right. Like a Power Play gym is going to be
located anywhere *near* Little Mexico."

Laughing, Jillian said, "Okay, okay. So it's a little
out of the way. What do I care? I've got the top down
on the Mustang. I can work on my tan. It's a beautiful
day. Not that you would notice."

She turned toward the door.

"Hey."

Jillian turned back.

"Be careful, okay?"

"Always." She blew him a kiss.

At her desk she gathered up her overstuffed tote bag, dropped a spiral notebook into it, and headed for the door. The Mirror offices were located downtown on Commerce, in a renovated warehouse. The atmosphere was funky and fun, with hardwood floors, twenty-foot ceilings, brick walls, and exposed pipes overhead, painted black. It had the bustle and buzz of all newspaper offices, with stacks of newspapers in every conceivable corner and busy people clacking on keyboards and talking on the phone and hurrying back and forth.

Jillian loved it, loved every aspect of it.

She even loved working downtown, with a forty-five-minute commute. A great deal of time and money had been spent on downtown Dallas in recent years. What had once been a derelict and decrepit part of the city was now a popular tourist area—from the cavernous shopper's paradise, the West End Marketplace, to Dealey Plaza and the Sixth-Floor Museum, an assassination-buff's dream located in the infamous School Book Depository. Downtown Dallas was slowly regaining the edge it had lost when all the fun seemed to have bled out of the city and into the suburbs. The Cowboys might be in Irving and Six Flags Over Texas in Arlington, but the old girl still had a little life in her.

Even though fighting traffic and the never-ending roadway construction sites to get there was a royal pain, Jillian loved the energy and pace of working downtown. She loved chasing down leads on a story so hot it made her blood boil. She loved zipping around the Dallas-Fort Worth Metroplex in her candy-apple-red '68 Mustang convertible. And she loved stripping away the facade of so many of the

city's movers and shakers, exposing them in the pages
of the *Mirror* for the phonies they were.

Though she'd been in journalism for well over ten
years, Jillian had never had such an invigorating job.
She'd worked for the *Village Voice* in New York, the
Washington Post, and the *Dallas Times Herald* before
it closed up shop. But most newspapers, she'd discovered to her immense frustration, had certain sacred
cows she was not allowed to touch, for one political
or financial reason or another. But the *Mirror* had no
sacred cows, and she'd sunk her teeth into her job
with relish.

Not only did she do at least one major investigative
story a month, but she had her weekly column, "Reflections," in which she lampooned whichever issue
struck her fancy. She'd been well rewarded, not just
financially, but with Dallas Press Club Katie awards,
Texas Headliner awards, Dallas Bar Association Phil-
bin awards, and the coveted H.L. Mencken Writing
award, given annually to one newspaper columnist in
America.

Jillian had made more than a few enemies along the
way. Most people, she'd learned, didn't like reading
the truth about themselves in the paper. And even
though she received many offers from rival papers and
even television networks, she turned them all down.
Nothing could compete with the satisfaction she had
right now, every day of her life.

Not to mention the fact that nothing could induce
her to leave the best-looking guy in the whole damn
city. Correction. The best-looking guy who was not
gay.

The best-looking guy who, the first time he kissed
her, made her knees buckle. Literally.

As Jillian tossed her tote into the white leather passenger bucket seat of the Mustang, she got in and
checked her makeup in the rearview mirror, lifting her
designer sunglasses for a closer look. She considered
having a boyfriend like Derek Thorsen to be another

little miracle of her lucky life. There he was, sur-rounded by gorgeous, buffed women all day long, and who did he choose? Jillian Ross. Go figure.

Not that she'd never had a man in her life. She could flirt with the best of them, and now that her twenties were behind her, she was certainly no virgin.

But this man . . . mmmhmmm. This man.

Jillian had read someplace that most women had at least one affair like this in their lifetime: at least one man who, while maybe not the most intellectually stimulating, nonetheless filled her with sexual excite-ment, a man who made her feel desirable, alive, sexu-ally on fire.

She'd read it, all right, but she'd never believed it would actually happen to her.

Supermodels, maybe. Movie stars six feet tall who weighed a hundred pounds. But not her.

While she reapplied her lip gloss, Jillian privately acknowledged that her looks were fairly striking—from the neck up. Unlike most redheads, her complex-ion was not fair or freckled. It was coppery, bronzed from all that Sunbelt driving around in a convertible. Her eyes were deep brown, but her hair was her best feature, hands-down. It fell in a tangled mass of au-burn curls down below her shoulders and flew like a banner behind her when she was careening along at seventy miles an hour on one of the huge freeway mix-masters that looped in and out of the city.

It was her body that was the problem. At five feet four inches tall, she had a classic hourglass figure that would have been considered sexy in Marilyn Monroe's day, but had been a constant aggravation to Jillian since junior high. Though the other girls had envied her big breasts, they didn't realize what a constant struggle she had with her weight, which fluctuated as high as a hundred and fifty pounds. She could hide it behind classic blazers and the ubiquitous black, but as the fashions grew more and more shrink-wrapped and the fashion models more and more emaciated, Jillian's battle of the bulge finally sent her, in near-despair, to a Power Play gym and into the capable hands of Derek Thorsen.

At thirty, he was four years younger than Jillian. He stood six-two and possessed not a single muscle that wasn't toned and buffed to near-perfection. His was the classic blond-haired blue-eyed beauty, and it didn't occur to her that he might be the least bit attracted to her, at least, not like she was to him.

But Jillian was nothing if not a workhorse, and she never flinched no matter how hard he drove her, until at last, her body began to grow strong as it trimmed down. Before long, she had more than one reason not to skip her appointments with Derek at the gym. She still weighed a hundred thirty-five, but much of it was muscle and she'd never looked better. And now she was living with Derek in his posh north Dallas bachelor pad.

Lookin' good, ol' girl, she thought. *Maybe it's the glow of love. Or maybe being in heat.* As she ripped out of the parking lot just in front of a ponderous Suburban and roared through a yellow light, she shifted gears with one hand while she pushed the autodial on her car phone with the other, guiding the steering wheel with her wrist.

"Hello?"

"Randi-girl! Are you ready to rock and roll?"

A muffled groan was her answer. "The baby kept me up all night long," said Randi Smith, Jillian's best friend and the single mother of an eight-month-old. "He's teething or something. God, I need a cigarette."

"Want me to bring you some?" Jillian weaved the Mustang between a bus and a pickup truck.

"I've got cigarettes, okay? I just don't smoke them around the baby is all."

"Okay, okay. You don't have to bite my head off."

"Sorry. I'm just tired."

"Well, we're gonna have us an adventure tonight, girlfriend. That'll perk you right up." Randi laughed in spite of herself. "Awww, you love it as much as I do," said Jillian. "You know it and I know it."

"I must. My mom says I'm crazy to keep doing this now that I've got the baby."

"Now, Randi. How many times do I have to tell you? Never listen to your mother."

"Yeah, and you know how much she loooves you."

Jillian laughed. "I consider the fact that your mother hates me a compliment."

Randi snickered.

"Listen, I'll be there in about twenty minutes, then I thought we'd run by and wish Derek luck on the new opening before we go to Little Mexico."

She waited for a response as she came to a stop at a red light. The man in the car next to her was staring at her. Randi said nothing. Jillian sighed. "I wish you'd give Derek a chance."

"Oh, you mean Goldilocks?"

"Don't be mean."

"He's a himbo. You know what that is, don't you, Jill? It's a male bimbo."

"He is not!" flared Jillian. "He's a very successful businessman."

"Yeah, thanks to Cricket."

Randi was referring to Derek's business partner, Cricket Andrews. She'd started out as yet one more perky aerobics instructor, had teamed up with Derek, and had helped to build their assets into the multimillion-dollar range.

"Anyway," said Randi, "I have this rule. Never get attracted to a guy whose hair is prettier than mine."

Jillian laughed. The light changed, and she peeled rubber, leaving the guy in the car next to her gawking. Derek's shoulder-length curls had been the source of many good-natured arguments between her and Randi. But then, Randi had never tangled her fingers in those golden locks while panting beneath that perfect body . . .

Still, Jillian couldn't resist defending Derek. "I

know you like to make fun of Derek," she said, "but I wouldn't be with him if it were only sex."

"Yeah, right."

"No, seriously," she insisted. "He has a sweetness about him that's very genuine. He's tender and kind. He gives away a lot of money to charities. Believe me, I've dated a lot of stockbrokers and lawyers through the years who had virtually no redeeming qualities beyond their bank accounts. They'd make fun of Derek, too, but I wouldn't trade him for six of them."

"Whatever," said Randi, who would remain stubbornly unconvinced no matter what Jillian said. "I've gotta go and make sure the baby-sitter's on her way."

"Okay," said Jillian with a sigh. "See ya in a minute."

She hit I-35 east, otherwise known as Stemmons Expressway, and floored it, slipping the Mustang in neatly between a lumbering delivery truck and a minivan. Her car was a thing of great pride and joy to Jillian. She loved tinkering under the hood and keeping it in optimum running shape. A classic car shop had replaced the tattered upholstery and the holey convertible top when she first bought it, and had installed a good tape deck and speakers. Every week she washed and polished it, cleaned the white leather seats, and vaccuumed the red carpet.

It was already hot and humid for early May, but nothing worse than Dallasites were already used to. Jillian popped in a Tom Petty tape and sang along uproariously to "Don't Back Down."

God, it was good to be alive.

She picked up Randi, who came out of the apartment like a pack mule, bearing cameras and lenses and other paraphernalia. She had the kind of body Jillian had always wanted, lean and lanky, and a boy-cut hairdo that accentuated her cheekbones. She wore very little makeup, which suited her. "Are you going to put up the top when we're there?" she fretted to Jillian. "I don't want any of my cameras to get ripped

off." Her gray eyes were clouded. She slipped on a
pair of dark shades.

"We'll lock 'em in the trunk," said Jillian. "Don't
worry about it."

Randi dumped the cameras in the backseat and got
in. As Jillian pulled out and picked up speed, Randi
reached over and turned down the volume on the
tape deck.

"What's the matter?" asked Jillian. "Got a
headache?"

Randi shrugged, cupped a cigarette in her palm
against the wind, and lit it, taking a deep drag. "Nothing. I don't know. I've just got a bad feeling, is all."

As she pulled out to pass an old station wagon,
Jillian frowned. "About what?"

"This Little Mexico assignment."

"Look, if you don't want to go, I can take the pictures myself—"

With an abrupt laugh and a shake to her head,
Randi said, "Yeah, right."

Jillian smiled. "Relax. You're just uptight because
you're tired. We'll have a ball. You'll see."

Randi cut a sideways glance at her. "God, I wish I
had your confidence."

With a short laugh, Jillian said, "It's all an act."

"No, I mean it. You're just such a warrior-woman. I
mean you're . . . fearless. Me, I'm scared all the time."

Shifting gears, Jillian cut in front of a BMW. "What
are you scared of?"

"Oh, everything. Something happening to Toby.
Something happening to me so I can't take care of
Toby anymore. Spiders. Tornadoes. Hang-up phone
calls. Getting kicked off of AOL."

They both giggled. "That's your problem right
there, Randi," said Jillian. "Too much virtual sex and
not enough of the real thing."

"Hey, if Goldilocks can match me up with some
hunky himbo who doesn't mind a baby around the

house, I'm all his! Until then, I gotta settle for roam-
ing around chat rooms in my alter-ego, Bambi."

"Bambi?" howled Jillian.

"Hey, don't knock her. She's got boobs as big as
yours."

They laughed together as Jillian whipped off the
expressway and threaded her way toward a tony shop-
ping center not far from the Southern Methodist University campus.

The parking lot was dotted with manicured trees,
and they followed stone walkways to the handsome
brick shops. The Power Play was tucked between a
mystery bookstore and a Starbuck's coffee shop. A
"Grand Opening!" banner was draped across the
front. White satin ribbons bedecked the glass door,
and inside were several stunning floral arrangements.
Jillian could hear Derek barking orders at the rear of
the gym, and with a nod at the front desk receptionist,
picked her way on plush blue carpeting through a
montage of work-out machines and hard-bodied men
and women dressed in Power Play T-shirts of blue and
gold. Randi trailed behind her.

When he spotted Jillian, Derek's face lit up with a
smile that still melted her knees, and he swept her off
her feet with his powerful arms into a suffocating bear
hug. That was one of the things she loved about him;
he was always so glad to see her. He never acted as
though he were too busy to be bothered.

"I didn't think you'd make it," he said, bending
Jillian over for a passionate kiss that embarrassed her
a bit. When he released her, Randi was staring at
the ceiling.

"Hi, Randi," Derek said, entwining his arms around
Jillian. "What do you think of the place?"

"Gee, I don't know, Derek. It's pretty much like
the other three, isn't it?"

With a smile that was completely unaffected by her
sarcasm, he nodded. Usually Derek wore his hair in a
ponytail at the gym, but tonight he had it brushed to

a silky glow. "Oh," he said to Randi. "I have a little surprise for you." He turned away from them for a moment, and Randi quirked a brow at Jillian.

"Here," he said with a boyish, beaming grin. He handed Randi a white envelope. He could hardly contain himself.

Randi opened the envelope and took out a letter, which she scan-read. Bewildered, she glanced up. "Derek . . . This is a membership to the Power Play."

"Yeah!" His grin grew.

"But I can't afford a membership." She gave a helpless glance toward Jillian.

"Oh, no! It's free! It's a free membership. My gift, Randi. I thought maybe you could use the break from the baby. There's already day care provided here at the gym while moms work out."

Jillian smiled at Randi. Maybe now her friend would be able to understand what she saw in a himbo like Derek.

"Not that you're not already in great shape," he hastened to add. "I just thought it would be a good stress-buster."

"I don't know what to say." The glance Randi threw Jillian's way was a guilty one, and Jillian couldn't resist an *I told you so* smirk in return.

"Thank you," said Randi, surprising them both by hugging Derek. "I couldn't ask for a nicer gift."

"You're welcome," he said. "Any friend of Jillian's, you know, is a friend of mine."

"Well . . ." Randi smacked the envelope in the palm of one hand. "Guess I better inspect the facilities, then." She grinned at both of them and began wandering around the club, looking over the equipment and talking to smiling employees.

"That was really sweet of you," said Jillian. "She's pretty stressed out these days, with the baby and all."

He shrugged. "Glad to do it. I like Randi."

That was another thing about Derek. He liked most everybody he met and had an open, trusting nature

Jillian found refreshing after hanging out with journalists all day long. He probably didn't even suspect Randi's true feelings toward him. And the irresistible thing about Derek's personality was that he had a way of winning people over eventually anyway. It was charming.

"The reception's at nine," Derek said to Jillian.

She blinked. "Derek . . . I'm working on a story. Remember? I can't come to the reception. I just came by to wish you luck."

A small thundercloud passed over his blue eyes. "But this is *important.* You know how much I like for you to be at my openings."

"I know, I know. But I've got to cover a rally in Little Mexico."

"What's that, a restaurant?"

Randi, who had rejoined them, stifled her usual snort. Pointedly ignoring her, Jillian said, "It's downtown. You know. The Rodriguez story?"

"Whatever." He pouted. "I just wish for once you considered my work as important as yours."

"I do. It's just that this is something I have to do."

"Fine." He turned to adjust the weights on a machine.

"I'll come by after the rally."

"You will?" He turned back, a sunny smile on his face.

"Sure."

"C'mere," he said, crooking his finger. "I wanna show you something."

She followed him through a set of double doors to a big blue-and-gold-tiled, echoing room that contained a beautiful turquoise swimming pool. "Oh, Derek!" she cried. "I didn't know you'd have a pool at this one."

"I know. I was saving it for a surprise. I know how much you like to swim."

"You big ol' sweetheart." She threw her arms around his neck, and he pulled her into a tight embrace that made her gasp, lifting her completely off the floor and pressing her to him until she could feel his erection.

"Derek!" she whispered. "Let me go! Somebody could walk in."

"I know. That's the fun of it." He kissed her some more, pressing her up against the cool tiled wall and moving his strong hands over her body until she felt the growing heat between her legs, until she forgot everything but him. God. Could there be anybody in the world sexier?

"Derek. I—we—can't . . . " Her heart was pounding, her otherwise distracted senses still alert to the slightest sound of a door opening or footsteps approaching.

Derek's propensity for initiating sex in risky, open places—elevators, parked cars, dressing rooms—both upset and excited her. Once he'd brought her to full climax while sitting side by side in a movie theater. It was like making out with your high school boyfriend in the living room while your parents watched TV in the next room. It made her feel young and daring and wild, and it never failed to scare her half to death.

His little blue silk boxer gym shorts were easier to get down than her slacks, but they managed, and he held her easily the whole time, right up against the wall, thrusting deep into her until she forgot all about Randi, forgot all about Juan Rodriguez, forgot everything but the power of this man and the scent of sex mingled with chlorine from the pool and Derek's dreamy, expensive aftershave.

This was Derek. He filled up her senses, crowded out her doubts, exploded inside her like the swirling stars she could see behind her eyelids when he rammed himself deep inside her.

It was the one area of her life over which she seemed to have no control, and that, she had discovered, was not necessarily a bad thing.

He pulled out of her, and crazily, she wanted more.

But the great thing about Derek was that there was always more to come. He couldn't seem to get enough sex. It was wild. She'd never known anything like this hunger.

Still, the real world beckoned.

Self-consciously, she fluffed her hair, ran her tongue over her lips now kissed free of lip gloss, and followed him out, studiously avoiding Randi's prying gaze and hoping their little romp wasn't showing all over her face.

"So, what do you think is wrong with little Toby?" she asked as they made their way back to the car. It was a pathetic attempt to distract Randi while she got her heart rate and breathing back to normal. This was the effect Derek always had on her.

If Randi wasn't fooled, she didn't let on. "He was running a mild fever and fussy all night. His nose was running, but the pediatrician said that sometimes it seems like they have a cold when all it really is is teething."

"Have you tried buying some of those water-filled plastic teething rings and keeping them in the refrigerator?" said Jillian. "It's cool on their gums."

Randi stared at her. "Where'd that come from? You don't have any kids."

"Little sister. I practically raised her. You remember stuff."

"I'll try that," said Randi. "Girl, you're full of surprises."

"You ain't seen nothin' yet," Jillian said with a sideways cocky grin.

"Hey, if I was gettin' laid as much as you are, girl, I'd be Superwoman."

Jillian blushed.

"I mean, the guy may be a dim bulb, but if he's a good lay, hell, that's all that matters."

"He's not a dim bulb!"

"Duh, what's Little Mexico—a restaurant?" she mocked in a deep voice.

"Look, Derek works fifteen hours a day. He spends his life at the gym. Just because we know all the crime spots of the city doesn't mean he necessarily keeps up with it. Anyway," she added reproachfully, "he did just give you a lovely present."

"That's true," said Randi with a guilty sigh. She glanced over at Jillian. "Does this mean I have to quit making fun of him?"

"You're incorrigible!"

"What do I know about it anyway? Nobody's ever screwed me at the movies."

"We didn't screw! Boy, you get mean when you're tired."

"Maybe I'm just horny." Randi gave her a sly grin. "We could go back to the gym. Maybe Derek could take care of it. Like, you know, additional services offered by the gym."

Jillian rolled her eyes, but before she could respond to that, the phone rang. Gratefully, she jerked it up. "Yeah?"

The voice was richly deep and melodius. "Is this Jillian Ross?"

"Speaking." Jillian braked behind a slow-moving Volkswagen and stifled a curse.

"This is Abraham Artemis. I'm gonna kick your little red-haired ass for sayin' such scandalous things about me in the paper."

Jillian laughed out loud. To Randi, she said, "It's Ash."

Randi grinned. "Put him on the speakerphone."

Jillian punched the button and hung up the receiver. She said, "Randi's here, and I've got you on the speakerphone, so you better be nice, Mr. Artemis."

They could hear laughter, and then in his usual drawl, Ash McGraw said, "How ya doin', Randi?"

"Oh, I don't get enough sex, but other than that, I'm fine."

"I can relate to that."

"You're the only one here who can."

"What . . . oh, you mean Jillian and Thor?"

Randi giggled.

"You two cut it out!" yelled Jillian, smiling as she passed the Volkswagen. Next to Randi, Ash McGraw was her favorite friend in the world. They'd gone to college together, nursed each other through broken relationships, and kept in touch even though they moved in different worlds. Ash was an arson investigator for the Dallas Fire Department.

Even so, they had a long and affectionate history. If Randi was Jillian's best girlfriend, then Ash was her best guy friend. "So, what have you been up to, darlin'?" drawled Jillian.

"Oh, nothin' much. A homeless guy set himself on fire. Seems he was huffin' paint and got a sudden craving for a cigarette. Talk about your basic crispy critter."

Randi rolled her eyes at Jillian.

"So where you headed? I tried your home number and got the machine. You're a hard gal to track down."

"Me'n Randi are headed out to Little Mexico to catch the Cinco de Mayo rally Juan Rodriguez is throwing."

"Little Mexico? You're armed, aren't you?"

"Of course I'm not armed." Jillian searched for her exit. "You know how I feel about guns."

"And you know how I feel about you racing around town and into areas cops don't go into without a 911 call."

"We'll be fine."

"Famous last words. What time's the rally?"

"At seven."

"It could get a little hairy, my friend. Especially if Artemis's thugs show up."

"Aww, that'll just make it interesting."

"Maybe I'll drop by, then. Somebody's got to keep an eye on you."

Jillian groaned. "Why do all you *guys* seem to think I need a keeper?"

"Hey, it's not just the guys," said Randi.

"Suit yourself, Ash." Jillian pulled off of Harry Hines Boulevard and began to work her way into the bowels of the city.

"Maybe I'll see you later, then."

"Okay. Bye."

"Randi? Keep an eye on her till I get there."

"Yes, sir." Randi grinned, and Jillian hung up.

They pulled over on a quiet, run-down street. Randi selected a camera and lens, and Jillian helped her load the rest of the cameras, along with the car phone, Jillian's tote bag, and some cassette tapes, into the trunk. Then they put the top up and fastened it to the windshield. Jillian was aware that anyone could slash through the sturdy canvas top with a sharp knife, but it was better than leaving the car open and vulnerable to theft.

She turned off the car radio, and they didn't say anything as Jillian slowly maneuvered the car down narrow, shadowy streets and past dark knots of people staring at them with suspicious eyes. It was dusk, the spooky time of day the cops liked to call "the witching hour."

They were running late, and Jillian found a parking place a block from the squat red brick collection of apartments that had been built with federal funds in 1941 to correct the disgraceful housing situation that existed in south and central Dallas at the time for the poor and minorities. As they got out of the car, Jillian noticed how badly lit the streets were. It was the first thing one realized about low-income neighborhoods; they were dark. Gloom collected in the corners. At the last minute Jillian undraped the press pass that she kept hanging on her rearview mirror, and put it around her neck. Maybe she and Randi would be able to work unmolested as long as people knew they were reporters. She locked the car and stuffed the keys in her pocket.

The skyscrapers of the city of Dallas glittered and towered over the tenement neighborhood like the lights of Disneyworld, just as beautiful and fantastic and just as inaccessible.

As they walked toward the rally, Jillian craned her neck for the sight of police cars. There were none. Neither were there any camera crews from any of the local television news stations.

"What's wrong?" asked Randi, who was clearly nervous.

"Nothing. It just never ceases to amaze me how little interest this city takes in any issues or events that involve minorities."

It was hot and muggy and still. Jillian strode quickly with her head up, eyes alert, and step firm. She had her game-face on now, no doubt about it. She was working, and that made this her turf. She'd walked some of the worst streets in the city covering stories, and felt she could handle herself just by being aware of her surroundings, keeping her guard up, and not taking any unnecessary risks. Most of the time she was left alone. She had come to count on that.

Jillian and Randi made their way through the periphery of the crowd that was gathering even as Juan Rodriguez was speaking. The atmosphere was close and tense. Sweat drooled between Jillian's breasts and gathered stickily in her armpits. There was an unpleasant odor in the air. Jillian considered it to be the stench of poverty. *You can read about poverty,* she thought, *see pictures of it, even see poor people gathered in places like the welfare office, but you've never known poverty until you've smelled the stench of it. It's sweat, filth, fear, and something indefinable but overwhelming.*

After a moment she withdrew a small spiral notebook and pen from another blazer pocket and jotted down her thoughts in a bizarre shorthand indecipherable to anyone but herself. Her words would appear in print later, pretty much as she had thought them on the scene.

Jillian looked around at the faces gazing up at Rodriguez. The older people seemed resigned, tired, defeated. The younger people—especially the young men—had faces twisted with rage and hatred and defiance. One young Latino man caught her eye and gave her a derisive, appraising glare. Jillian glanced away.

For the first time that evening, she felt a twinge of fear. She glanced over at Randi, who was checking the dim and fading light with a meter and muttering to herself. It was somehow reassuring, and Jillian tuned in to what Rodriguez was saying, pen poised over the notebook.

"For too long, the African-American power structure has run roughshod over the Anglos, who cowered in their politically correct fear. They gave in to the blacks time and time again so that they would not look like bigots." He shook his head. Jillian scribbled. "The Anglos act like black and white are the only two colors in the Crayola box, eh, amigos?"

The restless crowd murmured its dissastisfied response.

"In the meantime, the Latino high school dropout rate soars to thirty percent, and it may even be higher, once they are finished recalculating the numbers of Hispanic kids who drop out of the seventh or eighth grade.

"Time and again the success of bilingual education has been proven, but instead, some Hispanic children are thrown into classrooms where everybody in the class speaks English—even the teacher. Do you know what kind of despair that can cause a child?"

People nodded and shouted approval of his words.

"But Abraham Artemis, and the Black Panthers, and his buddies over at the NAACP, they don't want to talk about Hispanic children. They don't *care* about

Hispanic children. It's like, what's ours is *ours*, and what's yours is negotiable."

Angry Spanish conversations going on rapidly around Jillian almost drowned him out. Randi began snapping pictures.

"Everything the blacks have wanted in this city, they have gotten. Well, it's time for somebody to stand up and say that they are now *over*represented. We supported them in their fight, but where are they in *our* fight? When they deal with us, it is apples and orchards. They want to give us the apples while they keep the orchards!"

Jillian was jostled and fumbled to hold onto her notebook. The mob was getting angrier by the minute, shouting curses in Spanish—or what passed for Spanish in this part of Texas. It was more a hackneyed blend of Spanish and English known as Tex-Mex. Most Mexican-Americans Jillian knew could not speak or read classic Castillian Spanish.

"And the Anglos are no better!" cried Rodriguez. "Where are they now? Look around you. Do you see any whites here?"

A number of Hispanics turned and stared at Jillian and Randi. Randi didn't seem to notice, with her camera glued to her face.

It had grown almost completely dark. Though some lights had been strung over the hastily constructed stage, most of the area was in shadows. The air seemed to crackle from the heat and the tension.

Out of the corner of her eye, Jillian spotted a pickup truck easing ominously up to the edge of the crowd. A pile of cold-eyed muscular young blacks wearing bandannas on their heads poured out of the back of the pickup.

"Let's get out of here," said Jillian, her body going into full alarm.

A fight immediately broke out between a Latino gang and the blacks, and the crowd erupted into instant screaming chaos. Jillian was knocked to the ground. Someone stomped on her hand. Randi leaned over, grabbed a handful of red hair, and hauled Jillian to her feet. Someone yanked Randi's camera, which was hanging around her neck, pulling her almost to the ground.

"No!" she screamed. "Not the camera!"

The camera disappeared into the crowd.

"That's a four-hundred-dollar camera!" she wailed.

"Don't worry about it!" yelled Jillian. "The paper'll replace it. We've gotta get out of here!"

Interlocking elbows, they plunged forward through the melee in the general direction of the street where the Mustang was parked.

Firecracker pops . . . no, gunfire rang out.

Jillian whirled toward Randi. Her eyes were so wide with fright that Jillian could see the whites all the way around the pupils. Her face was pale in the humid murkiness. "Jill—"

And then her face disappeared.

It happened in just that way. One moment Randi was looking straight at Jillian, her face rigid with fear, and in the next moment, it was gone.

Blood, brain matter, eyeballs, and skin tissue splattered into Jillian even as she heard the deafening roar of the gunshot.

Randi slumped to the ground, dragging Jillian, whose arm was still interlocked with hers, down with her. Randi landed face first in the dirt.

All senses deserted Jillian. Time stopped. Sound, sight, smells . . . all disappeared. The world vanished into blackness for one brief, blessed moment, and then came roaring back, but somehow, Jillian wasn't all there with it.

"RANDI!" she screamed. "GET UP! WE'VE GOT TO GET TO THE CAR!"

Struggling, she pulled the inert body of her best friend into her arms. Randi's head lolled back. There was nothing in front of it but bloody pulp. One eyeball hung precariously by a thread from the one remaining eye socket that she had. It seemed to Jillian that Randi was going to need that eye, so she carefully replaced it into the socket.

"I'll get you some help!" she cried. "I've got a phone in the car. I'll call an ambulance."

Yes. That was it. She would dial 911 from her car phone. But she couldn't leave Randi here; not like this, she couldn't leave her, *she wouldn't leave Randi.*

Heart pumping raw adrenaline through every muscle in her body, Jillian pushed herself up, shouldered Randi's still, silent, heavy body, and began staggering for the car. Speed was everything.

Hurry. Hurry. Gotta get help. Gotta get help. Randi needs help. Randi needs that eye.

At the Mustang, she fumbled for her car keys and almost dropped them, then missed the car door handle lock three times before finally fitting the key in with violently trembling, bloody hands. A siren shrieked past, but Jillian took no notice of it. She laid Randi gently into the front seat, her head on the headrest of the white leather car seat.

Blood. There's so much blood. I never saw so much blood in my whole entire life.

Blood soaked Jillian's clothes, face, hair, and hands. It ran down the street, pooled in the floor of the Mustang, and dripped off the seat.

She reached over Randi's body for the car phone.

It wasn't there.

Locked in the trunk.

Jillian stumbled for the back of the car. The keys fell to the street. She dropped to her knees and began groping, groping and sobbing, groping and screaming, groping and shrieking for help, *help, help! HELP! HE-E-E-LP!!*

And then she was just screaming. Screaming and screaming and screaming.

This was how Ash McGraw found her.

Chapter Two

It was like driving straight into the mouth of hell.

As a former paramedic and firefighter, Ash had worked accident scenes and fires before, but never a riot. As he approached the scene, the air was filled with the scream of sirens as people fled on foot down sidewalks and streets, crisscrossing between cars, some of them brandishing weapons, some shouting curses, most melting into the darkness.

To become an arson investigator for the city of Dallas, candidates had to complete the sixteen-week police academy training before attending fire investigation school. Consequently, they were licensed law enforcement officers and as such, carried nine-millimeter firearms and had the power to make arrests. Ash preferred the Lasermax Glock 19 with a custom magazine grip extension, and as he drove slowly down the street toward the worst of the riot, braking off and on to avoid the runners cutting in front of him, he instinctively reached down and unsnapped his holster.

He was about a block away when Jillian's red Mustang showed up in his headlights, its passenger door ajar and the silhouette of someone sitting in the front passenger seat haloed in a crazy kaleidoscope of crimson and blue flashes from police cars. Since another car was parked in front of the Mustang, Ash had to leave his car angled into the street. Even as he released his seat belt, his gut was seized with an awful, nauseating sense that something was very, very wrong.

The moment his foot hit the pavement, he heard Jillian's screams—a high, piercing, animalistic keening that sliced open his insides and laid bare his soul.

Then he saw her.

She was kneeling in the street behind the Mustang, spotlighted by the headlights from his car. Her face, hair, and the front of her body were soaked in blood.

"Oh, my God!" Ash cried.

At first, he thought she'd been hit by a car. He rushed to her and knelt before her, placing his hands on either side of her face.

"Jillian," he barked in a short, sharp tone, forcing her to focus on him. Her pupils were blasted wide open.

"Where are you hurt, darlin'?" Ash wiped some of the blood from her forehead, but could find no wound.

She stopped screaming, but her entire body trembled so violently that Ash could feel the vibrations all the way up to his shoulders. He watched as she struggled to place his face in her shock-numbed mind.

"It's Ash, Jill. Ash. I'm here now." Expertly, he ran his hands down her arms. Where the hell was she hurt? Internally?

"R-r-r-randi," she stuttered through chattering teeth.

"She's in the car, darlin'." Tenderly, he took her wrist into his hand to check her pulse.

To his surprise, she yanked away from him and sprang to her feet, swaying as she did so.

"You gotta help her!" she yelled. "You gotta help her!" Her face was twisted with fury and panic, her eyes with their blasted pupils a ferocious black.

"Okay, okay." For a moment Ash was confused, until he hurried around and saw Randi's face. Or what was left of Randi's face.

During his years in turn-out gear, Ash had seen his share of gruesome sights. Once, he'd pulled two dead children out of a house fire, one under each arm. As a paramedic, he'd pried people's heads out of car windshields and had seen much that he'd rather not have seen.

But this was one of the worst things, ever.

Or maybe it was just worse because it was Randi, sweet, lovely Randi.

She'd taken what appeared to be a high-caliber gunshot at close or even point-blank range to the face. And it was just gone. An eyeball hung crazily from what remained of an eye socket.

To his horror, Jillian reached past him and calmly stuck the eyeball back into its place.

"You gotta help her," she repeated, tugging at his sleeve like a little kid. "You gotta help her."

Anyone still in possession of his faculties could tell at a glance that Randi was dead. Just the amount of blood, copious amounts of it all over the car and running down the street, would be the first clue.

Ash turned to Jillian and studied her face. He'd heard about psychogenic shock before, but he'd never seen a real case. From what he could tell, Jillian didn't *have* any faculties at the moment—her mind had been blown by the shock of what she'd witnessed. One thing he did know—if psychogenic shock was not treated, and soon, it could be life-threatening.

"Okay, darlin'," he said in his calmest, most soothing voice. He reached for his cell phone, then remembered that he'd brought a two-way radio. Sometimes in a riot situation or other major emergency, the 911 phone lines could get jammed. He could reach straight to the ambulances with his radio.

Pulling the radio from his jacket pocket, he said, "I'm going to call for an ambulance, see?" He held the radio, which was already set on an emergency frequency, in front of her face. "But I need you to wait right over here so that I can take care of Randi."

Taking her elbow in a firm grip, he led her to the curb, where he gently pushed her until she sat in the scraggly grass. Removing his jacket, he put it over her shoulders and tucked it under her shivering chin as though she were a child. As he did this, he sneaked a feel of the pulse in the carotid artery in her throat. There wasn't enough time to count beats, but he didn't have to; it was weak and thready, both bad signs. Her skin was clammy and cool.

For a moment, he cupped her ghosty pale, blood-spattered face in the palm of his hand, blinking back tears.

Then he hurried back over to where Randi's body sat slumped in the front seat of the Mustang, where he called in a request for two ambulances—one to handle Randi's body and call for the M.E., and one to take Jillian to the emergency room. Both would be slowed down by the chaos and confusion brought about by the riot. Where there was one gunshot wound, there had to be more, so Ash was certain others would be on their way to the hospital as well.

Just to be sure about it, Ash groped for a pulse, but Randi's face was such a pulpy mess he couldn't even find the right spot on her throat. He tried the wrist, to no avail. Her body was already cooling. Glancing around the Mustang, Ash paused to figure out what had happened. If she'd been shot in the car, there would have been blowback in the direction of the gunshot, on the seat or dash or wherever. There was none.

However, the blood trail clearly led back to the Little Mexico complex, and it slowly dawned on Ash that Randi must have been shot in the riot, which meant that Jillian had carried her all the way back to the car. He glanced over to where Jillian sat, shrunken and miserable, on the curb, dwarfed by his big jacket .

Unbelievable.

"Oh, Jilly," he muttered. "Poor kid."

All around them the night raged, throbbing with the shriek of sirens and the pulse beat of bloodred and other mesmerizing multicolor emergency lights,

pounding with the angry footfalls of a mob gone mad.
Quickly Ash returned to Jillian.

"I want you to wait in my car," he said, taking her
hands to pull her to her feet.

"No." She jerked her hands free. "You gotta help
Randi."

"I'll help Randi," he said. "You wait in the car."

"Why don't we wait in the car instead, gringo?"

Ash whirled, withdrawing his pistol from his holster
as he did so, and faced three young sneering thugs,
one of whom was posturing with a long, wicked knife.

"I don't think so," he said through clenched teeth,
assuming the stance with his gun. "Now, get out of
here before I blow your stupid little heads off."

As soon as they saw the tiny red dot of light from
the Glock's "laser" sight focused right between the
eyes of the kid with the knife, they ran.

Replacing the gun in its holster but leaving the holster unsnapped, Ash pulled the struggling, protesting
Jillian to her feet.

"Jillian—"

"No." She pushed against his chest. "No."

To Ash's relief, an ambulance appeared, turned the
corner, and headed straight toward them. As it pulled
to a stop alongside Jillian's car, two paramedics sprang
out. The one closest to the Mustang spotted Randi
immediately. As he leaned toward her, Ash called out,
"Let the next ambulance get her. This one needs to
go now."

The paramedic straightened, and their eyes met.

To Jillian, Ash said, "Honey, we're going to take a
little ride to the hospital and make sure you're okay."

"No. You gotta help Randi."

"It's okay. Another ambulance will be here in just
a minute."

"No. You gotta help Randi."

Placing an arm firmly around her waist, Ash began
to guide Jillian toward the ambulance, and all hell
broke loose. Like a wildcat, she turned on him in a

blur of fingernails and fists, hitting, screaming, tearing at him, her strangely black eyes feral.

The two paramedics leapt into action, each one taking an arm as they pulled her off of him.

"No! Nooo!" she shrieked through bared, gritted teeth, kicking out at Ash with her feet, twisting her body, flailing against the paramedics with all her strength.

To Ash's vast relief, a second ambulance slowed to a halt behind his car. Stepping forward, heedless of her sharp kicks, Ash put his hands on either side of Jillian's face and turned her head until she was forced to see the other ambulance.

"See? Here's the ambulance now. They're going to take care of Randi."

Almost immediately the fight went out of her, and she slumped between the two paramedics, who were still holding her.

"I'm an arson investigator with the city of Dallas and a licensed paramedic," said Ash to the men. "I'll take her. You better get the stretcher. She's about gone."

Putting both arms around Jillian, Ash held her as she trembled like a rabbit caught in a snare. Only when the other paramedics had huddled around Randi did Jillian allow herself to be helped onto the stretcher.

Inside the big patient compartment of the ambulance, one paramedic began working on Jillian even as the other pulled out into the choked street, blasting the horn along with the siren. After setting up normal saline with an 18-gauge catheter, he took Jillian's blood pressure while Ash covered her with a blanket, and propped up her legs on another folded blanket. He could see for himself the reading of the blood pressure gauge: seventy over forty and dropping.

"She's pretty shocky," said the paramedic as he fitted an N.R.B. (nonrebreather) mask over her face. "See if you can get a verbal response."

Ash said, "Jillian."

She was staring at the ceiling of the ambulance, which swayed slightly now as they broke free from the worst of the traffic congestion and picked up speed.

"Jill?"

Ash felt his breath catch in his throat and his chest turn cold and heavy.

"Jillian! Can you hear me?"

Though Jillian's eyes were wide open, she had gone somewhere far, far away from Ash, somewhere deep inside herself.

"It's a gated stare, man," mumbled the paramedic, who was taking her pulse. "She can't hear you now. It's like they're reliving it or something." He frowned. "Pulse is erratic."

Ash didn't want to believe it. Leaning over, he pressed close to Jillian, so close that his breath puffed her blood-matted hair. "Jillian!" he cried, dismayed that his voice broke, betraying his powerful emotions. With a firm swallow to get himself under control, he shouted, "Don't leave me! You hear?"

But her eyes stared right through him, black, cold, and empty.

His first fatality was unintentional.

He'd taken to cruising the parts of the city that were dominated by industrial warehousing and other anonymous buildings at odd hours of the day, scouting possible fire-setting locations. His first attempts were amateurish, to be sure, and cowardly—dumpsters, mostly. He only set the fires late at night, when there were unlikely to be any witnesses, and if he was careful, he could sometimes hang around in the area, hidden by black-on-black shadows, and watch the firetrucks rush in to put out his virgin efforts. Sometimes he even called the fire department himself.

The first few times were exciting, if only for the novelty, and because these little episodes were so very different from his usual methodical life. Modest though the fires might be, no one would ever suspect a respected psychiatrist and university professor of having been the arsonist. He'd done some research on the 'Net, and knew that the fire investigators would assume that the series of dumpster fires plaguing the city were the result of vandals—teenagers, most likely.

So he could move about in complete secrecy, committing his small crimes, exulting in his hidden double life.

But after half a dozen or so fires, the new began to wear off. The surge and tingle he'd felt in the beginning, watching the monster roar forth out of its prison, rearing its hot and fearsome head and glaring at him with a knowing glance, making him feel—if only for those brief moments—fiercely alive, was beginning to dampen. It was no big deal, after all. Just a stupid little dumpster fire. Sometimes the firefighters only used regular fire extinguishers to put it out.

This, he knew, disappointed the fire as much as it did him. Where was the challenge in that? Where was the fight?

He contemplated moving up, so to speak, by setting the warehouses themselves on fire, but these were sturdy buildings constructed of cement blocks and steel girders. Even if he wanted to set fire to the contents, he would have to break and enter, as well as use copious amounts of accelerants which, he learned, could be traced to the several stores from which they'd been purchased, and from there, to the possible purchasers. Too risky.

Not that he didn't relish the risk. He just wanted any risks he took to be calculated ones.

So he continued to set fire to the dumpsters, because at the moment, he couldn't decide what else to do and, in the meantime, didn't want to give up the fires altogether.

He needed the fires. Without the fires, he couldn't breathe anymore.

From the first feverish sigh against his face as he

awoke the flames from their dreamless slumber, to the scorching belch of black smoke and hot fury that warned him away before others might see him, he stood mesmerized, watching the hypnotic dance.

In spite of his cautious and clumsy attempts to maintain control by setting the fires within a contained metal structure like a dumpster, every fire was different. If he was lucky, unseen discarded aerosol cans would sometimes act like small explosive devices, sending a one-man fireworks show to blast into the black night and causing the flames to stand straight up and shake their fists in his flushed face.

Other times the fire would sneak insidiously around the shadowy corners of the dumpster, creeping unseen into various cracks and crevices on secret missions, only to leap up in several different spots at once, charging toward the middle to blaze forth, a warrior in full battle gear.

He never knew what to expect, and this kept bringing him back to the dumpsters, even though the aliveness he gained from the fires was beginning to diminish, and that scared him.

It scared him because the aliveness he felt from fire only made his regular every day deadness seem that much more unbearable. Each morning, he awoke to a paralyzing sense of numbness. As he stared into the overhead fan tracing lazy circles in the ceiling, he couldn't breathe.

He would take great gulps of air in a desperate attempt to convince himself that it was all right. He was still alive. But the breaths never seemed to reach into his soul.

At first the fires would exhale their scorching, heaving life into him, and his lungs would open up, and he could breathe again. But after a while, he found himself gasping even in the car on the way back home.

And then the man burned.

He never intended to kill anyone. It never occurred to him that somebody might actually choose to sleep in a dumpster. Or maybe the man had been clamboring around in there while drunk and simply passed out. He made no sound at first, no warning as to his presence in the dumpster when Keegan first set the fire.

It was the odor that first alerted him that something was different about this fire, something awfully, horribly different.

It smelled like meat, cooking.

Even as his brain registered that unthinkable thought, the burning man suddenly screamed—a torturous, agonizing, rawboned cry unlike anything Keegan had ever heard, and began a wild thrashing, his fists slamming into the sides of the dumpster with such force they left dents.

Frozen in place by the icy stickiness of horror that poured over his body, Keegan barely had time to realize what he had done before the terrible thrashing stopped, leaving only the triumphant guffaw of the fire and the throbbing of his heart in his ears.

The smell of roasting flesh assailed his nostrils, and he quickly whirled and vomited into the scrubby weeds.

Goosebumps of fear and revulsion needled his arms and legs, and he felt himself grow dizzy from his own high, panicky panting. Waves of heat billowed from the dumpster-turned-oven, scorching his brows. Quickly he stepped back, but the smoke followed him—borne, perhaps, on a finicky wind . . . or maybe reaching for him in hopes of entangling another victim in its sinewy web.

He didn't know what to do. It was far too late to try and save the man, and anyway, he would have to leave soon, before he was seen, especially now that the fire he had set had actually killed a man.

His heart continued to jackhammer against his rib cage, sending alarm signals throughout every sensory nerve in his body. Adrenaline coursed through his veins with every hammer pound of his heart. His fingers and toes tingled, his muscles hardened, and his loins surged.

Within his brain, he felt an explosion.

Not the painful, worrisome kind, but the kind that clarifies and crystallizes all thought, all sensation, all knowing.

He was alive.

HE WAS ALIVE!

Chapter Three

Parkland Hospital, which gained unasked-for fame so many years ago as the deathwatch facility for the mortally wounded President John Kennedy, now provided state-of-the-art trauma care, including two separate emergency room entrances—one for surgical-medical trauma and one for the kind of trauma Jillian was now suffering. Although there were gunshot wounds being admitted from the riot through the surgical-medical side, not all of them were necessarily fatal. With Jillian's rapidly dropping blood pressure, she was considered hypotensive, a potentially life-threatening condition, and was triaged with lightning speed and whisked away from Ash before he knew what was happening.

While awaiting word, Ash found a relatively quiet corner of the waiting room, pulled a cell phone from a jacket pocket with hands still bloody from touching Randi, and tracked down the phone number for the new Power Play gym.

After several rings, the phone was answered by a laughing young woman to the background noise of a party in full swing.

"I need to speak to Derek Thorsen, please," said Ash. "It's urgent."

"He's busy right now," chirped the laughing girl. "Can I take a message?"

"It's imperative that I speak with him now." Ash

spoke as clearly and authoritatively as he could, trying not to disturb the anxious people nearby who were waiting for word of their own loved ones. "It's an emergency."

"A what? *Stop that!*" she added with a giggle.

"An emergency." He raised his voice. "Get Derek on the phone *now*, do you understand me?" Several people around him gave him a sharp, worried glance.

"Okay, okay. Just a minute." The receiver clanked as if it had been dropped to the desk. The noise hurt Ash's ear and set his already simmering impatience into a slow boil.

After what seemed like a ridiculously long wait, Thorsen picked up the phone. "Yeah? This is Derek."

"Derek, this is Ash."

"Who?"

"Ash McGraw, Jillian's friend."

"Oh."

"I've got some bad news. There was a riot at Little Mexico tonight. Jillian's friend Randi was shot and killed, and Jillian's in the emergency room of Parkland Hospital."

"What? A riot at a restaurant? What are you talking about?"

Ash paused. "They weren't *at* a restaurant, Derek. Whatever gave you that idea?"

"I just thought . . . never mind. What happened?"

Ash sighed. "There was a riot. Randi got her head blown off right in front of Jillian, and it threw her into very deep shock. The doctors are working on her now. It's important that you get here right away."

"Oh, my God! Jillian got shot?"

"No."

"I thought you said she did."

"I said she was in the hospital. I didn't say she got shot. Randi got shot."

"Oh, no. Poor Randi."

"Yeah. But that doesn't mean Jillian's not in bad shape, Derek. You need to be here."

There was a long pause. "I don't know what to do," said Derek. "I mean, I appreciate you calling and everything, but I can't come right now. KRLD News is going to interview me for the ten o'clock news. They just got here with the cameras and stuff. We're opening a new gym."

Outrage washed over Ash like a cold shower. "Maybe you don't understand. Jillian could die."

"But I thought you said she wasn't shot."

"She wasn't."

"Then, she's not really hurt, is she? I mean, she just freaked out, is all. They can take care of that, can't they? I'd like to be there, really, but the TV people are here. I can't just walk out on them."

Ash ground his teeth together. Ingratiating asshole. For the life of him, he would never understand what Jillian saw in the guy. He said, "What's your problem? What part of the word *die* do you not understand?"

"Look, I didn't say I couldn't come at all. I'll be there after they get through interviewing me."

Ash lost it. Normally a man of exquisite self-control, he found himself shouting into the telephone, oblivious of the open stares of the others around him. "Listen, you vain, self-absorbed little peckerhead, I don't give a shit about your TV interview. If you don't care enough about Jill to get your ass down here now, then just stay the fuck away, do you hear me?" Then he hurled the phone to the floor, where it cracked and fell open, spilling its guts.

Panting, he looked around. A woman had pulled her small child into her lap and was cradling him as if Ash presented some sort of danger to the boy. A man glanced away.

A large black woman sitting nearby reached out and patted his coat sleeve. "It's okay, honey. She'll be all right as long as she's got you to look after her."

He stared at her for a moment, then said, "Thanks." Mumbling apologies to the others, he gathered up his crippled phone and stuffed it into his pocket. Too em-

barrassed to hang around, he paced the corridor outside. He couldn't get Randi's crumpled, faceless body
out of his mind. It was one thing to pull anonymous
victims out of a car wreck or a burning building, another thing altogether to stare at the lifeless body of
a friend. Thoughts of her baby came to him, and it
was all he could do not to cry. He rubbed the palms
of his hands over his burning eyes.

When he grew tired of pacing, he returned to the
waiting room.

A trim woman in a white coat wearing a stethoscope
around her neck appeared at the door. "Is there anybody here for Jillian Ross?" she asked.

Ash hurried over. "Yes," he said. "I'm her friend."

"Okay. We got her stabilized and sedated. She
should sleep through the night. Physically, she's going
to be all right. We'll keep her overnight, at least, for
observation."

"And mentally?" Ash couldn't resist asking, even
though he knew the answer.

She shook her head. "I can't say, Mr. . . ."

"McGraw."

"Mr. McGraw, she's suffered a terrible trauma. Different people handle post-traumatic stress in different
ways. I would recommend that she receive counseling
of some sort, but I'm not going to admit her to the
psych ward at this point."

"I understand."

"I'm glad you're here," she added. "She'll need all
the friends she can get."

He nodded.

"What about family?"

Ash shook his head.

She nodded. "Ms. Ross should awaken in the morning. You'll have a better idea of her mental condition
then." She turned to go.

"Can I see her?"

"She's being moved to a private room now. The
nurses at that counter over there can send you where

you need to go. Were you planning on spending the night?"

"Yes." He said it automatically, without thinking.

"Good. She may not remember anything about what happened when she wakes up. She may be disoriented and confused. It would help if she could see a familiar face. I'll tell the nurses that normal visiting hours don't apply in this situation."

"Thank you, Doctor."

With a brisk nod, she walked away, and he was left standing alone, staring at his bloody hands.

When Jillian first opened her eyes, she felt dead from the neck down, and wondered for a brief chaotic moment if she were. Her arms and legs felt impossibly heavy, and her head seemed disembodied from the rest of her. It took a moment for her to realize that she was lying in bed in a dimly lit hospital room, and she wondered why.

Then she remembered.

It came to her in a sudden, overwhelming, vivid rush of powerful impressions and memories so real she felt almost as if she were experiencing it all over again.

She felt the panicked crush of the crowd, the sweat under her armpits and between her breasts, the look of stark terror in Randi's eyes just before her face vanished in a bloody blur, the weight of her as she fell to the ground, dragging Jillian with her.

Randi.

At the thought of her, the flashback occurred all over again, and again, until all Jillian could see in her mind's eye was blood, blood everywhere, blood where Randi's face used to be, blood draining down the street as Jillian staggered to the car with her friend's body, blood on the white leather car seats, blood all over Jillian's clothes and in her hair, blood, blood everywhere.

A sob escaped her, and then she was wailing, a dry-mouthed, throaty keening of grief too terrible to express any other way.

There was a rustling beside her, and then Ash suddenly leaned over her. She hadn't even known he was there.

He gathered her in his arms and held her as she screamed and sobbed and gulped air, until she had exhausted herself and there were no more tears left. When he stepped back, brushing damp hair off her face, she saw that he had been crying, too, and it made her feel better somehow, not so alone.

She felt so tired, a weariness beyond words.

"The doctor said you might not remember what happened when you woke up," he said. Reaching for a styrofoam pitcher on the bedside stand, he poured her a glass of water and handed it to her. She drank it down gratefully.

"I wish I didn't," she said. "Remember, I mean. It would be easier."

He sat on the edge of her bed and took her hand in his. "It's not your fault, sweetheart," he said.

She glanced away from him. How did he know?

"This awful thing happened to you, too. It's a wonder you weren't shot as well. It's going to take you some time to learn to cope with it. Right now, the most important thing is for you to get some rest."

"I'm so tired," she said, still avoiding his steady gaze. *It was my fault,* she was thinking. *Randi had a bad feeling, and I ignored it. I took the mother of an infant into a life-threatening situation just to get a goddamned story. I wish I had been shot instead.*

Ash wet a washcloth with cool water and tenderly wiped her face with it. It felt so good that she closed her eyes.

"Go back to sleep," he said. "We'll talk later."

Jillian turned over onto her side and curled into the fetal position, pulling the covers up to her chin. She didn't want to sleep.

She wanted to die.

*   *   *

They let her take a shower the next morning. The water ran red down the drain with Randi's blood, and Jillian heard herself crying again, though she was hardly aware of it.

Here she was, taking a shower, washing her hair like she did every day, and yet, after everything that had happened, it seemed like such a bizarre thing to be doing. She shouldn't be sleeping and eating and showering. Not when Randi lay dead, her beautiful face gone forever.

She shouldn't be living, period.

Back in the hospital room, with Ash hovering solicitously, she stared at her bloodstained clothes with distaste. Jillian didn't want to wear them, ever again. She wanted to burn them.

"I can run out to your apartment and get you some clothes," he said. "There's time before they check you out. The doctor hasn't even been by yet."

Just then the door banged open, and in walked Derek with a massive flower arrangement and a gym bag over his shoulder. He set down the flowers, and Jillian flew into his arms. It felt so good, being held by him again.

"I called down at the desk this morning," he said, "and the nurse said you might want some clean clothes, so I brought you some."

"Oh, Derek!" she cried. "That was so thoughtful. Thank you." She unzipped the bag and pulled out her favorite warm-ups, sneakers, and socks. "This is just what we needed, isn't it, Ash?" she asked, glancing up.

Ash was standing stiffly to the side, glowering at Derek. Jillian felt momentarily piqued. It was one thing for Ash to dislike Derek, but this was hardly the time or place to express it.

"I'd have come last night," said Derek, "but they said you were sedated."

She nodded.

"How convenient for you," said Ash.

Jillian gasped. "Ash!"

"I've got to go," Ash said abruptly, leaning over to kiss her. "I'll call you."

As he turned to leave, she reached out and clasped his hand. "Ash . . . thank you. For everything."

With a contemptuous glance at Derek, he said, "It was truly no trouble at all. I'll be in touch." At the door, he stopped, glared back at Derek, and said, "Take good care of her." Then he left.

"Prick," mumbled Derek.

Too exhausted to deal with the tension between the two men, Jillian slipped on the clothing Derek had brought. Taking the shower and getting dressed had worn her out, and she stretched out on the bed.

"The riot was on the news," said Derek. "I'm so sorry about Randi. What happened?"

Jillian told him. She omitted nothing. When she was finished, he shook his head.

"I wish you would listen to me. I've been trying to get you to stay away from these dangerous places, but you just seem determined. Now look what happened."

She stared at him. His words, coming so close to her own piercing guilt, only deepened the wound. "Are you saying it was my fault?" she asked.

"I'm just saying you shouldn't have been there, Jill, is all. You could have gotten killed."

She turned her head to stare out the window. A weight settled onto her chest, so heavy she could barely breathe. She tried to take a deep breath, but could not fill her lungs. Her chest actually ached. *When a heart breaks,* she thought, *this is how it feels.*

"I was on KRLD news," he said. When she didn't respond, he said, "Jill?"

"Huh?"

"I was on TV last night. KRLD did a spot on the Power Play gyms for the ten o'clock news."

"Oh. That's nice, Derek."

"Yeah. It was pretty cool. They interviewed me for about twenty minutes, but they only showed like, a minute. Tiffany taped it, and it turned out pretty well. You should have been there," he added with a hint of accusation.

She couldn't think. Why was he bringing this up now? "I guess you're right," she said wearily. "I should have been there."

The vast, emerald green lawns of Restland Cemetery, which featured bronze plaques to mark the grave sites rather than tombstones in order to make it easier on the mowers, glistened under the powerful Texas sun as mourners gathered beneath the green-striped canvas canopy that covered Randi's freshly dug grave. The family was seated in a row of folding metal chairs in front of the casket, which had not yet been lowered into the earthen slash that would be the final resting place of a young, vital human being whose life had been yanked from her mid-stride.

Jillian stood mutely between Ash and Derek in the surrounding crowd as the minister droned on in dreamlike tones about eternity and salvation. It suddenly, irreverently, occurred to Jillian that Randi would have a real hoot at the idea of her mother's Baptist preacher having any final words to say about her. She could almost hear Randi's wicked laugh as she tossed back her head behind a cloud of cigarette smoke. *You guys all hang around,* she'd say. *There's going to be a baptismal after the service.*

Jillian almost laughed. Oh, God, she was going to miss her.

The service finally came to a blessed end as the minister bent over to hug Randi's mother. Jillian dutifully joined the line of people that formed to take turns paying their respects to the family. There was Randi's sister, Patty, and her husband. In her arms Patty was holding Toby, who gazed about him in uncomprehending wonder with clear, shining gray eyes. His mother's eyes.

As Jillian placed the palm of her hand against the

child's sweet soft cheek, she turned to Patty and said, "I am so very sorry."

She was going to say more, about how much she would miss Randi and how much their friendship had meant to her, when Randi's mother, who was seated next to Patty, shook off the embrace of a friend and whirled toward Jillian, springing to her feet. Randi's mom was a diminutive woman, not much more than five feet tall, with sharp features and a surprisingly loud voice. Her stricken face was mottled pink from crying, but her eyes glittered at Jillian with such force she nearly stepped back.

"How dare you," she said through clenched teeth, "show your face here today."

"Mom," said Patty in gentle warning. "Not here."

But the woman's eyes, widened with hatred, held Jillian's horrified gaze. "You killed her," she said.

Jillian's entire body turned to ice.

"You killed my baby!" screamed the woman. "And you orphaned poor Toby, and I hope to God you burn in hell for it!"

Placing both hands firmly on Jillian's chest, the little woman shoved her. Jillian stumbled backward, every nerve ending in her body now afire with humiliation and distress.

"Get out of here!" the woman cried. *"Get out!"*

Face burning, she stood stupidly, too shocked to move.

"I warned her about you!" the woman yelled. "I told her to stay away from you, but she wouldn't listen to me, and now look—" She broke into sobs. "Get out!" Still weeping, she shoved Jillian again, who fell against the hard surface of the coffin.

Ash stepped forward. In an infinitely calm voice, he said, "Okay, okay. I think that's enough. We're leaving now." Placing a firm arm around Jillian's waist, he pulled her against his side. The silent crowd parted for them. Jillian, stumbling along on stiff, clumsy feet, allowed herself to be guided through the people, most of whom averted their eyes. She could hear Randi's mom's wailing all the way out to the car.

Derek materialized from somewhere and opened the car door for her, and Ash helped her into the seat. Before pulling out of the car doorway, he looked her straight in the eye and said, "It's not true, you know. Randi's death is not your fault. The woman's grieving, that's all. Tomorrow she won't even remember it."

But I will, thought Jillian. *God help me, I will.*

It was so easy to get away with murder.

As he shaved each morning, he thought about how easy it was. All you had to do was pick a disposable victim, somebody nobody would miss. Make sure there were no witnesses, and take care to leave no evidence behind. Then live an exemplary life.

It was so easy.

Keegan Sloane had waited for days in a state of hypervigilance, certain that at any moment there would be a knock at his office door or the doorbell would ring at home, and there would be a couple of homicide detectives from the Dallas Police Department or maybe some guy from the Dallas Fire Department, and they would say, "Dr. Sloane? We need to ask you a few questions about an arson fatality we're investigating."

He'd pored over the newspaper every morning and watched the TV news every night, looking for some sign that investigators were stepping up the pressure to find the man's killer. But the newscaster announced the death as an accident. There was a shot of the burned-out dumpster in the background. The sight made him sick but excited him at the same time.

A week later, the man remained unidentified, and his death had long since been overtaken by other, more demanding stories, like that tiresome riot over in Little Mexico.

He couldn't believe it. He had actually burned a man to death and gotten clean away with it.

Nobody suspected anything—not even his family. At first, he'd been a nervous wreck, certain that his guilt and anxiety showed all over his face and in every mannerism, but no one noticed a thing. It was kind of sad, really. Here he was, going through hell, and the people closest to him had no clue.

He'd always felt alone in the world, but Jesus, this really took the cake. Of course, the good news was that it worked to his advantage. As long as even his family remained blind to his secret life, then so would the rest of the world.

In the final analysis, there was one more necessary element to getting away with murder.

It was important to make it look like an accident.

He added that factor to his mental checklist. Because before he had even decided on the matter, he already knew: he was going to do it again. Oh, yes. He was definitely going to do it again.

Chapter Four

In the days following the fiasco at Randi's funeral, Jillian hid from the world in Derek's apartment. She spent most of her time curled up in bed, watching monotonous daytime TV with mindless inattention. In the evenings, when Derek was home, she made an effort to present a sane self to him. She would bathe and dress and throw together some kind of meal, and she would pretend to listen while he chattered on about his work on the informercial or comings and goings at the various Power Play gyms.

But none of it was real.

At night, insomnia punctuated her screaming nightmares and scattered fragments of dreams that left her battered senseless by dawn. Every time she closed her eyes, she saw the bloody pulp that had been Randi. Daytime naps did nothing to restore her old energy. Instead, she found herself too exhausted to face even the simplest tasks. She left the answering machine on to screen her calls and did not return any of them. It took entirely too much effort to carry on a conversation with anyone.

She couldn't feel, couldn't think, couldn't function. Work was out of the question.

Sometimes she found herself eating for comfort, and took to hiding chocolates and other forbidden treats from Derek's prying eyes in order to avoid the criticism that was sure to follow. Since she had stopped

exercising along with everything else, she soon started
to gain back the weight she had fought so hard to lose.

She and Derek took to bickering about little things.
It was not that he was entirely insensitive, but he was
just too busy himself to notice the depth of her despair. For the first couple of weeks, he tried to be
patient with her, and she was grateful for that. When
he did ask for sex about two weeks after Randi died,
Jillian gave in—gratitude, again—but her lovemaking
lacked passion. Mainly, she just wanted to get it over
with so she could be left alone again. He didn't seem
to notice, or if he did, he didn't say anything about it.

Still, the arguing continued, and she wondered if
their sex life had something to do with it.

A couple of times Ash came by, pounding on the
door and yelling that he knew she was in there and
to let him in, but she pretended to be gone. She
couldn't face him. Especially not him. After all, hadn't
he warned her not to go to Little Mexico that night?
And hadn't she blindly ignored him, too?

She was drowning. And too damned tired even to
tread water.

One afternoon, a full month after the riot, Derek
came home early and caught her in bed.

"What's wrong?" he asked. "Are you sick?"

A voice in her mind screamed at him, *What's
wrong? What's wrong? You dare to ask me what's
wrong?*

She said, "I'm just tired."

"You need to get some exercise, that's all," he said,
grabbing for her hand. "If you'd get up and start moving around, you'd feel better." He tugged at her.
"C'mon. Let's go to the gym, and I'll take you through
a workout. You haven't been in a long time."

"I don't feel like working out."

With a loud, long-suffering sigh, he said, "That's the
problem. You're getting lazy. You have to get back
into the habit. C'mon, Jill."

She resisted, and he let go of her hand. After a

smoldering moment, he said, "Cricket's having a reception at her house tonight for all of our Power Play staff. You should come. It will do you good to get out of the apartment for a while."

Jillian could not imagine anything that would "do her good" about attending another mindless, boring reception at Cricket Andrews' perfect little *House and Garden* show-off abode. It was the kind of house where if you set down your glass—on a coaster, of course—it would be immediately whisked away and loaded into the dishwasher out of sight. She'd never felt comfortable there.

"You go on," she said. "Maybe next time, okay?"

He gave another melodramatic sigh. "Fine," he said. "If you want to sit around here and feel sorry for yourself, then fine. But honestly, Jill—" He knelt beside her. "If you'd do a workout with me, I know you'd feel better. Exercise is the best thing for you right now."

"How do you know what's the best thing for me?" she asked, her voice sharper and more bitter than she'd intended. More quietly, she added, "You don't know anything."

"I know you're getting fat again," he said, and the words hurt.

This was the flip side of Derek's charming personality, she was learning. He could use words as sweet seductions or as sharp weapons.

"I know you don't do anything but lay around the house all day watching soap operas and crap on TV. I know your boss calls here every other day wanting to know when you're coming back to work. And I know I'm getting sick of it. It's time you snapped out of this, Jill. I know your friend died, and I'm sorry, but life goes on, pal." He got to his feet and glared down at her.

Jillian was surprised by her rage. She didn't know where it came from. It boiled up from some inner simmering cauldron and drove her out of bed and onto her feet, facing him with clenched fists. "You don't know a goddamned thing!" she yelled. "You never had anything bad happen to you in your whole miserable life! Why don't you go watch your best friend's face get blown off right in front of you and see how well YOU deal with it!"

Her entire body sizzled and snapped with heat and tension, and it was all she could do not to haul off and hit the man. She was beginning to wonder what she'd ever seen in him beyond the obvious.

"I don't have to take this," he said. "I do *not* have to take this!" He turned and stomped from the room and out of the apartment, slamming the door behind him.

Still trembling, Jillian seized a china vase and hurled it after him. It smashed against the door.

Her whole world, it seemed, was disintegrating around her. She had to get out. She didn't know where she would go, but at that moment she had to get out of the apartment. Jillian grabbed her tote, stuffed her feet into a pair of Keds, scrounged for her car keys, and hurried out the door. All she wanted to do was drive, music blasting, with no destination in mind.

She had not driven the Mustang since the riot. Her only forays outside were to a supermarket within walking distance of the complex. The Mustang was parked in her usual slot in front of the building, next to the empty space that usually held Derek's Lexus. The white top was up.

She was moving too fast, too unthinking, to remember.

Jillian had flung open the car door and actually sat down behind the wheel before she saw.

The car had not been cleaned. Crusted pools of blood covered the white passenger seat and stained the red carpet brown. It had soaked down into the seams of the leather, and there were rusty droplets of it on the gearshift knob and between the seats.

Jillian took one long look, then whirled and, leaning out of the still-open car door, vomited.

She hadn't thought there were any more tears left in her, but there were, and they coursed down her cheeks as she found herself rocking back and forth in the car seat, sobbing and saying, "I'm so sorry, Randi, I'm sorry, I'm sorry," over and over again.

There was no escape then. Nowhere to go to get away from the pain, the relentless guilt, the overpowering terror of that moment, the regret, the grief, the rage, the tumult and turmoil that roiled inside of her until she wanted to scream. Sometimes, her face buried in her pillow, she did.

She was going to have to sell the car. They'd have to replace the upholstery on the passenger seat and the front floorboard carpeting, but whatever the case, Jillian would never be able to drive the Mustang again. She knew that now.

Finally, she dragged herself out of the car and back into the apartment, where she fell into bed once more, too exhausted, too spent, to care. She would call Ash. Tomorrow, maybe, or the next day. He would be the best one to help with the transaction. She'd have to buy another car, some suitable form of transportation. And she'd have to go back to work in order to pay for it. But she wasn't going to think about that now.

She wasn't going to think about anything now. If she was lucky, she would sleep, and if the gods were with her, she wouldn't wake up screaming.

Ash was relieved to hear Jillian's voice when she called to ask his help in selling the Mustang. For her to ask for help—any help—was a good sign, and it gave him an excuse to visit her and finally be allowed into the apartment. Before going up, he stopped to look over the Mustang, and was enraged to see that Derek had not bothered to clean up the blood. Even if he was squeamish about it, the asshole could have turned the car over to professional detailers and let them do the job. It was unbelievably thoughtless of him to have left it for Jillian to see.

It took awhile for Jillian to open the door for Ash, and he struggled to hide his alarm at her appearance. The weight gain and absence of makeup did not bother him as much as the deadness in her eyes and voice, the slow, tired manner, and the listless way she discussed the sale of the car she had once loved so much. Jillian Ross was normally a woman of great vivacity and vitality, a woman who loved life and lived it with gusto. This wild child, this gifted writer, now shuffled across the room and folded herself into an armchair like a wounded animal.

"What kind of car would you like to trade for?" he asked, as if the car were what mattered in this room.

"I don't care," she said with a limp-wristed wave of her hand. "Something that gets good gas mileage, I guess. Something affordable."

"Okay." He studied her for a moment. "The demons are running loose, aren't they?"

Her dark-rimmed eyes widened. "What are you talking about?"

"It's never easy to confront your own mortality, Jilly," he said. "The first time it happens, especially if it involves the violent death of a friend, it lets loose a swarm of demons in your mind. They torment you all day long, blaming you and making you feel guilty and hopeless." Leaning forward, he propped his elbows on his knees and gestured with his hands as he talked. "Look, sweetie, I've been there. I've walked into the jaws of the beast and left a friend behind. And I've got my own demons."

"How do you get rid of them?" she asked quietly.

"You don't. You just learn to cage them up."

"Do they stay caged?" she whispered.

He held her gaze with his own. "Not always." It was an honest answer.

She nodded.

"How do you get them into the cage?" He could barely hear her now.

Ash thought for a moment. "Well, I guess the first thing you have to do is forgive yourself."

"I can't." Her voice was sharp and clear.

"You have to. It doesn't do any good to blame yourself. It doesn't change anything. What happened, happened. It's over now, and you can't change that, and you can't bring Randi back."

Leaning her head back against the chair, she closed her eyes and said, "I know."

"You just have to find a way to honor your friend with your own life. Randi wouldn't be this hard on you, Jill. She loved you, and she would never want you to punish yourself in this way."

"I can't help it," she said. "I can't get past it. I've tried. It's just . . . devouring me."

"I know. It's going to take some time, is all."

She nodded, but said little else. After a while, he took the keys to the Mustang, gave her a long, hard hug, and left.

Keegan Sloane came home from work one evening to find his study door ajar. Light spilled from the room into the hallway. He pushed open the door and stepped inside. His wife, Eleanor, was stooped over a box of books he had stored beneath his desk. She'd pulled out the box and was examining the titles: *The Nature of Fire, Dynamics of Fire, Arson.*

"What are you doing?" he asked in his sharpest, most commanding voice.

With a start, she turned to face him. "I-I just wondered . . . wh-what you were doing with these books," she stammered.

"And I'm wondering what you're doing snooping around in my study." Crossing the room, he snatched a book out of her hands and dropped it into the box.

"I wasn't snooping."

"Eleanor. This is my office. These are my things. Have you ever caught me prying into your things?"

"Well, no, I—"

He took the box and stuffed it back beneath his desk. "You have entirely too much time on your hands. For a schoolteacher, you spend a pathetically small amount of time on class preparation. I should think your students are suffering for it."

She blushed and bit her lip.

"If you're bored, then why don't you get involved in the PTA like the other teachers?"

"You know how shy I am, Keegan."

He sighed. "Ah, yes. The shy excuse. Here we go again."

"There's no need to belittle me."

"Is that what you thought I was doing? Once again, you seem to have misinterpreted me, my dear." He put on a smile. "I was only teasing."

"It didn't feel like teasing."

"That's not my problem, now, is it? I can't help it if you are too sensitive to understand a joke." He put a hand to her elbow to guide her from the room. To his surprise, she stood her ground.

"I want to know why those books are in our house, Keegan." Her voice quavered at the end, and she dropped her gaze from his own penetrating one.

He thought quickly. "If you must know, Eleanor, I have a patient who is having trouble with impulses of pyromania. I'm only trying to help him. And now you've made me violate patient confidentiality. I hope you are satisfied."

"I'm sorry!" she cried, putting her hand to her lips. "I didn't mean to—"

"But you did, and that's what comes from prying. You should be ashamed of yourself."

"I'm sorry," she repeated.

"Yes," he said, once again guiding her toward the door. "You should be." Slump-shouldered, she walked out. At the doorway he flicked off the light. As he

pulled the door shut behind them, it occurred to him
that he was going to have to put a lock on the door.

Derek was working late, and Jillian had channel-
surfed until she discovered *Power Up Your Life With
Derek and Cricket*, the very infomercial she'd been
hearing so much about in recent months. There they
were, the Golden Couple of the fitness industry.
Cricket Andrews, as blond as Derek, was a petite dy-
namo, one of those relentlessly energetic people for
whom the word "pep" had been invented.

She'd been a cheerleader in high school and college,
and it showed. What no one but a few insiders knew
was that Cricket was also the brains behind the
multimillion-dollar fitness enterprise she and Derek
had built. It was Cricket who hired and fired the managers at the various Power Play gyms, Cricket who
had assembled a team of attorneys to handle legal
matters as the franchise grew into not just gyms, but
a line of workout clothes, the infomercial, and cur-
rently in development, a syndicated radio call-in show
for Derek.

While Cricket ran the business, Derek, who had
never been to college but nevertheless was possessed
of the considerable gift of gab, took care of the PR.
He made the society pages frequently as he worked
the party circuit, the charity balls, and other events
where he could promote the tony Power Play gyms,
which had become *the* place for upper-middle class
executives and their spouses to see and to be seen in
their stretch Lycra and spandex.

"Don't touch that remote!" Cricket was saying.
"You don't know it yet, but you've just found the
answers to some of your most pressing and worrisome
questions. Isn't that right, Derek?"

"Absolutely, Cricket." Derek, his long hair pulled
back in a practical ponytail, was resplendent in his
royal blue and gold Power Play workout clothes: spandex biker shorts and a short-cropped, sleeveless shirt

that showed off what muscle-building aficionados liked
to call his "six-pack"—the coveted washboard abdom-
inal muscles. Gazing into the camera with sincere blue
eyes, he said, "Questions like, Why does my life feel
so out of control? Why am I so tired all the time?
What can I do to help myself quit eating compulsively,
or smoking, or drinking too much?"

Jillian glanced down at the Hershey's chocolate bar
in her hand and took another guilty bite.

"Here at Power Play," said Cricket, "we know *exactly* how you feel. We've all been there, and our licensed, professional fitness experts are eager to help
you work out an individual, personalized program that
will empower you to get your life back on track."

"And there's no greater feeling," added Derek,
"than knowing that *you* are in charge of your life,
you're in control, and believe me, nobody can ever
take that away from you."

"Wanna bet?" muttered Jillian. A sharp knock at
the door startled her, and she stuffed the candy back
into its wrapper and crammed it behind the sofa cushions. It could be Derek; he could have forgotten his
keys or something.

She shuffled to the door and peered through the
peephole.

It was Cricket Andrews.

Surprised, Jillian opened the door. Cricket was
dressed as usual, in tight spandex shorts, a blue Power
Play sweatshirt, and spotless white Reeboks. Although
it was dark out, sunglasses were perched atop her
head, arranged in the fluffy folds of her short blond
hair like a barrette. She did not look perky and happy
or infomercial-ready. In fact, she looked anxious and
worried.

"Jill, is Derek here?"

"Uh, no. He's working late tonight."

"Do you know where? I couldn't get him on the
cell phone."

"I'm not sure, Cricket. I didn't really ask him where he was going to be tonight. Is something wrong?"

Cricket jingled the car keys she held in her hand. The woman was incapable of sitting or standing still. She pursed her lips, as though debating with herself about what she should say.

"Would you like to come in? He should be here soon."

"Well . . ." Cricket stepped through the door and stopped, staring at the TV. "Would you turn that off?"

"Sure." Jillian picked up the remote and turned off the television. This was very strange. Although she and Cricket were hardly girlfriends, they'd always been friendly. "Can I get you anything?"

"Water, please, if you don't mind."

"You bet." Jillian crossed into the kitchen to the refrigerator and pulled out a blue bottle of Ty'Nant Spring Water. She reached into the cabinet for a glass.

"That's fine, thanks." Cricket had followed Jillian into the kitchen and took the bottle from her. She unscrewed the cap and took a long drink.

"Are you all right?" asked Jillian.

"No, to tell you the truth, I'm not." Cricket drummed her fingers on the edge of the counter. "I really need to talk to Derek, and I don't want to do it over the phone. Would you tell him to come by my house in the morning before he goes to the gym? I'll be up early."

Jillian's reporter instincts went on full alert. "What's going on?"

"I can't tell you. You'll be on Derek's side no matter what I say."

"That's not necessarily true. I'm a journalist. I'm perfectly capable of making up my own mind."

Cricket finished the bottle of water and set it down on the kitchen counter. "Some people at the office are spreading lies about me," she said. "They're saying I've jacked around with the books, that I haven't been paying taxes and stuff."

Jillian's breath caught in her throat.

"It's not true," continued Cricket. "But I'm afraid they got to Derek before I could."

Jillian thought a moment. "If the allegations are false, you should be able to prove your case quickly just by showing them the books," she said reasonably.

Cricket glanced away from her. "It's not that easy, I'm afraid."

She was lying.

Jillian had covered too many instances of fraud in articles for the *Dallas Mirror*. She'd been lied to by the best, and over the years, had developed a fine-tuned instinct for when she was hearing untruths.

"What are . . . they . . . saying, exactly?" she said, keeping her tone even and nonjudgmental, as she always did when interviewing liars.

"Oh, all kinds of crap!" Cricket began tapping her foot irritably. "Like I didn't pay social security taxes on employees, or that I invented Power Play employees so that I could cash the false paychecks, or that money that should be going to pay operating expenses is disappearing. Stuff like that. None of it is true. Not one word."

"Well, who's making the accusations?"

Cricket shrugged. "One of our investors. And our accountant. That guy's a prick, anyway. He's been hitting on me for months. I should have known it would come to this."

More lies. Jillian knew, just from this brief conversation, that the Power Play franchise, and possibly Derek as well, were now in serious trouble. If the accountant and one of the investors were calling into doubt Cricket's methods, then questionable figures must have come to their attention. It was a classic liar's defense to counter the accuser with an accusation of some sort that was meant to divert attention from the *real* problem—hence the remark about the accountant "hitting on" Cricket.

And Derek, poor, trusting Derek, would be caught in the middle.

"I just want Derek to hear my side before they get their fangs into him," said Cricket.

I'll bet you would. "I'm sorry he's running so late. Would you like to wait for him?"

"No, no. Just give him my message, will you?" Cricket brushed past Jillian and walked rapidly through the living room, as if she couldn't wait to get out the door.

She knows I don't believe her, thought Jillian. *I failed to show enough righteous shock in my reaction to her story.* "I'll tell him you came by," she said. "And that it's urgent he see you."

"Thank you," said Cricket. Then, dropping the dark shades over her eyes, she walked out into the night.

Chapter Five

The news of the Power Play financial scandal hit the local papers and television news only a few days after Cricket's visit to the apartment. Within the month after the news broke, Derek and Cricket were embroiled in an acrimonious and very public business divorce. Their only communication, it seemed, was in "he said–she said" news pieces.

Derek didn't help matters when he took out a restraining order forbidding Cricket access to any of the Power Play gyms. He followed through a week later by having her arrested when she came to one of the gyms to talk to him.

Cricket responded by filing a motion of contempt against Derek. After that, Derek and several investors sued Cricket Andrews, claiming she had mismanaged funds, breached her fiduciary duty, misappropriated corporate assets, failed to pay federal taxes, and then misrepresented the tax liability to the investors.

Cricket countersued, claiming Derek had cheated her out of her fair percentage of the partnership, that a subordinate made the tax "error," and that Derek was "emotionally and verbally" abusive to her.

Meanwhile, the IRS claimed they were owed $250,000 in unpaid employee social security taxes.

Under normal circumstances, Jillian would have been one of Derek's staunchest and most supportive allies, ferreting out information for him and listening uncritically to his anti-Cricket tirades. But caught in the quicksand of her own devastating post-traumatic depression and unable to pull herself free, Jillian found herself overwhelmed by the crisis. She couldn't cope with Derek's demands for attention and sympathy. Her mind often drifted when he rambled on about his troubles.

One night, when he'd been ranting and raving about some new development, Jillian said, "If you'd learned to read a spreadsheet and checked the books yourself now and then, you might not have been taken advantage of in the first place."

"But I *trusted* her!" he yelled. "Can I help it if I'm too nice?"

"No," she said, and muttered, "but there's a fine line between being nice and being *stupid.*"

"What did you say?"

"Nothing."

He stalked off into the kitchen, and a moment later thundered, "What are all these dishes doing in the sink? I can't believe this!" Rounding the corner of the doorway, he pointed at Jillian and said, "What the hell is the *matter* with you? All you do is lie around feeling sorry for yourself, when *I'm* the one in trouble!"

Jillian felt a pang of guilt. In spite of the fact that they weren't getting along these days, he had a point. "You're right," she said. "I'm sorry. I'm trying to pull myself together." Then and there, she decided to make a real effort—for her own self if not for Derek. This situation with Cricket had been a terrible strain on him, and she was being no help at all.

After all, he'd tried to be patient with her after the riot, and she hadn't made things any easier. She longed for the old days between them, the playful banter, the hot sex. Maybe it wasn't all lost, but she knew it was up to her to salvage the remnants of the relationship.

The next morning, Jillian got up, cleaned the apartment, shaved her legs, dug out her bathing suit—which crimped a bit now that she'd regained so much weight—and decided to surprise Derek at the new gym—the one with the swimming pool. She'd not been there since the night of Randi's death. Remembering Randi's teasing visit there with her the night of the riots was too painful.

She drove over in her new hunter green Saturn. Ash had done a good job. The car was a demonstrator model, and he'd helped her get it for a song. It didn't have the panache and spirit of her old Mustang, but it had a better sound system and handled well. He'd also found a buyer for the Mustang and had gotten her a good price. She'd never seen the car again after Ash drove it away that day.

The late June day was blazing hot, even for Dallas, which reminded Jillian of the convertible and other things she'd rather not think about. She parked the car and sauntered in with her gym bag as if she worked out every day. The girl behind the desk started to speak, then recognizing Jillian, waved her on through. This was a weekday, and not one of the gym's peak times. A few women lumbered along on the treadmills, wearing headphones and bored, intense expressions, while one other worked a weight machine as if in training for a Nautilus competition. Concentrating fiercely, she didn't notice Jillian, either.

Jillian glanced around for Derek, but didn't see him. She started to ask the receptionist, then changed her mind. She'd find him. It would be a pleasant surprise, and after her swim and shower, maybe they'd have a fruit smoothee or something.

As she swung through the doors into the sparkling aquamarine sanctuary of the pool room, Jillian heard something that froze her in her tracks. Slowly she swiveled her head to the right.

Derek, his back to the door, his blue satin Power Play gym shorts dropped to his ankles, buttock muscles straining, held one of the young Power Play girls—Tiffany, wasn't it?—against the wall exactly as he had done Jillian so many forgettable weeks before, fucking her brains out.

The tableau froze. Tiffany was the first to spot Jillian, her mouth forming a shocked little "o."

"Jill!" she cried, in that familiar way some people have who call you by a nickname when they really don't know you well enough to do so. Obviously, that was the name Derek used when talking to Tiffany about her.

Derek stopped.

Jillian spun on her heel and slammed through the doors, half running through the gym with such urgency that even the weight lifter stopped to take note.

By the time Derek made it out the front door, Jillian was peeling rubber out of the parking lot.

By the time he got home, she was gone.

Sometimes he tried to psychoanalyze himself, or at least the dead self, the dead true self that hid behind the alive false self even as it slowly devoured all that he was.

He would take out the dead self as if it were a mysterious shrunken object one might find in a child's treasure box. He would turn it this way and that, examining it, trying to figure out what it might be.

The whys, he understood. As a psychiatrist, he already knew that he hated his mother even as he loved her. Her crazy strength had somehow held them together even through the bouts of drunkenness and dementia. His father's abandonment, he knew, had left him fatally scarred, disfigured for life. Like the tragic phantom of the opera, his true self had hidden away from the world, into the bowels of his being where, over time, it eventually died a quiet and unnoticed death.

The death of his true self also killed any true emotions he might have felt, the sorts of emotions one might label "normal." Did he love his wife? He'd stayed married to her all these years, hadn't he? Surely that might be construed as a form of love, mightn't it?

Did he love his son? He never treated his son in the way his mother had treated him, and God knew, he'd never abandoned the boy. That had to be love; in any event, it was more than he'd ever received as a child.

What about his work? His work, in the final analysis, was his salvation. He did feel some measure of satisfaction from his work, and that was the closest thing to happiness he was likely ever to encounter— a mild contentment in the routine, and in the knowledge that he was good at it, in spite of his flawed character. His false self was doing a good enough job, it seemed, for both of them, at least in his private practice.

He tried not to let the other facts bother him too much: the fact that, although he was a university psychology professor, he was teaching in a third-rate commuter college of a university, the fact that he'd been passed over for department chair not once but twice, the fact that although he'd published in a couple of professional journals, his articles came and went without any particular notice from the psychiatric community.

Even more significant, perhaps, he was never asked to present a paper—or even to serve on a panel—at any of the professional conferences. He tried not to think about it.

He tried not to think about it a lot.

There were other things he tried not to think about, but it was impossible not to. Something was different. Scary.

What had changed in recent months about his personal situation was the nature of the deadness. Whereas always before it had been a black hole at the core of him, now it seemed to be, for lack of a better term, growing. He had noticed that it was getting harder and harder to maintain the false self.

His true self, his dead self, seemed to want to take over.

And it terrified him.

It took Ash several days to track Jillian down. He found her at her old rental house, located in a neighborhood in Dallas that had once been grand but was now aging and comfortable. She answered the door sooner than he expected, after his having spent numerous futile visits since the riot pounding on Derek's door in attempts to see her. She smiled at the sight of him, which he took as a good sign.

"I didn't know you kept your old place while you were living with Derek," he said. It was not what he had intended to say, but there it was.

She shrugged. "He had one of those high-dollar yuppie interior decorators who would have cringed if I'd dared interlope with any of my junk. And it was only a couple months. By the time I'd made up my mind about the move becoming permanent, we'd already broken up." She quirked a sad grin at him. "Story of my life. Come on in."

The small house—more like a cozy cottage—was so like Jillian in so many ways, and it felt good to be seeing her back in this place rather than in Derek's sterile postmodern soulless suburban digs. Jillian's home reflected her eclectic interests and her full-tilt approach to life that she'd had ever since they'd first met on the University of Texas campus—what, fourteen, fifteen years ago? It was hard for Ash to believe it had been that long.

The walls were crammed with framed movie posters: Tyrone Power in *The Mark of Zorro*, William Holden and Gloria Swanson in *Sunset Boulevard, The Postman Always Rings Twice* starring Lana Turner and John Garfield, Alan Ladd and Veronica Lake in *The Blue Dahlia*, *Laura* starring Gene Tierney and

Dana Andrews, and of course, Bogart and Bergman in *Casablanca*.

Overstuffed bookshelves covered every available space not taken up by movie posters. Like Ash, Jillian loved true crime and thrillers, including classics by Sir Arthur Conan Doyle and Edgar Allan Poe. There were also books on every conceivable subject, as though she'd never sold any of her college texts, as well as tattered old childhood favorites, ratty dictionaries, finds from the half-price and antique bookstores, and functional writer's volumes such as Strunk and White's *The Elements of Style*.

A TV and VCR was stashed on one shelf, surrounded by toppling videos, many of them containing old movies she'd taped off the movie classic network to watch when she had time.

A desk holding a handsome computer rig was nestled against the bay windows of the living room, and it, too, was covered with sentimental mementos she'd saved over the years, including her considerable collection of Daffy Duck figurines, and photos of family and friends, including one of Ash in full turnout fire-fighting gear standing next to Jillian, who was also dressed in full turnout. That one was from a story she'd done once on firefighter training—he'd suited her up and taken her into a burning building during a real training exercise and she'd loved every minute of it.

A blue pitcher sat next to the computer, containing an inexpensive bouquet of flowers in various shades of yellow she must have picked up at a supermarket florist, and on every surface that didn't have books or videotapes could be found votive candles in various stages of melt. Sunshine spilled through the sheer draperies, gleaming off the yellow flowers, bouncing from the blue pitcher, and soaking warmly into the books like a still-life tableau. All that was missing, it seemed, was a cat.

The comfortable little place, which also featured a

small, sunny kitchen, a cramped bedroom, and a temperamental bathroom, was cluttered and disheveled, but Ash still felt no small measure of relief, seeing her back here in her own element rather than stashed in Derek's apartment like one of his trendy possessions du jour.

He'd never liked that guy. Come to think of it, he'd never had much use for any of Jillian's boyfriends.

Which brought him back to the reason for his visit. He took a seat in a too soft armchair, got up, and switched to the couch. Jillian curled up in the armchair catercorner to the couch. Now that he was able to take a closer look at her, he could see that she still did not look well at all. Not that recent events had helped any.

"I heard about Derek," he said. "I'm sorry, Jilly." It was a name he seldom used with her, and he knew she understood that he meant it only in the most tender way.

She shrugged. "It was my own fault. He was going through a hard time, and I neglected him. I was too wrapped up in my own problems."

And why was that? Ash wanted to shout. *If he hadn't been such an asshole to you when you needed him most, you might be back on your feet by now.* Instead, he said, "Don't blame yourself, Jillian. Could be the relationship had just run its course."

"I miss him," she said.

God knows why, he thought. He said, "It'll get easier, sugar."

Again, she shrugged.

After a moment he said, "Have you thought about going back to work? It could be just the thing to help in your recovery."

"I need to, I know," she said. "Especially now. I don't have that much money. It's just that . . ."

"What?"

"Well, it's not like I'm standing there riveting bolts into a car on an assembly line or something. I mean . . . my work depends upon my *imagination*, Ash!" A look of genuine fear came into her eyes. "Everything I do, I do in my head. And when I try to . . . access . . . that part of me . . ." Her voice dwindled off, and then she whispered, "There's just nothing there."

This was more serious than even Ash had realized. What Jillian was describing went far beyond mere "writer's block." This was deep, clinical depression.

She went on, almost in a monotone. "Every time I hear a siren, I see it all over again. Every time I try to go to sleep, I see Randi's . . . face . . ."

He reached over and patted her knee. "It's hard for me, too. I want you to know that. And that's normal. It doesn't mean you're crazy or anything."

She nodded. "I know. It's just . . ."

He waited.

"I hate myself, is all."

"Jillian—"

"I can't help it. Randi's mom was right. It's my fault Randi's dead, my fault Toby's motherless. And what led to that whole thing in the first place? My work. Or, at least, my drive to do my work in just my way, without any regard for the consequences. I mean, it's one thing to risk your own personal safety for a story—especially if you're single and childless like me. But to risk the life of a *friend*. And, Ash, she didn't want to go! She really didn't want to go. She had such a bad feeling about that rally, and I *ignored* her! I overlooked her own fears, her own instincts for self-preservation for my own selfish interest. And I just can't get past that."

He looked down at his hands, trying to think what to say that could help her.

"When I hear a siren, I just . . . I get so *afraid*. Sometimes my heart pounds so fast and so hard I think I'm going to die. And you know what the worst part is?"

He was afraid to ask.

"The worst part is that sometimes I wish I *could* die. And I miss her so much. She's been a part of my life since we were little kids. I don't think a day in our lives ever went by that we didn't talk on the phone. I was Toby's godmother before—it just hurts so bad!"

"I know." He leaned forward and took her hand in his. It was cold and lifeless.

"And then when I caught Derek and that girl . . . God, that was so humiliating. But the thing is that mainly all I could think was 'Well, Jillian, looks like you've fucked up all over again.' "

"Now, wait a minute," protested Ash. "*You* did not fuck up anything. That was all Derek's doing, babe."

"Maybe. But he had good reason."

Ash rolled his eyes. "Nobody's *ever* got good reason to cheat on someone who cares for them. If he couldn't live with the way things were, he could have had the common decency to break up with you. That would have been more merciful."

"He probably didn't want to hurt me."

"Aw, bullshit, Jillian! He wouldn't break up with you because he *needed* you for some pathetic little-boy reason. He was using you, probably from the start."

"That's not true."

He let out a melodramatic sigh.

She sprang to her feet. "I don't want to talk about it anymore. You just don't understand."

Oh, but I do, thought Ash. *I just wish you did.*

He changed the subject. "I went by the Mirror offices and spoke to Miles yesterday."

"How are they doing?" She wiped her eyes.

"He's lost without you, Jillian. He really needs you back. Says the place is a madhouse without you."

In spite of herself, she smiled. "That sounds like Miles." Staring at the floor, she said, "I need more time."

"It's been, what, two months already?"

"Something like that."

"Okay then. Would you let me help you?"

"How?" She gave him a suspicious glance.

"What you're going through—it's more than just grief or depression. It's actually post-traumatic stress syndrome."

She looked up in surprise and doubt. "You mean like what the Vietnam vets experienced?"

He nodded. "Sort of. Not exactly, because the trauma they experienced was ongoing and lasted for months. But what you went through was a single very traumatic, violent event that threw your entire system into shock." He paused, and when she didn't say anything, he went on. "It's something firefighters have to deal with all the time. I've had to do it myself—remember that time we lost three guys in that terrible fire?"

She nodded.

"I blamed myself, just like you do. We all did, all of us who felt that if we'd done something different or been in some other place, we could have prevented the tragedy."

"I remember," she said quietly.

"Okay. Then maybe you remember that the fire department has professionals on call. People who are specially trained in trauma counseling. There are psychiatrists who volunteer their time to the department for the firefighters who may need it. There's one I know of who's real good. He's a psychiatrist who specializes in PTSD. He's had a lot of success in helping people cope with the aftereffects of trauma."

"Do you know him? Did you go to him after you lost your friends?"

He shook his head. "No. He wasn't on the list at that time. I've just heard that he's good. From guys who've been to see him."

Jillian shook her head. "It's not that I'm opposed to some sort of counseling, Ash, it's just that I couldn't possibly afford it."

"But you can. I asked Miles about it. He checked with your health insurance policy, and this doctor is covered by it. All you have to pay is a modest co-payment, fifteen or twenty bucks."

She frowned. "But isn't that for a limited number of sessions?"

"It depends. If you need more time with him than the policy covers, then the *Dallas Mirror* will pick up the slack. They consider it a disability payment, and Miles considers it well worth the investment if it will get you back to work. He says their circulation has actually dropped since you quit writing for them. He checked it out with the main office and everything."

Biting her lip, Jillian thought over the offer. "Sweet Miles. I can't imagine a better boss." After another quiet moment, she said, "I know I need help. I can't seem to get past this on my own. I've tried." She gave Ash a bleak smile.

"If you go into therapy with this guy, will you go back to work? Even on a part-time basis?"

"My work would probably suck, you know."

"Jillian." He grinned. "Your work sucking is like a normal writer's work shining. And that's a direct quote from Miles."

She laughed. "All right. Where do I find this guy?"

With a satisfied nod, Ash dug around in a jacket pocket for the name, which he'd scrawled on a piece of scratch paper. "I just happen to have . . ." He handed it to her.

Jillian leaned over and read aloud, "Keegan Sloane, M.D." She glanced up. "And he's supposed to be pretty good with nutcases like me?"

Reaching over, Ash rubbed her cheek with his knuckles. She leaned her face into his hand.

"The best," he said. "Dr. Sloane will change your life."

PART II

Flashpoint

One fire burns out another's burning,
One pain is lessen'd by another's anguish.

William Shakespeare
Romeo and Juliet

O eyes, no eyes, but fountains fraught with tears;
O life, no life, but lively form of death;
O world, no world, but mass of public wrongs;
Confused and filled with murder and misdeeds.

Thomas Kyd
The Spanish Tragedy, 1594

Chapter Six

By the time Ash McGraw arrived at the fire scene, the worst part of the fire had been knocked down. He sent word to the firefighters that he wanted them to delay overhaul until he'd had a chance to do a preliminary investigation. Before approaching the building, a warehouse in an industrial area of the city, Ash made a note that this was the same general area where he'd investigated a fatal dumpster fire not long ago. An unidentified man, presumed to be homeless, had been found dead in the dumpster by firefighters, his body in the pugilistic pose of fire victims, who always looked as though they'd done hand-to-hand combat with the beast.

Ash would have been forced to render the death as "accidental," if it had not been for one crucial piece of evidence: a small puddle of vomit discovered beside the dumpster. The lab had ordered a DNA test, and found that it did not match that of the victim. That meant that, even though there had been no one around when firefighters arrived, and even though no trace of accelerants could be found at the scene, and even though the victim was found in autopsy to be inebriated almost to the point of unconsciousness—there had been somebody else at that dumpster.

Perhaps he'd set himself on fire some way, and a companion had panicked and fled the scene, but since Ash was never able to determine in what way the fire had started, he remained disturbed. As far as he was concerned, there was a fatality and someone else had been present either before or after the fire. Ash was not ruling out murder, although until he had more evidence, there wasn't much he could do about it.

Now here he was again, in the same neighborhood. He didn't like it.

Like the other fire, this one had occurred in the depths of night. There were few spectators. Ash wrote down the license plate numbers of all the vehicles in the area and briefly questioned the handful of witnesses, making notes as to their dress and general appearance and taking down their names and addresses for future formal statements. Any one of them, he knew, could be an arsonist.

But as he jotted down their comments and explanations for their presence on the scene, no alarm bells sounded in the depths of his mind. Ash did not think an arsonist was among them.

Before beginning a cursory examination of the exterior of the building, Ash opened the rear doors of his Suburban, which was crammed with the tools of his trade—everything from cameras and tape recorders to brand-new, specially treated empty paint cans (good for evidence collection), glass jars, hypodermic syringes, gardening tools, various meters and detectors, graph paper for sketching, a hundred-foot measuring tape, debris-sifting screens, powerful hand lamps, a fingerprinting kit, disposable plastic gloves, heavy elastic bands, evidence tags, a video camera, sealing wax, plastic evidence bags, sterile sponges, rope, compass, aluminum foil, crime scene and fire line tape, and signs that read NO TRESPASSING—PER ORDER OF THE FIRE MARSHAL!

He kicked off his sneakers, tossed them into the trunk, and withdrew a pair of steel-toed protective boots. He was already wearing the distinctive white arson investigator coveralls and heat resistant bunker coat with identifying shoulder patch. Pulling on the

boots, he grabbed a hard hat and checked to make
sure his credentials were in his pocket and his side
arm locked in the glove compartment of the car. Then
he hung a camera around his neck and went to work,
beginning with a quick shot of the gaggle of spectators.

There were a couple of uniformed police officers on
the scene, and Ash requested that they secure the area
and allow only a minimum of fire personnel past, at
least until he was able to check over the scene. He
questioned them briefly, to see if they'd noticed anything unusual or suspicious upon their arrival, or if
they'd witnessed anyone running or driving away from
the area, but they'd seen nothing out of the ordinary
except for the fire itself.

He then questioned the fire captain on the scene as
to his observations concerning the extent and color of
the smoke and flames when they arrived. (The gray
to brown smoke and yellow to red flames made it
appear that there was no gasoline, turpentine, kero-
sene, or other accelerants present.)

Ash also questioned the fire captain about witnesses, as well as which areas of the structure were
involved in the actual burning. The fire had been reported by the police, which Ash already knew from
his previous interviews with the officers on the scene.
Though the firefighters had not spotted any accelerant
containers or smelled a discernible odor that would
alert them to the presence of any, they'd called Ash
in to investigate when they realized the fire appeared
to have two separate and distinct points of origin—an
almost sure sign of arson. That made the fire "suspicious," and that made it Ash's responsibility.

He thanked the fire captain and began to work his
way around the building. He would be able to tell
more in daylight, to be sure, but the beam of his hand
lamp could still reveal charring patterns and other telltale signs of fire patterns or ignition sources. As he
walked, he checked for any evidence of incendiaries,
but found none.

Heat emanated from the building in waves, carrying with it the acrid, choking stench of smoke, ash, charred wood, melted plastics, and other chemicals released when a building is destroyed by flame and ultrahigh temperatures. Sweat drooled down the back of Ash's neck and between his shoulder blades. In the background he could hear the firefighters working the scene, shouting to one another, banging equipment around, occasionally laughing. The noise was like the sound of the surf to a fisherman, comforting and homey.

At the rear of the building, Ash spotted a door. When he got up close to it, he could see that it had been forced open by some tool—possibly a crowbar. After whistling over one of the uniforms to secure the exit, Ash took several photographs of the jimmied door, then pulled on a pair of rubber gloves and entered the building through the door. He found himself in a small office area that featured a large window overlooking the warehouse storage area.

The office was untouched by fire and showed only minimal smoke damage, though water dripped from the ceiling and soaked the floor. Crouching, Ash shone his light over the surface of the water pools, looking for signs of oily substances floating on the surface, but none appeared. He sniffed the water, but noticed nothing unusual. He would withdraw samples of the water with a syringe later, or possibly soak some up with a sterile sponge and have it analyzed at the lab.

Ash rifled through the desk and file cabinets, looking for signs of theft. He found the petty cash box. It was unlocked. Within, he counted about two hundred dollars.

So the "suspicious fire" was probably not an attempt to cover up a burglary.

Next he turned up a book of financial records and set that aside. He'd go over it later and see if he could find any evidence of financial decline, coded entries, or signs of other transactions that might point toward insurance fraud.

There did not appear to be a burglar alarm, but Ash did discover a smoke detector. However, no batteries were in it. He couldn't tell if it had been tampered with or if the owner had just been careless about replacing the batteries. Ash made a note to question him about it.

Leaving the office, Ash continued his interior examination of the building, working closer toward the fire damage. In order to examine V patterns on the walls, Ash had to work his way up and down aisles of boxes and shelves of merchandise. The area closest to the office was undamaged except for smoke and the water used by firefighters to extinguish the blaze. Closer in, heat damage was visible, along with signs of charring, and there was a great deal of debris where that section of the roof had collapsed.

He had almost reached the point of maximum destruction when he tripped over something in the floor and almost fell headlong, sending the hand lamp tumbling to the concrete floor. It fell on its side.

Staring unseeing into the beam of light lay a man, his body blackened by soot. He lay on his stomach, his face turned toward the light, his arms splayed out by his sides with the palms facing up.

Kneeling next to the man, Ash played the light over the body. There were signs that the skull had been caved in by something—possibly the same crowbar that had forced open the back door. Ash knew that in extreme heat, the human brain swelled, causing the skull to "explode" outward. By the time this event occurred, the human in question was long since dead, usually from smoke inhalation or carbon monoxide poisoning rather than from fire.

But this was not a question of extreme heat swelling the brain—firefighters had arrived soon enough to knock down the blaze before that could happen, and the skull was fractured inward, not outward.

Naturally, now that he'd discovered a fatality—further cursory examination of the body revealed him to be a security guard—Ash would follow Dallas Arson Investigator procedure. He would notify the police, call in the crime scene search team, and alert the medical examiner.

But Ash already knew what they would find. This man had not died battling the beast. The beast had been cheated of that small satisfaction.

The poor man had been murdered, by someone far less powerful than the beast, but every bit as deadly.

When Jillian arrived for her first appointment with Dr. Sloane, she was shown into a small room with table and chairs by an assistant who explained that before she met with Dr. Sloane, she must fill out a questionnaire and insurance forms. After that she would be given two diagnostic tests: the Minnesota Multiphasic Personality Inventory, or MMPI, and the Beck Depression Inventory. The doctor would take a few minutes to evaluate the test results, and then he would meet with Jillian to discuss her treatment.

The Beck Depression Inventory was very simple and took only a few minutes to complete. Its basic purpose seemed to be to evaluate the effects of Jillian's distress on her sleeping and eating habits, her body image, and her general mood. The questions were easy to answer and, Jillian suspected, presented a fairly clear picture of her depression.

The MMPI was another matter. Here it was often difficult for Jillian to know how to answer them since they were true or false with no variation as to degree. For instance, Jillian had never liked her mother's poodle and used to like to tease it until it barked and ran to hide under her mother's chair, but when Jillian encountered the statement, I like to tease animals, she hesitated. If she put "true," would that make her sound like some nasty little sadist who enjoyed tormenting innocent little creatures? But if she put "false," would some other answer in the lengthy test reveal the presence of her mother's poodle and make her look like a liar? After all, she liked animals—it was just that little dog who drove her nuts. Or maybe it was the way her mother had behaved with the dog that she didn't like. Whatever. She put "false."

Jillian did not like the MMPI test, and was surprised that it took a whole hour to complete. After that, she sat in the comfortable waiting room and nervously flipped through magazines. No one else was in the room. Jillian wondered if Dr. Sloane had some sort of private exit from his office for the privacy of his . . . what? Clients?

Patients.

Here she was, a patient. She'd never been in therapy before, and she was anxious about it. Jillian had long prided herself on her independence. Now she not only needed help, but she had to accept it from a stranger who would be privy to the most intimate details of her life. Revealing those details was not something she looked forward to doing.

"Jillian?"

At the sound of her name in the quiet room, Jillian jumped. The magazine she was reading slid to the floor, and she fumbled for it, irrationally annoyed that she had to stop reading an article when she was only halfway through it. Almost in the next moment, she forgot what she'd been reading.

The receptionist showed her into an office that was decorated in soothing shades of blue and gray. Three wing-back chairs faced one another in a triad in front of a large, neat desk. The man seated behind the desk rose to greet Jillian as she entered the room.

Dr. Sloane was not what Jillian expected. She'd thought he might be an older, distinguished, bearded gentleman of imposing stature and was surprised when Sloane turned out to be early forties, five-nine or ten, and slender, with thinning brownish hair, a plain face, and expressionless brown eyes. His handshake was rigid and dry, and in that moment, Jillian wondered how such a man could ever help someone as strong-willed as she was.

He gestured her into one of the dark blue chairs and sat opposite her with a yellow pad balanced on his knee.

She crossed her legs, suddenly unbearably nervous. This was too intimate, too personal. She wanted to run away.

"I have evaluated your tests," he began, "and they show a significant indication of depression, so I should have no trouble arranging for your treatment with your health insurance provider."

She nodded. This wasn't the way they did it in the movies.

"Now," he said, "why don't you tell me what brought you here in the first place?" He fixed his brown eyes upon hers, and she felt trapped. Suddenly she found she couldn't fidget or look away or use any of the other tricks people used to avoid intimacy.

"Um, my boss recommended that I come and see you because I haven't been able to work."

"You're a journalist, I believe?"

"Yes."

"And you're experiencing writer's block?"

"Well, it's worse than that. I just . . . I can't seem to function . . . ever since the riot." Her heart was pounding. It was all she could do not to jump up and flee.

"You were covering a riot for the paper?"

"Well, it wasn't supposed to be a riot. It was a political rally in Little Mexico, and I was doing a story on the main speaker."

He nodded. "I remember hearing about the riot in Little Mexico. Back in May, wasn't it?"

"Yes." Her mouth was so dry she could barely move her tongue to speak.

"Several people were killed."

To her horror, tears swelled into her eyes and spilled over. She brushed angrily at her cheeks.

"Tell me what happened." The room was very quiet. His voice was soft, almost hypnotic.

Almost against her will, Jillian found herself telling Dr. Sloane everything, about how Randi hadn't wanted to go and how she had laughed off her friend's doubts, about the look of terror on Randi's face when the rally turned violent, how her face disappeared in a crimson mist of blood, how Jillian woke up in the hospital with Randi's blood in her hair, how Randi's mother had accused her of killing Randi and had shoved Jillian against her best friend's coffin.

The breakdown.

The breakup with Derek.

Her shutdown.

She didn't know when she started to cry, but she was sobbing and shaking, desperate to leave, desperate to stay. Or maybe just plain desperate.

Sometimes Dr. Sloane jotted notes on his yellow pad. Sometimes he just listened. Mostly he didn't say anything, allowing Jillian to release the flood of words that had been pent up in her for so long.

When she came to a stop, he waited a moment before speaking, and his tones were measured but not condescending. Jillian found his voice infinitely comforting.

"You've been through a terrible ordeal," he began. "It might interest you to know that there are several critical elements used to define trauma when it is addressed in the Diagnostic and Statistical Manual, or what we shrinks call the *DSM*—it's a sort of reference that categorizes various forms of psychological disorders and conditions and mental illnesses," he said. Ticking them off on his long fingers, he listed them. "If the event is defined as life-threatening, overwhelming, or sudden and unexpected in nature, then it is considered to be traumatic."

Jillian blew her nose with a tissue from a box on the doctor's desk.

"The term post-traumatic stress disorder, as it is known today, did not come into widespread use until the Vietnam War, although soldiers have long been traumatized by war. They were called 'shell-shocked,' or they were treated for exaggerated grief response. But by studying the veterans of the Vietnam War more closely, we were able to discern a pattern of symptoms that we have since noticed in all types of trauma—even battered women and accident victims."

She dabbed her eyes and took a deep breath.

"It's common for someone to experience flashbacks or intrusive thoughts, in which they vividly reenact the experience in their minds, which brings back all the same fears and psychological distress that was experienced at the time."

Jillian nodded.

"Another common symptom is avoidance, or wanting to escape the experience by pretending that it didn't happen and refusing to talk about it with loved ones."

That got her attention.

"It's also common to experience a state of hypervigilance and other panic symptoms, and to feel that all your old assumptions about life have been shattered. Self-blame—to the point of excessive guilt—is also a natural reaction of trauma survivors."

Jillian spoke up. "I don't think I'm blaming myself because of the trauma. I think I'm blaming myself because it was my fault."

He nodded. "I want to examine that, Jillian. I want to discuss it in full in future sessions and see if we can find a way you can live with these thoughts."

She liked what he said, the fact that he was not judgmental or argumentative, and that he was objective. She was beginning to feel a measure of relief.

"There is another condition associated with post-traumatic stress," went on Dr. Sloane, "and that's called 'chronic dysphoria.' This is when life reaches the point that it's simply a matter of day-to-day endurance, inability to concentrate, inability to sustain intimate relationships—it's as if the person has curled up into a little ball within herself and can only survive each day by enduring it."

Jillian nodded. "I look forward to bedtime, but then I can't sleep because I'm afraid of my dreams."

"I'm going to help you with that, Jillian. Let me tell you what you can expect from treatment. First, we will deal with this current crisis of yours, the inability to work or function socially. We will get you stabilized, and that may include the use of medication.

"The second phase involves working through the trauma and dealing with all the baggage you brought with you out of that trauma—the guilt, the shame, the despair."

For the first time since the riot, Jillian felt a small measure of hope.

"Now, I must warn you," said Dr. Sloane, "getting through the trauma phase is hard work. You may even feel worse—but you must remember that it is temporary. We will get through it."

"How long will it take?" asked Jillian doubtfully. "I've heard of people being in therapy for years and years."

He smiled. "The field of psychiatry is changing and growing and learning. We now focus on what makes a patient stronger, not what made them weak in the first place. PTSD treatment, if it's done right, can take two or three months of weekly sessions, depending upon how you cooperate and how you apply what you have learned in the sessions."

That was a big relief. Jillian, who was well aware of her own driven, achieving personality, liked to have a goal to work toward and responded better to the idea of a time frame than to an open-ended equation.

"And finally, we enter the integration phase, where you learn how to adjust to the changes you've experienced in your life that were brought about by the trauma. You also explore the impact of the trauma on loved ones, and you focus on problem solving and getting back into the swing of life."

"But I'm not ever going to be the same again," she said sadly, "am I?"

"You may find that you don't want to be the same," he said. "You will most certainly be wiser, and in some ways, a better person."

"That's not saying a lot," she said disparagingly, surprised at the bitterness in her voice. "I got my best friend killed. Let's hope I don't do that again."

"Don't be so hard on yourself," he said. "I know you feel helpless and hopeless right now," he added. "It will get better."

"I hate myself," she whispered.

"I know," he said quietly. "But we're going to work through this. I'll help you."

He glanced at his watch, and Jillian was genuinely surprised to find that her time with him was up.

"Is this time good for you?" he asked. "If so, you can make an appointment for next week with my assistant."

No, she thought. *I want to come back tomorrow and get this show on the road and get over this thing and put it behind me and get on with my life. I want to stop seeing blood every time I close my eyes.*

"This time next week is fine," she said.

"I'm going to prescribe a mild antidepressant for you," he said, scribbling on a prescription pad. "It will take a few weeks to take effect, but it will help to stabilize your moods. You should be able to cope better, too." He tore off the prescription and handed it to her.

"Thank you," she said. She wasn't sure what else to say. "So." She glanced up from the paper and into his eyes. "I'm not crazy?"

"No, you're not crazy," he said with a soft smile. "Just human."

She gave him a shaky smile and left. On the way out to the car, she thought about Ash, and about how good to her he'd been, how he'd tried to help her cage up her demons.

She might call him, she thought, and tell him that things were going to work out just fine.

Chapter Seven

Keegan Sloane sat propped up in bed with the television remote control in his hand and his heart in his throat. His wife—who could sleep through anything—lay snoring softly beside him, unaware that she shared her bed with a murderer. The late-night news was reporting that the security guard had been found murdered in the burned warehouse.

This was not good.

He'd thought the fire would have burned the body to the point that nobody would know the man had been dead before the fire got to him. Though Keegan was still careful to avoid using accelerants that could be traced to him, he'd carefully set the fire in two different locations so that they would burn together and destroy the building over the top of the dead guard's head.

What happened?

He should have hung around longer, watched to make sure everything was all right.

But the guard had scared him so badly that he'd spent the rest of the night reacting to that fear, and it had made him careless.

God, it was a close call. He'd already forced open the back door and was in the process of setting the fire when he heard the guard. As far as he could tell, there was just that one door leading in and out—the great doors, which were used to load trucks during the day, were of course closed and locked at night, and that little back door was the only way out.

He was trapped.

What was he supposed to do? Hang around in there until the guard spotted him and hauled him in for breaking and entering? They might even be able to figure out he was an arsonist, and put two and two together about the homeless man in the dumpster.

What was he supposed to do?

It was self-defense, pure and simple. He had not entered the warehouse intending to kill the guard. It was the guard's own fault. If the guard hadn't threatened him like that, by showing up and snooping around, he would still be alive.

Besides, that guard was armed. It was kill or be killed. Or it could have been. One never really knew in a situation like that. The guard could have seen him and been spooked and shot him. It could have happened in just that way.

He had had no choice, really.

And then, after he came up behind the guard with the crowbar . . . well, he was just so shaken. Squad cars often made rounds in the warehouse district, looking for suspicious signs—they could have driven up and spotted the forced-open door and come in to investigate. He didn't have any choice but to hurry up and get the hell out of there.

Sloppy. Careless. Stupid.

Still, he didn't think the arson investigator or the cops would find anything linking him to the crime scene. He used gloves. He set the fires in a clever way that would be very hard to pinpoint, and he never used accelerants. There were no witnesses that he knew of.

That's what made arson such a delicious crime, when he stopped and thought about it. It was so easy to get away with. If they didn't have fingerprints or a witness or accelerants to trace back to the place and time of purchase, it was virtually impossible to catch an arsonist. While they could prove that the fire was not accidental, they could not prove who had caused it. And even when they knew the arsonist, it was very hard to prove in a court of law without either an informant or a pattern of other fires or a witness or physical evidence.

Sometimes they could prove that someone had a motive for setting a fire, such as insurance fraud. But random fires like the warehouse fire were bitches to solve.

So he was probably okay.

But he was through with warehouses. With cops and security guards making rounds, it was too easy to get caught. That dead guard had been a close call, one he did not want to repeat.

Residential. Now, that was the way to go.

Ash was on his way back to the warehouse when he suddenly remembered that he was supposed to have lunch with Jillian. Cursing under his breath, he reached for his car phone. It had been insane of him even to make the date in the first place. City of Dallas arson investigators (not "fire investigators," because they handled only those cases believed to be arson) routinely worked some 3500 cases a year. It's a wonder they ever ate lunch at all.

He'd only agreed to it because she asked, and he'd been so surprised—pleasantly so—that she appeared to be crawling tentatively out of her cave. She was still so fragile. It was almost as if Jillian herself had died in the riot, because he scarcely recognized her these days. All her old verve and vitality, wild edge and crazy sense of humor, seemed to have been snuffed out of her.

Dammit. He hated to let her down now.

"Hello?"

"Hey, Jillian. It's me."

"I was beginning to wonder when you'd call. We never did pick a restaurant."

Her voice sounded lighter than usual—not exactly happy, but better. Ash grimaced. "That's what I called about. I can't make lunch today."

"Oh, no! I was really looking forward to it. I haven't gone . . . anywhere . . . in so long."

"I know, babe. I hate to let you down like this, but I'm working a fatal today, and time is of the essence. I just can't get away. I'm on my way over to the site now."

There was a brief silence. Then she said, "Are you not going to be able to eat at all?"

"Probably not. It's okay. I'm used to it."

"Well . . . I was wondering . . . Do you think it would be okay if I picked up a couple burgers and brought them out to you? I've never seen you work an arson investigation. It would be interesting."

Ash maneuvered the Suburban into a parking place near the warehouse and cut the engine. The warehouse looked like all buildings that have been decimated by fire: haunted. "I wouldn't mind you coming, really, but there's nothing nastier than a fire scene. You'd get filthy."

"So? I don't have anything better to do. I could dress for the occasion."

He hesitated.

"I won't get in the way, if that's what you're worried about."

The loneliness in her voice touched him. "Okay," he said finally. "Bring boots that you don't mind ruining. Same with the clothes."

"Oh! It'll be fun!"

"Yeah, it's a real laugh riot," he said grimly, but she didn't seem to notice. He gave her directions to the building with mixed emotions. This was a criminal investigation, a homicide. Bringing a civilian onto the scene wasn't exactly the end of the world, but it wasn't very smart, either.

If it had been anybody other than Jillian, he'd have said no straightaway. But she was sharp and savvy. As a journalist, she'd done worse, no doubt. She knew better than to tromp around and destroy potential evidence. The crime tech guys had already been out anyway.

Besides, maybe it would help her take her mind off her troubles.

Ash decided to wait for Jillian in the car, since he would not want to eat once he pulled on his boots and started working the scene. It was a baking hot July day, and he rolled down all the car windows to catch what little breeze there was. He moved the car, parking it beneath a small tree for a spot of shade, and sat looking at the blackened building, thinking.

Despite the appearance of two points of origin and the dead guard, Ash had made sure to rule out all possible accidental causes. He had thoroughly examined the electrical and heating systems, as well as the type of storage and even whether the guard had smoked. (He had not.)

Nothing presented itself as an accidental cause. Even though Ash had suspected from the beginning that the fire was arson, he had to rule out any possible accidental causes so that if the arsonist should be caught and brought to trial, no slick defense attorney could get the defendant off by even hinting that Ash had failed to look for accidental causes.

The failure to determine that a fire was *not* an accident had let more than one arsonist walk. Indeed, there was no more difficult crime than arson to prove in a court of law—because much of the evidence was often simply burned up. Even if an investigator could prove arson as the cause, he still had to prove that a particular defendant was the torch—which was sometimes even more difficult. Jurors tended to give the benefit of the doubt to the defendant if he was not seen fleeing the roaring fire with a container of gasoline in his hand.

What Ash was having trouble figuring out now was the motive for this particular torch job. He had already questioned the owner of the warehouse and had gone over the financial records he'd found, and there seemed to be no insurance fraud or other financial gain that he could see. There were no building or code violations. Neither had there been a messy divorce or other emotional background to the owner's life that might account for a spite or revenge fire. Ash had done a police background check on the owner as well, and not only was his record clean, but there had been no other history of fires in his life.

Juvenile vandalism could be traced as the cause behind many fires, but this particular fire did not fit any pattern of juvenile vandalism—it wasn't near a school or a neighborhood frequented by kids, and the fire had been set too deliberately, too carefully to fit the usual profile of drunken teens slopping gasoline into a church or school or rival gang neighborhood.

That left two possible motives: crime concealment and pyromania.

On the one hand, it would seem obvious that the fire had been set to cover the crime of the security guard's murder.

But why was the security guard murdered in the first place?

The building's owner had provided Ash with an inventory of the building's contents at the time of the fire, and nothing had been stolen that Ash could detect. The petty cash had not been disturbed. This building was in no way a front for drug trafficking or any other criminal activity.

The security guard was a retired cop, trying to supplement his retirement pay with an extra job. He hadn't been a cop in ten years. Nobody knew of any enemies who might have stalked him or wanted him dead. He wasn't a drinker, and there'd been no trace of alcohol or drugs in his blood found from the autopsy. His credit record was clean, and there was no history of gambling or other secret problems in his background.

It was Ash's hunch that the guard had interrupted the arsonist, but before he discovered the firebug in the act, he'd been struck from behind and killed. In his initial examination of the body at the scene, there was no soot in the victim's mouth, which meant he had not inhaled smoke, and his lips were not cherry-red, which indicated an absence of carbon monoxide in his blood—a finding later backed up by the autopsy. Poor guy was probably dead by the time he hit the floor—the blunt object had struck his skull with such force that his brains were visible, oozing from the wound.

Somebody killed him, apparently, because he happened to be in the wrong place at the wrong time.

But something else niggled at the back of Ash's mind. There was the matter of the homeless man, burned to death in the trash dumpster not far from this warehouse.

If there was one thing law enforcement officers did not like, it was coincidences.

Either this torch was unlucky enough to have accidentally caused the deaths of two men while in the course of setting his fires . . . or he was developing a taste for blood.

"I haven't had this much fun since Randi 'n me used to make mud pies and feed 'em to my little sister," said Jillian with a grin. She was squatting on her haunches with a sifting screen in her hands in the midst of soot, ash, and burned debris, sorting and sifting through piles of it in search of anything Ash might consider "suspicious." Ash knelt nearby with a soft clean paintbrush in his hands, brushing ashes away from a corner of the warehouse.

The sun, which slanted through the fallen roof of the building, was broiling, and there was little breeze. Dallas in July wasn't much cooler than the fire itself.

He looked up and quirked a lopsided grin at her. "You were a sadistic little kid," he said.

"Which made journalism the perfect career choice, don't you think?"

He laughed, and Jillian winked at him. This was the closest she had come to feeling like her old self since the riot. The hot, difficult, methodical work was therapeutic, and she was still buoyed by the encouragement she'd received from Dr. Sloane. Since Randi's death, she'd learned to live life in increments of moments, and this moment was good.

Ash leaned back and dragged a filthy hand across his sweating forehead, leaving a muddy streak. *"God!"* he cried. "He's a sneaky son of a bitch!"

"Who?"

"Who? Him. This torch. I can't get a handle on the bastard."

"How do you mean?"

He sighed. "There are certain methods of fire setting that are known to both arsonists and investigators. And each arsonist has a favorite method—call it a trademark, if you will. If he's just doing it for profit, he's as likely to use gasoline as anything—something easy. If he's a pyro, he'll get creative on us, but he won't think of anything we haven't already thought of."

"But this one has."

"I don't know. And I need to figure it out, so that if there's another fire like this one, I'll know what to look for."

"You think he'll do it again?"

Ash nodded. "Oh, yeah. He may have already done it, and I just haven't realized it yet. But I will, and that's a promise."

She was thoughtful. "What kind of guy would do a thing like this?"

"Well, it depends," he said. "There are different types of fire setters. Some are compulsive and immature—they just want to see what will happen if they set a fire. Others get off on fires sexually. Then there are the antisocial types who are pissed off at the whole world and want to strike back. Any of them can appear normal and go about their daily lives without even their spouses being aware of their hobby."

"You're kidding. Wouldn't a lover smell smoke on them or something?"

"Not if they use a time-delay device. And if they're already firefighters, she wouldn't think anything of it."

"I can't believe that firefighters would set fires!"

He shrugged. "Unfortunately, it's true."

"What would you say is the one overriding characteristic of all fire setters?"

He mocked a fierce frown. "Is this an interview?"

"I can't help it. I'm curious."

"Uh-oh."

She threw a piece of charred wood at him.

"Okay, okay. Hmmm. That's a toughie." He flapped the paintbrush back and forth on his knee, then said, "I guess if I had to pick one thing common among torches, it would be that they feel inadequate."

"Inadequate?"

"Yeah. They feel like failures in their private or even professional lives. They may not look like failures, necessarily, to other people—but they feel like it deep inside. Setting fires makes them all-powerful, godlike."

"Wow."

"I mean, look what all you set in motion with a fire. It's not just the awesome majesty of the flames themselves, but here come all these huge trucks with lights and sirens screaming down the street and people racing back and forth. It's high drama. And you can start it all with just one little match."

Nodding slowly, she said, "But this—" She waved her hand to include the burned-out building. "This went beyond the drama of fire trucks and police cars. This took a man's life."

"Yes."

"And from what you've told me, it was the arsonist himself who killed the guard."

"Most likely."

"I mean, geez, Ash, he could have hidden from the guard just as easily. He didn't have to kill him."

"You're right."

"So you've got somebody who gets off on a whole lot more than just setting fires."

He sighed. "It would appear so, yes. However, the guard may have surprised him, and he panicked."

"Either way, though, now he's murdered, so this fire may not be the last one he sets that leaves a fatality."

"Right again. And if my suspicions are correct, then he's killed before." He told her about the suspicious dumpster fire and the dead homeless man.

Suddenly what she was doing no longer seemed like a lark. It now assumed much greater importance in her mind. She said, "Maybe you'd better explain to me in a little more detail what I should be watching out for here." She held up the sifting screen.

"You bet."

"Because the sooner you find him, the sooner you'll get a killer off the streets," she said solemnly.

"Now you're gettin' it, babe." Ash reached out and ruffled her hair, which probably left it streaked in black, but she didn't mind at all.

Chapter Eight

When the first few days after the warehouse fire had passed and no arson investigators had come knocking at his door, he at first experienced a great relief.

Then the deadness hit.

It was not just a depression. It was more a smothering. He couldn't breathe. It wasn't a panic attack or spell of anxiety, either, because he'd treated enough of those to know the symptoms. This was a blackness, a paralyzing numbness that shut him down so effectively that he had to cancel all his appointments for two days—or rather, his assistant rearranged his schedule. He was incapable of talking and had barely been able to make his request of her. Nasty flu bug, he said. She was sympathetic and solicitous. He couldn't get off the phone fast enough.

For the next four days, the two he'd missed from work and a weekend, he lay in his shuttered bedroom, the covers pulled up to his ears, suffocating from sheer terror.

It was as if his soul were being sucked into the vortex of a black hole lost in the empty vastness of space and time.

For years now it had hidden in the center of him like a sinful secret. In fact, it had become in some ways a silent companion to him, something he could always count on. His false self had very effectively masked the deadness, but lately, his false self wasn't enough. It wasn't nearly enough.

The blackness was growing.

I'll be lost, he thought frantically. *God help me.*

But he knew there was no God.

What if it swallows me? he thought. *What if this is all there is?*

But he knew that it wasn't.

There was that moment. That exquisite moment of exhilaration, of the terrible beauty of rage and fear and the awesome force of death over life.

That moment when he'd swung the crowbar with all his might into the skull of the security guard, that crack, that satisfying power, the fury and the glory.

And then . . . the funeral pyre blazing into the heavens, proclaiming his power for all to see, his magnificent triumph. The fire pushed the blackness back. It conquered the deadness because fire was a living thing.

The phoenix of him was alive, rising from the ashes of the dead.

But it was not without cost. Because the aliveness he'd felt in those moments served only to exaggerate the rest of his dead life, to make his daily existence even more unbearable.

Was the newfound aliveness somehow causing the deadness to grow? Or did the growing deadness provoke his need to feel alive, if only for one brief, shining moment?

Was there no other way?

Where? How? By jumping out of planes? Climbing rocks? Rafting rivers?

Child's play. Games for little boys who never outgrew their toys.

And commonplace. Boring. Anybody could jump out of a plane.

But who could unleash the beast? Who could hold the power of life and death in his hands?

Who among them all could beat back death?

Indeed, it was the only way.

"I shall show the powers of darkness bound," Milton wrote. "For only in destroying I find ease to my relentless thoughts."

On Monday, he was able to breathe again, and after that, there was no looking back.

Jillian was still a little nervous for her second appointment with Dr. Sloane, but not as much as she had been during the first. Still, they had not gotten into anything intensely personal that first visit beyond the riot, and she expected to this time.

"Tell me a little about your background," he began.

She thought a moment. "It was pretty typical for a middle-class suburban upbringing," she said. "My dad was a mid-level manager at a mid-size company, and my mom was a housewife. I had a much younger sister—ten years younger than me."

"So you were the oldest."

"Yes."

"In some ways, that would give you the characteristics of an only child, since you were without siblings for ten years, but it would also endow you with the characteristics of the firstborn."

She nodded.

"Go on."

"Not long after I got my driver's license, my mom went back to school to finish her degree and then went to work. I became her built-in nanny, housekeeper, and kiddie chauffeur."

"So you assumed adult responsibilities when you were still very young."

"Yeah."

"Which explains why you feel such intense guilt at your friend's death. You feel responsible now, just as you did then."

Jillian paused. "I never thought of it quite like that before."

"Were you paid for your household help?"

Jillian shrugged. "It was weird. I never really got paid, but my folks bought me a used car that I could run errands in and they gave me a generous amount each week for school lunch money, which was sort of like an allowance. In the summers, I always seemed to have plenty of cash, but I couldn't go anywhere or do anything with my friends because I had to take care of my sister. Sometimes I would have friends over or I'd take her with me, but it wasn't the same. All my friends seemed so spoiled and carefree—even the ones who had after-school jobs."

"How is that?"

"They didn't have to come home from work and straighten the house or cook for their families."

"You must have resented that a great deal."

"I didn't think about it so much at the time, but as I got older and looked back on it, yeah, I resented it. I felt like my folks got away with some pretty cheap labor."

He glanced down at a sheaf of papers in his lap. "Your questionnaire says your parents are dead."

"Yes. They were killed in a car wreck six years ago."

"I'm sorry."

"It was harder on my sister than me, because she is so much younger. That first year after they died, she got married to a guy in the Navy. They're living in Hawaii now. She's got four little kids I never see."

The room was silent for a moment. Dr. Sloane said, "So you don't feel as if you have anyone to whom you can turn now for support and comfort?"

She glanced away for a moment, collecting herself. "Randi. Randi was always there for me. When the *Dallas Times Herald* went belly-up, I lost the best job I ever had, with no prospects in sight. The only other local paper was the *Dallas Morning News*, and the competition for available jobs over there was very hot. Naturally, white males got the best ones. I couldn't even work circulation for months. If it hadn't been for the *Dallas Mirror* coming to town and recruiting me, I'd have been homeless by now, I guess. And if it hadn't been for Randi, I don't know what I'd have done," she said, dismayed at the sudden flood of emotion that accompanied the words. She swallowed and focused her gaze on a nearby lamp until she felt more in control.

"Tell me about your work, Jillian. I'd like you to put into words what it means to you."

"Oh," she said with a sudden heartfelt smile. "It's as if I come alive. I expect it's much the same way an actor feels when the curtain parts or the director yells, action! When I'm chasing down leads on a hot story, my whole body tingles. It's like . . . like I'm fulfilling my purpose in life, you know? Like I'm on a mission. I guess that sounds silly," she added uncertainly.

"Not at all."

"Writing . . . It's the one thing I'm really good at. I love every aspect of it. I love the research, the interviews, the chase. I love beating the deadline, my fingers flying over the keys and my words singing over the wire." She hesitated. "That's what it's like. Singing."

Staring at the lamp for a moment again, she mused, "I'll never forget the first time a story of mine appeared in print. You always think you'll be thrilled at seeing your byline, right?"

He nodded.

"But it wasn't that, really, that thrilled me, Dr. Sloane. It was my words. Ideas, taken from the ether of the mind, now appearing in black and white, and those ideas, those words, are then read by hundreds or even thousands of people! My God! What an amazing privilege!"

She stopped, flustered at herself, half expecting him to snicker at her or tease her in some way, but his gaze on her was intent and his expression was one of respectful attention.

"I can take this . . . gift . . . this talent with which

I was blessed . . . and I can influence people. I can make a difference with my life. How many people can say that?''

He said, "Jillian . . . are you aware of the change that comes over you when you talk about your work? You become more animated, your cheeks flush with color, your eyes sparkle. In short, you become a completely different person than the defeated woman who walked into my office.''

Her breath caught in her throat. "But that's just it. I know what my work means to me, and I can discuss it, but I can't *do* it anymore." Her heart began a slow, distressed pounding in her throat. "It's as if I died along with Randi.''

Dr. Sloane tapped his pen against his yellow pad. "How do you know you can't do it anymore? Have you tried?''

"I haven't wanted to try. That's the thing. I haven't felt the *fever*, you know?''

"Perhaps you're hung up on stale assignments you'd been following before the riot. Has anything fresh and new caught your interest?''

Ash and the warehouse fire immediately popped into her mind. "Well . . . there is one thing.''

"What? Tell me.''

"I have this dear friend, who's named Ash McGraw. He's an arson investigator for the Dallas Fire Department. It's funny, you'd think he got his name because of what he does, but the truth is that his mother was like, this fanatic about the movie *Gone With the Wind*. She named his sister Scarlett and Ash Ashley, and he said that after he got his first playground bloody nose, he insisted that everybody call him Ash.''

She chuckled, knowing she was rambling, but enjoying having somebody to talk to anyway, when she glanced up and into the eyes of Dr. Sloane.

He'd grown very still, and his eyes glittered. That was the word for it: *glittered*. For a second, another word leapt into her mind: *reptilian*.

Jillian, old girl, you've really lost it, you know that?

"Your friend," prompted Dr. Sloane, and even though he spoke, his head did not move.

Strange.

"Well, Ash was investigating a warehouse fire the other day? You might have heard about it on the news. They found a murdered security guard in the building?"

"I remember hearing something about it, yes," he said, and to Jillian's hypersensitive mind, his tone of voice seemed to have taken on a note of impatience, as if he wanted her to hurry up and get on with the story.

So she did.

"Anyway, Ash felt sorry for me and actually let me help him investigate the fire, even though technically, it's a crime scene."

"How do you mean, he let you help? He called you while the building was still burning?"

"No, no. Nothing that exciting. A few days after the fire, he let me come onto the scene and help him sift through the ashes. He was trying to figure out how the arsonist set the fire. I've never known anything about the subject, and I must admit I found it fascinating."

Dr. Sloane leaned forward. "It is indeed fascinating. Tell me more. How can sifting through the ashes help your friend discover how the fire was set?"

"Well, there are certain . . . devices . . . with which arson investigators are familiar that can serve as a source of ignition for the fire. That's what they call the start of a fire," she couldn't resist bragging, "ignition."

"Interesting. But wouldn't the fire destroy that evidence?"

"That's what I thought, too. But actually, most people don't understand the nature and dynamics of fire and of fire suppression—that's what the firefighters do," she supplied helpfully. "Most people think a building just incinerates in a fire and leaves nothing.

But it depends on what is in the building in the first place—how flammable it is—and how soon the fire-fighters can get the blaze knocked down. Sometimes a whole room is preserved intact without even so much as smoke damage simply because the door was tightly shut."

"But if the ignition device *starts* the fire," said Dr. Sloane, "then wouldn't it burn up, too?"

"Sometimes. It depends on the device. Sometimes it can catch a nearby substance on fire but not burn itself, and the arson investigator can find it in the rubble."

"I see."

Jillian smiled. This was really neat. She had no idea her therapist would be so interested in the subject.

"So . . ." he consulted his notes, "are you going to write about the fire investigation?"

"I don't know," she said truthfully. "It would depend on what Ash wants me to do, of course. And it would also depend upon whether this is the work of a serial arsonist."

Dr. Sloane sat up straighter in his chair. "What makes him think it's a serial arsonist?"

"He's not sure, really, but there was a fatality, you see, and in that same general area a few weeks ago, a homeless man burned up in a dumpster. Ash thinks the two may possibly be related."

"Has he found any connection between the two?"

She shook her head. "Not so far. It's just a theory right now. Gut instinct, I guess you'd call it."

Dr. Sloane discreetly consulted his watch. "I'm afraid our time is almost up. Jillian, I'm going to give you a homework assignment of sorts."

"Okay," she said doubtfully.

"Since this arson investigation has piqued your interest and got you to thinking about writing again, I think it might be crucial to your recovery."

"Really?"

"Absolutely. You want to start working again, don't you?"

"Of course. But I don't know. Ash may not want me publicizing this case, and I don't know what Miles would think. That's my editor," she added.

He waved his hands in the air dismissively. "I don't want you to worry about that right now. All I want you to do is pursue this story wherever it leads. See if you can feel that tingle again." He smiled at her.

She smiled back.

"Then I want you to come back next week and tell me more about what you've learned. Pretend I'm your editor, and you're pitching the idea to me." He leaned back in his chair. "Let's see if we can ignite a little fire of our own."

She laughed appreciatively. "Thanks, Dr. Sloane. I think that may be just what the doctor ordered."

He smiled again. "Me, too." And his eyes glittered.

Chapter Nine

The powerful and terrible allure of fire was not something that many firefighters could articulate to anyone who had not known its hypnotic attraction, thought Ash. But they all felt it. If they didn't, they would find a much easier and less dangerous way to make a living.

It was usually within the controlled confines of carefully set training fires that firefighters first fell, mesmerized, under the spell of the beast. In that situation, they could often stand back and watch the fanciful dance of flame and fury without the urgent pressure to rush forward and immediately extinguish it. They could see for themselves its awesome, spellbinding beauty.

No firefighter ever questioned that fire was a living creature. In fact, the term "firefighter" came from the fact that in order to put out a blaze, the men and women had to literally fight the fire; they had to step into the jaws of the beast and do hand-to-hand combat with it.

Every single fire, no matter whether it was the work of a clever arsonist or a strike of Mother Nature or a tragic accident, was different. Like the firefighters themselves, each fire had its own personality, its own quirks, its own strengths and weaknesses. No one ever knew, from moment to moment after pulling up to a fire scene, what to expect.

A raging forest fire could vault with the muscular glory of a gymnast right over the roof of a house, go from tree to tree, and spare the house while destroying the forest around it. A man could fall asleep in bed with a lit cigarette in his hand, and the resulting fire could incinerate the bed and the man with it but spare the house. A curious child could strike a match in a clothes closet and twenty minutes later, a two-story, two-hundred-year-old house could be leveled.

And, oh, the beast was a tricky, deceptive devil. He could have you convinced that a fire was completely stamped out, only to rise again hours later in savage triumph from nothing more than a glowing ember.

Most people didn't know these things about fire. They underestimated it and took foolish chances with it. They thought they could beat it. They thought a ten-dollar smoke detector was an unnecessary nuisance, that if a fire crept into their home by night, they would discover it on their own and get themselves and their families out safely.

But they did not know the sinister weapons all fires had at their disposal: quiet, deadly fumes that could render a person unconscious before they ever saw smoke or felt heat. And smoke. House fire smoke was something no one who had not seen it up close and personal could understand.

Hollywood did not help matters. Movie-set fires were always fueled by natural gas, a clear, clean accelerant, and were controlled by fire wranglers through hidden burners. So on TV and in the movies, people could see their way through a fire to find loved ones; they could stay in a burning building as long as they needed to in order to serve the plot.

A real-life house fire was entirely different. In real life a house could be completely blacked out with thick, choking smoke no less than *two minutes* after the start of the first flame and long before the fire itself made its sneaky, delayed appearance.

There was no time.

Without smoke detectors, people had no time to get out before they were rendered unconscious and even dead from smoke inhalation. Many times, their bodies would be found without a single burn on them.

A ten-dollar smoke detector with a fresh battery could warn a family and give them just barely enough time to awaken, grab their children, and flee before the beast could suffocate them with smoke.

Oh, how the beast detested smoke detectors.

These thoughts never failed to depress Ash as they turned over in his mind, again and again, at the site of every fatal fire. On this hot night in July, Ash stood impotently and watched as grimy, solemn firefighters emerged from a fully engulfed suburban home carrying two small dead children in their arms.

The beast had won again, and Ash could fancy him laughing as the powerful flames billowed skyward and bloodied the clouds overhead.

Another word for *power* was *potency*.

And nothing was more potent than the beast in all his engorged glory.

This was the power that held them in its thrall; the potent power of life and of death, and the battle to defeat the beast.

On this sweaty night, Ash had a miserable foreboding that the real war had only just begun.

Setting house fires was turning out to be far more challenging than Keegan had anticipated. In fact, he had yet to set his first house fire. There were complications he had to take into consideration—barking dogs, vigilant neighbors, and the nature of fire itself.

In order for his fires to do the maximum damage, they had to be set in such a way that billowing smoke or flames did not attract the attention of passersby. Once they dialed 911, firefighters would arrive within minutes and could extinguish the blaze before it had accomplished Keegan's purpose.

That meant the fires had to be set within the house.

Keegan was no cat burglar, and most city people were savvy about locking their doors and windows at night or when they were gone. Selecting a house and figuring a way to gain entrance so that he could disable the smoke detectors—if they had any—and set the fire so that it would be fully enaged before any firefighters arrived, was proving to be exceedingly difficult.

He thrilled to the challenge. It made him feel alive.

At first he concentrated his efforts on low-income neighborhoods, since those houses were less likely to be equipped with high-tech security systems. But this proved to be emotionally unsatisfying. It was too . . . workmanlike. Not enjoyable at all. In fact, he didn't even set any of the houses he had in mind on fire.

It took him awhile to figure out why.

When he did, he didn't want to admit it to himself. After all, he was no sociopath. He'd interviewed a few once in a prison for a case study while in his psychiatric residency, and he wasn't like any of those men at all.

The very thought gave him the creeps.

Still, the fact was that choosing a house to burn was just no fun at all.

That's when he realized that he had been going about it the wrong way.

He should be concentrating not on the structure itself . . . but on its occupants.

And yet that challenge proved so daunting that, at first, he backed away from it, like a threatened animal retreating to its hole.

For a few weeks he found himself sleeping more and more at home and even catnapping at the office, for the work of maintaining his false self was growing

increasingly exhausting. All the living who surrounded
him, he came to realize, merely mocked the deadness,
and he found it almost impossible to tolerate the presence of those individuals who radiated life's vibrancy
and energy—the bubbly, the peppy, the cheerful, the
animated, the lively. It was as if the brightness of their
life force served to dim his own weak light even
further.

He became obsessed with them, resentful, jealous,
and envious. They were the soul-eaters, thieves in the
night who stole from him what few precious reserves
of life he had left. In their presence he was lessened—
if such a thing were possible.

Around the shy, the depressed, the weak, the vulnerable—he could function. His false self could easily
fool them; they did not notice the lie that was his
daily existence. With his patients or his family—people
whom his silences could intimidate—the false self
could hold the deadness at bay.

But when in the presence of the extroverted and
the ebullient, he felt himself totally eclipsed and the
false self shamefully exposed beneath the scrutiny of
their own bright lights.

Surely they must know this. How could they be so
self-involved as to not notice?

They had to know. And if they knew, then they
must be doing it deliberately. They must be sucking
up the life force available in any room for their own
self-aggrandizement, like putting out all the lights so
that only a spotlight might shine upon them, and
them alone.

His mother had been just that way. All her emotions
were dramatic to the extreme, and they all served to
make her the center of attention. It made no difference what the emotion was; her expression of it was
what mattered. If she was angry, she stormed through
the house in a towering rage that made the young
Keegan cower in his room while she smashed things
and screamed and cursed. If she was sad, she would

cry hysterically and inconsolably, leaving him feeling helpless. And if she was happy, she was giddy and giggly and funny and bright. She would seduce him with her sparkle, and he would forgive her anything. Then, without warning, she would vanish into the cloud of another melodramatic mood.

He never knew what to think or how to act. And when he did react, it was usually too late. He would be laughing when her mood had already soured and turned nasty, or he would offer her pity when she had already moved on to good humor. No matter what he did or said, it was always wrong. What did she want from him? He never knew.

So he withdrew and sent his soul into hiding. Now it was lost.

The live ones always wanted more, more, more. And no matter how much you gave them, it was never enough. They would take and take until there was nothing left of you, and then they would mock your emptiness.

He couldn't stand them anymore, the live ones.

He wanted to make them dead.

Jillian still bought her vitamins at the same health food store as Derek, so she should not have been surprised when their paths crossed one day and she found herself standing toe-to-toe with him next to a display of mineral supplements.

He was still as attractive as ever, but gone was the boyish exuberance, the buoyant self-confidence. He appeared to have lost weight, and his eyes had a haunted look to them.

"Hi, Jillian," he said. "How've you been?"

"Oh, just peachy," she said bitterly, glancing around for a quick escape route. "I've got to go."

"Look, I know you're angry," he said, reaching for her arm.

"Damn right I'm angry!" she cried. "But I'm not

about to discuss it with you here." She turned to leave with some modicum of dignity.

"Jill, please."

Something in his tone stopped her. She stood awkwardly. "What is it?"

He shrugged. "I'm ruined," he said simply, and the depth of despair in his eyes hit her full force.

"What?" The finality of the statement came as a genuine shock to Jillian. "What are you talking about?"

He picked up a bottle of creatine mono-hydrate powder and stared unseeing at the label. "It's Cricket. She stole everything, Jill."

Jillian had been following the feud between Cricket Andrews and Derek only halfheartedly. After all, that was a part of her life she was trying to put behind her. "Surely it's not all that bad, Derek."

"I've got to file for Chapter 13 bankruptcy protection. How bad is that?" he answered bitterly. "All this time, I *trusted* her, and she was robbing me blind. We've got to close two of the gyms," he added, his voice slow and heavy.

"Oh, Derek. I'm so sorry to hear that. I really am." Jillian didn't know what to say. The situation was much worse than she had assumed. It mitigated some of her anger, in spite of herself.

He set the bottle back on the counter and stared over the top of her head. "I can't believe I could have been so stupid," he said.

"Don't be so hard on yourself," she said, echoing Dr. Sloane's words to her. "You couldn't have known. No one could have."

"But you were right," he said with a heavy sigh. "If I'd learned to read a stupid spreadsheet, maybe I'd have seen this coming."

"I'm sorry I said that, Derek," she said sincerely. "Embezzlers can be notoriously clever at covering their tracks. And you had people whose job it was to watch out for signs of trouble—like your accountant and your gym managers."

"I don't know." He rubbed a hand over his eyes. "I just feel so *betrayed,* you know? Like if we had been married and I had caught her in bed with another man or something." He blinked. "I mean—I never slept with her or anything—"

Jillian smiled. This was the Derek at whom Randi had loved to poke fun. "I understand what you mean," she said. "A business partnership is very much like a marriage, and when someone you trust . . ."

A woman came wandering over to the mineral aisle and browsed the shelf. Derek and Jillian moved away from her. Derek said, "I know I'm not the smartest guy in the world. I didn't go to college or anything. But I worked my *ass* off, Jill! You know I did!"

"Yes," she assured him. "You did work very hard."

"I built something out of nothing. How many people who didn't go to college can say that?"

She smiled at him. It was a sad, knowing smile.

"And that greedy little *bitch* . . ." His fist clenched at his side. "She got us in trouble with the IRS. She defrauded our customers. She stole from me. And you know the worst part?"

She waited. Jillian was growing increasingly distressed at the depth of Derek's rage, and yet, curiously, she could understand it.

"The worst part is that people associate the Power Play gyms with Derek Thorsen. Not just the name, I mean, but with *me.*"

His eyes moistened, and he pursed his lips. "She dragged me and my name through the mud. And now people will never be able to think of the Power Play gyms without thinking, Derek Thorsen, that crook."

Jillian started to protest, but he cut her off.

"I didn't have anything but my name. And Cricket Andrews stole even that."

"Don't be silly!" cried Jillian. The woman on the mineral aisle turned a snoopy ear in their direction. They moved to another aisle. "Derek—people understand what happened. They don't blame you. As soon as all this legal mess is straightened out, you can rebuild. People still trust you to help them get into shape. That hasn't changed. They'll trust you again."

He shook his head, and Jillian sighed. She'd forgotten how mulishly stubborn the man could be. He stood in front of her, clenching and unclenching his fists in a completely unconscious way. This was typical of Derek, she thought. Whereas Jillian herself might react to traumatic life events by turning her guilt and anger inward and blaming herself to the near point of suicide, Derek would turn those same emotions around and lash outward.

He had never been abusive to her, but she had seen displays of his temper. With his bulk and rippling muscles, he could be frightening.

She placed a soothing hand over his fist and squeezed it. "Derek. Maybe you just need somebody to talk to."

"I'm talking to you, aren't I?" he said, his face surly.

"No, I mean someone who could help you sort out all these feelings."

"What, you mean a shrink?" He snorted. "Shrinks are for sissies. Forget it. I plan on handling things in my own way. You'll see."

He pulled his hand away from hers, then, at the look on her face, his expression softened. "It's good to see you again, Jill."

She glanced away from the intensity in his eyes.

"Maybe we could . . . you know . . . get together for dinner or something and talk about things. I miss you. Maybe we could think about getting back together."

"And maybe you'd better talk to Tiffany about that first," said Jillian, making no attempt to hide the bitterness in her own voice.

"She's nothing," he said, oblivious to the irony. He made no attempt to apologize for his own betrayal of Jillian, which was not lost on her.

"Take care of yourself, Derek," she said. "I'll see you around."

She left without buying anything.

Though he didn't spend much time in it, the office of Lieutenant Ash McGraw was located in downtown Dallas, not far from the brick streets, lofts, tattoo parlors, and dramatic wall murals of Deep Elum, in the old Municipal Building, which at one time had housed the Dallas Police Department. He entered the gray brick building through the front door, crossed the linoleum-floored lobby with its handsome framed photographs of historic fires, and took the stairs two at a time to the fourth floor. Pushing through the unassuming doors with frosted glass on which was stenciled ARSON & BURN UNIT, Ash followed a narrow hallway. He passed a gaggle of colleagues who were discussing last night's multi-alarm, which had caused the deaths of the two young children.

Preliminary findings pointed toward accidental causes, meaning this particular case was closed. Technically, anyway. You could never close your mind on dead children, especially when a ten-buck investment could have saved their lives.

Ash's office was in the same mess it had been when he first moved into it three years before. Framed diplomas and certificates were still leaning against the wall on the floor, waiting to be hung. A jumble of extension cords snaked up over the door and around the corner to accommodate the demands of modern computer technology. A sooty fire helmet with the name MCGRAW painted on it rested atop the overstuffed file cabinets. Buried somewhere beneath a pile of papers on Ash's desk was a charred piece of two-by-four—a souvenir from the first fire Ash had ever fought.

The only thing Ash did have hanging on his wall
was a framed movie poster Jillian had given him de-
picting a scene from the seventies Paul Newman disas-
ter flick, *Towering Inferno*. She'd wanted to give him
one from the more recent fire movie, *Backdraft*, directed by Ron Howard and starring Kurt Russell and
William Baldwin, but Ash wouldn't have the thing.
He'd found the movie so riddled with outrageous inac-
curacies—such as Kurt Russell's character going into
a burning building without his SCBA (Self-Contained
Breathing Apparatus)—that he'd refused the poster,
saying it would only piss him off every time he looked
at it.

Not that *Towering Inferno* was any better, but at
least it didn't pretend otherwise.

Ash dug through the papers on his desk until he
unearthed a creased Dallas map on which he'd put
red X's on the locations of several mysterious dumpster fires. These fires had occurred in the industrial
area of the city in recent weeks, including the fire that
had killed the unidentified man. Charting the location
of the warehouse where the security guard had been
murdered, Ash drew another X. All the X's were located in the same general area.

He was becoming increasingly convinced that all the
fires had been set by the same torch.

Staring at the map, Ash pondered what he per-
ceived as the growing intensity of the fires. The first
few had scarcely attracted the attention of the fire
department, much less arson investigators, because
they had been easily extinguished with a minimum of
property damage. Then they required an engine truck
to extinguish the blaze.

Then the homeless guy burned up.

Then the warehouse and the security guard.

Ash recalled a lecture series he had attended once
by a renowned serial killer investigator from Washington State on the subject of "signature" killings. There
were certain hallmarks of each murder, the same re-

gardless of choice of victim or location, that were known among astute investigators as "signatures."

It occurred to Ash that these fires shared similar signatures.

Although the first small dumpster fire and the warehouse fire would seem on the surface to have little in common, the truth was that they shared a number of characteristics. No detectable accelerants were used. The cause was suspicious but still unidentified. There was no usable criminal evidence and no witnesses. No apparent motive.

The only difference between the first dumpster fire and the warehouse fire was intensity—a man had been murdered and the building burned down around him. Everything else was the same.

The lecturer from Washington had mentioned that signature killers often "practiced" their crimes by starting out, say, with window peeping, moving on to rape, and gradually escalating to sexual homicide. The fantasy—fed by peeping—was the springboard. Each time the killer killed, he learned something new. A mistake made that almost got him caught in an earlier crime would not be repeated in a later one.

Police investigators often missed related clues between crimes because they considered the M.O., or modus operandi, to be different. They would not consider the window-peeping reports in a neighborhood to be significant to the sexual homicide in a nearby neighborhood, when actually, chances were good that these crimes had been committed by the same man, working up his nerve and improving his skills.

Ash believed that this torch was working up his nerve, practicing his skills, learning from his mistakes.

He would kill again, Ash was almost certain of it. In fact, he almost leapt from his chair and charged into the office of his deputy chief to report his findings and request assistance from an arson task force.

But he kept his seat. What did he have, anyway? A

few dumpster fires, one suspicious death, and one "arson with bodily injury, including death."

A few X's on a map.

It wasn't enough. Not nearly enough.

Meanwhile, this particular torch was getting better all the time.

Chapter Ten

Jillian was driving seventy miles per hour along a Dallas mixmaster in her cherry-red Mustang with the top down. The weather was sunny and warm, and the wind lifted her hair off her neck while the buttery sun toasted her skin. Randi was sitting beside her, and they were talking.

"I saw Derek the other day," said Jillian.

"Oh, God. The himbo?"

Jillian laughed. "Yes, the himbo. And, yes you were right and I was wrong."

"I never thought I'd live to hear those words," said Randi.

Something about the remark didn't sound right to Jillian, but she couldn't think what.

"By the way," said Randi, "when you saw Derek . . . was it before or after I died?"

Shocked, Jillian turned her head toward Randi and discovered to her horror that Randi did not have a face. Instead, the front of her head was a bloody, pulpy mess—Jillian could actually see her brains—and an eyeball was hanging by a single thread, watching Jillian.

Randi did not have a mouth—only a blood-filled hole, and the hole was moving. Staring at Jillian with the dangling eyeball, Randi attempted to speak, but Jillian could not understand what she was saying.

Jillian began to scream. At least she tried to

scream—tried with all her might—but no sound
emerged. Growing increasingly terrified, Jillian struggled to get the scream out, and finally it broke free in
a strangled, deep-throated cry, which grew louder until
finally, her eyes opened and she could escape the hysterical grip of the nightmare.

Her T-shirt was soaked with sweat, and the sheets
were damp, snarled beneath her in knots. Her heart
was hammering so hard that she could feel her chest
jerk, and she was panting. Too frightened to go back
to sleep and afraid to lie there in the dark, Jillian
turned on the bedside lamp. But the light did not scare
the demons away.

Every dream-image was branded into her brain. She
couldn't stop them from coming. The riot was all
around her and in her—she could smell her own sweat
and fear.

And Randi. Jillian was haunted by the idea that
Randi had tried to say something to her, and she could
not understand what.

It's just a dream, she thought. But it wasn't. It had
been too vivid, too three-dimensional.

Flinging back the covers, Jillian laboriously untan-
gled her legs from the twisted sheets and got out of
bed. Pacing the length of the room, she tried to take
deep breaths, willing herself to calm down, but nothing helped.

She went all over the house, turning on lamps, and
poured herself a glass of milk, then left it sitting on
the counter, forgotten.

I'm losing my mind.

Back in the bedroom, she sat on the edge of the
bed and, impulsively, reached for the phone. After
four rings, Ash answered.

"Y'llo?"

"I'm sorry!" she cried, near tears. "I know it's
late—"

He was instantly alert. "Not too late. It's, what?

Three a.m.? I've had three whole hours of sleep. What's wrong?"

She hesitated. It sounded silly to her now. "I shouldn't have bothered you. It's really nothing."

"You're not bothering me. And it is something, or you would never have called. I know you, remember?"

She nodded, forgetting that he couldn't see her, feeling suddenly like a little kid.

"Was it a bad dream?"

Exhaling a pent-up sigh, she said, "How did you know?"

"Let's just say, been there, done that. For two years after I lost my buddies in that bad fire, I dreamed about it. One time I'd dream that I was able to rescue them, and I'd feel so relieved, and then I'd wake up and have to deal with the fact that they were dead all over again. Another time I'd dream that they were screaming for me, and I couldn't get to them. Just as bad."

"Oh, Ash. We were friends then, and I had no idea you were suffering so much."

"It's not the kind of thing you can discuss with somebody who's never been through it."

"No kidding."

He waited. She said, "It was so awful. Randi and I were just driving along in the Mustang with the top down, and she didn't have a face. Nothing there but a bloody mess. And she was trying to say something to me but I couldn't understand what."

"Poor kid," he murmered. "I know how scary these dreams can be. But listen—it's normal, okay? All part of the trauma. Hasn't your shrink said anything about that yet?"

"I haven't told him about the dreams."

"They're always worse in the beginning, those dreams. You just gotta work through them. When you start to get on your feet, they'll get better."

"If I had a dog or something . . ." she mumbled, thinking aloud. "It's just so quiet around here."

"I think the solitude is good for you right now, Jilly," he said. "When you wage armed combat against the demons, you gotta go one on one."

She sighed. "You're probably right. It's just . . ."

"What?"

"It's just . . . as if she was trying to tell me something. You know. Like from beyond the grave or something." It sounded ridiculous now, said out in the open rather than harbored in her feverish neurotic mind.

"Darlin', that wasn't Randi talkin'. That was the demons. When Randi gets ready to say something, she'll say it. But you gotta get those demons caged up first."

She sighed. "Not having too much luck, at the moment."

"What does your shrink say?"

"Actually, now that you've brought it up, he says that since I've gotten interested in working with you and all, I ought to pursue that. Maybe write about it."

Long silence was her answer.

"Or not. I mean, I don't have to do a piece for the paper, Ash. Just for myself, you know. To get the juices flowing again."

After another lengthy pause, he said, "If I let you work with me, will you promise that anything you learn would be strictly off the record unless I say otherwise?"

Surprised and thrilled that he would even consider allowing her to tag along with him on the investigation of the warehouse fire, she said, "Of course! Geez, you can trust me. I would never trade on our friendship for a story." *I've already sacrificed one friend on the altar of my ambition,* she almost said.

"Okay then," he said. "If this guy thinks it's a good

idea, it probably is. I'd do anything to help you, Jill. You know that."

"Yeah," she said with a smile. "Even talk to me at three in the morning."

With a noisy yawn, he said, "You think you can get back to sleep now?"

"Yeah," she lied. "Ash . . . thanks. You know. For everything."

"Don't mention it. You just get better, okay?"

"Okay."

They hung up, and Jillian went through the house, turning off lamps. She discovered the milk and drank it. But back in her bedroom, she still couldn't face the dark.

Not as long as all those demons were still out there, prowling through the shadowy corners of her mind.

She tried to sleep, but every time she closed her eyes, all she could see was Randi's mutilated face. It was as if the image were branded into her brain, burned into the backs of her eyelids, and there was no escaping it.

Finally, kicking off the hot sheets, she threw on some clothes, grabbed up her car keys, and fled into the night.

He'd been following her for some time now, and he was surprised at how easy it was. People never seemed to pay any attention to their surroundings when they went about their daily routines, he had discovered. It simply never occurred to them that someone might be watching.

At first it was scary. What would he say if he were caught? What could he possibly say? Then it became a game, even kind of fun. Cloak and dagger stuff.

He'd had a hard time making a selection, and then he decided that there was something to be said for convenience. For one thing, he had her address and phone number in his files. For another thing, she was beginning to get on his nerves. In her weekly sessions with him, she seemed to chirp like a nervous little bird, punctuating her remarks with a high-pitched, staccato laugh. It was a nervous, insincere laugh, an unconscious gesture of insecurity.

Everything in her life, it seemed, was a moment for high drama. In the stories that she relayed to him, it seemed she was always positioned as either the victim or the hero, or her favorite: the heroic victim.

Self-absorbed, vain, shallow. A user of those foolish enough to love her.

A soul-eater.

In time, he came to despise her.

She lived in an exclusive neighborhood where the houses were set some distance apart and surrounded by trees and shrubbery. If there were any children living there, they were tucked well out of sight. Nobody ever seemed to be at home, and when they were, they paid no attention to their neighbors.

He parked his car in a park a few blocks away. Dressed in jogging clothes and with his everyday, unassuming appearance, he found it easy to blend in. The hooded sweatshirt he wore provided a good place to tuck the binoculars, even if it was hot.

It did not take him long to figure out that she went jogging every night at the same time, and that she was always gone the same length of time. She even ran the same route—the exact same route—every night. He could practically clock her in his mind.

And she did not lock her door. Typical of her type of vanity, this invincible belief in her own indestructibility.

Perhaps she thought it an inconvenience, carrying house keys. Maybe she just felt safe. Whatever the reason, he had enough time to slip through the sliding glass door overlooking the patio and explore the house.

It gave him time to find the smoke detector and remove the battery.

It gave him time to seek out the best place to set the fire.

It even gave him time to sit and think and plan.

The excitement was almost unbearable.

It was a small article in the *Dallas Morning News,* buried deep inside the fold, no more than four or five paragraphs long. Ash might have missed it altogether if it weren't for the headline: SPONTANEOUS FIRE.

A local fire chief, Ash read, of an exclusive bedroom community suburb of Dallas, had ruled a house fire that had taken the life of a young divorcee as having been caused by spontaneous combustion.

Someone driving down the street past midnight had spotted the flames and called 911 on his car phone. Firefighters had not discovered the woman's body until after the worst of the fire had been knocked down. Autopsy revealed that death had been caused by smoke inhalation. The fire chief—who doubled as the local fire investigator—had ruled the fire accidental, caused by spontaneous combustion that had started, he said, in a laundry room, in a basket of clothes hot out of the dryer.

Ash could not believe what he was reading. The whole thing was ludicrous. Some fire investigators did not believe that spontaneous combustion was even possible. Others conceded that it was, but only under the most extreme conditions—say, in an unairconditioned building in the depths of a hot summer, maybe in a closed cabinet full of oily cleaning rags. Even then, it was a long shot.

But in a basketful of clean clothes? Even if they were hot out of the dryer, they would cool the longer they sat—there would be no reason for them to combust without the presence of an accelerant such as cleaning oil to fuel the heat.

If the fire had not been fatal, Ash would have shaken his head in disbelief at the stupidity of some people, but the presence of the dead woman sent

alarm bells ringing all over his body. Officially, there
was nothing he could do. This was out of his jurisdiction. Even if the fire chief was a complete idiot, it was
not Ash's place to supersede his authority.

That didn't mean he couldn't take a little drive out
to the suburbs.

Impulsively, right before he left, Ash called Jillian
and asked if she'd like to go along. She was so delighted at having been invited that Ash felt a little
guilty for neglecting her in recent days.

On the drive over, Ash said, "I know this may
sound impossible to you, but let me do the talking."

She cut a sideways glance of mock shock at him
and said, "Who, *moi*?"

"Yeah, *you*," he said, laughing. "You're not the reporter here, digging after a story. You are an observer.
Just stand back and observe the master at work."

She rolled her eyes and shook her head.

They found Chief Dan Corruthers fairly easily in
his spotless, well-appointed office. He was at least
forty pounds overweight and wheezed as he rose from
his chair to greet them. His short-sleeved white shirt
strained at the buttons, and Ash glimpsed a pack of
Marlboros in the chest pocket.

"What can I do for you, Lieutenant McGraw?"

"As I told you over the phone, I'm an arson investigator for the Dallas Fire Department. This is my
friend, Jillian Ross."

They shook hands, and Ash said, "I was curious
about the fatal fire you had the other night."

Corruthers nodded. His hair was combed straight
back, and his scalp was sweating. "You mean the
spontaneous combustion. Beats anything I ever saw."

"I wanted to ask you about that," said Ash, "because to tell you the truth, I don't think I've ever
seen a genuine case of spontaneous combustion in my
entire career."

"Well, that's what it was," said Corruthers with an
expansive gesture of his hands. "It wasn't electrical.

No presence of accelerants—we've got a dog to sniff that stuff out, and he didn't alert anywhere."

"And you're certain it started in the laundry room."

"No, I'm certain it started in the laundry *basket*. The whole thing was just melted. The laundry room itself was gutted. Lady's bedroom was just down the hall. Smoke got her."

"That's what the paper said."

Corruthers smiled. There were damp spots under his arms even though the office was well air-conditioned.

"Um, I was curious, Chief Corruthers," popped up Jillian, ignoring Ash's threatening glance. "Did you notice any smoke detectors?"

"One."

"Was it working?" interjected Ash before Jillian could say more.

Corruthers blinked. His eyes, between the folds of fat, narrowed and hardened. "What do you mean, was it working?"

"I just wondered why the lady didn't awaken when the smoke detector went off."

The chief shrugged. "I dunno. Could be the smoke was already too thick when it set off the detector. Could be the battery was dead. People sometimes go years without changing the batteries. They might as well not have them." He smiled at Jillian.

"Did you check?" persisted Ash.

Corruthers shifted in his chair. "What are you getting at?"

"I was just wondering, that's all."

"Look." Corruthers placed the palms of his hands flat on his orderly desk. "If you're suggesting arson or murder or something, you're wrong. She died of smoke inhalation. There were no accelerants in that house. Case closed." His annoyance was clear.

Ash felt himself go into a slow burn. The jerk had not even checked the smoke detector to see if it was working. "Mind if we take a look at the house?"

"Be my guest. But it's already been overhauled and *thoroughly investigated*. You won't find anything." He got to his feet. It was a dismissal.

"Thank you," said Ash.

"It was nice to meet you," said Jillian.

They walked out to the car. "What a jerk," she said.

"That's the trouble with fire investigation," said Ash as they got in the car and began to thread their way down wide, curving, sunlit suburban streets. "In these small towns, especially, you've either got to rely on overworked state fire marshals or somebody like this guy with very little training. Hell, he may have only actually investigated five or six fires in his entire career and never a fatal."

"Huh," she mused. "I had no idea there could be so much variation in fire investigation."

"You can't imagine," he said. "I don't think there's any other area of criminal investigation that has a higher level of frustration. You run up against this kind of crap all the time. It's amazing."

"Do you think this might be the same torch who killed the security guard?"

"I don't know," he said honestly. "There's just something hinky about it. A fatality. No accelerants. No obvious cause."

"Hinky?"

He grinned. "It's an old cop term. Means somethin' don't smell right."

"But it doesn't fit the pattern of the others. I mean, it's not in the same area as the dumpsters and the warehouse," she pointed out.

"I realize that," he said. "But if this guy is clever enough to fool fire investigators for this long, he's clever enough to know that as long as he enters different jurisdictions, he can get away with murder for who knows how long. City of Dallas, and its crack arson investigators, stop at the suburban lines. Here it is."

The blackened, gutted house looked tragic and forlorn in the manicured neighborhood, and Ash had no doubt the neighbors would get rid of the unsightly mess as soon as it was decently possible to bulldoze it. There were a few people rubbernecking from the sidewalk when Ash and Jillian drove up, and they watched curiously as Ash and Jillian got out of the car and pulled on heavy boots. Out of the corner of his eye, Ash surveilled them, making mental notes for future reference.

As he and Jillian picked their way through the charred wreckage, it took them awhile to uncover the smoke detector, which was slightly melted. Ash had to get a screwdriver and use a hammer to pry the thing open. He was not surprised by what he found.

The battery had been removed.

Chapter Eleven

"So, how have you been since we last talked?"

Jillian settled lower in her chair. "Oh, good days and bad days, I guess you could say." She sighed and glanced into his eyes. "I'm having terrible nightmares, Dr. Sloane."

"Tell me about them."

She described the dream in which she and Randi had been driving down the expressway in the red Mustang, only Randi did not have a face.

Nodding, he said, "Dreams are an excellent gauge as to where you are in the recovery process." He made a note in his yellow pad. "These kinds of vivid dreams, which are almost re-creations of the traumatic event, signal that you are still early in the recovery stage, and that you are overwhelmed by the experience. Your subconscious is trying to master it, and is struggling. This is a signal that you still have unresolved issues you need to work through."

"Yeah, like why am I alive," she muttered, and the remark surprised Jillian. This was the first time she had questioned her own survival of the event that had taken Randi's life.

"Survival guilt. It's very common," said Dr. Sloane. "People from plane-crash survivors to prisoners of war wonder why they were spared when others died. Sometimes they feel as if God must have singled them out from everybody else, and they feel unworthy of the privilege."

"Yeah!" she cried, then bit her lip. "Only God didn't choose to kill Randi. I don't believe that."

"Then, who did?"

She hesitated. "The person who pulled the trigger?"

He smiled, his eyes unreadable.

"But Randi wouldn't have been there if I hadn't made her go. She'd have been home with her baby, which is where she belonged."

"And yet she chose to go with you, didn't she? It was Randi's choice to go, wasn't it?"

She stared at her hands.

"We're all responsible for our own choices, Jillian."

He waited, giving her time to process that statement. Then he said, "So. How did you do on your homework assignment?"

"Oh!" She smiled at him. "I asked Ash if it would be all right if I tagged along with him, and he said yes! I was so amazed."

"Good. And how did it go?"

"It's very interesting. We went out to the scene of another fatal fire the other day. The local fire chief had ruled the cause as spontaneous combustion, but Ash wasn't buying it. The guy said the fire started in a basket of laundry hot out of the dryer."

"And Ash disagreed, I take it?"

"Definitely. He said there was no way the laundry could have been hot enough to combust without some sort of fuel present, and anyway, we found out that the smoke detector had been tampered with."

"Oh? In what way?" He was jotting notes on his pad, as though he were only half paying attention.

Jillian said, "The battery had been removed."

"I see. And how did he know that the homeowner had not removed them?"

"Well, she could have, of course, but people don't usually remove the battery from smoke detectors until they are replacing it with a fresh battery. After all, when you buy a smoke detector, it already has the battery in it. There wouldn't be any reason for people to remove the battery from one and leave it unworkable."

"Hmmm. What did the fire chief think?"

"He wasn't pleased that Ash was poking around in his jurisdiction. He'd already ruled on the cause of the fire, and he wasn't about to change his own ruling."

"I don't understand. Maybe I missed something. Why was Ash, er, poking around in another jurisdiction?" He glanced up from his pad as though he were only mildly interested in the answer.

"That's the interesting part," she said, leaning forward in her chair. "Ash thinks the same guy who burned down the warehouse and killed the security guard also set this fire."

He nodded. "That is interesting." Jotting another note or two on his pad, he said, "What can he do with this information? Provided he's correct, of course?"

She leaned back in her chair with a sigh. "That's the frustrating part. He can't do anything about it. It's not his jurisdiction, and unless he can prove that this is the work of a serial arsonist, he can't even get help from his own department."

"That's too bad." He paused again, seemingly deep in thought. "Jillian, I'm disturbed that you seem unable to move past your survivor's guilt about Randi's death. The nightmare that you described is a clear signal to me that you are having some difficulty dealing with this tragedy."

She frowned. "You don't think the nightmares will fade away in time?"

He pursed his lips. "Without . . . more intense . . . help from me, I'm afraid it's possible that you may not be able to advance through this first crucial stage of grieving."

This was distressing news. Jillian didn't know what to say.

"If it's all right with you, I'd like to start seeing you

twice a week for a while. At least until we get through this first, very difficult phase of your recovery."

Jillian felt a sense of great relief. "To tell you the truth, Dr. Sloane, I'm glad you think so. I still seem to be . . . floundering. I mean, Ash has been a great help, and going to these fire scenes with him has been a real lifesaver for me, but I'm still not sleeping worth a damn and God knows I'm still not writing."

"Exactly. I think we have more ground to cover than I thought when I first evaluated you. You don't seem to be making the kind of progress I had hoped for." He pulled out his prescription pad. "I'm going to change your medication. Stop taking the other pills for now. They were mild antidepressants, but I'm going to precribe an antianxiety drug instead that has had successful results when used with trauma patients." Scribbling the prescription, he added, "And why don't we change our appointments to Tuesdays and Thursdays for a while, shall we? Is that all right with you?"

Jillian nodded. "I'm not happy that it's taking me so long to get over this, Dr. Sloane, but I am so thankful to have you. You always seem to say just the right thing."

He smiled and passed her the prescription. "I appreciate that, Jillian. You may not be thinking that when we roll our sleeves up and get to work, you know," he added. "Getting through this next phase of your treatment may be traumatic."

She bit her lip.

"Still, while you go through this process in our sessions, I think the best thing for you to do in your downtime is to continue working with this young fire investigator. You seem to find it stimulating."

"I hate to admit it," she said with a smile, "but I do."

"Then I think you should continue accompanying him on his investigations, since he's been kind enough to agree to it. In future sessions, we'll examine how

you can apply some of the things you're learning on
these jaunts to your recovery."

"Like a phoenix, rising from the ashes, eh?"

As if she had goosed him, Dr. Sloane jumped,
blinked, and dropped his pen. As he groped beneath
his chair to recover it, he said, "That's a very good
allusion, I think."

She got to her feet and so did he. "Thank you, Dr.
Sloane," she said. "I don't know what I would do
without you."

Sometimes he thought he was going mad.

If a psychiatrist went insane, would he know it?

And yet, he had seen the insane before. They did
not hold down reputable positions in the professional
world, teach classes, and return home to their families
each night and read the newspaper. The truly insane
did not wear a mask of sanity with which to fool the
world—not even the strongest medications could
make them appear normal.

So he was not insane, after all. And he had already
determined that he was not a sociopath.

There was no label, it seemed, for a living death.
No probing articles in the medical and professional
literature for the suffocating blackness that closed in
tighter and tighter around his soul each and every day.
No happy pills to make it all go away.

There was only the terrible, beautiful beast and the
hot breath of life he breathed into Keegan's body and
mind each time he reared his magnificent head. Keegan had come to need the beast as the beast needed
him. To burn was to live.

The rest of the endless days and nights of Keegan's
life were becoming increasingly unbearable to him.
Getting out of bed in the mornings, facing a new day,
was a loathesome chore. He couldn't breathe. He
couldn't breathe.

He began to envy those who seemed to live life so
effortlessly, who seemed to enjoy the simplest aspects

of each day, and to do it with verve and laughter and eyes that sparkled. Obviously, they had never felt the suffocation, the blackness of the living death. Why? WHY?

Why were some spared this living-dying hell of an existence? What had they done to deserve their easy laughter, their spontaneity, their joie de vivre?

Soul-eaters.

They took it for granted. They didn't know what they had. They didn't deserve it.

He resented them, hated them. He recoiled from their presence.

It was unbearable.

It took Ash some weeks to realize that he was spending more and more time with Jillian because he enjoyed her company and not because he was trying to help her get through a tough period in her life. As emotionally fragile as she was right now, she was still sharper, spunkier, and funnier than anyone else he knew. And prettier. Definitely prettier.

When had he noticed? He couldn't say; didn't know, really. They'd been good friends for a very long time. Maybe he'd always had a secret crush on her. Whatever the reason, he found it a pleasure to take her along to fire scenes. She was quick and alert, and it was nice to have somebody to talk to, for a change.

Of course, if the deputy chief found out, Ash's ass was grass, but he'd jump that hurdle when he came to it.

For now, he found himself glad of her help. Nothing he asked her to do was ever too filthy or boring. She'd dig right in until they both reeked of smoke and soot, but when she smiled up at him, her hair would glint in the sun like a brand-new copper penny, and he'd feel himself growing warm from something other than the Texas heat.

Sometimes he wondered what it would be like to kiss her. He'd catch himself watching her and glance away, embarrassed. She needed him right now, needed him to be a friend, not some goony guy pawing all over her like a pimply teenager. She was vulnerable; the last thing she needed was for him to change the nature of what made them close.

Of course, that wasn't all. He wasn't that noble. The truth of the matter was that he was afraid. Afraid that if he ever made a real pass at her, she'd scurry into her little hole like a scared bunny rabbit and that would be the end of their friendship. If that happened, he didn't think he could bear it. Far better to keep his distance and retain her friendship and respect.

Maybe later, he thought. When she was stronger. Maybe then he could risk it. For now, he'd have to be content with the pleasure of her company, and the sunlight gleaming off her hair.

Jillian stared at the numbers on her pocket calculator, glanced back at her checkbook, then gazed down at the bank statement. She'd refigured three times, and the numbers were always the same. If she did not get to work—and fast—she would not be able to pay next month's rent, let alone the utility bills or even the cable TV bill.

She groaned. *What am I going to do?* She had to work, and yet she couldn't work. The paper was covering her therapy as a form of disability, but she was not on salary, not as long as she was not submitting work. Maybe she should start looking for a receptionist job or something—anything—that would bring in some money.

Drumming her fingers on the desk, Jillian stared blindly out the window. This was scary. This *was* a nightmare.

"Maybe you're being too hard on yourself," she muttered. "It doesn't have to be perfect." After all, journalism was who, what, why, when, and where. She could hammer together the nuts and bolts of an article—column inches of copy that would bring in some income. She didn't have to shoot for the Pulitzer.

Back at the office, she knew, were all her notes and research materials on the Juan Rodriguez story, the one she'd been working on when she and Randi went to Little Mexico. She wouldn't even have to complete the interview with Rodriguez's ex-wife in order to put something together for Miles. Of course, it meant she would have to return to the *Mirror* offices downtown.

The very thought filled her with dread.

It was bad enough, imagining herself having to meet and greet all those people who would wonder how she'd been and if she was back for good, but to return to that place a mere ghost of herself was almost an unbearable prospect. Not to mention delving into the story that had led to the riot and Randi's death.

But she needed money, and she needed it now. She was in no condition to begin in-depth research on another story, nor could she afford the time.

She would have to sit down at the computer and write again. There was simply no choice in the matter.

I can't do it, she thought, struggling with the overwhelming despair that threatened to wash over her again.

But numbers—unlike words—didn't lie. And the numbers in her checkbook were forcing her hand.

In a near-panic, Jillian almost called Dr. Sloane to seek support, comfort, and advice. But the truth was that there was nothing he or anybody else could say that would change the situation. Either she had to go back to work or she had to find some other job. End copy.

One step at a time. She got to her feet and dragged herself into the shower. Her hair was badly in need of washing, and she hadn't shaved her legs in two weeks. There was no need in showing up at the *Mirror* offices looking like a bag lady. *I'll wear my favorite red blazer. Maybe it'll cheer me up.*

One thought that offered a small measure of comfort was that writing could be done anywhere. There was no need to stay at the office while working on the story. She could gather up the materials and notes, bring them home, and work on them without fear of interruption from some well-meaning coworker who wanted to chat.

She pulled on a pair of "fat jeans" and put on the red blazer. It was tight in the shoulders, and she could no longer button it, a fact that depressed her so deeply it was all she could do not to cancel the whole trip. She had to try on two more jackets before she found one that was presentable. *I look so awful,* she thought as she stared at herself in the mirror. *They're going to make fat jokes about me behind my back. God, I hate myself.*

It wasn't exactly a pep talk to get her out the door. That took a little more gumption.

Midday traffic was heavy, and Jillian chose to concentrate on her driving rather than think too much. Naturally her customary parking space was taken, and she had to drive around the lot in search of another. So much for being irreplaceable. She wondered who was jockeying for the choice assignments in her absence.

"Jillian's back!" cried the receptionist the moment Jillian stepped through the front door. Before she had walked ten feet, she was surrounded by well-wishers smiling and hugging and genuinely glad to see her, in spite of the competitive nature of their business. It was gratifying, but also so terribly distressing that she wanted to run out of the building and hurry back home again. These were her friends, but even returning their smiles seemed a tremendous, exhausting effort.

It was dreamlike and agonizing, as if Jillian were a part of it and yet not a part, observing herself even as she observed others. Even as she smiled back and made small talk and even exchanged quips with them, she walked separate and alone. This should be the one place in the world where she felt comfortable, where she belonged, but instead it was just another situation that demanded more of her than she could give.

Slowly she made her way back to her cubbyhole, which looked, strangely, as if she had only just left it for a cup of coffee. Even the computer was on, the screen saver silently swirling a kaleidoscope of color. Old *Mirrors* were stacked up on the floor next to her chair, and a hodgepodge of notes and assorted paperwork cluttered the desk.

Jillian took her old seat and called up the Rodriguez file on her computer. She printed up the preliminary outline for the story that she'd done before the riot and stuffed it into her tote bag, along with cassette tapes of interviews, copies of documents, and assorted notes.

"I can't believe it."

Jillian looked up to see Miles standing beside her desk, beaming at her like a proud papa.

"They said you were back, but I didn't believe it."

"Well, I'm not really back. Not here, anyway. At least, not yet," she added at the look of dismay that crossed his face. "I thought I'd see if I could go ahead and put together that piece on Juan Rodriguez. At home, I mean. I thought I'd write it at home." She felt so lame.

"That's a great idea!" he enthused. "I don't see any reason why you can't freelance for us while you're . . . recuperating. And Rodriguez has announced his candidacy for city council, just as we knew he would. This is terrific!" He smacked his hands together. "How soon do you think you can have it?" he asked, ever the editor.

Jillian felt a momentary panic. She hadn't considered deadline pressures. "I don't know," she stammered. "Maybe a week? Or two? I mean, I've already done the groundwork. All I have to do now is put it all together." She could hear the lack of confidence echoing in her own voice and glanced away from his piercing gaze.

"Take all the time you need," he said gently. "I'm just glad to have you back."

"You may not be so glad when you read the story," she mumbled.

"What?"

"Nothing." She got to her feet. Miles took the opportunity to hug her.

"You'll be fine," he whispered in her ear. "Trust the talent."

She nodded doubtfully, and he stepped back.

"If you need anything at all," he said, "call me."

"I will." Jillian felt suddenly swamped by sentimental gratitude. After all, most any other employer would have fired her by now. She blinked against the emotional tide. "I can't thank you enough for all you've done for me," she said, glancing away.

"Nonsense. I'm just selfish. I'll do anything to keep my best reporter. Nobody else sells more papers." He gave her a devilish grin, and Jillian couldn't help but grin back.

"Okay if I e-mail the final copy to you?" she asked.

"No problem. Whatever works for you is fine by me."

"All right. I'll be in touch, then."

"You bet."

Jillian made her way out of the building. By the time she reached her car, she was trembling. She wondered if this was the way stuntmen felt when returning to the set after suffering a terrible accident while doing a movie stunt. They couldn't let their fears hold them back, not if they wanted to make a living.

By the time she made it home, Jillian was absolutely drained of all energy. Tossing her tote bag onto the bed, she pulled off her tight clothing, then fell across the bed on her stomach. When she turned her face to the side, she was staring at the bag full of work.

It had to be done. She *had* to do it. There were bills to be paid. Miles was counting on her.

It was too much.

Turning her face in the opposite direction, Jillian closed her eyes and drifted into a restless sleep.

Chapter Twelve

"There's one thing I really miss about typewriters," said Jillian.

"And what's that?" said Dr. Sloane, staring at her in that same inscrutable way.

"You can't rip a page out of a computer, wad it up, and hurl it onto the floor when the writing is going badly."

"Oh, so you've decided to start writing again?" He smiled. "Is it the fire story?"

She shook her head. "No. This is purely bill-paying stuff. I'm trying to complete an assignment for the *Mirror* that I'd started before the riot."

That was always the way she said it: *before the riot*, or *after the riot*. Never, *before Randi died*.

"I see. And I take it the writing's not going well."

She sighed. "I tried half a dozen different lead paragraphs, and they all stunk. So ever since then I've been transcribing tapes from interviews. There's nothing creative about transcribing tapes. Any moron could do it."

"What makes you think the paragraphs . . . stink?"

She shrugged. "I just know."

"Have you considered writing through it? Going on in spite of the fact that you don't like the way it's going? You can always go back and revise."

"I guess." She stared at the floor.

"Or perhaps you could consider writing something else. Have you worked any more on the fire story?"

"It's not really a story," she said, glancing up at him. "I mean, all I'm doing right now is following Ash around while he investigates these fires."

"And how is the investigation going?"

Jillian smiled. This was one thing she really liked about Dr. Sloane. He was always so *interested*. She couldn't think of another soul who would give a shit. Except for Ash, of course. She said, "Well, there haven't been any more fatalities that fit this particular signature. Ash is beginning to wonder if the arsonist has left town."

"I'm sorry. What is a signature?"

"Oh!" She laughed. "Here I am throwing around these technical terms like a big shot when I barely know what they mean myself." She explained the meaning of the term as Ash had explained it to her.

"I see." Dr. Sloane nodded. "So, is the investigation closed?"

"Oh, no. An investigation like this is never closed until they make an arrest and, hopefully, get a conviction."

"Does he have any . . . suspects?"

"Not really. Anyway, he's the only one in the department who thinks all these fire fatalities are related. His boss is pressuring him to move on to other cases, and that's pretty much what he's been doing."

"And, in the meantime, you're working on this other story."

"I'm trying. I get so easily distracted, though. Like a little kid. The other day I turned on the TV, which I shouldn't have been doing anyway since I was supposed to be working, and there was Cricket Andrews with her own infomercial. It made me feel so bad for Derek."

"Tell me about Derek. I don't believe you've mentioned him before."

She told him everything.

Tapping his pen on his lips, he said, "I believe I've seen those infomercials. They come on at odd times, like Sunday mornings, right?"

"Right."

"She's the one with the hundred-watt smile who practically bounces out of the television screen, isn't she?"

Jillian laughed. "That's a fair description, all right. I used to like Cricket. Now when I think about what she's done to Derek, I can hardly stand the sight of her."

"You still care for this man."

"No. Yes. Oh, I don't know. As a friend, maybe. I feel sorry for him, I guess. I could never be with him again." When Dr. Sloane made no response, she said, "Anyway, the point is that I'll do anything to keep from writing, even watch one of Cricket's infomercials."

"Or perhaps you could say that you would do anything to keep from working on the article at hand," he said.

"Same difference, isn't it?"

"Not necessarily. I thought we agreed that you should pursue the fire story, since that was where your enthusiasm lay?"

"Well, yeah—I mean, I find it very interesting, but I can't pay my bills with that."

"Why not?"

"Because, for one thing, I promised Ash that anything I learned during the course of this investigation would be strictly off the record. And for another, I don't have an assignment from the *Mirror* on the fire story. I've got one on Juan Rodriguez."

"But you are incapable of completing that assignment."

Jillian hesitated. She had never said she was *in*capable of writing the article, just that she was having difficulty doing so. "Don't worry," she said, "I'll do the assignment."

"How can you be sure?" he persisted. "So far you haven't done anything on it except busywork."

"That's true . . ." she began doubtfully. Maybe Dr. Sloane was right. Maybe she *couldn't* do the Rodriguez story. After all, the old Jillian would have been done with the damn thing by now.

Now she was really worried. "What am I going to do, Dr. Sloane?" she asked plaintively. "I've got to pay my bills somehow."

"And yet the Rodriguez story is holding you back. After all, it was because of pursuing that story that Randi died."

A dagger to the heart would have hurt less than Dr. Sloane's words. He was right, though. Wasn't he? She thought a moment. "If I decided to actually write the fire story, I'd have to ask Ash first."

He quirked an eyebrow, but said nothing.

"What?" she asked anxiously.

He shook his head. "It's really not my place."

"Of course it's your place. It's why I'm here. Now . . . what?"

"It just seems to me that if you asked your friend's permission to work on this story, it would give him the power of censorship over your work."

Censorship. Jillian hadn't thought of it in that way before. All the same, it didn't seem right. Doubt flooded her mind. She said, "I can't keep something like this from him."

"Then, wait until you've written the story and allow him to read it. Otherwise, he won't give you the same kind of access he has to date."

Jillian had to admit that Dr. Sloane had a point. Still . . . "I don't know what to write, what angle to give the story."

"Don't worry about it," he said. "Something will come to you. You can even bounce ideas off me during some of our sessions. Would that help?"

"Immensely!"

"Good."

It was funny, though. Jillian had expected to feel good about things now, more hopeful. Instead, she felt more confused and anxious than ever. For the life of her, she couldn't say why.

Insomnia, he had found, could sometimes be one's friend.

He'd gotten past the compulsive sleeping, and now it seemed he never slept at all. When he dozed, he was simply unaware of it. He would awaken suddenly, surprised to have slept.

He was sitting up in bed late one night, as usual, flipping TV channels on the remote control while his wife slept beside him.

And there she was.

The perky blonde who never stopped smiling, who literally bounced when she spoke.

"Don't touch that remote!" she cried. "You don't know it yet, but you've just found the answers to some of your most pressing and worrisome problems!"

As he watched her, with her relentless fake cheeriness and phony concerns for the well-being of his viewers—a soul-eater if there ever was one—he slowly began to realize the truth.

She really did represent the answer to his most pressing and worrisome problems!

As far as Ash McGraw was concerned, this was definitely a hostile fire.

Insurance investigators used two terms to describe fire: "friendly" and "hostile." A "friendly fire" was one that did not progress beyond its "assigned" limits. A woodstove fire, for example, would begin at the stove and burn the areas closest to it, including walls, floor coverings, or furniture.

But a "hostile fire" was one that extended well beyond its limits. A hostile fire would burn down a house.

By the time Ash had arrived at the scene, the upscale house was fully involved, and there were two engines—a ladder truck and a utility vehicle—working the fire. He had been called when firefighters came across unburned wads of newspaper just inside the sliding glass door at the rear of the house. Other piles of papers had caught fire, and the fire had spread, most likely due to the gasoline soaking the papers, which still gave off a strong odor.

They'd found the owner of the house in a nearby bedroom and had brought her out to the yard, where they were working feverishly with the help of paramedics to revive her. Ash caught only a glimpse of her in among all the people working on her, and her face was black with soot. After twenty minutes of futile effort, they loaded her in the ambulance—still pumping her chest and blowing oxygen into her lungs—and screamed off toward the hospital, but the consensus was that she was a goner. A room-by-room search of the residence had turned up no other occupants except a cat, which they had been able to revive. A neighbor took the pet.

There wasn't a lot Ash could do by way of fire investigation while the firefighters were still actively battling the blaze in a powerful effort to prevent its spread to neighboring homes. While he waited, he decided to question the neighbor who had taken the cat. She lived next door, and there was still a light on in the kitchen when he tapped discreetly on the back door, holding up his badge in the window. After the lady parted the curtains and saw the badge, she opened the back door.

She was pretty, if somewhat disheveled at this late hour, her robe wrapped tightly around a shapely body, dark, expensively frosted hair smoothed back behind her ears. Her name was Sandra Cunningham, and her husband was asleep, she said, in spite of all the excitement. She fretted over the cat, a pretty calico whose eyes held the look of shock.

Ash introduced himself and asked, first of all, if the

cat needed to see a vet. This thought hadn't occurred to the woman, who was obviously distraught by the evening's events. Ash informed her of a twenty-four-hour emergency animal clinic a couple of miles away, and she promised to take the cat.

"I just can't believe she's gone," she said, bursting into tears and fumbling in the pocket of her robe for a tissue. "It's just too terrible."

"You knew the victim?" asked Ash. A positive ID would be made later, he knew, but it would help to know now, so that he could begin to question family or a boyfriend or ex-husband—anyone who might have a motive for her death.

"She was my personal trainer," she said, attempting to blow her nose through the sobs. "She was just the greatest lady in the world. She helped me so much. I know she had some business problems, but I never believed the rumors about her. I can't believe why anybody would want to hurt her."

"What makes you think somebody hurt her?" asked Ash sharply.

The woman dabbed at her eyes. "I heard one of the firemen say that somebody had put newspapers in the back door, poured gasoline over them, and set them on fire." While she cried some more, Ash secretly cursed the bigmouthed firefighter.

"I don't know what I'm going to do without her."

"What was her name?" prodded Ash.

With a shudder, she said, "Cricket. Cricket Andrews."

For a moment he stared at her as if he hadn't heard her correctly. "The woman who offers those exercise videos through the infomercials?"

She nodded. "She used to be partners with Derek Thorsen."

Used to be, thought Ash. *That is the operative term.*

PART III

Flameover

About, about in reel and rout
The death fires danced at night.

> Samuel Taylor Coleridge
> *The Rime of the Ancient Mariner*

Death, violent death, and painful wounds
Upon his neighbors he inflicts and wastes,
By devastation, pillage, and the flames . . .

> Dante Allegheri
> *Inferno,* Canto XI

But I in none of these
Find place or refuge, and the more I see
Pleasures about me, so much more I feel
Torment within me.

> Milton
> *Paradise Lost,* Book II

Chapter Thirteen

Night.

It seemed to exist for no other purpose than to torment Jillian. She tried over-the-counter sleep-inducing medications, but they had no effect. She moved the television into her bedroom, thinking that watching late-night TV would lull her to sleep. Sometimes that seemed to work—until she awoke suddenly, usually following a nightmare, to a blank, hissing screen. She'd glance at the clock, turn off the TV, puff up her pillows, roll over . . . and lie awake. That was the worst.

Silence seemed to wrap itself around her like a burial garment.

In the stillness of being completely alone in the dead of night, the demons would swarm, chasing her thoughts around in the darkness until, driven nearly mad, she would roll out of bed, pull on a pair of jeans with the rumpled T-shirt she'd worn to bed, jam her feet into a pair of sneakers, and take off in the Saturn, following the city lights until she felt sleepy.

After that, she'd drive home and nap until the blinding light of dawn woke her.

It was hard to tell whether the constant fatigue that dogged her was the product of depression or simple sleep deprivation. Then one morning, Jillian was shuffling about the house in a ratty T-shirt and panties after another tattered and torn night of attempted sleep, foraging for coffee with the TV babbling in the

background, when she caught the name "Cricket"
from the local news. She stumbled into the living
room, empty coffee mug in hand, and stared uncomprehending as film footage of the flame-consumed
house filled the TV screen and the announcer's voice-
over explained that Cricket had been found dead in
the fire. Arson was suspected.

This couldn't be happening. It was too unreal.

Mug still in hand, Jillian yanked up the phone and
dialed Ash's office number. Of course he wasn't in it,
and she left a voice mail. Then she called his car
phone and, after six rings, left a message there.

Jillian didn't know what to do. She tried to busy
herself by making coffee, but it was no use; she had
to know what was going on. Knowing he would be
peeved at her for it, but unable to stop herself, Jillian
called Ash's beeper.

It took him longer than usual to return her call, and
yes, he was peeved.

"Is everything all right?" he said breathlessly as
soon as she answered.

"Yes, I'm fine. But, Ash—I had to know, what's
going on about Cricket? This can't be our same guy,
can it?"

"I can't talk to you right now," he said flatly. "It's
an open, ongoing investigation, I'm just about to question a suspect, and I've got a lot to do to get ready.
You interrupted me."

"I'm sorry," she said. The old Jillian wouldn't have
cared if she'd interrupted an arrest, as long as she was
getting the information she sought. The new Jillian
was anxious about making Ash mad at her. She cursed
herself and pressed on. "Surely you can tell me if you
think it's the same guy."

"No." Now he was really getting annoyed.

"No, what?"

"No, it's not the same guy. I've gotta go."

"But how do you know?" she said recklessly.

He sighed. "Newspapers soaked in gasoline. Jillian,

I've got to get back to work. I'll talk to you later."
He hung up before she could say another word.

It took a few more beats before Jillian thought of
Derek. She called him. An unfamiliar female voice
answered the phone.

"Hello?"

"Uh, this is Jillian Ross. Is Derek home?"

"Oh, Jillian," the woman gushed, as if they were
old friends. "This is Summer. Do you remember me?
From the health club?"

As if there were only one club. "Sure," lied Jillian.

"Anyway, Derek's not here, and I'm so worried."

"Why?"

"These cops came by to talk to him about Cricket.
He went back to the station with them to answer some
questions about her."

"I don't think you have anything to worry about,"
soothed Jillian. "It's natural for them to want to ask
Derek some questions since he and Cricket were once
so close."

"No, you don't understand. Derek and Cricket had
this big fight yesterday down at the club in front of
everybody. It was awful. He told her she'd ruined his
life. She's such a bitch!"

Ash had said he was getting ready to interview a
suspect. Suddenly, Jillian felt queasy and hot all over.
Did Ash think that Derek had set the fire? How could
he? Derek had his faults, but there was no way he
could have done anything like that.

"Don't worry." she said. "Tell Derek when he gets
home to call me, okay?"

They said good-bye and hung up. Jillian began to
pace around the small apartment. No wonder Ash had
been so annoyed by her phone call. He'd been getting
ready to question Derek right then.

She told herself that Ash was a pro, he would
straighten all this out, he would know that Derek was
not involved.

But the more she tried to convince herself, the less she believed it.

Ash took his time jotting notes to himself, organizing his thoughts, and planning his approach to the interview. Though he'd told Jillian he had a suspect, the truth was that Thorsen was still just a witness and was only being interviewed, not interrogated. As yet, he was not under arrest. But as far as Ash was concerned, he was a suspect, all right.

Derek Thorsen waited for him down the hall in a small room they used for such purposes. It was kept very plain: a gray metal table, a few folding chairs, and a video camera. There were no friendly pictures on the walls, although some clown had put up an old Smoky the Bear poster with its admonition, "Only *you* can prevent forest fires!"

Derek was staring at the poster when Ash entered. Massive biceps bulged from the tight sleeves of Derek's Power Play T-shirt, and his neck looked like a buffalo's. Ash was not in the least discomfited by the man's bulk. In his opinion narcissistic muscle-bound power lifters like Derek looked like freaks.

"Can I get you anything before we get started?" he asked perfunctorily.

"Do you have any bottled water?" asked Derek. "Evian or anything?"

Ash paused, then said, "I'll see what I can find." He went out into the corridor, filled a paper cup with tepid water from the drinking fountain, and took it to Derek. "Best I could do," he said.

Derek took the cup and sighed.

Ash ground his teeth together. He did not like Derek Thorsen. Thorsen was one of those types whose smooth charm, ingratiating manner, and good looks gave him lots of points with the ladies. Women fell for him quickly, and he knew it.

But guys like Thorsen didn't fare as well with their fellow men. It was said that male psychopaths could charm women and female psychopaths could charm men, but that their own gender instinctively distrusted them. Not that Thorsen was a psychopath. Basically, he was just a jerk. But he routinely got away with all kinds of crap with women that Ash, for one, would never tolerate.

He hadn't liked the man from the moment they met, but his behavior toward Jillian on the night of the riot and his treatment of her afterward had put him on Ash's shit list for sure.

For a moment Ash pretended to busy himself with the video camera so that he could surreptitiously observe his subject.

Derek was nervous. Very nervous. His fair-complected face was reddened and sweating, and he fidgeted while he sat, bouncing one knee up and down rapidly while picking at his fingernails.

"Before we begin," Ash said, "I've got something I need you to sign. It's just a formality." He took out a sheet of paper and read aloud: "You have the right to remain silent. Any statement you make could be used in a court of law against you. You have the right to have an attorney present. If you cannot afford an attorney—"

"Am I *under arrest*?" cried Derek, his face suddenly ghost-pale.

"No," said Ash calmly. "I'm just asking you a few questions, but you do have rights that I am legally bound to discuss with you first. Now . . ." He glanced back down at the sheet. Naturally he had long since memorized the Miranda warnings, but he always read aloud from them so he could never be accused of leaving something out. "If you cannot afford an attorney, you have the right to have an attorney furnished free of charge."

"Do you think I need an attorney?" interrupted Derek.

"That's up to you," said Ash. "And finally, I must tell you that if at any time over the course of the interview, you wish to request an attorney or refuse to provide further information, that is your right." He looked into Derek's worried face. "Do you understand these rights?"

Derek nodded.

"Okay. Sign here, please." He gave Derek a pen.

Derek scrawled his name with a touch of arrogance, as if he were providing an autograph.

"Date it, please," added Ash.

Derek scribbled the date next to his signature.

"Thanks," said Ash, whisking the paper out of sight. For the record, he stated the date and time and location of the interview, though he knew that was already provided on the tape. He never liked to take any chances where there was a fatality involved.

"Okay. Derek, first of all, I'd like you to tell me a little bit about Cricket Andrews."

"What do you wanna know? She was a bitch."

More arrogance. Either that, or stupidity. Surely he knew he was suspected in her death. The least he could do was appear sorry that she was dead. It was not an auspicious beginning for Derek Thorsen.

"I'd like to know a little about your relationship with her."

"I never had relations with her," said Derek emphatically. "We were business partners only."

Ash refrained from rolling his eyes. Guy was a moron. "Were you friends?" he asked.

Derek shrugged. "I guess. Until she cheated me and lied to me and stole from me."

"Are you referring to your recent business problems?"

"Damn right. The little bitch fucked me over pretty damn good, is all I can say."

"How did you feel about that?"

"Royally pissed, of course. How would you feel?"

Ash ignored the question. "You recently filed for bankruptcy, is that correct?"

"Cor-rectamundo."

"Do you believe it was Cricket's fault that you had to file?"

"Absolutely."

Ash consulted his notes. "According to court documents, Cricket maintained that you were abusive toward her."

Derek's face flushed. "She's a damn liar. I never laid a hand on a woman in my life."

"I think she was referring to . . . let's see . . . she called it verbal abuse."

"Shit." Derek rolled his eyes. "It was the other way around, you ask me. She cussed me all the time."

Ash continued to study his notes. "You took out a restraining order on her that prevented her from entering the Power Play gyms, is that correct?"

"Yeah. I didn't want her coming around, stirring up a fight, and yelling and cussing in front of the customers. It was embarrassing, and it hurt business."

"But she came by yesterday, didn't she?"

Derek gulped down the water and began shredding the paper cup. "Yeah. That was a bad scene."

"Tell me about it." Ash leaned back in his chair.

"She came over raising high holy hell because my lawyers had taken out an injunction that would pull her infomercials off the air. At least until our legal problems were worked out. She was screaming and cussing me, saying I was a limp dick and all this stuff, and that she was going to ruin me."

"Why didn't you call the cops?"

Derek stared at him as if he were nuts. "What for?"

"She was violating her restraining order. You were within legal rights to have her removed from the property."

Derek rolled his eyes. "I could take care of it myself."

Suddenly Ash leaned forward, close to Derek, invading his space, jamming his knee against Derek's, getting in his face. "That's what you did, isn't it, Derek? You took care of it all right, didn't you?"

Derek tried to lean back out of Ash's way, but there was no place to go. He began to stammer. "Wh-what are you t-talking about?"

Like most of those *big strong* bodybuilders, thought Ash, Thorsen was a pussy. He was scared shitless. "You know what I'm talking about, asshole," he said.

The whites of Derek's eyes became more pronounced. "You think I set that fire?"

"No, Derek. I don't think you set the fire," said Ash. "*I know* you set the fire. I know that the gasoline used was bought from the gas station you frequent near your apartment. I know we found your fingerprints all over her house. And I know you wanted her dead."

"I never!" cried Derek, his body trembling so hard that his hair shook. "I didn't!"

"Your girlfriend says you were really pissed off at Cricket after the fight. She says you went out last night and you didn't tell her where you were going."

"Yeah, but I didn't do nothing to Cricket."

"She says she could smell smoke on you when you got back to the house," lied Ash, watching closely.

"How? What? I didn't do it! For Chrissake, I didn't do it!"

Ash sat back in his chair and said calmly, "Prove it."

Derek stared at him with fear-widened eyes.

Ash said, "Take a polygraph. Show us you're telling the truth."

"What's a poly—oh, you mean like a lie detector?"

"Yeah. Like a lie detector, Derek. Take a lie detector test for us and prove that you were nowhere near Cricket Andrews' house last night. I can set it up easy," he added.

Derek's lips had tightened into a thin white line.

Ash waited, his eyes fixed on Derek's, who kept glancing away.

Finally Derek said, "I don't want to answer any more questions. I want to call my lawyer. Right now."

He crossed his huge arms across his chest and said
no more.

It was his son's twelfth birthday, the age at which
Keegan's dad had left.

For years Keegan had given little thought to his
dad's abandonment, but the older his son, Ian, became, the more acutely Keegan was reminded. Although Keegan understood only too well how the man
would want to be free of his wife, he could never
come up with a satisfactory explanation for why he
would leave his only son.

Was I that obnoxious as a child? Keegan wondered.
He didn't think so. He and his dad had enjoyed some
good times down at the firehouse, hadn't they? So
how could he do that? How could he just walk out for
a pack of cigarettes one night and never come back?

For a time he had fantasized about finding his father, hiring a private investigator, and figuring out,
once and for all, what had happened to his dad.
Maybe even why. But he'd long since given up on the
idea. If the man wanted to be found, after all, he
would show himself, wouldn't he?

Eleanor had baked a very nice cake for their son,
and she brought it out now to the dinner table from
the kitchen, her face beaming in the candle glow. It
was a plain face, but a decent one. In all their married
life, she'd never made any demands on him, never
questioned his silences and his moods, and for that he
was grateful. He felt a tenderness toward his wife, a
certain loyalty akin to what some people felt for a
beloved family dog. He would never abandon her; that
was his private promise, and it was the closest thing
to love he could muster.

Ian was a bit more complicated.

They'd gotten him when he was four weeks old, and
Keegan had often wondered what had happened to
the infant in those four weeks. He didn't cry much,
but he seemed listless and not much interested in Kee-

gan. As a toddler he was insecure away from his mother and frightened of many things. He often cried in the night, and against Keegan's wishes, Eleanor would bring him into their bed.

He was a bright boy, but frail and small. Keegan had secretly hoped that he might raise one of those robust, athletic boys who could do all things and be all things that Keegan had not been. But ironically, the child seemed as introverted as Keegan himself had been. Though he did well in school and the teachers liked him because he never made any trouble, he had few friends and preferred to spend most of his time alone in his room, playing computer games.

Keegan sometimes wondered if his son was gay.

Ian was opening a present that Keegan had selected for him—an intricate fantasy computer game involving characters taken from Tolkien's *Lord of the Rings.*

As he tore off the wrappings, Ian gasped. "Oh, Dad! I've been wanting this! How did you know?" Before Keegan could answer, he leapt from his chair and threw his skinny arms around Keegan's neck in a surprisingly tight embrace.

Keegan did not know what to do. This was the most affection the boy had ever shown toward him.

Eleanor smiled at them.

At that moment an emptiness so vast it had no horizon yawned in Keegan's soul. This was the kind of moment fathers lived for. He knew—as a psychiatrist and keen observer of human behavior—he knew he should feel something right now. His heart should be warm with love and pride. He should feel the urge to hug the boy back.

Something.

Anything.

Awkwardly he patted Ian's hand. "I noticed you were reading Tolkien. It occurred to me you might like the game," he said stiffly.

Eleanor's smile faded.

Keegan couldn't bear the reproach in her eyes and glanced away.

Oddly enough, Ian did not seem to notice. "Mom, may I go play my game now?"

"You silly boy," she said, turning her attention to the child. "Don't you want to open the rest of your presents?"

"Oh!" he cried happily. "I forgot!" He smacked his hand on his forehead clownishly, set the computer game aside, and ripped into another present while his mother looked on indulgently.

Maybe he did feel something, after all, reflected Keegan as he watched over his little family. Misery. That is what it was. Misery that, even here, even now, he could not manage to feel like a member of the human race.

Chapter Fourteen

Ash McGraw leaned against his car in front of Cricket Andrews' ravaged house, thinking.

The crime-scene people had come and gone, packing off their gruesome treasures to the lab. Ash had diagrammed the scene and photographed the charred ruins from every angle, particularly the fire's point of origin at the rear entrance and the site where the body had lain. At the time, it was still being treated as a crime scene, with yellow tape stretched around the perimeters and a patrol unit on hand to keep intruders out.

From his pocket Ash withdrew the three-and-a-half-by six-and-a-half-inch loose-leaf notebook he carried everywhere with him while working a fire. Its lined pages were filled with his precise printing—an accountant's handwriting, Jillian said.

Inside were tiny index dividers into which he categorized all the information he gathered during the course of the investigation. They were labeled WHO, WHAT, WHERE, WHEN, HOW, and WHY.

Under "WHO," he had listed the witnesses he'd rounded up and notes he'd taken during their statements, such as the next-door neighbor who took the victim's cat, and who had reported the fire in the first place, and the man walking his dog an hour before the first report of the fire, who identified Derek

Thorsen's black Lexus as having been parked in front of the house at that time.

In the "WHAT" section, he'd noted evidence that had been collected and analyzed so far, such as the gasoline sold near Derek's apartment where he often filled up the Lexus, and his fingerprints all over the house.

In the "WHERE" category, Ash had written down the street address of the burned house, described the upscale neighborhood where it was located, and noted its proximity to Derek's apartment complex, including the exact time in minutes it took to drive from Derek's apartment to Cricket's house. He also included dimensions of the house and a description of the structure prior to the fire.

Under "WHEN," he'd noted how long it took to extinguish the blaze, and the weather conditions at the time. (Hot, humid. Clear skies. Wind 5–10mph NE.)

The "HOW" section was used to analyze how the home was attacked. It appeared that the sliding glass door at the rear of the house had been jimmied open—fairly easy to do if a security rod was not inserted from within. Wadded newspapers had been scattered around, doused with gasoline, and set afire. Studying this page, Ash realized something he'd forgotten to do. He went into the house, which was completely destroyed only at the rear of the building, and searched until he found a smoke detector. He pried open the disk. Its nine-volt battery was intact.

So why didn't she wake up?

Autopsy results were not in yet. Ash was anxious to find out if there was any evidence of foul play in Cricket's death other than the fire.

"WHY." On the surface, the motive seemed fairly clear to Ash. If Derek had quarreled with Cricket and set fire to her home in a fit of rage and frustration over their rancorous business divorce and his financial woes, then "revenge" would be the one-word explanation for motive.

A few things did bother Ash, though. If Derek had indeed set this fire, then why hadn't he made some attempt to keep it secret? Why park right in front of the house after having been seen arguing publicly with her, and why set the fire in such a clumsy and obvious way that he would be clearly implicated?

Stupidity?

That seemed logical enough to Ash at the moment. One thing he had observed about Derek Thorsen— there was no subtlety to the guy, no sinister cleverness, no sneaky use of charm. He displayed his feelings in much the same way he showed off his body—unself-consciously.

So maybe he did it, but felt badly enough about doing it that he made no attempt to hide the crime.

Wandering back into the living room, his big boots squishing over the water-soaked carpet, Ash stood in the large room, every available surface covered with blackened soot, including the delicate silk peach blossoms arranged in a chrome vase. It had once been a beautiful room, done in warm shades of apricot and cream. Now it looked as dead as its occupant.

In spite of a powerful gut feeling, Ash knew that so far, he did not have a real case against Derek Thorsen. He could imagine a defense attorney attacking everything he had gathered in a courtroom: So Derek Thorsen visited Cricket Andrews before the fire? That did not mean he set the fire. So he was seen arguing publicly with her that day? That did not make him an arsonist—or a murderer. So his fingerprints were in the house? He'd visited her, hadn't he? And not just on that day, but many times in previous years. So the fire was set with gasoline from the same station he frequented? Thousands of people got gas at that station over the course of a year.

Ash took some time and searched the living room, looking for more than the crime-scene guys might have had in mind—looking for something, anything, that might incriminate Thorsen. He found nothing.

Flipping through the notebook, Ash realized that he *did* have enough information for something other than a brief preliminary report.

He had enough probable cause to go before a judge and request a search warrant for Derek Thorsen's house, car, and garage.

It took Jillian several days to catch up to Ash. She surprised him with a pizza as he was working late at the office.

"What are you doing in this neck of the woods?" he cried with a delighted smile.

She went around the desk and gave him a one-armed hug as she set down the pizza box. "I missed you. And I was in the neighborhood."

"At this time of night? Yeah, right." He lifted the lid of the box. "Oh, good. You got thin crust."

Helping herself to a slice of triple-cheese and pepperoni, she perched on the edge of his desk. "I was down at the *Mirror* offices. I'm trying to work up the gumption to finish the Rodriguez story, and I needed something from my desk. It's easier to go at night, when there aren't as many people around."

Leaning back in his chair, he quirked an eyebrow up at her but didn't say anything. That was one of the great things about Ash. He usually knew when to talk and when to keep quiet. After wolfing down one slice and helping himself to another, he said, "So how's it going?"

"Oh, fine." She took a swig of Diet Coke.

"I mean the writing. How's it going?"

"Slowly. Very slowly." She didn't mention her conversation with Dr. Sloane and his suggestion that she pursue the fire story without Ash's knowledge.

"You'll get there," he said. "You're just rusty, is all."

She glanced away. After a moment she said, "I talked to Derek."

He sighed. "Jillian, you know I can't talk to you about that case."

"Why not?"

"Because it's an open case, still under investigation. You know that."

"So are those other fires. You talk to me about them."

"That's different."

"Why?"

"Because they're unsolved." He grimaced, as though regretting the words the moment he said them.

"Are you telling me that as far as you're concerned, you've solved the Cricket Andrews case?"

"That's not what I meant, Jill, and you know it."

"No, I don't know it, Ash! As far as I can tell, you're convinced Derek did it, and you're trying to convict him instead of finding out who really set that fire."

He tossed a half-eaten piece of pizza back into the box. "What makes you so sure he *didn't* do it?"

"Oh, for crying out loud!" She jumped off his desk and paced around the office. "You can't honestly believe Derek Thorsen is capable of murder!"

"We're all capable of it," he said quietly.

Jillian stared at him. She stopped pacing. Finally she said, "Look, Derek's got a temper, I'll grant you. I've seen it myself. And maybe I could imagine a scenario where he and Cricket were having a knockdown dragout fight, where she was cussing him and he was cussing her and push came to shove and maybe, yeah, maybe he'd be capable of striking her or doing something that would cause her death in the passion of the moment. But this situation is completely different. This is an evil act that took forethought and planning and a cold disregard for human life. Derek has his faults—and I'd be the first one to admit that—but deliberate murder? I just can't see it."

"No one who is close to a murderer can ever see it," he said.

She rolled her eyes. "Jesus."

"Goddammit!" He slammed down a can of Pepsi. "No matter what I believe or don't believe, no matter what *feeling* I have about a case, I have to base that case on evidence that will stand up in a court of law. No more and no less. Evidence. And right now the evidence is screaming loud and clear that Derek torched that house. Whether you like it or not, that's just the way it is."

"What if there was other evidence? That pointed in another direction?"

He narrowed his eyes. "Are you telling me you have other evidence?"

"No." She jammed her hands down in her jeans pockets. "I just mean . . . if you *had* other evidence, would you investigate it or shove it under the carpet because it didn't back up your theory about Derek?"

"For God's sake, Jillian! What do you take me for? Of course I would investigate other evidence. But I'm telling you, there *is* no other evidence. And that's all I'm going to say." He shoved the pizza box away from him.

Jillian stared at the floor. She felt depressed and frustrated. Of all the things to come between her and Ash, the last she would have expected would be Derek. They'd broken up weeks ago. She and Ash had grown very close in the time since then. And now they were fighting over him. If it hadn't been for that stupid fire . . .

She sighed. "I guess I'd better be going. You've got a lot of work to do, and I need to see if I can get anything done on the Rodriguez story."

He nodded. "Sure. Thanks for bringing the pizza. It was nice."

A miserable new tension stretched between them. "I didn't mean to make you mad," she said, and felt instantly foolish for sounding so junior high. It was all part of the new, ridiculously insecure Jillian.

He waved his hand in the air. "Don't worry about it. It's no big deal."

But it was a big deal, and they both knew it.

That night Jillian slept even worse than usual. It took her hours to drift off. Jagged dreams pierced her rest—she would dream that she was quarreling with Ash, then wake up angry and confused.

And then, in the black velvet time of night known only to night watchmen and insomniacs, she opened her eyes to the solution as though it had been in front of her all along.

Ash had said he would investigate any new evidence that might serve to clear Derek.

Therefore, she would search for new evidence.

At first she planned to wait for morning. It would, after all, be the sane thing to do. But once the idea had occurred to her and she'd obsessed about it to the point of full wakefulness, Jillian decided that, since sanity was hardly her strong suit these days anyway, she'd act on the impulse now.

She was so excited by the idea, at finally being in control of *something*—even if it was crazy—her hands shook as she pulled on the pair of rubber boots she'd bought to wear with Ash to fire scenes.

By now she was used to driving late at night, and she knew the way to Cricket's house since she had been there before with Derek. On the way, she reflected that it felt good to be heading someplace with a sense of purpose and direction. Not only might she clear Derek's name, but if she found anything, she might restore the positive feelings between her and Ash that this awful case had disrupted.

Cricket's upscale neighborhood was buttoned down for the night and completely silent. Not a soul stirred. Feeling like a burglar, Jillian drove once past the house without stopping. Garages were located to the rear of the residences, and for her to pull up and park out front might draw undue attention, though Jillian didn't see any lights on anywhere beyond the handsome gas lanterns in several yards and a few streetlights.

She decided to park behind Cricket's house in the rear drive. Even then, she drove very slowly so as not to alert anyone but the occasional dog. Counting houses, she doused the headlights as she approached Cricket's.

Intermittent clouds dragged ragged edges across the half-moon, leaving just enough moon glow to give the house a haunted appearance. Because of the steeply pitched roof and the location of the fire, the house had appeared whole and unharmed from the street. But from behind the front facade, Jillian found a building that resembled a gutted carcass.

Carrying a heavy-duty flashlight, Jillian let herself in through the gate in the redwood fence and then stopped. In their efforts to suppress the blaze, fire-fighters had trampled every flower bed. Debris littered the lawn and floated in the pool. The rear of the house, especially the den that opened to the pool, had been eviscerated by the blaze, and the back part of the roof was charred black.

The sliding glass door, shattered by firefighters, had been covered with plywood loosely nailed in place. Using another scrap of wood for leverage, Jillian was able to pry up one corner and slip underneath it, into the house. Picking her way slowly around fire-damage litter and through the gaping door, she swallowed. She had not been close to Cricket, and she did not like the way the woman had defrauded Derek, but she would never have wished a violent death on the vibrant, hardworking lady.

Shining the powerful beam of the flashlight around, Jillian could tell even in the dark that the beautiful redwood and brick home was completely destroyed. Because the firefighters had arrived as soon as they did and fought the fire as aggressively as they had, the heat within had not reached the point of total incineration, but everything in the den, the adjoining bedroom where Cricket had slept, and portions of the kitchen were burned or melted into misshapen lumps.

Crunching through the remnants of Cricket's home, Jillian found herself shivering in spite of the warm night. Following Ash around on his job, Jillian had wandered through other burned-out buildings, but this was different. She had sat in the lovely living room with Cricket and Derek and had eaten dinner on the glass-topped table in the formal dining room. Though Jillian had made private fun of Cricket for her obsessive neatness and constant push to impress, rather than welcome, her guests, this had once been a cherished home.

And it had become a tomb.

Jillian could only imagine the horror of that night. Had Cricket awakened? Tried to escape? Had she coughed and choked during her last moments, fighting for breath, desperate for help, only to die alone?

The place was creepy. Jillian found herself jumping at the slightest noise, whirling in the darkness as if someone were at her shoulder. She hurried, as best she could, through the rest of the house. Most of it had been ruined by heavy black smoke and then flooded with water used to put out the fire.

The odor of gasoline, mixed with soot and ash and charred wood, was still gaggingly strong.

It smelled like death.

Jillian felt suddenly sick and more than a little foolish. What in the hell was she doing here? She was no arson investigator. What could she possibly hope to find that the crime-scene technicians and Ash had not found? She didn't even know what she was looking for.

She stood uncertainly in a hazy swath of moonlight that fell through a hole in the roof, looking around, feeling guilty, like a vulture picking over the remains of the dead.

Then the glow of the flashlight and her gaze dropped to something that simply did not belong.

She knew Cricket Andrews. The woman was compulsively organized about every aspect of her life. Her home was always spotless. Granted, trampling firefighters and the fire itself had ravaged the home, but even so, it was not normally a cluttered residence. The appointments were sleek and modern, and nothing was ever out of place.

In the formal dining room, the glass-topped and chrome table was blackened and fingerprinted by soot and crime-scene people, but it was closer to the front of the house and out of the way of the worst of the fire damage. Something caught Jillian's attention, and she drew closer.

In the middle of the table was a powdery pile several inches high of some substance that, at first glance, resembled dirty sand.

It wasn't ashes or anything having to do with the fire. Whatever it was, Jillian was certain that Cricket would never have gone to bed and left a mess like that on her dining table. Jillian leaned forward and poked at the powder. It was soft, and beneath the sooty outer layer it was rusty in color, like cinnamon.

Jillian leaned over and sniffed, then stood up, baffled.

It *was* cinnamon. A simple household spice that people liked to mix with sugar and put on toast or sprinkle into their cocoa or atop an apple pie. This wasn't just a mess that might be left over from baking. This pile of cinnamon represented two or three boxes of the stuff, dumped in the middle of the dining room table for no discernible reason.

Cricket never baked and even if she had she'd have done so in the kitchen. She *never* would have left a pile of cinnamon on the spotless glass top of her dining room table and gone to bed. No matter who had put cinnamon there or for what reason, Cricket wouldn't have been able to sleep until she'd cleaned it up. Derek used to tease her about it.

Derek.

According to Ash, Derek had been present that night. Though Derek denied it, Jillian had heard news reports that he'd been at Cricket's house that night and that they had quarreled.

But why would he leave a pile of cinnamon? He seldom set foot in the kitchen. He might not even know what cinnamon was.

Obviously no one who'd been in the house as part of the investigation had found anything unusual about a pile of cinnamon on a dining room table, but to Jillian, it was like a flashing sign. Withdrawing a small camera from her pocket, she took pictures of it from several angles and distances. Then, balancing the flashlight on the table for light, Jillian drew a quick sketch in her notebook as to the position of the spice.

This is crazy, she thought. *Getting psyched over a pile of cinnamon on a dining table.*

And then, with a touch of grim humor, she found herself chuckling dryly. *So what if it's crazy? I'll just tell my shrink.*

Chapter Fifteen

He'd gotten away with murder three times, and he no longer lived in fear for the knock at the door that would reveal police detectives or an arson investigator asking where he'd been or what he'd been doing on certain nights. It never ceased to amaze him, how easy it was to get away with murder. It was the dirty little secret never revealed in the movies or on television programs. It was exhilarating! It was empowering.

In the movies, the detectives or the fictional FBI profilers always talked about how intelligent serial killers were, as though they stood somewhat in awe of them. In fact, it didn't require much intelligence, just a certain care in planning. And the false self, of course. The false self was crucial in maintaining the facade. Even for smart investigators, it was human nature never to look beneath the facade unless one had some compelling reason, and it was Keegan's ongoing mission never to give anyone a compelling reason.

This last murder, now, that was a sheer stroke of genius. Not only had he taken care to change his method of fire setting, but he'd set up a fall guy for the crime and gotten clean away with it.

With each killing, he got smarter and smarter.

So, the little thought occured to him, does this mean you consider yourself a serial killer?

Of course not. He was no sexual sadist, some

twisted pervert like Ted Bundy or Jeffrey Dahmer. He was the phoenix, rising from the ashes.

That was a whole different thing.

Ash McGraw managed to flag down Assistant District Attorney Mary Atherton on the sidewalk in front of the mammoth, ultramodern Dallas County Courthouse.

"I want to be sure that if I arrest Derek Thorsen on the Cricket Andrews arson murder, we've got enough to indict him and take this to trial," Ash said to the diminutive ADA.

ADA Atherton was short, plump, gray, and motherly. She fooled defendants all the time. They were never quite prepared for her keen intelligence or her no-bullshit trial manner. In all her years at the courthouse, she had never lost a murder case. She stopped, glanced at her watch, and said, "Autopsy reports?"

"Asphixiation. *Before* the fire. There was no soot in her air passageway or her lungs."

She nodded.

"I think he suffocated her, maybe with a pillow in her bed, then set the fire to cover the crime. I've got extensive documentation of a clear pattern of animosity between Thorsen and the victim for weeks before her death."

"I want real evidence, Ash, not circumstantial. This is a capital case."

By "real evidence," Ash knew she meant solid physical evidence that would place Thorsen securely at the crime scene. "Thorsen's fingerprints were all over the place," he said. "The gasoline used as an incendiary device was purchased at the same gas station frequented by Thorsen, and a search of his garage revealed an empty gas container with his fingerprints on it."

"Aw, c'mon, Ash. You know as well as I do that if you'd found that gas can at the scene of the fire with his fingerprints on it, now *that* would be real evidence. Finding it in his garage is nothing."

He glanced away from her piercing gaze. She was right, and he knew it. He sighed. "Direct evidence in the form of witness statements placing his vehicle at her residence an hour before the fire was reported."

"Who called in the fire?"

"Lady next door."

"Hmm." She thought a moment.

"And Thorsen and the victim were witnessed by several Power Play employees having a loud argument that afternoon in which Thorsen accused her of having ruined his life."

"Circumstantial. Circumstantial. You don't have anything else?"

He grinned. "Guy refused a polygraph."

"Gee, thanks, McGraw. That's real handy, since the jurors will never know it." She rolled her eyes. "Statement from the suspect?"

He shrugged. "Right up till the time he requested his lawyer."

"Anything on it?"

He hesitated, then grinned. "Denials."

"Talk to him again."

"It won't do any good," he protested. "He'll have his attorney there for sure."

"Doesn't matter." She started walking again, faster this time, and Ash stretched his long legs to keep up. "Lean on him. Put some pressure on him. Make him nervous. See what happens. You got a crime report?"

"That *and* a follow-up," he said, handing her a thick file of copies of his reports and witness statements.

"Let me read through this and think about it," she said. "Meantime, you see what you can get out of the guy. I'll get back to you." She disappeared into the building.

Well, that was something. Usually if she thought the case was bullshit, she just came right out and said it to his face.

Back in his car, Ash retrieved a message on his phone from Jillian. She'd found something that might be of interest to him about the Andrews case and could he come by later?

He drove straight to her apartment. He had no idea what she was talking about and didn't expect much, but he welcomed the excuse to see her and make up for their argument of the other night.

She came to the door without makeup. She'd lost the tan she'd always had driving the Mustang, and now he could see the fine dusting of freckles across her nose. Her wild coppery hair was pulled back in a ponytail. It made her look like a little kid.

"Hi," she said, smiling.

He returned her smile. "Hi."

She let him into her cluttered living room. The TV was on, which bothered him. It meant that in all likelihood, she had not been working. He was beginning to worry that if she didn't do something pretty soon, she might face eviction.

"Okay," he said. "What's up?"

"I want to show you something." She rummaged through the papers on her desk to produce a photo-development envelope, from which she withdrew several snapshots. "You said you would consider other evidence that might clear Derek of Cricket's murder."

He nodded warily.

She handed him the photographs. He stared at the first one. He had absolutely no idea what he was looking at. There were four different shots of the same thing, and none of them made any sense to Ash. "What?" he said.

"I took these at Cricket's," she said. "After the fire."

He stared at her.

She pointed to one of the photos. "This is Cricket's glass-topped dining table. It's a formal dining room, see, and I found this on it."

He continued to stare at her. "What are you talking about?"

"I know it doesn't look like much," she said, "in the photos, I mean. But what it is, see, is this big pile of cinnamon. Right smack in the middle of her dining room table."

Controlling his temper with great effort, Ash said, "Am I to understand that you went to the crime scene without my permission and took photographs?"

"Okay. I knew you'd be mad about that, but—"

"Jillian. I cannot believe you would do something like this." He was so angry he could barely think straight. "What on earth did you think you were doing?"

She looked annoyed. "You're not paying attention. There's a big pile of *cinnamon* on Cricket's *glass-topped dining table*. She would never leave a mess like that in her formal dining room. Somebody else had to put it there."

Slinging the photos onto her desk, where they scattered like autumn leaves under a cold wind, Ash said sarcastically, "I don't suppose you happened to have a Subdivision 10 evidentiary search warrant signed by a district judge that allowed you to continue the investigation, did you?"

She blinked at him.

"Have you lost your mind?" he shouted. "Do you realize the evidence you may have destroyed? How *dare* you go to a crime scene of one of *my* investigations without me!"

"The crime-scene techs had already been there," she explained.

"The fucking crime-scene techs are not investigating this crime!" he yelled. "I can't believe you did this."

"I'm sorry!" she cried. "But the least you could do is *listen* to what I'm trying to tell you and *look* at these photographs!"

With a disgusted groan that came out sounding

more like a growl, Ash shook his head, turned on his heel, and slammed out the front door.

Jillian was so distraught by the fight with Ash that she almost forgot her therapy appointment and was a few minutes late. She'd realized that Ash would be put out with her for visiting the crime scene without him, but she'd never dreamed he would be so outraged. Even worse, he was so underimpressed with the photos that she now felt like a complete idiot for having taken them in the first place. How silly it all must have appeared to him. Here he was in this high-profile capital murder case, and she was trying to get him to look at a pile of cinnamon on a dining room table.

"I'm sorry I'm late," she said breathlessly as she took her seat. "Ash and I had a big argument, and I lost track of time."

Dr. Sloane frowned in sympathy. "What were you fighting about?"

She sighed. "I'm afraid Ash was right this time. I meddled in one of his investigations and tromped around the crime scene when I should have *known* better. The crime scene is sacred to investigators. They don't even like other cops messing around there."

"What were you doing?"

"Oh, it's that case concerning my old boyfriend, Derek, and the arson murder of his former business partner. I don't think Derek did it, and I was trying to find something that might help. You know, something that would clear him or at least cast some doubt."

"And did you? Find anything?"

She hesitated. The truth of the matter was that no, she hadn't found a damn thing, and that was the main reason she was feeling so miserable. She shook her head. "It was really stupid."

"Did Ash say that?"

"In so many words."

"He has a great deal of power over you, hasn't he?"

Jillian stared at the doctor. "Power? Well, no. I mean . . . *No!*"

"Then, why do you get so upset whenever you anger him?"

"That's just because . . . well, we're friends. Nobody likes to make their friends mad."

"True, but they don't necessarily fear losing the friendship. You seem to think that if you make Ash mad at you, he will withdraw his support of you, much in the same way a child fears angering a parent and being abandoned because of it."

"Oh, Ash isn't like that. He wouldn't bail out on the friendship just because I screwed up. Not even if it jeopardized a case."

"How can you be sure?"

"Well . . ." Jillian stammered to a stop. "I trust him."

"If you trust him, then why are you so worried about the argument?"

"I . . . uh . . . I don't . . . know."

Dr. Sloane had not blinked during the entire conversation, and the effect was almost hypnotic. In any event, she was confused again.

"People only have as much power over you as you are willing to give them, Jillian."

"But this isn't a power struggle, Dr. Sloane."

"Isn't it? Ash has the power over the investigation, doesn't he?"

"Well, yeah."

"Therefore he has power over the destiny of your old boyfriend, whom you say you still care for."

"I guess so. In a way. Yeah."

"Are you so convinced that your old boyfriend is innocent?"

"Absolutely. He could not have possibly done this crime."

"How do you know?"

Jillian bit her lip.

"For all you know, this man Derek could be leading

a false life. He could even be manipulating you with his protestations of innocence. Maybe he's even jealous of your friendship with the arson investigator."

She rolled her eyes. "I think he's got a few more pressing matters on his mind right now."

"All the same, he could be using you."

Jillian considered this. "I hadn't thought about that." Now she was confused again.

"Whose friendship do you value more at this time? Derek's or Ash's?"

"Oh, that's easy. Ash McGraw and I have been friends ever since college. He's the only person I know who stuck with me throughout the whole riot situation and saw me at my worst and still believed in me." She swallowed.

"He's also encouraged your writing, hasn't he?"

She nodded.

"Before all this trouble with Derek arose, you were enjoying accompanying Ash to fire sites, weren't you?"

"Oh, yes."

"Then, perhaps you should give your friend Ash the benefit of the doubt. After all, he is the expert. If he is so certain that Derek murdered his old partner, then you might consider the fact that he may be right."

Everything in Jillian's being fought against believing that Derek had murdered Cricket. She rubbed her forehead. Ever since the argument with Ash, her head had been splitting.

"One thing is for sure," went on Dr. Sloane. "As long as Ash is angry with you over this matter, he will never allow you to go with him to another fire site, and you won't be able to work on the fire story."

"Maybe I should drop it anyway," she said. "It's not worth sacrificing the friendship over."

"There you go again. Abdicating power in the relationship."

She shook her head. "That's not what I meant."

He smiled.

"It's not!" Jillian was growing increasingly frustrated. "This has nothing to do with power!"

"Doesn't it?"

"Of course not. It has to do with trust."

"Trust is empowerment, my dear. If Ash had trusted you in the first place, he would not have gotten so angry with you for visiting the crime scene."

Jillian closed her eyes. A feeling of profound depression settled on her shoulders.

"And if you fully trusted Ash, you would relinquish control of the investigation to him, which is where it belongs."

She sighed. "I do trust Ash."

"If you trusted him, Jillian, you would not fear his taking away his affections from you. You fear that abandonment because of what happened at the riot. In a way, Randi abandoned you by dying."

She said, "That doesn't make any sense, Dr. Sloane."

"Think about it. It will."

Her eyes filled with tears. "I don't know what to do. I'm so confused."

"Are you taking your Xonok?"

She avoided his gaze. "I don't like the idea of taking a mind-altering drug."

He chuckled. "Nonsense. All Xonok does is correct a chemical imbalance in your brain that resulted from the shock of the trauma and the sustained stress of the past several months. It's only a temporary measure, to help you through this rough period. Once you're on your feet again, you may stop taking it. But I want you to be faithful until then," he added, his voice a firm reprimand. "I must be able to trust that you are cooperating fully in your treatment for me to be able to help you."

"Okay," she said, defeated. "I'll take it. It's just . . ."

"What?"

"I've heard that the drug can have side effects, that it can make some people violent or suicidal."

He waved his hand dismissively. "Ratings-grabbing media sensationalism. If I thought the drug was in the least bit dangerous, I wouldn't prescribe it."

"All right."

"In the meantime, you might consider patching things up with your friend. Working on that fire story has done more for you than any medication. Besides, his friendship is important to your recovery, as well."

"Of course," she said. "I was wrong, anyway. I owe Ash an apology."

"Good. Trust him with the investigation, which is his domain, after all. But when it comes to your own work—the fire story—just remember that he can have only as much power over you as you give him."

Jillian rubbed her head again. "But aren't you asking me to do two different things?"

"What do you mean?"

"Aren't you saying that I should trust Ash with the investigation of Derek's case, but at the same time, I should sneak around behind his back and work on this fire story he doesn't want me to write? I mean, if I apologize for what I did, and then use the friendship to get information on different cases for a story, isn't that being manipulative?"

"Not at all," he said. Other than an unconscious tapping of the pen on his pad, he sat very still. "I'm asking you to trust your instincts where your own work is concerned, just as Ash trusts his with his work. From what I've seen here in this office, it would appear that your instincts are telling you that this fire investigation story may be just what you need to jump-start your stalled career and put you back to work, earning a living doing what you love."

"Maybe," she said slowly. "But judging from how angry he was this afternoon, if he thought I was using any of the information I'd learned while accompanying him on his investigations for a story I promised him I wouldn't write . . . well, I shudder to think what would happen."

"Remember, you're doing this story for your therapy. There's no need to even show it to Ash until it's done. And in the end, it may not be a story for publication anyway. It may just be an exercise in healing."

Jillian was doubtful. What she really wanted to do was drop the fire investigation altogether, after seeing Ash so angry that afternoon. But maybe Dr. Sloane was right. Maybe she was investing Ash with too much power over her and her emotional security.

"Do you trust me, Jillian?" asked Dr. Sloane suddenly.

Surprised, Jillian said, "Of course I do."

"I don't know," he said. "I sense resistance whenever I try to help you."

"I'm not resisting," she protested. "At least, I don't mean to."

"Good," he said. "Then, I'll see you day after tomorrow. And don't forget to take your medication."

"I won't," she said, and trailed out of the office like a chastened child. At the door she stopped.

"What is it?" he asked pleasantly.

"I just . . . wondered . . . why it is that the more time passes since . . . the riot . . . the worse I feel? I don't seem to be recovering from this post-traumatic stress stuff. I'm still not working, and I can't seem to get myself together. And when I come to see you," she added bravely, "I wind up more confused."

He smiled. "That's perfectly normal, Jillian. Remember, I said that when we worked through this stage of the recovery process, you would feel worse for a time?"

She nodded doubtfully.

"Recovering from trauma is hard work. I know it may seem as if you aren't making any progress, but don't worry. You are. Trust me."

Chapter Sixteen

He had begun to develop a ritual that he repeated with each fire. The ritual allowed him to prolong the anticipation, build the excitement, and prepare his mind, spirit, and body for the task at hand. It also enabled him to look forward to the next fire even as he savored the success of the last one. He found the ritual to be almost as exciting as the fire setting itself.

In this way, the deadness was kept at bay in much the same way a campfire could hold back the darkness and frightful nighttime creatures of the forest.

The number 500 began to assume great importance to him. As the phoenix lived 500 years before self-immolating in its own funeral pyre, so he chose 500 hours as the length of time between each fire: on the 20th day and the 20th hour.

Twenty was, after all, divisible by five.

Besides, this gave him time to select his next honoree. They were honorees, after all, not victims. Sacrifices to the great Beast.

The Assyrian phoenix honored its dead sire by rising from the ashes of the funeral pyre and, as soon as it had gained sufficient strength, carrying its own nest—the sepulchre of the fallen bird—to the temple of the sun, where it was consumed in flames.

It was, therefore, an honor to be selected.

Once the honoree was chosen, he then had to assess the appropriateness of the selection. Did this person live alone? Where? If he or she lived in an apartment, then the title would have to pass to someone else, because Keegan had little control over an apartment fire. Extensive security systems in the house, or personal habits that were prohibitive to the mission could also exclude someone from the ranks.

Once the selection was made, it was then necessary to familiarize himself with the daily routine of the honoree as well as gain entry to the home, if possible, in order to seek out the best possible location for the altar.

The method of fire setting varied, depending upon what Keegan had learned from previous fires.

Although he greatly preferred that the fire work its ultimate magic on the honoree, he also respected the fact that fire had a life and a will of its own; it could not be manipulated to his purpose. Therefore, he used chloroform to subdue the honorees, since he had learned that ether left no trace and was difficult to determine in autopsy. Otherwise, having learned his gruesome lesson early on with the warehouse security guard, he preferred as little personal contact between him and the honoree as he could manage.

All this preparation was taking up an increasing amount of time. Without telling his wife that he had done so, he cut back on his clinical practice and reduced his course load at the university. This enabled him to be away from the office off and on during the course of the day, as his preparation demanded. Getting away from the house at night proved to be ridiculously easy. All he had to do was tell his wife he was teaching evening courses at the university. It never occurred to her to question or doubt him.

Ceremonial night was, of course, the most exhilarating part of the ritual. Sometimes the excitement was so unbearable, he could hardly hide it from his family. Fortunately, his wife was an early riser and went to bed by ten each night. To ensure no interruption, he always sprinkled a few grains of Seconal in her tea after dinner on those nights.

On the 20th day, the 14th hour—the numbers "four" and "one" equaled "five"—he retired to his office, where he locked the door and lit his ritual cinnamon-scented candles. There he would sit in the dark in front of a candle and gaze into the flame, suspending all thought. He would allow the flame to enter into him, and he to enter into it, until he felt the stirrings of life deep within his loins.

Sometimes—and he was ashamed to admit this to himself—he would even masturbate. The orgasm was like nothing he had ever felt during his infrequent sexual encounters with his wife, and served to heighten his excitement even further.

On the 15th hour—a number that, when divided by five, equaled three; as the three corners of a pyramid, a symbol which represented fire—he would take out the sacred pouch that contained ashes from each of his fires. Dipping his moistened fingers into the ashes, he made the sign of the pyramid on his forehead.

He was then ready to go.

In a locked safe behind his desk, he kept a backpack filled with the items he would need to ignite the blaze. He always carefully extinguished the candles before leaving his office.

The last thing he wanted to do was cause an accidental fire in the home of his sleeping family.

On ceremonial nights, he always parked his car at the curb in front of the house rather than in the garage at the rear, so that he could quietly start the engine and drive away without awakening his wife or son. He always drove carefully and obeyed all the laws, because by the 18th and 19th hours, it was always the depths of the night and he wanted to do nothing that would draw attention to himself for any reason.

He dressed in black jogging clothes so that he could blend into the shadows, but if he was seen, he could appear to be a resident out on a late-night run. No

one ever seemed to notice him because he always
looked as though he belonged.

Barking dogs could be a problem, but he ignored
them, knowing most of the residents did as well, and
never lingered in one spot long enough to arouse
suspicion.

By the 20th hour he was always in place, ready.

The moment of ignition was so excruciatingly exquisite that he soon abandoned time-delay methods so
that he could watch.

The intimacy of that moment, the intensity, made
him feel more purely alive than at any other time in
his life.

If his method was particularly covert, he could stay
awhile and watch the fire as it awakened from its
slumber, reared its beautiful head, stretched, and
began to explore the house. Occasionally it was so
exciting that he couldn't help himself—he had to masturbate again. He always brought a washcloth for that
purpose and took it away with him, so as not to leave
any potentially incriminating evidence behind.

The power! The glory!

By the time the fire engines came shrieking down the
street and the neighbors came spilling out of their
houses to watch and wonder, he was usually already
back at home in his own bed, beside his slumbering
wife, with his thoughts reeling and his heart thumping
and his senses tingling and his mind shouting *I am alive!*

Jillian forced herself to hammer out the Juan Rodriguez story, and it was the worst writing experience of
her life. She approached the computer each day with
dread and double questioned each line she wrote—
when she wasn't staring off into space. Finally, she
took the rough outline of her notes and strung the
paragraphs together with weak transition sentences,
enough to put together something to send to Miles.

She waited.

When two days had passed without word from him,

Jillian knew she was sunk. Too cowardly to face him or even talk to him on the phone, she sent a tentative e-mail asking if he'd received the article.

His return message was cursory: *Yes, I did get it, and it seems a bit rough to me. If you don't mind, I'd like to suggest the following revisions.*

His suggested revisions, point by point, left scarcely a paragraph untouched. Revising was a necessary part of writing, but Jillian hadn't had an article torn apart so thoroughly by an editor since college.

It hurt.

It was humiliating, for a journalist of her stature and experience to be treated like a raw beginner, but Jillian couldn't muster up any outrage toward Miles because she knew he was right. She'd turned in substandard work so far beneath her usual caliber that she was surprised he had accepted it at all.

She came to loathe Juan Rodriguez and everything about the story. Ironically, she missed Randi's insightful photographs, which would have taken up valuable space and skillfully illustrated what Jillian was trying so clumsily to say. She wondered bitterly who had stolen Randi's camera and what had become of the photographs she had taken just before her death. Her last photographs.

Morbid, miserable thought.

Forcing herself back to the task at hand, Jillian had to admit that she welcomed Miles's suggestions because she seemed incapable of thinking on her own for this particular piece. Using his e-mail like a connect-the-dots drawing, she made all the changes he suggested and e-mailed the result back to him.

That's better, he responded. *The check's in the mail.*

It wasn't exactly a ringing endorsement, but it was editorial acceptance of a piece of work she had done and for which she was being paid.

Awkward though it might be, it was a step forward. Now what?

She should have felt elated, but she still felt terrible.

The quality of her work had suffered so badly and her fragile self-esteem was so imminently bruisable that she feared she might never write again with the old passion and ferocity.

While sitting at her desk contemplating that depressing thought, Jillian decided to straighten out her desk drawers.

That was when she came across a small spiral notebook, open to a page upon which she had jotted in her own crazy shorthand: *You can read about poverty, see pictures of it, even see poor people gathered in places like the welfare office, but you've never known poverty until you've smelled the stench of it. It's sweat, filth, fear, and something indefinable but overwhelming.*

The page was smudged with blood.

Jillian's hands began to tremble, and her mouth went dry. These were the words she had written on the night of the riot, while Randi stood beside her taking pictures.

Without stopping to think, she opened a new document in her computer and copied the words out of the notebook.

Then—almost against her will—fresh words began to flow.

When my friend Randi and I went to cover the Cinco de Mayo rally in Little Mexico for the Dallas Mirror, we thought we understood the consequences of poverty ignored. We thought we realized what it meant to be disenfranchised, dissatisfied, disenchanted. We were journalists, after all. We covered stories like that every day; I with my little spiral notebook and my big ego, and Randi with her small camera and her powerful talent.

But the tragic truth is that we didn't understand anything.

At least, I didn't. I didn't understand that your best friend could die in a bloody mist before your eyes when someone who really understood poverty and ignorance and frustration and rage exploded.

I thought I knew death.

On that terrible hot, sweating night in May, I found that I didn't know anything.

I didn't know that a young, vibrant, beautiful mother of a sweet baby boy could die in my arms because someone neither of us had ever met chose that moment to lash out at an indifferent world.

I used to be indifferent. I'm not anymore.

Now I'm just different.

She stopped and read over what she had written. It wasn't long enough to be a "Reflections" column. Nevertheless, she copied the piece over to her e-mail file and sent it straight to Miles.

Fifteen minutes later, the phone rang. Jillian now relied on her "Caller ID" device and her answering machine to screen calls, but when she saw the number to the *Mirror* show up on the readout, she picked up. "Hello?"

"Jesus, Jillian," said Miles. "I'd have called sooner but I couldn't stop bawling."

"So you think it's pretty good?" she hazarded.

"I'm running it. As is. It's the most powerful piece you've ever done."

Staring at the blood-smeared notebook, Jillian sighed. She felt strangely numb. "Thank you," she said, and they hung up.

Maybe she was on the way back. It seemed as if it was going to be a very long journey.

Rolling her head around on her shoulders, Jillian shuffled into the kitchen. The bottle of Xonok was sitting on the kitchen counter. She picked up the bottle and fingered it.

On the one hand, she'd just done a piece of work her editor was proud of. Wasn't that a sign of healing?

On the other hand, she still felt like crap, and she knew she had a long way to go before she was anywhere near ready to return to work full-time. And Dr. Sloane had insisted that she "cooperate" with him.

She got out a glass of water and swallowed a pill.

Chapter Seventeen

It never ceased to amaze him, how some people actually went to bed in the city without locking their doors at night. Granted, it very rarely happened in the finer neighborhoods, but in some poorer ones—the ones you might suspect would be the most vulnerable to crime—some of the people simply didn't bother, or else were careless and forgot. Perhaps they thought there was little worth stealing in their humble cottages. Maybe they were simply stupid. Either way, it was a lucky break for him that his chosen honoree was one of the careless ones.

It was so easy as to be almost disappointing.

He simply slipped through the front door—pretty as you please—and stood in the darkness, filled with dark exhilaration at knowing that he had actually crept into someone's home while they slept and now held total power over them.

At this point he could do whatever he wished. He could simply leave. He could steal some momento of his presence. Or he could even have a little fun—rearrange things on a bookshelf or tabletop, for instance, like a stealthy little poltergeist.

But he was not here to make mischief.

Young people did sleep so very soundly. It was an added advantage. He supposed he could tromp around all he liked without fear of discovery, but all the same, he was cautious as ever.

How raw and vulnerable they appeared in their sleep, his honorees. Not always innocent, but always helpless.

This was that point of exquisite hesitation, that hovering doubt, as he stood by their beds, gazing down at them, listening to their breathing, contemplating their dreams. He could walk away if he chose.

But he never chose to walk away. Not with the beast coiled, sinewy and waiting to be released.

Admittedly, sometimes he had to take a moment to screw up his courage. The moment of the chloroform—that was the most dangerous, fraught with the terror of discovery. But the beast never failed him. He was always given almost godlike strength so that he could subdue the thrashes of even the strongest honorees.

This night, however, seemed to get off on a sour note when his honoree showed surprising muscular strength. In the struggle, he was almost overcome and, indeed, was struck a glancing but quite painful blow on the shoulder blade. This angered him and gave him the spurt of adrenaline needed to finish the job.

But the battle had unnerved him. Perhaps sensing weakness, the beast seemed reluctant to show itself. He had one hell of a time setting the fire—and then! The blaze came roaring to such furious life that he was almost trapped himself!

Certainly there was no time to satisfy his urges into the washcloth, not when he had to run for his life as the blaze seemed to explode forth with a power and rage he had never before seen.

What was wrong? Had he dishonored the beast in some way? What had he done?

All the next day, he obsessed about it, until he hit upon the problem.

It was her. That girl, that reporter who was seeing him for PTSD. She was defying him. And to defy him was, of course, to defy the beast. This was unacceptable!

She needed discipline, and he knew just how to give it to her.

With a heavy heart, Ash McGraw stood in front of the blackened, stinking wreck that had once been someone's home. Fatal fires always saddened him, but this one more than others because the occupant of the small, modest rental house had been a young college student who was working his way through school by sacking groceries at the local supermarket. Judging from interviews Ash had conducted so far, the kid hadn't had an enemy in the world. Everyone who had met him had liked him immediately. So friendly and full of life had he been, in fact, that patrons of the supermarket sometimes stood in his line even when another checkout was open, just so they could visit with this personable young man.

He was friendly, funny, bright, and wholesome. And now he was dead. Initial autopsy reports showed he had died of smoke inhalation and had no alcohol or drugs in his system. Since there were no smoke detectors in the home, it would appear that the young man had died in his sleep when a fire broke out in his home. Absence of accelerants pointed toward accidental causes.

The trouble was, Ash couldn't find where the accident had occurred.

An examination of the exterior of the structure indicated that all windows and doors had been closed at the time the fire broke out. There was no sign of forced entry.

Working his way inside the house from the area of least fire damage, Ash checked the ceiling to see if he could determine the area of the most serious damage. From there, he looked for the telltale "V" pattern along the standing walls, which would narrow his search to the area of the fire's origin and its flash point.

Interviews with firefighters told him that flameover

had taken place very early in the fire—within the first couple of minutes of onset. He stooped down and, with his pocketknife, pulled back a corner of the carpet. The concrete underneath showed "spalling," or hairline cracks, which demonstrated the high heat of the fire and the high rate of speed of the fire's spread. The doorjamb that separated the living room from the bedroom where the young man's body had been found also revealed "alligatoring," or cracks and ridges appearing in the charred surface of the wood. Again, using his pocketknife, Ash peeled away a section of the wood char to ascertain its depths, which might provide a clue as to how fast the fire had spread. It could be that some kind of accelerant was used that had eluded his investigation so far.

The ceiling light fixture had burst, and the lightbulb within it had melted to a point. It was common for the remnants of melted lightbulbs to point straight toward the fire's origin. A fire-gutted sofa squatted beneath the melted lightbulb. Ash knelt before the sofa and promptly sneezed. Not many things smelled worse than burned polyethylene sofa cushions.

With a heavily gloved hand, Ash tilted the blackened sofa frame backwards at an angle. Something thudded to the floor behind it. Uprighting the sofa again, Ash went around and discovered a glob of melted candle wax.

It was common for house fires to start when people left candles unattended. Even the hottest fires did not completely obliterate the wax, and fire investigators could usually pinpoint the fire's origin.

But something about this find wasn't right. Who would light a candle and place it directly on a sofa? And then go to bed?

Ash had observed many acts of colossal stupidity in his years of investigating fires. Like the woman who had put a copper penny behind a fuse in the circuit breaker of her home because it annoyed her whenever it tripped the power off. Since copper, an excellent

conductor of electricity, completed the circuit, she
ended up burning down her house. He couldn't count
the morons who had used automobile gasoline for
cleaning purposes right next to a hot water heater—
and promptly blown themselves to smithereens. Or
crack addicts who'd set themselves on fire while free-
basing cocaine.

But something about this wasn't right. By all accounts, this young man was responsible, sensible, hardworking. He was a goal-setter, an achiever, a good
student. At the time of the fire, he had not been drinking or doing drugs.

Why on earth would he light a candle, set it on the
sofa, and go to bed?

From the fire patterns in the burned sofa, he had a
hunch the candle had been placed against the back of
the sofa with the express purpose of catching it on
fire. Since the sofa was placed against a window, the
curtains would then catch fire from the sofa, and the
foam cushions—made of an oil-based substance—
would melt very quickly into their original liquid form
and automatically ignite as surely as any gasoline. No
wonder flameover had occurred so fast once the fire
started.

The entire one-story, four-room structure would
have been blacked out with thick smoke within five
minutes.

The young college student, asleep in his bed, never
had a chance.

Something wasn't right.

Sitting back on his haunches, Ash let his gaze wan-
der around the room. Corners seldom showed much
fire damage, so his attention was drawn to one corner
with a neat pile of ashes. It looked as though a wad
of paper had incinerated to the point of fine ash, but
even the ash was symmetrical.

Crossing the room, Ash squatted in front of the
unusual pile and poked at it with the pocketknife he
still had open in his hand. The pocketknife left a small

dent in the pile that showed itself to be brown. Ash didn't know of any ashes that were brown inside and soot-colored on the outside. He leaned down and sniffed.

When he did, every hair on the back of his neck stood straight up and goose bumps crawled over his entire body.

Cinnamon.

Jillian's first thought of suicide came as she was driving on a freeway overpass. *I could just floor it, and go soaring straight over the side like* Thelma and Louise.

It wasn't a thought as much as an urge, a frightening pull toward the precipice. *Snap out of it,* she told herself. *What's the matter with you?*

She was tired. Maybe that was it. Since submitting the two written pieces to Miles, she'd been feeling increasingly exhausted, despite the welcome income that allowed her to stave off the wolves a bit longer.

He'd discussed a few more ideas for articles with her by e-mail, but nothing sounded interesting to Jillian. Dr. Sloane was probably right. She needed to work on the fire story, but after her last confrontation with Ash, Jillian was not eager to provoke him again.

The old depression, always lurking in the shadows at the back of her mind, had crept into the forefront again, though she wasn't sure why. Seeing her work in print again should have lifted her spirits and convinced her she was on her way back from hell, but for some maddening reason, it hadn't seemed to matter at all.

Nothing much did.

Even worse, she was growing forgetful and fuzzy. Sometimes she couldn't remember if she'd taken a Xonok or not and would have to take another just to be sure. A dull headache settled into the back of her head like a noxious cloud, and she was unable to

shake it no matter what over-the-counter remedy
she ingested.

Hideous nightmares plagued her sleep.

Finally, in desperation, she called Dr. Sloane's answering service over one weekend. Dr. Sloane called
back almost immediately, full of concern. When she
explained how she was feeling, he responded by increasing the dosage of Xonok.

Jillian didn't mind. The never-ending headache and
the lack of sleep seemed to sabotage what little work
she was able to do, and this was causing her a great
deal of anxiety. The Xonok was soothing. It helped
her forget how stressed-out she was. Before long, she
began to depend on the drug, and was grateful to Dr.
Sloane for prescribing it.

Once, she thought about taking all the pills at once.
She might mellow out altogether then, she thought,
and all her problems would go away.

Before she could act on the thought, however,
Ash phoned.

"I called to apologize for blowing my stack about
the pictures you took at the Cricket Andrews crime
scene," he said.

"It's okay," she said. "You were absolutely right. I
never should have meddled in an ongoing investigation like that."

"Do you still have the photographs?"

Jillian found that curious. She told him she did.

"Why don't you meet me for lunch?" he offered.
"Bring the photos, and let me make it up to you for
being a jerk."

They set up a meeting place and time, and Jillian
started to get dressed.

A little thrill scissored through her insides. She told
herself it was just Ash, just good old Ash, but she was
excited to be seeing him; thrilled, in fact, that he had
called her.

The thought brought her up short. She'd been dash-
ing about, grabbing articles of clothing and tossing

them aside in a mini-panic as she searched for just the right thing to wear. Now she stood stock-still in the midst of the whirlwind of her own manic activity and faced the fact that until now had eluded her:

She was falling in love with Ash.

There was no mistaking it. She'd been in love before and knew the signs. But something about this time was different. This was no mad rush of sexual attraction. Ash had been her friend for years. Throughout the trauma of the riot and Randi's death and everything that had happened since, he'd been irreplaceable, a rock.

Maybe *this* was the mysterious "power" that Dr. Sloane had alluded to. She loved Ash, and it was more than just friendly affection. When she had angered him and he'd slammed out of the apartment, it had felt as if he'd taken a piece of her soul with him. Never had her home seemed more empty.

Now he had called her, and she was going to see him again, and it made her giddy with joy.

As she applied her makeup more carefully than usual, Jillian wondered where Ash stood in all this. That he cared for her was obvious, but Ash was a good person. How could she be sure he wasn't just being kind to a good friend?

Jillian was so nervous that she jabbed the mascara wand into her eye and had to start all over again. She took a Xonok to calm her nerves.

They met at Dick's Last Resort, located downtown, not far from Dealy Plaza and the old red brick School Book Depository, where an assassin had once lurked so many years ago. Dick's Last Resort liked to brag that it had "no dress code, no taste, and certainly no class," and was a welcome change for anyone sick of trendy yuppie coffee shops who wanted a mess of ribs or a big fat order of catfish. On Sundays, you could hear live gospel singers while you chowed down on a crab leg brunch.

Ash was waiting for her at a table covered with

butcher paper. When she saw him, her heart sang. He gave her a one-armed hug, and when she lifted her face to kiss his cheek just as he turned his face toward hers, their lips connected for one soft, brief, electrifying moment. In that heartbeat, Jillian *knew*.

At least she thought she knew. Struck suddenly shy, she fumbled with her menu and with ordering, and imagined that Ash seemed just as awkward as she did.

"It's good to see you," he said, his smile warm. Were his eyes really alight, or was she just wanting them to be?

"I hate it when we fight," she said.

"Me, too."

"Everything just feels . . . wrong." She glanced away from the intensity of his gaze and worked her napkin between her fingers under the table. She was fully aware that the sexual tension between them—which they had always treated with teasing jokes and innuendo but never acted upon—had heightened since her breakup with Derek. At times, when they were poking through a burned-out building, their bodies would brush up against each other, and they'd both jump back as if burned. And sometimes she looked up and caught him looking at her in ways that good buddies didn't normally look at each other.

Not that she wasn't looking back. In fact, it was not uncommon on some of her more restless nights for her to dream she was making love to Ash. She always hated waking up then.

Now here they were, circling like curious animals in a mating dance. Neither one of them seemed to know how to act.

They talked of inconsequentials, as if skirting the edges of subjects neither was quite ready to approach. Sometimes Jillian felt like a teenager on a first date, even though she'd had lunch with Ash countless times.

Finally she said, "I brought the pictures. Do you want them?"

"Yes."

She groped in her tote bag and produced the envelope. "I guess it's stupid."

With a shake of his head, he pulled out the photographs she had taken at Cricket's house after the fire and studied them.

After a moment she remembered the diagram she'd drawn, and produced it as well.

"About how high was the cinnamon pile, would you say?" he asked, frowning in concentration.

"I'd say maybe six inches. Why, Ash?"

He sighed. "Because I found one just like it at the site of another fatal fire."

She gasped, and her whole body went cold. "Oh, Ash!"

"Yeah. Oh, Ash is right. I can't imagine anything more out of place at a fire scene, but when you tried to tell me, I wouldn't listen. I was so pissed off that you'd gone back to the scene without me—"

"You were right."

"Maybe. But I can't help thinking of a dog marking its territory." He grinned suddenly.

She smiled back. "You're cute when you're mad," she said impulsively, then blushed.

"Oh, yeah? And you're cute all the time," he said and both their words hung in the air between them, and she knew that he knew that something subtle had changed, that the relationship would never again be quite the way it had been before.

Then the phone in his jacket pocket rang.

They both jumped. Ash answered quietly. While he spoke, Jillian picked at her food and wondered what was going to happen next.

"I gotta go," he said, his face a sketch of apology.

"I understand."

"If it's all right, I'd like to come see you tonight after work."

"Yes. I'd like that."

"Okay."

They stared at each other. Jillian had the sense that

something profound and wordless had passed between them, that they'd crossed over some invisible line, some magical boundary understood only by friends and lovers. They knew where it was but couldn't describe it, exactly. But they both knew when it had been crossed.

He paid for the meal, and for once, she didn't argue over the bill or insist on going dutch. She let him pay and again, it felt oddly like a date. He walked her out to the car. Right before she got in, she had an impulse to kiss him, but didn't.

She still didn't know how to act around him.

With men, Jillian had always been confident, even bold on occasion. She was good at picking up signals and even better at giving them, but all the rules had changed with this one.

She drove home in a fog. As soon as she let herself into the apartment, she saw as if for the first time the mess it had become in recent weeks. Immediately she set about straightening things up.

So preoccupied was she by the situation with Ash and his upcoming visit that night that she forgot to listen to her telephone messages for a full hour. On her way into the kitchen with her hands full of empty soft-drink cans, the blinking light caught Jillian's eye and she pressed the button impatiently, juggling cans and thinking of other things.

The voice was deep, male, and unfamiliar. It said, *I'm going to kill you, cunt.*

PART IV

Knockdown

What if the breath that
  kindled those grim fires
Awakened, should blow them into
  sevenfold rage,
And plunge us into the flames?

      Milton
      Paradise Lost, Book II

. . . the communication
Of the dead is tongued with fire
Beyond the language of the living.

      T. S. Eliot
      "The Dry Salvages" (1941)

Chapter Eighteen

Ash knocked softly on the office door of his deputy chief, James Dixon. Dixon, on the phone, waved Ash into the office. Like Ash's office, it was cluttered, with few homey touches other than framed photos of his wife and three strapping sons. Dallas arson investigators were too busy to have much time for decorating their offices. Dixon was a big man, standing six foot six with a burly build and a Marine Corps buzz cut. He could be intimidating when he wanted to be, with his booming bass voice, but he was a decent man and good to work for.

"This is a matter for the ATF," he was saying, "but have the HAZMAT people call me anyway. We can coordinate a task force, if we have to. Okay. You bet."

He hung up. "That goddamned train explosion last week. The one that caused the three-alarmer?"

Ash nodded.

"Jurisdiction is a nightmare." He sighed, scribbled himself a note on a desk littered with similar missives, and said, "What can I do for you, Ash?"

Ash took a deep breath. "I think I'm dealing with a serial killer. Arson is his weapon of choice. I need help, and I'll take it from anywhere I can get it—state fire marshals, Dallas PD, whatever. I want to stop this bastard."

"Jesus." Dixon blinked. "What do you mean, arson is his weapon of choice?"

"Well, I admit that's simplistic. The truth is that some of the victims died as a direct result of the fire and some were killed and then the house burned around them. I'm convinced he incapacitated them in some way first, either with chloroform or suffocation with a pillow, something."

"Wait a minute. I'm confused. Isn't the M.O. the same?"

"No, and that's the genius of it," said Ash, leaning slightly forward in his earnestness. "He changes his M.O. from fire to fire so that there's no distinctive, traceable pattern. He never uses accelerants. Correction. He used an accelerant once, to throw off investigators and frame somebody else, but it was him, I'm sure of it. The other times, he made the fires look like accidents."

Dixon leaned back in his chair and shook his head. "You're not making much sense. He uses accelerants, he doesn't use accelerants. He makes the fires look like accidents. What makes you so sure they're *not* accidental? Is there any connection among the victims?"

Shifting his weight uncomfortably in his chair, Ash said, "No, sir. No connection that I can find so far."

Dixon frowned. "There's no doubt that there have been an exceptionally high number of fatal fires in this city this summer, but a serial killer? C'mon, Ash. You gotta give me a little more than what I've heard so far."

Starting at the beginning, with the homeless dumpster victim, Ash laid out the sequence of events in his investigation. The only part he left out was Jillian's presence at the scenes. He simply let the deputy chief think that Ash had taken the photographs of the first cinnamon pile.

As he talked, Ash felt himself growing increasingly nervous. The chief wasn't buying it. The expression on his face went from incredulity to skepticism to doubt. When Ash told him about the cinnamon, he seemed to be barely suppressing amusement.

"So let me get this straight. The causes of most of these fires is either undetermined, or you have not been able to rule out accidental causes?"

Miserably, Ash nodded.

"And you think that, what, a pile of *cinnamon* at two of the fire scenes puts a serial killer there?"

"Right."

"But there's nothing similar about the M.O.'s, and there's no connection between the victims that you can tell."

"That's correct."

"And you think that some diabolical psychopath is insinuating himself into all these houses and finding some way to set fires that one of the best arson investigators in the business can't ascertain?"

There was nothing Ash could say.

"And I'm supposed to call up CAPERS," the chief said, using the acronym for the Dallas Police Department's Crimes Against Persons division, "and tell them I need one of their busy homicide detectives to come over here and help us solve these serial killings, which have taken place in all these accidental fires. Oh, and one fire that was made to look like arson to throw us off the track, but it wasn't really arson. Or maybe it was arson, but the arsonist was so good he just wanted us to think that it was arson in order to cover up his murder."

Ash sighed. "Something like that."

"Look, Ash, I sympathize. Really, I do. This has been a bitch of a summer, and all these fatalities are jacking up the stress and strain on you. I don't know why you can't pinpoint the causes of most of these fires. All I *do* know is that in order for us to get a conviction in a court of law, we need to prove three things." Ticking the items off on his big fingers, he said, "First, that a fire did occur. That's easy enough. But then you have to prove that the burning was due to incendiarism. And third, you have to prove that the accused individual was responsible for that criminal action."

Ash knew all this, and the chief knew he knew it. He swallowed another sigh.

"Now, from where I sit, you've only got proof that one of these fires was incendiary, and that was the Cricket Andrews fire. We're on the verge of making an arrest on that fire, and now you claim that Derek Thorsen was not responsible, and some serial killer who wanted to frame him for some undisclosed reason did it. But you have absolutely no evidence and no way to prove it in court. In fact, even if I was willing to go along with you on the serial killer thing—and I gotta tell you, I'm not—we still have no way on earth to prove that one individual committed all these crimes. There's no connection to the victims. No physical evidence. No nothing. Do you see, from where I'm sitting, how crazy all this sounds?"

"Yes, sir. I do."

"Then, you can see the position I'm in. I can't possibly pull together a task force on a case as flimsy is this. The way I see it, you'd better get back into these individual fires and see if you can pinpoint the causes. My guess is that you'll find that they were indeed accidental. It just got to looking spooky to you, that's all, because you're so tired. We're all carrying bigger caseloads this summer. These fatals are a bitch to investigate."

Closing his eyes, Ash forced himself to ask, "What about the cinnamon, sir?"

Dixon laughed. "Take it to ADA Atherton. See what she thinks. If she doesn't laugh you out of her office, then come back and see me." Chuckling, he turned back to his paperwork.

There wasn't much to do then, but leave.

He didn't know if the deadness was becoming more excruciating to bear, or if those who were so vividly alive around him were becoming more unbearable to be near. Either way, it seemed as if he were surrounded by potential honorees.

At home, and in his clinical practice, he had more control over his environment and the people with whom he surrounded himself. It was quiet. He and Eleanor had little to say to each other anymore, and Ian spent most of his time in his room. At work, his patients were needy, vulnerable. He saw them one at a time, and they never met in the waiting room, so there was little talk among them. It was orderly, manageable.

But at the university, students filled the corridors outside his campus office and his classroom with their restless, slender, tight young bodies and their youthful, free-flying spirits. They jostled one another and made crude jokes at each other's expense, laughed loudly and pawed at one another like rutting deer. To his horror, some of the young ladies actually tried to flirt with him, as if such lewdness would get them better grades.

Some of the professors were no better. They fancied themselves "cool" and young at heart. Sometimes you couldn't tell them apart from the students, and at least one of them, he knew, had a tendency to sleep with the prettier coeds who were willing. He didn't know if that influenced their grades or not. He preferred not to think about it.

In the teacher's lounge, they liked to tell ribald jokes and gripe loudly *ad nauseum* about the college administration. Some of them were noisy and rude. It was impossible to find any peace and quiet there. He would fix himself a cup of coffee and take it to his office, where he preferred to work alone with the door shut. His hours were clearly posted; if the students wanted to see him, they could make an appointment just like his patients.

More and more, the world around him began to overwhelm him. He didn't know if the deadness was crowding him out or surrounding humanity crowding him in, but either way, there was so much of it, so much, and he was finding it increasingly difficult to hold himself together. Every morning he awoke suffocating as the deadness sucked out a breath more from his lungs. He had to lie there in bed and will himself to arise, to knit together the false self mask and emerge into the world encased in a fragile bubble of self-control.

There, over the course of the day, the cacophony of the live ones would intrude and encroach, closer and closer, nearer and nearer, threatening to pop the bubble at any moment and leave him exposed. More and more, he couldn't stand it.

The fire was his only sanctuary. The fire was sacred. The fire was real.

There, at the altar, the phoenix would find blessed release and would emerge, empowered, fierce and fully alive and never in need of a mask or a bubble.

The fire was his only sanity.

By the time Jillian opened the door to Ash that evening, she had gotten over the worst of the shock from the death threat. Investigative journalists were used to threats from disgruntled readers, but usually the threats involved lawsuits, not killings.

For a brief moment she had entertained the theory that the threatener was the serial killer who was setting all the fires, but she quickly dismissed that thought. He would have to be brilliant indeed to know that she had anything to do with the arson investigations.

Ash arrived earlier than she had expected, and she could see his dejection at a glance.

"What's wrong?" she said before he even sat down.

With a heavy sigh, he said, "I talked to Chief Dixon today about the arson-killer investigation." He plunked down onto the sofa.

"And?" She sat next to him, their elbows touching.

"And he thinks I'm crazy."

"Did you tell him about the cinnamon?"

"He thinks the cinnamon is *especially* crazy." Weary, he rested his head on the back of the sofa and closed his eyes. His entire posture was one of defeat. "I don't know. Maybe it is crazy."

"You don't think that. And neither do I."

Cutting her a sideways glance, he grinned. "What do you know, anyway?"

She thought for a moment. "Maybe more than you think."

"What do you mean?"

Go for it, girl. She hesitated. "Well . . . I've kind of been getting back to work, you know."

"Oh!" he cried. "I'm sorry! I've been meaning to tell you that I read your column about the riot. I thought it was brilliant."

She smiled with pleasure. "Really?"

"Back to your old fightin' form, I think. Maybe even better."

She nodded. "Then, that's what I want to talk to you about."

He looked at her with wary eyes.

"My shrink says that if I want to get back to work full-swing, I should write about what interests me."

"Sounds like good advice."

"Yeah? Well, the only thing that really interests me is this arson investigation."

"Now, wait a minute. You finished the Rodriguez piece. I read it."

"And I hated every minute of it. Plus, it was crappy."

Ash started to protest.

"Just listen for a minute. Your boss thinks this whole thing is crazy, right?"

"Right."

"If you could have anything you wanted right now as far as this investigation is concerned—other than catching the guy, of course—what would it be?"

"I asked the chief for help. I'd like a task force."

"Okay. What better way to get that help than to make this a high-profile case? And what better way to make it high profile than a front-page story in the *Dallas Mirror*?"

Pulling back from her, Ash crossed two fingers, held them up in front of his face, and said, "Get thee away from me, Satan."

Jillian laughed. "I'm serious."

"You're also the press. It's risky enough, just having you for a friend." He was only half joking. "They teach us in cop school that there's no such thing as *off the record*."

She rolled her eyes. "Have I ever used our friendship in that way?"

He mock-sulked, but she could tell he was listening.

"Think about it," she said. "This is your chance to use me, to use my power. If we publicize the case, it could bring in some tips from readers. It could also put pressure on the deputy chief to upgrade the status of the investigation."

"Yeah, and it could backfire, and I could be drawing unemployment."

"Who says you have to be involved? Reporters never reveal their sources."

"Don't be silly. Everybody knows we're friends."

"But they won't know how much you told me and how much I snooped out on my own. After all, I took the cinnamon photos at the Cricket Andrews fire."

"A little fact I neglected to mention to my boss."

"Don't worry about it. Your secret's safe with me. I'm just saying, let me go public with this, Ash. Let me do a proper investigative piece."

He leaned forward, put his elbows on his knees, and buried his face in his hands. "I don't know."

She grinned. "Trust me."

He shook his head. "My mama warned me about girls like you."

She leaned into him with her body and gave him a

shove. Playfully, he shoved back. They started a wrestling match. Ash soon overpowered Jillian and loomed over her where she lay back on the couch, holding her wrists with his hands. They were both laughing.

Ash kissed her. It was a quick peck on the lips, like friends do. But he did not release her. He was very close. There was a question in his eyes.

Jillian answered it by letting her body go limp and lifting her head slightly. He lowered his face and kissed her again, a slow, melting kiss that sent hot, pulsing energy throughout her body. She opened her lips and took his tongue into her mouth, tasting him, savoring him. With a soft moan, he let go of her wrists and tangled his hands in her hair.

The fire spread.

Arching her body into the curve of his, she could feel his excitement and clasped him closer. The chemical reaction between them was explosive, as if all their sexual energy had been pent-up as tightly as the erection she could feel straining against his jeans. Still kissing, they rolled onto the floor, knocking over the coffee table with a crash, and grappled at each other's clothes like starving people in a bread line.

She leapt to her feet, pulled her shirt off over her head and, reaching behind her, sprung her breasts from the restraints of her bra with one yank. She was still laughing, feeling wild and deliciously uninhibited—not the least bit shy as she normally was with a new lover. He pushed her up against the wall, his mouth and tongue devouring her face. A lamp tipped over and clanged onto the floor.

She was ripping at his jeans, and he was kicking off his sneakers. In his sock feet, he put his arms around her waist and lifted her off her feet, carrying her into the bedroom where they fell in a tangle onto the bed with such force a painting was dislodged and swung crazily on its nail.

They continued kissing and caressing with a wild urgency that was still somehow measured—a controlled burn. He would be stretched out the length of her and then they would roll over and she would be on top of him, exploring every nook and cranny, every part of him.

"I love your body," he whispered.

"You don't think I'm fat?"

"I think you're all woman, voluptuous and soft and curvy in all the right places. If I wanted to take something into my arms that was all bones and narrow hips and flat chest, I'd go for boys."

She giggled, and then she cried. No one had ever paid her a nicer compliment, or made her feel better about herself.

When he pushed himself inside her, she was so wet and ready that even the condom she'd produced from somewhere didn't slow the rhythm. Then he withdrew, lowered his head and worked her with his tongue in a way she had never imagined possible.

She lost all control, cried out, bucked against him. When she thought the tension was too unbearable to go on, he plunged back into her and they moved together in perfect synch until they were both shuddering, bodies sweating, chests heaving, hearts pounding.

He collapsed onto her, his face buried in her throat. She held him tightly against her. She had never known such purity of joy, such peace of soul.

"Jillian," he whispered. "I love you."

She nuzzled the top of his head. "I know. I love you, too."

At that unfortunate moment, the phone rang. He started to move from her, but she held him fast. "Let the machine get it," she said contentedly.

They heard her voice drawl, "Hello. Please leave a message, and I'll have my machine call your machine. Thanks."

There was a beep, and then, *"I'm going to kill you, bitch."*

Chapter Nineteen

"What the hell?" Ash pulled away from Jillian and leapt to his feet, but by the time he had made it to the phone and snatched up the receiver, the caller had disconnected. He listened to the message again, but couldn't make out anything distinctive. The Caller ID said merely OUT OF AREA, which could have meant anything from a cell phone call to blocked long distance.

Still naked, he returned to the bedroom, where Jillian had sat up and pulled the sheets over her breasts.

"Do you have any idea who that was?" he asked. It had not been his intention to make the question sound like a police interrogation, but his tone was sharp.

"No."

"Has he left other messages like this?"

"One. This morning."

"Why didn't you *tell* me?" he cried.

"Because . . . we got to talking about the serial killer investigation as soon as you walked in, and then, well, there wasn't exactly an opportunity for it to come up." She grinned.

He felt exposed and foolish, standing there butt-naked when he was trying to be businesslike. Turning away from the door, he searched for his jeans and found them inside out on the living room floor, his underwear under a chair. He pulled on his briefs and then his jeans, and returned to the bedroom.

Sitting on the edge of the bed, he said, "Jillian, this is serious."

"I know it's serious!" she said irritably. She reached for a robe, pulled it on, and got up from the bed. "But what am I supposed to do about it when I don't even know who it is or what the hell I've done to piss him off?"

She headed for the kitchen, and he followed her. "Could it be something you wrote?" he asked.

"I don't know," she said with a shrug. "Usually they just sue me."

He saw her take a prescription bottle from the kitchen cabinet and swallow a pill with some tap water. "What's that?"

"Xonok," she said. "Dr. Sloane prescribed it for me."

"He's got you on *tranquilizers*?" Ash had never known Jillian to take medications of any kind beyond aspirin.

"They're not tranquilizers," she said. "They're more an antianxiety thing." She opened the refrigerator. "Want a beer?"

"Are you sure you should be drinking when you're taking tranquilizers? Alcohol's a depressant, you know."

She slammed the refrigerator door. "Ash, for God's sake! Stop treating me like a child! And I told you, they're not tranquilizers."

"I thought that's what antianxiety medication was."

"Well, it's not," she said, but she didn't seem sure to Ash. She brushed past him into the living room, her face a study in controlled anger, and began uprighting furniture they had knocked asunder.

Ash was determined not to follow her again, but he did anyway. "Look," he said, "I'm not trying to treat you like a child. I'm just worried. Some psycho's leaving death threats on your answering machine. He may be stalking you. I just . . . don't want anything to happen to you, that's all."

Her expression softened. She came up to him and put her hand on the side of his face. "This is stupid, us arguing now," she said.

"I agree." He turned his head and kissed her hand.

"You sounded so . . . coplike . . . all of a sudden, and it made me defensive."

"I didn't mean to," he said honestly. "Occupational hazard, I guess."

She nodded, then turned away from him and perched on the edge of the couch, putting her face in her hands. "I have the worst headache," she murmured.

"Would you like me to get you some aspirin?" he asked. He was concerned. Jillian was a robust, healthy woman who seldom even caught colds.

"It won't work," she said. "I've had it for weeks. Nothing gets rid of it."

Ash felt a stab of fear. He sat next to her and rubbed her shoulders. "This doesn't sound right," he said. "You need to see a doctor."

"I called Dr. Sloane—he's an M.D., you know."

"What did he say?"

"He said I was just stressed out and increased the Xonok dosage."

Ash frowned. He started to protest but decided against it for the time being. He didn't want to provoke another argument between them. But somewhere deep inside, he felt the vague reverberations of a warning bell.

Jillian practically bounced into Dr. Sloane's office.

"My, you look happy today," he commented with a smile.

"It's the strangest thing, after all that's happened, but I never dreamed I could feel this happy *ever*, much less now, after . . . you know, the riot and all."

"So, tell me about it."

"Everything just came together for Ash and me. And you know, I was such an idiot. All this time, Ash was perfect for me, but I never paid any attention to him that way because, well, because he was my friend, my buddy. He was just Ash. I think it's the Vanilla Guy syndrome."

"Oh? I haven't read about that in the psychiatric literature," Sloane said, and she couldn't tell if he was teasing or serious.

"Vanilla Guys. You know. The good guys who treat women right and are faithful to them and who go to work each day and come home and watch TV. Women are always moaning about how there aren't any good men in the world, when all along, there they are, right there."

"Why do you suppose that is?"

"Because morons like me get hung up on the Hot Fudge Guys. Bikers or bodybuilders or race car drivers—I don't know. Guys who seem exciting and a little dangerous. And what do they do? Stomp on our hearts and cheat on us and dump us. And what do we do? Go running to the Vanilla Guys to whine about it." She grinned.

"So women think Vanilla Guys are boring."

"I guess so. You ask, What do you want to do tonight? And he says, I thought we might rent a movie and just spend the evening being together. And you're thinking, Yuk, I wanted to go dancing! I'm in the mood to party!"

"Sounds like you have to do some growing up to be ready for the Vanilla Guys of the world."

She stared at him. "Well, yeah. You're right. And I've done a lot of growing up in recent weeks."

"It's a sign of emotional maturity that you have learned from past mistakes and are ready for a mature relationship. You were just playing at it before."

"I guess I was. I didn't realize it before. Hey, this therapy stuff's not bad!"

He smiled at her and said, "What do you think was the catalyst that brought you and Ash together?"

She thought a moment. "The obvious thing to say would be the riot and all, but I don't think it was that as much as it was the fire investigation. By letting me into his world, it became more of a give-and-take between us. When I was all fucked up because of the riot, it was mostly Ash doing the giving."

"And what do you think you've given him concerning the investigation?"

"A sympathetic ear, for one thing. He went to his boss the other day, his deputy chief, and Ash told him that he thought that most of these fatal fires he's been investigating have been set by one person."

Dr. Sloane grew very still. "And what did the deputy chief say?"

She shrugged. "Basically, he laughed him out of the office. Ash didn't have any evidence, no probable suspects, no connection between victims—he didn't have a case, really. And he knew that, which was why he went to the chief in the first place."

"I don't understand. If he didn't have a case, how did he think the deputy chief could help him?"

"Ash wanted a task force, help from people like the ATF and the Dallas PD homicide people, maybe the FBI and the state fire marshals."

"I see. And I take it he's not going to receive that help."

"Well . . . not yet." She grinned. "That's where I come in."

"Oh?"

"I convinced Ash that it would benefit him if I did a thorough investigative piece for the *Dallas Mirror*. Going public would draw all sorts of media attention to this case. It would put pressure on the brass to give him the help he requires, and readers may phone in tips that could help crack it."

Dr. Slone frowned. "Jillian, I thought we agreed that this writing exercise was going to be something you did privately, for purposes of improvement over the course of your therapy. You weren't even going to mention it to Ash."

"I wasn't going to mention it to Ash because I thought it would piss him off. But now that things have developed the way they have, I knew the time was right to bring it up to him. I had to do some convincing, but he's on board now. I'm excited about it. After all Ash has done for me, now I can take my talent and experience and contacts and help *him*. Plus, I can go around with him while he investigates. We could be together, both doing our thing. It's great!"

He shook his head. "You don't seem to understand. Your mental and emotional state is very fragile right now. You're not ready for the pressures such a job would put on you. There could be repercussions you're not expecting."

"I can handle it, Dr. Sloane," she persisted. "It's what I *do*."

He was silent for a moment, watching her in that intense way he sometimes had that always unnerved her. "Tell me. Have you been experiencing any cognitive problems? Short-term memory loss? Confusion? Brain-fog?"

She stared at her hands. "Okay. Yeah. All those things, plus a killer headache."

"You see?" A smile so fleeting she thought she had imagined it played across his face. "Your body is demonstrating signs of stress and strain that you should heed. You should not push your recovery too hard or too fast. You could suffer a bad setback."

Jillian was confused again. "But, Dr. Sloane . . . I felt so good about this idea. And so did Ash. I know I can help him."

He finally blinked. "I know you can. In time. But I don't think this is the best idea for you right now. Why don't you just continue in the vein we first suggested, that you go along with Ash on his investigations, collect information as you would for an article, but postpone the actual writing and publishing until you are stronger?''

"I don't know . . ."

"In the meantime, I'm going to give you a prescription for a medication that should help you with the side effects you may be suffering from Xonok.''

"I don't want to take any more pills, Dr. Sloane,'' she protested.

He watched her. "Are you ready to give up the Xonok? You've told me that you find it soothing and helpful.''

"I do, but—"

"Then, trust me.'' He chuckled. "I'm not going to make a junkie out of you.''

"I know,'' she said weakly.

He tore the page off the prescription pad and handed it to her. "Take care of yourself,'' he said. "And I'll see you next time.''

The chief had sent Ash back to the drawing board, and he started with the murder of Scott Lancaster because that was the most recent fatal fire that he thought was tied to the serial killer.

Scott had attended college at one of a number of commuter community colleges that had sprung up like sandbags to handle the flood of suburbanites who wanted to finish a college degree while working full-time and raising a family, bouncing back from a divorce, upgrading outdated job skills, or simply moving up from hourly wage slave labor to a job that offered benefits.

The younger students who attended were made up of kids whose high school grades and test scores hadn't been good enough for a name university; kids not even sure they wanted to go to college but whose parents had urged them to take a few hours; and kids who couldn't afford to leave town.

Scott had fit into the latter category. He'd been living rent-free in a small house owned by his grand-

mother, while working and going to school full-time.
His grades were good, and he stayed out of trouble.
His dream was to transfer to the University of Texas
and study architecture.

Then his house burned down around him, and he
died at the age of twenty.

With a copy of Scott's class schedule in his hand,
Ash was working his way through Scott's class professors, interviewing them in hopes that something might
come up that could give him a lead.

Sloane. Scott had taken a course in Introductory
Psychology, and his professor was a guy named
Sloane. The name jumped out at Ash as the name of
Jillian's shrink, the one on the fire department list.
For a moment he thought it might be the same guy,
which could serve as a red flag, since arsonists fre-
quently had ties with fire departments, usually as vol-
unteer firefighters or even as investigators.

But Jillian's Dr. Sloane was a practicing psychiatrist,
an M.D. Surely if he were teaching psychology, he'd
be someplace like Baylor School of Medicine and not
here at this two-bit junior college teaching basic psychology courses to a bunch of goof-offs more interested in the next keg party than the intricacies of brain
synapses. Besides, it was Ash's impression that Jillian's
shrink ran a full-time practice and did not teach on
the side.

The college was fairly new—ten years or so—and
the facilities were pleasant. Nonetheless, the corridors
all looked alike, and it took Ash a while to find the
professor's office. The door was closed, but there was
a small rectangular window in it. Ash could see that
the light was on and Dr. Sloane was sitting at his desk,
working. Most of the profs left their doors open when
they were in. Ash glanced at the posted office hours.
Apparently Dr. Sloane didn't like to be disturbed unless you had an appointment.

Ash was about to make himself an appointment.
He knocked. Through the small window, he saw the

professor glance up and frown, then go back to work. The message was clear: Don't bother me unless I've already said you could bother me.

Ash took out his badge, smacked it up against the window, and knocked again, sharply.

Sloane glanced up again—clearly annoyed this time—saw the badge, and jerked, dropping his pen beneath the desk. He bent down to find it, and when he sat up again, his face was drained of color. He coughed and called, "Come in."

Ash pocketed the badge and entered the office, his glance taking in the methodical arrangement of books on the shelves, the orderly desk, the absence of family photos and framed degrees. Sloane could move out, and the room would hardly miss him.

Sloane got to his feet. He was slight in build, washed-out in coloring, thinning of hair, and his handshake was stiff, resisting a firm grasp.

Ash disliked him on sight.

"I'm Ash McGraw, arson investigator with the Dallas Fire Department."

"Oh?" said Sloane, fidgeting with papers on his desk. "Please sit down. Forgive me for my rudeness earlier, but you can't imagine how distracting these kids can be when they see you in your office."

"It's all right," said Ash, taking a seat on the other side of the desk. He noticed that there was only one chair, which would discourage multiple visitors. "I'm investigating the death of one of your students, Scott Lancaster."

Oddly enough, Sloane gave no sign of recognition, nor did he nod or make sympathetic noises or ask about the progress of the investigation, as some of the other teachers had done. He simply stared at Ash without blinking. Creepy guy.

When he seemed to realize that Ash was waiting for some comment from him, Sloane said, "I have a lot of students, Mr. McGraw. I didn't really know Scott until his death rather got my attention."

This was unusual. From what Ash had gathered, Scott was a charismatic young man whom everybody seemed to notice. He said, "I was wondering if there was anything you could tell me that might be helpful to the investigation."

"Like what? I'm afraid I don't know very much."

"Like, did you notice any animosity between Scott and any of his classmates? Was he having any personal problems that were affecting his grades? Had he had a recent breakup with a girlfriend?"

"I'm sorry, Mr. McGraw. I don't delve into the personal lives of my students. I don't know any of them very well, to tell you the truth." His tone made it clear that he didn't *want* to know them.

"Okay." Ash jotted a note in his trusty notebook. "How about Scott's behavior in class? Had you noticed any changes recently? Was he sleeping through class? Arguing points with you? Making sarcastic remarks to others? Disrupting class in any way? Anything unusual that you may have observed?"

Sloane shook his head. The color was returning to his face, but he still looked pale, ill even. There was a thin sheen of sweat on his forehead, although the air-conditioned office was cold. "The boy came to class, took notes, and left." His speech was clipped. A tiny vein had appeared on his temple. Ash could see it pulsing.

The guy's behavior was strange, no doubt about it.

Ash decided not to make too much of it. Some people feared law enforcement officers even when they themselves were not in any trouble. Sometimes his presence alone could make people nervous. He was used to that, but usually better educated people did not react in that way.

Still, something about the guy's demeanor bothered him. He would be remiss if he didn't ask. "One more question, Dr. Sloane."

Sloane tapped a pen against a yellow pad.

"Do you ever do volunteer counseling for the Dallas Fire Department?"

Sloane blinked, once, twice. "No. Why do you ask?"

Ash shrugged. "I was just wondering. We have a Dr. Sloane on our list who helps firefighters recover from trauma."

"Sloane is a common name."

"Yes." Ash sat for a moment longer. Sloane volunteered nothing more.

"Okay," he said, withdrawing a business card that he handed across the desk to Sloane. "If you think of anything else, give me a call anytime. I've got voice mail, and I check it three times a day, so if you need me to call you, I'll get back to you before the end of the day."

Sloane took the card. "Thank you," he said. His fingers were shaking.

Ash got to his feet. Though he stood barely over six feet tall, it seemed as if he were towering over the man. And if he didn't know better, he'd say the man was cowering before him.

Weird. But then, as far as Ash was concerned, all shrinks were weird.

Chapter Twenty

The night came when he lost control.

Everything that night was agitated and hyper-real. It was as if he had become disconnected from himself, there and yet not there, committing the deed and yet apart from it. Things he could touch, taste, see, and hear assumed an otherworldly cast, a soft-focus blur indistinct and surreal.

The difference, he believed, was caused by fear.

The visit from the arson investigator had frightened him badly, jarred him back to the real world of police and lawyers and courtrooms and prisons. Before, he'd operated in a gleeful, solitary world of his own making, absolutely free to move about as he pleased, choosing his honorees and worshiping at the shrine of the Beast.

But he was not alone, after all, in his little world. He was being pursued.

So far, he had eluded detection, but the arson investigator had reminded him that he might not always. This gave his ceremony a note of desperation unknown in previous ceremonies.

And it ruined it.

Something wasn't right. The fire wouldn't burn properly, though he reset it three times. He couldn't figure out what he was doing wrong. And then—horror of horrors—he heard a noise from the bedroom and realized that he had not killed the honoree after all, but only rendered her unconscious. He had to get out quickly before he was caught. In his haste, he stepped on the cinnamon pile and scattered it in all directions.

In this anxious state, his need for the ritual unsatisfied, he went in search of another honoree that very night, without his usual caution, care, and planning. He had to! He couldn't be expected to wait another 500 interminable hours, could he?

Lucky for him she was on the list of potentials, and he had done preliminary reconnaissance, so he knew she always kept a bathroom window cracked open in hot weather.

Badly shaken and fearful of getting caught after his earlier bad experience, he overreacted, bludgeoning the honoree to death in her bed. Then, anxious to the point of near-hysteria that he wouldn't be able to set the fire properly again, he set several, all over the house, so he could be sure it would burn.

It was all so rushed; he couldn't enjoy the ceremony at all. Consequently, he was left profoundly depressed—almost to the point of suicide.

The deadness mocked him. It seemed to say, *Did you really believe you could escape me? Did you really think you could outsmart me?*

And it censured him. It said, *You let that arson investigator get the better of you. You let him catch you unprepared. You allowed him to ruin everything. You are worthless.*

It tried to smother him. He was afraid to go to sleep, afraid he would not be able to get enough air and he would die.

That's when he knew two things: one, he could not let this arson investigator destroy everything he had worked for, everything he had built and believed in. He had to defeat the investigator before the investigator defeated him.

And two, he couldn't possibly wait 500 hours before another ceremony.

                         *   *   *

Jillian gave a great deal of careful thought to what Dr. Sloane had said to her in their last session, and concluded that the good doctor, while well-intentioned, was simply mistaken. She believed herself to be much stronger in her emotional recovery than he did, and furthermore, Ash needed her help.

Ash was scheduled to be out of town for three weeks, teaching an arson investigation course in Austin. Jillian figured that would be a good time to write and publish the article. Hopefully his absence would spare Ash the worst of the political fire from on high, and she would be free to work without distracting visits that made her forget everything except taking him to her bed.

Their physical relationship had come as a complete—and very pleasant—surprise. The fact that it had been built on trust and friendship removed many barriers that often sabotaged new relationships. Not only did Jillian feel completely free and uninhibited in bed with Ash, but the solid foundation of their relationship made any game playing completely unnecessary. She felt absolutely comfortable with him. The more time they spent together, the more she loved him.

The only problem with the article came in the writing. Jillian's attention span seemed to be growing ever shorter, and as her forgetfulness worsened, she found herself struggling to maintain a coherent train of thought. The ever-present headache was no help.

Still, she was reluctant to take the new medication Dr. Sloane had prescribed, even though she did have it filled. It waited for her in the kitchen cabinet, next to the bottle of Xonok.

One night, as she rubbed her burning eyes in front of the computer console, an evil thought insinuated itself into her mind, and she found herself arguing with it.

If you can't work, it said, *then why don't you just do us all a favor and kill yourself?*

No! Not now! Not when Ash and I are getting together.

You're a burden to Ash. All he ever does is take care of you. He could be free to find somebody who's not as fucked up in the head as you are.

But Ash doesn't want anybody else! He loves me. He would be devastated if anything happened to me.

Give him the chance to find out and see what happens. He could find somebody who deserves him and not some screwed up fat girl like you.

The thoughts frightened Jillian, and she got up from the computer. Her head was splitting, and she lay down for a while with a cool rag on her forehead, trying to quiet the cacophony of voices in her mind. She was tired. Exhausted, really.

As if the thoughts in her own head weren't destructive enough, the death threats kept coming. Jillian turned off the ringer on her telephone and turned down the volume on the answering machine. At night she would scan through the messages, trying to ignore the nasty voice.

When she couldn't work anymore, she would doze for a while, then get up and work for a time, then sleep some more. This seemed to be the only way in which she could make any real progress on the article. The result was surprisingly good. As usual, it was too long, and it took her a couple of days to revise it down to a length Miles could live with. She e-mailed the article to him.

By that time she was in pretty bad shape, and decided to give in and take the other pills Dr. Sloane had prescribed. By then she would do anything to get rid of the excruciating headache. It was, quite simply, driving her mad.

Within half an hour of taking the new medication, the headache was gone.

It was a miracle.

When she didn't take the next prescribed dose, the headache returned with a screaming vengeance. Jillian immediately took one of the pills, and half an hour later the headache was gone again.

Normally Jillian might have questioned taking pills on an indefinite basis to keep from having a severe headache, but she was in no state to question anything. After that, she took the pills twice a day, as prescribed, along with the Xonok.

The fact that she soon found herself wandering through her days in a dreamy fog no longer seemed so important.

SERIAL KILLER SMOKES CITY: WILL THE DALLAS FIRE DEPARTMENT GET BURNED? Ash read the sensational headline on Jillian's story along with her prominent byline, superimposed on a full-page color photo of Cricket Andrews' house ablaze. Ash had provided the photo, after much convincing by Jillian. She had overnighted an early copy of the *Dallas Mirror* to him in Austin.

The inside story contained another full page, a black-and-white montage of photos of various fire scenes that Ash believed were connected, and on the opposite page, a two-inch headline: SMOKING CITY: AGAINST ALL ODDS, A LONE DFD ARSON INVESTIGATOR STRUGGLES TO TRACK DOWN AN ELUSIVE AND DIABOLICAL SERIAL ARSONIST WITH MURDER ON HIS MIND, WHILE DFD BRASS DRAGS ITS FEET. BY JILLIAN ROSS.

When he saw the front page, Ash cringed, and the glaring inside headline only made him squirm more. It had never been his intention to make Chief Dixon or anybody else at the DFD look like fools, and he was uncomfortable with the Lone Ranger image the headlines gave him. Jillian's article, however, turned out to be thorough, well written, and fair.

The lead paragraphs read:

Dallas Arson Investigator Ash McGraw is a man on a mission.

Over the course of this long, hot summer, he has struggled to make sense of the unprecedented number of fatal fires that have plagued this city—half a dozen with suspicious or undetermined causes that have wound up in his case file alone, and those in other jurisdictions that he believes may be connected.

Therein lies the mystery: none of the fires started in the same way; none of the victims were connected; none of them fit anything that might be construed as an "M.O.," or "modus operandi," which means, literally, the method of operation that the criminal employs while committing the crime. So when McGraw told his boss that he thought the fires had been set by the same "torch"—fire investigation lingo for an arsonist—he was laughed out of the office. The boss thought he was crazy.

Turns out he just may be crazy like a fox.

Interspersed with the many ads that filled the *Dallas Mirror* in its centerfold, semi-tabloid style, the article, which amounted to a cover story, spanned six pages and was illustrated with numerous photographs. As he had requested, she'd taken care to present Deputy Chief Dixon, ADA Atherton, and others as reasonable people who simply required more hard evidence than he could produce. Ash had never wanted to get the deputy chief in serious trouble. All he wanted was to jump-start the stalled investigation and bring in some fresh leads—maybe even draw the kind of help he needed. He was nervous about the repercussions, to be sure, but was made desperate enough by the growing pile of corpses to take the gamble.

At the very least, even if he got fired, they might catch the torch.

The article contained all the information Ash had learned in his investigation except for one salient fact: the cinnamon piles. He had explained to Jillian that it was always necessary to withhold at least one crucial fact of an investigation when cooperating with journalists, because there were nuts in the world who got off on confessing to crimes they hadn't committed—using details they'd read in the paper or heard on the news. The secret facts could then be used by law enforcement to weed out the false confessions.

Even so, it was a compelling piece, and in one of the first voice mails Ash returned from a system clogged with messages, he hit pay dirt.

A Dallas CAPERS detective, Lieutenant Sam Peterson, had been investigating a bizarre assault case that had made no sense to him until he'd read the article in the *Mirror*.

"I didn't know if this was a case of vandalism, or interrupted robbery, or nuisance, or stalking, or *what*," he told Ash. "A woman woke up in the middle of the night with somebody holding a cloth over her mouth and nose soaked with some noxious liquid—I'm guessing chloroform. For some reason, she had the presence of mind to hold her breath, and then whoever was attacking her covered her face with a pillow, trying to suffocate her. She played dead, but then the chloroform took effect and she passed out. Apparently the guy left her for dead.

"When she woke up a little while later, she took out the gun she keeps in her bedside stand and stumbled into the living room. At first she thought she'd been robbed, but then she figured out that the bastard had tried to burn her house down. There were three or four places where he'd obviously tried to start a fire. She called 911, and when the patrol cops realized what they were looking at, they called me.

"I couldn't make any sense out of it. I thought about calling you guys, but I figured I'd wait until I'd exhausted all the leads I could think of that might point to an old boyfriend or a nutcase neighbor. She has a brother who is mentally handicapped, and I

.

thought it might be him, especially since there was no sexual assault.

"Then I read that article."

This was the best news Ash could have hoped for. Not only had the victim survived the attack, but she was now a live witness he could interview. He thanked Peterson, who promised to share his case files with Ash as soon as he returned from Austin.

There was also more disturbing news—apparently there had been another fatal fire on the same night as the assault on the woman Lieutenant Peterson was investigating. Another arson investigator was handling the case, and Ash rolled his eyes and shook his head when he found out who: Salvadore Garcia. Garcia was a prick, with a chip on his shoulder who wouldn't let anybody tell him anything. He'd been jealous of Ash ever since Ash got promoted before he did, and Ash knew without asking that Garcia would share no information on this case—not even if he, too, believed it might be the same torch.

But that wasn't what really bothered Ash. What really bothered him was that the killer had apparently struck twice in the same night. Maybe he had murdered the second woman when he realized he'd failed to kill the first. Or maybe the fire was the key. Maybe his failure to get the blaze going had driven him, in frustration, to try again.

Or maybe—and this hardly bore thinking about with Ash stuck hundreds of miles away—maybe he was losing control. If that were the case, more innocent people were going to die, burned to death in their own beds just to satisfy some arsonist's sick fantasy.

If the killer was losing control, he would start acting sooner and sooner between killings, giving investigators no time to gather facts and check out promising leads before striking again. He could easily overburden the system, or even worse . . . move somewhere else and start the whole cycle over again.

Things were heating up. They were too hot to be left to chance. Ash picked up the phone again and started trying to round up a substitute instructor for his remaining classes. He had to get home before the whole damn city started to burn.

Jillian's phone began ringing almost as soon as the paper hit the stands. Most of the calls were from other reporters who were eager to file stories of their own. By ten p.m., the local TV news was broadcasting segments, using file footage of unrelated fires or fires they had filmed at the time.

By the second day after the story hit, Jillian was beginning to worry about the wave of attention that was bound to smack into Ash when he returned to town. She was relieved that he seemed pleased by what she had written, but she wasn't sure he fully appreciated the barrage of reporters who were circling the city like seagulls, watching for him to appear and throw out some scraps.

She was also worried about the slur that had lately begun to affect her speech. Jillian found herself dealing with the clamoring hoardes as if from a great distance. It was a real struggle to hold a thought, and often she couldn't understand their questions. Afraid they might think her drunk, she stopped returning calls.

She began to despair. Here she'd done all the work, and she couldn't even remember the facts of her own article. There was always a letdown for Jillian after publication of a major piece: depressing thoughts about whether she could have done better, or whether her work was making any difference. But this was something more. This was scary—or it would be if she didn't feel so cut off from her own emotions.

A few days after the article broke, Jillian was sitting on the edge of the bathtub, shaving her legs. She nicked her knee, and the cut began to ooze blood.

Staunching it with a piece of toilet paper, Jillian was
fascinated to realize she felt so little pain.

   She began to wonder what it would be like to slit
her wrists, and decided to make a few practice cuts,
just to see.

Chapter Twenty-One

A few days after the night he had attempted two ceremonies, Keegan came home from work to find his wife, Eleanor, packing.

"Are you taking a trip?" he asked, stifling the spike of excitement at the thought that, with his wife and son absent from the home, he would have more freedom to prepare for the ceremonies.

Eleanor turned from the closet with a stack of dresses folded over her arms. "I'm leaving you, Keegan," she said quietly.

He stood stock-still, shock so profound it nearly stopped his heart, riveting him to his place in the open doorway of their bedroom.

"Ian starts the seventh grade in a few weeks," she went on. "He will be in a new school then, and Lord knows he's made very few friends here anyway. It's a good time to take him back to Boston, where we can be near my mother. I'll enroll him in school up there. It will be a fresh start for both of us," she said, and it was clear from her tone that by "both of us," she meant her and the boy, not her and Keegan. She stood very still, watching him.

Keegan was stunned to discover that he felt utterly shipwrecked, cast upon the rocks without hope of rescue. All he could think to say was, "You can't."

"Oh, yes I can." This seemed to unstick her. She bustled over to the bed and lay the dresses down next to an open suitcase. Without looking back at him, she said over her shoulder, "Our marriage is dead, Keegan. Surely you know that. You haven't touched me in months. We never talk. We're not even friends anymore." Her voice broke at that.

"But . . . the boy . . ."

"You never loved him. Maybe if your sperm count hadn't been so low and we could have had a child of our own . . . I don't know. But you've always seemed to regard him as more of a nuisance than a beloved son."

"That's not true," he protested.

She whirled from the bag, and the fury in her eyes caught him so by surprise that he staggered backward. "It *is* true! How can you deny it? You never spend any time with him. You never show him the slightest affection. You don't even discipline him—not that he ever needs it, and not that you would notice! He's a sweet, dear boy, and I *won't let you destroy him!*"

Keegan didn't know what to do or what to say. His wife was normally the most complacent, malleable individual he'd ever known. He never had the slightest trouble getting her to give in to him in a disagreement. Most of the time she deferred to him anyway, to avoid a confrontation. He'd never seen this fierce side of her. Having never observed the maternal instinct in his own mother, he was caught by surprise at seeing it in his wife.

"I'm not destroying him," he said, dismayed by the weak defensiveness in his own voice. "I've always taken good care of both of you."

"Keegan, there is a lot more to a marriage and fatherhood than simply going to work and coming home every night."

"But my father *didn't* come home," he snapped. "And I would never abandon you! Never! And yet *you* abandon *me!*"

He hadn't meant for the last remark to come out sounding quite so needy, but he couldn't help it. This *was* abandonment! In all their years together, it had never once occurred to Keegan that his wife might wind up doing to him what his father had done when he was just the age Ian was now.

Oh, the bitter ironies of life.

His wife sighed and brushed a wisp of hair from her eyes. "This is not something I'm doing *to* you, all right? It's something I'm doing *for* Ian and me."

"No." He shook his head. "If you weren't doing it *to* me, you'd have brought it up before now." Hot rage washed over him. It was the first acute emotion he'd felt in years, and its power frightened him. He took a threatening step toward her. "I would never leave you. And yet you leave me." The words came out like spit.

She stood her ground. Coldly, she said, "And have you noticed? Not once have you used the word *love*."

He stopped.

"You haven't said, 'I love you, Eleanor,' or even protested that I can't take Ian away from you because you love him. And that's the bottom line, isn't it? You don't love either one of us." Her eyes pierced the red haze that threatened to engulf him.

He blinked.

"I feel sorry for you, Keegan," she said in a tone that left no doubt she did not feel sorry for him. She turned away again, busying herself with packing.

"Ever hear the story of the cobbler's family who had no shoes? He was so busy making shoes for everyone else in order to make money that he neglected his own family."

Closing the suitcase, she snapped the locks with finality. "I would say that right now, you are barefoot, Keegan. You spend your days counseling people who need psychiatric help, and yet you are blind to your own sickness. You need help, and I sincerely hope you get it."

Carrying the suitcase, she brushed past him. "I'm

going to help Ian pack," she said. "And I would appreciate it if you would stay out of our way."

While Keegan stood outraged and helpless, she walked down the hallway away from him. She did not look back.

When Ash drove back into town, he avoided the office, not yet ready for a confrontation with his boss. He'd been playing a deliberate form of telephone tag with Chief Dixon for several days in hopes that time would cool the heat. Instead, he drove straight for the DPD police headquarters building at Harwood and Main to meet with Lieutenant Peterson.

Peterson's cluttered desk was surrounded by other cluttered desks in CAPERS. Most of the other detectives were out working cases, as Peterson would have been if he hadn't agreed to meet with Ash. Due to Peterson's obvious Texan accent over the phone, Ash was surprised by the man's predominantly Asian features. He was wiry and compact in his mid-thirties, and his handshake was firm. He had the appropriate file on his desk and handed it to Ash without preamble.

Ash read the reports and studied the photographs with interest. "He's getting careless," he mused, tapping a photo with his fingertip. "Left burned-out matches scattered around. That's not like him."

"It's not like him to leave live victims behind, either, is it?" asked Peterson wryly.

The lab report on the matches was inconclusive. At least Peterson had done his job, which would make Ash's job a lot easier. He scanned the report of the interview with Dixie Balboa, the victim. It was written in ponderous cop-ese, but Ash was able to catch the gist fairly quickly.

He glanced up. "Did she mention anything about cinnamon?"

Peterson blinked. "Cinnamon? Like the spice?"

"Yeah."

"Not that I remember. But we never did get around to trading recipes." He grinned.

Ash told him about the cinnamon piles.

"Jesus! What the hell?"

Ash shook his head. "Damned if I know. He may be performing some kind of ritual. I figure he must be bringing some of his own, because people don't keep that much of the stuff around in their kitchens."

"No kidding. I don't guess I've ever seen that much *anywhere*."

Scrutinizing the crime-scene photos, Ash said, "Mind taking a little ride with me out to the house? I'd like to interview Dixie if it's all right with you."

"I thought you'd never ask." Peterson got to his feet. "She'd be at work right now. She's a cashier at a Safeway over on Greenville Avenue."

"So let's go buy a few groceries."

Peterson was smart and very interested in the "Firebrand" case, as the press had taken to calling it. Ash enjoyed talking to another investigator about the case without having to defend himself or endure being looked at as though he were crazy. Ash supposed he had Jillian to thank for that, but he reminded himself that Peterson was a cop, not an arson investigator. Ash still had to run the gauntlet back at the office.

They could hear Dixie Balboa before they saw her. She was loud of voice and hearty of laugh, and everything about her was ample, from her bra size to her teased and curled bleached-blond hairdo. Peterson and Ash stood off to the side and watched her with the customers. She seemed to have a laugh and a chatty bit of gossip for everyone, and always a piece of candy or sugarless bubble gum for the children. Even the surliest businessman or the most frazzled young mother wound up smiling by the time they left the store. It was hard to imagine anyone bearing ill will toward Dixie. Had the killer succeeded in his mission, she would have been sorely missed.

It occurred to Ash that Scott, the young college

student, had also been a supermarket cashier who was popular with the customers.

But then, there was the security guard and the homeless man and Cricket Andrews and . . . Ash sighed.

When there was a lull in the business at Dixie's cash register stand, Peterson took Ash up to her and introduced him. "Oh, I read about you!" she cried. "It like to have give me a heart attack, thinkin' I might've been murdered by some fire nut."

"I'm sorry," he said. "I hope the article didn't cause you too much distress."

"Nah." She waved her hand. "Tell you the truth, it kinda made me feel better that it wasn't nobody I knowed. That was worst, thinkin' that somebody coulda wanted me dead for some reason. I couldn't begin to think why."

Anxiety shadowed her dark brown eyes, and Ash wondered how people dealt with such a brutal invasion of their privacy and personal safety as to have someone assault them in their own beds as they slept.

"Ma'am," he said, "there are victim's advocacy groups who can help you through this trauma. You've survived a terrible experience, and you don't have to deal with it alone." He thought of Jillian, started to recommend her therapist, then thought better of it.

"Thank you," she said, "but all I need is Jesus. He'll get me through anything. Well, that and my .38." She grinned, and her eyes twinkled.

Peterson said, "She's got a Concealed Carry permit, a license for the gun, and I understand she's a helluva shot." They exchanged smiles.

Ash smiled, too. "Too bad you didn't catch him for us, Dixie."

"Well, I damn sure tried!" They laughed.

"We won't keep you from your work," said Ash. "I just need to ask you if you noticed anything out of the ordinary in your living room that night. I mean after you called 911, and you were waiting for the police. Did you see anything that struck you as completely out of place?"

"You mean other than the fires that nut tried to set?"

"Yeah. Other than the fires."

"I damn sure did," said Dixie. With an apologetic glance toward Peterson, she said, "I never did bring it up when we were talkin' because it seemed so silly. It didn't seem like it had anything to do with what happened to me, and I didn't want you to think I was crazy."

"Of course I thought you were crazy," teased Peterson, "but that wouldn't have affected my judgment."

She gave a loud whooping laugh, and Ash knew she was going to be fine. Investigators of violent crime seldom joked and teased with crime victims because the subject of their discussions was usually so upsetting. Sometimes they had lost loved ones or had been badly injured themselves. Investigators were usually sensitive to that fact and kept their jokes to themselves, unless the investigation went on for many months and they had established a familiarity with the victims, a friendship even. With the many cases in their files to be investigated, that didn't happen often.

For Peterson to be joking with Dixie this early in an unsolved crime investigation meant that she had shown him a strong sense of humor that, they both knew, was the healthiest way anyone could cope with trauma or stress.

"Okay," she said. "Now, I admit I'm not the best housekeeper in the world. My mama's always teasing me about how she's gonna call the health department. Anyway, there I was, sittin' there with my gun in my hand, jumping at every little creepy noise, thinkin' that lunatic was gonna come back and try to finish the job with me, and then kinda hopin' he *would* come back, if you know what I mean, when I noticed this big nasty mess all over my carpet. It was cinnamon! Can you believe it? Like the spice. Scattered all over my carpet. I like to have never got it vacuumed up."

Ash exchanged glances with Peterson. "Did you say it was scattered?"

She pondered this. "Well, it was like somebody had poured it all out into a big pile and then had kicked it over, like a mean little kid in a sandbox, you know what I mean?"

Ash nodded.

She bit her lip. "Does that sound crazy?"

Peterson patted her arm. "Not at all, Dixie. You've been a great help. Could be you'll help us catch this guy after all."

"Will you tell me?"

"What?"

"Will you call me and tell me when you catch him?" The shadow had crossed over her eyes again, and she added sheepishly, "I'm havin' a little bit of trouble sleepin' nights."

"Right away, Dixie. You'll be the first person I call," said Ash. "In the meantime, if you're not too attached to the place, you might consider moving. It sometimes helps victims who've been assaulted in their own homes to move someplace and make a fresh start."

"You're prob'ly right," she said. "I was thinkin' about movin' anyway. The owner's been lettin' the place get kinda seedy. I could move in with one of my girlfriends and be able to afford a nicer place. Maybe an apartment with security."

"That's a good idea," said Peterson. "Keep me posted so I don't lose track of you. We may need you to testify someday in court."

"I will. But there's one thing."

"What?" they said at the same time.

"Well, I don't like to think o'myself as a *victim*. That word makes me feel all helpless and scared. I like to think o'myself as a *survivor*, 'cause that's what I am, anyway." She lifted her chin bravely.

Both detectives found themselves nodding. "You're absolutely right," said Ash. "You're going to be all right, Dixie."

"I already am," she said, and though Ash admired her courage, he knew she was not all right, not really, and probably wouldn't be until they'd caught the bastard who had robbed her of her peace of mind and the sanctuary of her home.

Ash set up another interview with her at his office later in the week, when they would be free to talk in more detail. He also wanted to inspect the house himself and examine where the fires had been set—or almost set. Ash had a long way to go before he was finished with Dixie Balboa.

Chapter Twenty-Two

It was not a good day for Jillian. Not only did it require Herculean feats of concentration just to drive her car to Dr. Sloane's office, but when she got there, the atmosphere of his inner sanctum had changed. This time a barely suppressed rage lay coiled behind the dark stillness of his eyes with the sinister energy of a snake about to strike. It frightened Jillian and rendered her mute.

For an eternity of minutes, utter silence prevailed. He did not speak, and Jillian could not. Finally, in a voice hushed with menace, Dr. Sloane said, "I thought we agreed that you were not going to publish the fire story."

"I know," she said, mesmerized by his tone and the glitter in his eyes, much like a hapless rabbit who is about to become a reptilian dinner. "But I thought—"

"*You* thought?" he said. "I wasn't aware that you had come to therapy because your thought processes were all that sound. After all, *you* thought it would be a good idea to cover the Cinco de Mayo rally in Little Mexico, right? Randi had her sensible doubts, as did Ash and your boss, but *you*, Jillian Ross, *thought* it would be a good idea."

Jillian flinched as if a snake had indeed sunk venomous fangs into her soft flesh.

"And, of course, we all know what happened to Randi, don't we?"

Jillian recoiled. "How can you be so cruel?" she cried, her eyes brimming with sudden tears. "I don't understand."

"Oh, I think you do understand. Your decisions and your actions got your best friend killed and left an innocent infant motherless. Then you came to me for help, but you have resisted everything I've tried to do to help you. If you really wanted my help, you would follow my suggestions."

"I don't mean to resist—"

"The only conclusion I can draw is that you are continuing on your own path of self-destruction. Now your actions may have destroyed another friend who cares about you and has tried to help you."

"What? What are you talking about?"

"I asked you not to publish the fire story. You did it anyway. Did it ever occur to you that the story might draw the attention of the killer? That he might target your own friend, Ash? Or, as usual, were you concerned merely with your own ego and career advancement?"

His skill at exposing her deepest, darkest vulnerability and using it against her brought only a weak, defensive response. "Ash can take care of himhself," she said, struggling not to slur her words.

"I'm sure he can. Just as you took care of yourself at the riot. But then, you are an expert on the psychopathology of the human mind, whereas I, a licensed psychiatrist, don't know what I'm talking about."

"I didn't say that!"

"You didn't have to. You failed to heed my advice, and now you have drawn the attention of this criminal to not only your friend Ash but yourself as well." He waved his hand dismissively. "But I would expect no less from someone who is so bent on self-destruction."

Self-consciously, she tugged at the sleeve of her blouse in an attempt to cover the razor wounds. "I was trying to help Ash," she pointed out, but her reasoning no longer seemed to make any sense to her.

Now, *how*, exactly had she thought the article might be of help to Ash? In vain, she attempted to gather fleecy clouds of thought as they drifted across the blue vapor of her mind.

"I don't recall Ash asking for your help," Dr. Sloane said, his sharp words piercing her careful bubble of concentration. "As I recall, you brought the whole matter up and even had to do some convincing to get him to go along. Like Randi, he cares for you and wants to please you."

Jillian remembered something, something significant that would dispute what the doctor was saying, but just as suddenly, the memory was gone. She put her head in her hands. "I'm so confused. My head—it's like I'm in a fog all the time. I can't work anymore. I feel as if I'm dishin-disintegrating."

He nodded. "This is the very thing I feared would happen if you stressed yourself over the article. It's too soon in the psychic healing process. You've pushed things too hard, and now I fear you may be approaching a psychotic break." He caught her wrist in his hand. Pushing up the sleeve of her blouse, he said, "What is this?"

"Nothing." She pulled her wrist free. "I cut myself."

"Jillian. Did you try to kill yourself?" His frown punctuated the stern words, emphasizing them while his eyes burned into her.

"No!" she said, her face turning hot. She glanced away.

Dr. Sloane sighed and shook his head. "This still amounts to self-mutilation. This is serious. I'm afraid it's more serious than I previously thought, and far more serious than you realize."

"What?" She shook her head as if to rid it of cobwebs.

"If you do not improve, Jillian, I'm afraid we are going to have to consider hospitalization."

"What do you mean? Are you talking about committing me to an *asylum*?"

He smiled. "We don't call them asylums anymore, my dear. And you needn't be afraid. It's simply a place and a time where you may get some rest, away from the pressures of trying to make a living, where people can help you get well."

Jillian tried to protest, but her thoughts were too ethereal, too scattered for her to make any sense of them, much less put them into words. Suddenly she felt very much afraid but was having trouble remembering why.

He began scribbling on his pad. Without looking up, he said, "Well, did the fire story generate the kinds of leads you had hoped it would? Is Ash any nearer to finding the culprit?"

The abrupt change of subject was jarring. Jillian stumbled along, trying to keep up. "I don't know," she said. "Lots of people call in when something like this gets publicity, but they have to check everything out to see what's real and what isn't. And Ash has been out of town. To do . . . to teach . . . a conference . . ."

Getting such a long speech out required a great deal of effort, and Jillian was already beginning to forget what she had just said. "Ash has been out of town," she said. "He's been . . . out of town."

Dr. Sloane peered at her. "I'm going to write you another prescription," he said. "This will help to calm you down. I'm afraid your nerves are in a very fragile state right now, which, of course, was my worry all along."

Jillian was too exhausted to argue. She felt utterly weak from the session, as if the doctor had stuck a needle in her arm and drained out all her lifeblood. "I'm not getting any better," she said blearily. "Am I?"

He leaned over and patted her hand. "You have to trust me, my dear. I know I may seem harsh at times, but believe me, I'm only doing what I think is best for you. Once you stop resisting me and allow me to help you, I think you will find that you are doing much better. Soon we'll be able to put this whole matter behind us."

"Do you think so?" she said pitifully.

"Don't you worry." He smiled as if the entire session had been a pleasant success. "Soon this will all be just like a bad dream."

Now that was something Jillian could believe. It already felt like a bad dream.

There were two Keegans.

It was delicious. Brilliant. There was the buttoned-down Dr. Keegan Sloane, teaching little morons at the college or counseling mental defectives in his office. There was no life to this Keegan, no reason, it seemed sometimes, to go on. Maintaining this Keegan required tremendous discipline and self-control. He held this self together with tight, invisible threads that would snap on a weaker man.

And then there was the Keegan of the Beast.

With his wife and son out of his hair, he could perform the beginning of the ritual ceremony naked, in front of the fireplace. No more skulking about with candles in the privacy of his office. Now he could do it right, and it was glorious.

This was the Keegan who made it all happen, who held together the deadened Dr. Sloane until he could come alive. This was the *real* Keegan Sloane.

First, he experimented with various household substances until he had formulated a creamy chalk out of cinnamon. Sitting in front of the fire, he would breathe deeply until he felt himself drifting into the trance. Then, he would take the cinnamon-chalk and draw a line from the inside of his left wrist, along the underside of his arm, across his chest, then down the other arm to the other wrist.

After that, he would draw a line from the base of his throat, all the way down his chest and abdomen—making a cross of the other line—and then bury it in the bushy base of his penis. When the cross was complete, he would draw the fire-sign triangle upon his forehead, between his eyes. The triangle pointed upward, signifying flames as well as masculine power.

On the wall above the fireplace, he drew a crude sketch—for he was no artist—of the fire-bellowing chimera, the mythical creature that was said to have the head of a lion, a goat's body, and the tail of a dragon. This excited him, for it was a rendition of the beast that he could live with.

He would sit cross-legged in front of the fire, breathing in its scorching heat until sweat dripped from his nose and chin. (It was, after all, summer in Dallas.) There were times when he could swear the Beast winked at him and whispered to him.

This was no delusion, he told himself. This was real!

A delusion was a form of madness in which things appeared and voices spoke that did not exist, but fire was *real*, was it not? Here right in front of him, scalding his skin.

The Beast hissed to him things like, "Sssson of fire, your ssssacrifices have been powerful and majestic. Risssse up like the blesssssed phoenix in all your blazing glory, and honor me again!" And it would sizzle and pop in excitement and anticipation. He would touch himself, and his penis would spring to engorged life—splendid in ways he'd never known with his wife.

The Beast never criticized him for his mistakes, the way his mother always had. And the Beast, unlike his father, could rise up whenever he wanted. The Beast was loyal to him in ways his wife would never have understood when she betrayed his trust and abandoned him as his father had done. And the Beast never dropped veiled insults about intimate things like his low sperm count.

With the Beast, he had all the potency he would ever need.

The Beast empowered him, glorified him, *transformed* him!

The Beast annointed the honorees and made sacred the ancient sacrifice.

When it was time to leave and complete the ceremony, Keegan always knew that the Beast would never fail him.

Ash tried to reach Jillian several times after he returned to town, but all he got was her answering machine. He hadn't seen her in almost two weeks, and he ached to hold her, but three more fatal fires in quick succession took up his every waking hour. Finally, he consoled himself with the thought that she believed him still down in Austin anyway and he would see her when she was expecting to see him.

Two of the fires turned out to be accidental in origin, but the third contained all the signatures that he had come to expect the Firebrand to leave behind, including the telltale cinnamon pile. He'd had the substance tested at the Southwest Institute of Forensic Sciences lab just to be sure, and that's what it was all right, plain household cinnamon.

Ash now searched for cinnamon first thing when investigating a fatal fire. If he found it, he assumed the fire was the work of the Firebrand, and began a careful search for evidence—anything that might lead him to the doorstep of the clever torch.

One observation he made was intensely disturbing to Ash. The killer no longer seemed to distance himself from the actual killing. Bludgeoning his victims in bed now seemed to be his method of choice, and though he never resorted to the use of accelerants, he was also more likely to set multiple points of origin for the fire. Surely he knew that this was a red flag to investigators of an incendiary cause of fire. So either he was beginning to want to take credit for his work, or he was getting more desperate, more in a hurry to see the fire fully engaged.

Both signs indicated to Ash that the Firebrand's urgency to kill and burn were increasing.

The good news was that the latest bludgeoning finally caught the attention of DFD brass. They could see for themselves the similarity between several of the most recent fires. They didn't want to hear about cinnamon piles, but they were finally willing to allow Ash the help he needed in the investigation.

In fact, he was spared the ass-chewing he'd been dreading since returning to town. Too many fire fatalities had occurred since the publication of Jillian's article, which only served to validate it. Ash figured it was just a matter of time before one of the suits found some way to take credit for the Firebrand investigation.

He didn't care if the governor took credit for it. He just wanted the bastard stopped.

So Ash finally got his task force: ATF Special Agent Moses Washington—the only fed Ash had ever found to be worth a damn; Dallas arson investigators Kathy Williamson and, much to Ash's chagrin, Salvadore Garcia, who had kissed many asses for the privilege; and best of all, DPD CAPERS detective Sam Peterson, who came at Ash's special request.

The first meeting was productive in that Garcia finally coughed up the information that the first bludgeoning victim was a student who had attended the same junior college as Scott Lancaster.

Ash could have put his hands around the man's throat for that tidbit; Garcia *knew* that Scott and the victim in his case, Jennifer Johnson, had attended the same school, but he had failed to share that piece of information with Ash just because he was a son of a bitch. Jealous over the attention Ash was getting from the *Mirror* article, he chose to bide his time until he could insinuate himself onto the Firebrand Task Force.

Turf wars, petty jealousies, and pissing contests were common in the world of law enforcement and criminal investigations, but Ash had never had the time or the patience for them. Politics was not his

game, and he secretly (or maybe not so secretly) de-
spised those who played it.

The first known connection among the victims.

This was the first real break in the case. Had it not
been a Friday afternoon, Ash would have fairly flown
to the college, but he decided to let it ride over the
weekend while he tied up some other loose ends and
spent some time with Jillian. They would start fresh
on Monday morning, and they would move like a jug-
gernaught without pause until they had brought down
the killer. Ash was sure of it.

Finally, he'd had enough. Words on reports were
beginning to run together, and the crime-scene photos
he was poring over in his office seemed blurry to him
until he realized it was just his own weary eyes. He
was tired; he was stupid-headed; he was horny; and
he wanted to see Jillian. He hadn't seen her since . . .
what? Was it nearly three weeks? Must be. Time flew
when you were having fun.

Anyway, he wanted to see Jillian and drink a beer,
and not necessarily in that order.

Leaving another message on her machine that he
was on his way, Ash picked up a six-pack of beer and
a pizza and pushed fires and murders and all other
thoughts out of his mind on the drive over. He was
officially off work. And he couldn't wait to take her
in his arms.

At the door he juggled beer and pizza and pounded,
humming under his breath and waiting with a shit-
eating grin on his face.

And waited.

Glancing around the building to make sure her car
was in the single-car drive, he pounded a couple times
more and waited, wondering if she might be in the
shower and silently cursing the fact that the pizza was
getting cold and the beer warm. He had just raised
his fist to do some more pounding when the door
swung open and she stood in the darkened doorway,
swaying slightly and squinting out at him.

Ash felt the six-pack slip from his sweaty grasp and clatter to the porch. Speechless, he stared at the apparition in front of him as if it were a ghost instead of the woman he loved.

She didn't even look like herself. Her hair was unwashed and matted around her face, which was oddly puffy, as if she'd had dental surgery. Her eyes were unfocused, the pupils mere pinpricks, and sunken-in dark smudges that appeared to be smeared mascara, he finally realized, were the shadows of exhaustion. Her oversized T-shirt was stained, as if she'd been wearing it for several days or even longer. She didn't smell very good and neither did the apartment.

"Jillian!" he cried. "Darlin', what's wrong?" He waited for an answer, rather than barging in—there was no telling what he'd find inside.

"I guesh it's time to get up," she said. She did not give him the ebullient greeting he'd been expecting. She did not throw her arms around his neck or even make some off-color wisecrack about his absence. She did not do any of those things because she was not herself.

"Are you sick?" He felt her forehead, but it was clammy and cool, not hot.

"Yeshterday it was three o'clock," she said, lifting a hand to brush a tangled strand of hair out of her eyes. To his horror, he spotted the telltale scars of a suicide practice run. All paramedics knew to spot them, and when they came upon a real suicide, it was not uncommon to find such practice marks near the fatal slash.

"Dear God," he said. He picked up the beer and elbowed his way past her into a filthy apartment—the kind of nasty he used to see in crack houses. Living in a tenement in poverty did not breed this kind of filth; being high or stoned all the time did.

Drugs.

Tossing the pizza box on a coffee table covered with trash, Ash knelt in front of Jillian, who had sat down and was staring dully at him out from under a curtain of dirty hair. Taking her hands gently in his own, he turned over her wrists and counted the scars, then reached up and tucked her hair behind her ears. "Darlin'," he said quietly, "what have you been taking? Would you show me?"

"Aren't you out of town?" She blinked. A lot.

"I'm back, baby, and I'm here to take care of you. Now, I need you to show Ash what kind of drugs you've been taking, okay?"

Irritably, she shook off his hands. "Jush pershcrishion."

"Pershcrishion? You mean like Percodan?" He thought a moment. "Oh! *Prescription!*"

He knew where she kept her prescription medications, and headed straight for the kitchen, where he dug through just about every dirty dish the woman owned to discover three bottles of drugs, all prescribed by her psychiatrist.

The Xonok, Ash knew, was already under fire through various lawsuits and controversies. The other two he'd never heard of.

Why was she taking them?

He went back into the living room to ask, but she'd stretched out on the couch and was sleeping deeply, her mouth open and drool oozing down her cheek.

As a former paramedic, Ash's first instinct was to call Dr. Sloane and report what he considered to be an emergency, but something made him hesitate.

Panicked thoughts jumped around in his brain. Should he scoop her up and get her to a hospital? Call an ambulance? Let her sleep it off?

Each of the bottles was half full, which indicated that she had not attempted suicide by taking all the pills. He studied the bottles. Picked up all three. Read the labels. Two had come from one pharmacy, but the third was from another. Why?

Somewhere, Ash knew, Jillian had a *Physician's Desk Reference.* Most journalists kept them on hand.

Stumbling over piles of dirty laundry and scattered stacks of unread newspapers, Ash dug through her shelves and her desk until he found it. Then he looked up the medications.

It was just as he had suspected. The third drug was contraindicated for use with either of the first two. Any pharmacist would have known that and would not have filled the prescriptions without checking first with the doctor.

But the doctor didn't want to be checked up on.

Ash had trained himself to remain calm and clear-thinking in an emergency. It did not appear, from what he'd read, that the dosages she was taking, even in combination with the other two, were potentially fatal. However, the possible side effects were alarming:

> *Side effects may include extreme drowsiness, confusion, slurred speech, depression, severe headache, disorientation, lethargy, irritability, short-term memory loss and forgetfulness, even hallucinations. When used in combination with the above mentioned drugs, symptoms may mimic mental illness. If patient displays two or more of the side effects mentioned above, discontinue use.*

Without talking to Jillian, Ash had no way of knowing if Dr. Sloane was aware of her manifestation of these side effects, but he was still unwilling to phone the doctor to find out.

Why?

Over the years Ash had honed his instincts to a fine point and had learned to trust them.

Connections.

Jillian was seeing Dr. Sloane. Dr. Sloane, a licensed medical doctor, had prescribed a combination of drugs for her that was clearly not only contraindicated, but dangerous. Surely he knew better. But from what Ash could tell from the label listings, the prescriptions had actually been renewed, which meant he had continued the combination.

Why?

He was supposed to be a good shrink, according to the fire guys who'd been to see him. That's why he was . . . *on the fire department list.*

Sloane.

He'd interviewed a Dr. Sloane, too. Scott had taken a psychology class under a Dr. Sloane.

Yanking the phone out of his jacket pocket, fumbling with it even though Jillian had a phone sitting right on the countertop, Ash paged Salvadore Garcia.

To his surprise, Sal called right back. Obviously, he considered Ash's butt worth kissing. He'd keep that in mind.

"Sal. When you were going over the class schedule for Jennifer Johnson, did you notice if she took a psych course?"

"I don't remember, Ash. Wait a minute while I go get my notebook."

Ash waited. He walked into the living room and watched Jillian breathe. While he waited, he took her pulse. The beat was strong, if slow, but not alarmingly so. Her breathing was unlabored. He checked her pupils. Still small, but even. Her color was good. He'd let her sleep, for now.

"Okay," said Sal. "Let's see." Ash listened to the sound of pages turning. "Yeah. Psych 101. She had it at 2:20 on Tuesdays and Thursdays."

So she was not in Scott's class. His had met on Mondays, Wednesdays, and Fridays.

"Did you make note of her instructor?" asked Ash, whose own heart was tripping along like a Geiger counter.

"Yeah. Sloane."

Ash's whole body went cold, then hot, then cold again. Needle-points of self-incrimination burned his skin.

"All right," he said woodenly. "Thanks, Sal."

"What's this about?" asked Sal, who obviously expected payback for being such a good boy.

"I'm not sure. I've got to check a few things out, and then I'll talk to you guys on Monday."

"Oh." In other words . . . *So you're playing it close to the vest, then. Asshole.*

"I'll talk to you later, Sal." Ash hung up before Sal could make any protests. For a long moment he sat watching Jillian snore.

Jesus.

As far as Ash could see, all the fires that they considered to be the work of the Firebrand had only one thing in common:

Jillian.

She'd been there from the beginning, palling around with Ash, tagging along on his investigation.

And all along she'd been in therapy.

He made another call, dreading the answer he already knew in his heart: What was the full name of the shrink on the fire department list? He'd long since lost the piece of scratch paper with the man's name on it.

Keegan Sloane, M.D.

Keegan was the first name of the psych professor Jennifer and Scott had had.

Ash hurried into the kitchen, picked up a pill bottle, and called the pharmacy number listed. When the pharmacist answered, Ash had only one question: Which Dr. Sloane had prescribed the following medication for Jillian Ross? Ash was her husband, he said, and he needed to contact the doctor about the drug.

"Keegan," answered the unsuspecting pharmacist.

In that moment the planet ceased its orbit, and life as Ash had known it stopped.

Bas-relief. He saw it all in 3-D.

Agitated and distraught at his own carelessness, Ash paced the living room for a few minutes, cursing himself, hating himself for his myopia.

Your instincts warned you, came the self-accusation. *In that goofy college prof's office, your instincts warned you. You asked him, and he lied, and you didn't bother to check it out.*

Of course, now that he went back over it, Sloane's nervousness that day made perfect sense. If Ash had been paying only *half* of the attention he should have, he'd have cued in on the lie, too.

But he hadn't, and it almost got Jillian killed.

Ash set his jaw until his teeth hurt.

It was not going to happen again. He'd catch the son of a bitch before another soul got hurt, if it was the last thing he did.

PART V

Ash & Funeral Pyres

The fire which seems extinguished
Often slumbers beneath the ashes.

> Pierre Corneille (1644)

Out of the dusk a shadow,
   Then a spark . . .
Out of the dead, cold ashes,
   Life again.

> John Bannister Tabb
> "Evolution" (1845–1909)

To burn always with this
   hard, gemlike flame, to
maintain this ecstasy,
   is success in life.

> Walter Pater (1873)

Chapter Twenty-Three

Keegan, the "son of fire," became obsessed with the chimera. He went to the bookstore and bought as many books as he could find that contained its image. Then, through a friend of Eleanor's, he managed to track down an old-fashioned opaque projector from a nearby school and borrow it one weekend.

He washed off the crude sketch he'd made on the wall over the fireplace. Using the opaque projector, he placed one of the books beneath its hot magnifying glass and superimposed a beautiful likeness of the chimera in its place on the same wall. Then he stood upon a step stool and traced the lines of the Beast onto the wall. Afterward, using the book as a sort of paint-by-number guide, he painted the creature in vivid and lustrous acrylic colors of royal blue and polished gold and sunset orange and ruby red—all colors of fire.

For added effect, he gave it a background of flames. The result was magnificent.

He couldn't stop looking at it. He especially enjoyed watching it by the light of flickering candles he placed on the fireplace mantel. He liked it so well, in fact, that he decided to make as many images of the chimera on the walls of his house as he could. Not a room was spared.

It took him all weekend.

It was delightful! Thrilling! He'd never seen anything like it, and it was all his!

It had turned out to be a good thing that his wife
and son were gone. That left him with virtually unlim-
ited time to spend with the Beast, experimenting with
ways to bring Him to roaring life, and sorting through
lists of potential honorees. So absorbed did he become, in fact, that he decided to take a few days off
from both his jobs in order that he not be interrupted
in his important tasks.

The second summer session had just ended, and it
would be several weeks before the fall semester began
at the community college, so that was an easy absence
to arrange. Taking time away from the whining lot of
clients he treated was quite another, but he left the
job up to his secretary and gave her the time off as
well. What the hell. He was feeling generous.

Finally, *finally*, he had time, precious time all to
himself. Alone in the house, he could paint his body
and dance naked in front of the fireplace, paying hom-
age to the Beast and offering up prayers to the magnificent chimera. Sometimes, in the candlelight, it
seemed to come alive.

And as the Beast assumed more life, his own deadness began to recede.

At last he had conquered death, and he was *alive!*

A fierce headache awoke Jillian and served notice
that it was time for another dose of medication. She
struggled into a sitting position and stared in blurry
confusion at Ash sitting in the chair across from her,
his head dropped back onto cushions, eyes closed.

"Ash?" she said.

Instantly awake, he sat up straight. "Jilly? You
okay, darlin'?"

"Of coursh I'm okay, but my head hurts." She staggered to her feet. Ash sprang up immediately and offered his arm, which she shook off. "I'm okay, I

shaid," she snapped, but nonetheless, the room reeled, causing her to list somewhat to the side.

She shuffled toward the kitchen.

"I can get you anything you need," said Ash reasonably. "Why don't you sit down and tell me what you want?"

Ignoring him, she headed straight for the kitchen cabinet and soon came to a disoriented halt. All the dishes had been washed and put away, the counters wiped clean, the trash taken out. All she could think of to say was, "I had everything where I wanted it!" She knew this didn't make any sense, but it seemed like the thing to say at the time.

Stumbling a little, she reached for the cabinet where her medicines were stored and opened it.

They were gone.

Seized by panic, Jillian shrieked, *"Where are my medicationsh? I need 'em! Give 'em to me!"* The voice sounded as though it were coming from somewhere else. She grabbed her head and moaned.

Ash stood very near and put his hand on her arm. "Those medications are killing you, Jilly. Haven't you noticed? You've been so much worse since you started taking them."

She wasn't listening. She'd begun slamming open cabinets and drawers.

"Jill. Stop it! Listen to me!"

"Shut up!" she yelled. "You're makin' my head hurt!"

"It's the Xonok, Jill!" he shouted. "Headache is a side effect of the drug. You've gotta get it out of your system!"

"You don't know what you're talkin' about!" she screamed. "Give 'em to me, you fuckin' bastard!" She flew into him, pummeling him with her fists, but her arms were heavy and weak, and her blows had all the strength of a mosquito bite. She felt her knees give way. Ash caught her in his strong arms and half carried her to the sofa. She started to cry.

He knelt in front of her. "Baby, don't you see what's happening to you?" He touched her cheek gently. "It's Dr. Sloane. He's prescribing medicines that are making you crazy. Look at yourself!"

Setting her chin like a little kid, Jillian said stubbornly, "Dotor Shloane has helped me a lot. You don't know. Pleashe." More tears spilled. "Let me have the medishines. My head ish comin' off."

"Fine. Here." He withdrew a couple of the bottles from his shirt pocket, tapped out the pills in the palm of his hand, and handed them to her. "It's your funeral." With that, he disappeared into the kitchen, where he quickly reappeared with a glass of water and another couple of pills. "Take some of this aspirin," he said. "It will help." He hesitated. "Dr. Sloane said so."

"Okay." She took the pills, lay down on the sofa, and looked up at him. "Aren't you out of town?" she said, but by the time he had answered her, she was asleep.

Ash figured he could count on at least two hours of sleep from Jillian. He settled himself at the newly clean kitchen table with her pill bottles in hand and a box of baking soda. The prescriptions came in capsule form. Carefully, working like a scientist in a very grave experiment, Ash poured out half of each pill's medication and replaced it with powdered baking soda, a task he had already begun before giving her the pills.

He intended to increase the amount of baking soda with each day's dosage until the pills were nothing but placebos. This would allow Jillian to get the drugs out of her system in a slow, measured way and prevent the danger of sudden withdrawal from addictive narcotics.

As he labored with an Ex-Acto knife, cutting Jillian's drugs, it was all he could do not to get up from the table, track down that son-of-a-bitch Sloane, and shoot him.

Ash and Jillian had been good friends for more

years than he could count, and now they were lovers. She was vibrant, intelligent, beautiful, mischievous, hardheaded, irreverent, talented, frustrating, and wild. But drugs had never been her thing. He'd seen her a bit tipsy from beer or champagne from time to time, but he'd never seen her stoned.

And he had never, ever seen her like this.

Ash was uncomfortably aware that, as a law enforcement officer, if he had been called to a domestic situation involving the Jillian asleep on the sofa now, he would automatically peg her for either a drug addict or a mental case. He'd have her sent to the psych ward for an evaluation, where the sudden withdrawal from the drugs in her system would cause what would appear to psychiatric professionals as a total breakdown. It would take very little time, from that point on, for Dr. Keegan Sloane to have his star patient committed.

This was not just serious, it was downright terrifying, like something from a Hitchcock movie.

After Ash had completed that task, he went around the house and collected everything that Jillian could potentially use as a weapon against either herself or him, and hid it. Then he dug through her desk until he had unearthed her appointment book. Juxtaposing that with his notebook entries on each fatal fire, Ash was disappointed to find that a discernible pattern did not automatically emerge. In other words, Sloane didn't schedule an appointment for Jillian and then rush out and set a fire.

However.

Jillian had started hanging out with Ash during his investigation of the warehouse fire. He had talked to her then about the fact that the torch never used accelerants and often made the fires appear to be accidental.

After her next appointment, Cricket Andrews had been killed. And an accelerant had been used. In fact, it had been used in such a way and at such a time as to throw clear suspicion toward Derek Thorsen.

Had Jillian talked to her therapist, not just about the fire investigation with Ash, but about Derek and his feud with Cricket?

If so, then the so-called Firebrand had used that intelligence in a very cunning way. At that time, and for some time afterward, Ash had persisted in his belief that Derek had set the fire, and had made no effort to connect the Firebrand to the Andrews fire.

With a deep, self-recriminatory sigh, Ash put his head in his hands. He didn't regret including Jillian in his work. It had been the best thing for them, and had drawn them together. He would never trade for that particular joy. But at the same time, he'd been played for a complete fool by Sloane, with all the flair and skill of a gypsy.

All through this maddening investigation, Ash had been haunted by the fact that the arsonist seemed always to know Ash's last move so that he made a different one next, in a macabre dance of death.

The torch had been in the lead.

Turning from Jillian's desk, Ash watched her thoughtfully as she slept. Poor kid. Nothing but a footprint on the floor for the bastard to step on.

But Ash had changed the music. He was in charge of the dance floor now, and absolutely nothing was going to be the same again.

"Hang in there, sweet girl," he whispered to the sleeping Jillian. "When we get through all this . . . I'll take you dancing."

Chapter Twenty-Four

Jillian awakened in her own bed. Her headache was reduced to a manageable dull stone behind her eyes rather than the piercing throb that had driven her to the kitchen cabinet more times than she cared to remember. The first thing she noticed was how badly she needed a shower; the second was that she felt more clearheaded and less heavy-limbed. She got out of bed without feeling faint and headed straight for the bathroom.

It wasn't until she was standing beneath the hot, pulsating shower that she remembered—or thought she remembered—that Ash had been in her apartment. Could it have been a dream?

A knock at the bathroom door caused her to jump nearly out of her skin.

"Jillian?"

So it hadn't been a dream.

"Yeah?"

He came into the bathroom, but did not playfully pull back the shower curtain or climb in with her as he might have done. "How're you feeling?" he asked.

"Not bad," she said. "Pretty good, considering what a fog the past few days have been." Or was it weeks? Surely not. Some things were still a blur.

"I'm leaving you a cup of coffee here on the sink," he said.

"If you don't mind," she said, "I'd rather wait until I've had a bite to eat and taken my medication."

There was a long silence. Then the door opened and closed, and he left without saying anything.

Jillian found that curious, but she was beginning to tire from the long, hot shower and got out to dry off and comb out her hair. She brushed her teeth, dried her hair, pulled on a loose T-shirt and pair of comfy shorts, and went in search of Ash.

She found him in the kitchen, scrambling eggs. She lifted her face for a kiss, hugged him, then nibbled on a piece of toast while she headed straight for the kitchen cabinet to get her medication. "Were you here yesterday?" she asked, tapping pills into her hand.

"I was," he said. "And all night the night before. It's Sunday morning."

"You're kidding." She took the pills. "Oh! How was your trip?"

"Fine," he said.

"This is really nice, by the way," she said. "I didn't expect to wake up and find you here."

"No, I don't expect you did," he said as he spooned the eggs onto her plate. "You were pretty out of it."

"I know. I must have had the flu or something." She sat down and dug into the eggs.

Ash sat across from her. "Jillian."

She glanced up.

"You didn't have the flu. You were drugged."

"What?" She stopped chewing.

"Those drugs Sloane prescribed for you. They're deadly when taken in that particular combination. He had you drugged."

Swallowing the eggs, she said, "What are you talking about?"

"Those pills he's got you taking. They've had you stoned out of your mind for days. He's using them to manipulate you and try to control your mind."

"Are you crazy?" she cried. "I took them yesterday, and I'm fine today. And I just took another dose, and

I'm still fine!" Or pretty fine, anyway. Maybe not up to snuff completely, but she would be once she was fully recovered from the flu or whatever it was. She shook her head and took another bite.

He said nothing.

"Anyway," she said around a mouthful, "what reason would he possibly have to drug me and manipulate me? It's not like he's some cult leader or something."

Ash took a sip of coffee and did not answer.

"Honestly, I can't believe you." She shook her head and laid down her fork. She'd lost her appetite. Damn, she was so frigging tired! What was *wrong* with her?

"Did you try to kill yourself?" asked Ash abruptly.

"What?" Too late, she remembered that the T-shirt had short sleeves. She put her hands in her lap.

"I've been doing some research into these drugs," he said. "One of the side effects is obsessive thoughts of suicide."

"Why are you picking on me?" she whined. "I just don't feel very well, that's all." After a moment she said, "It's just crazy. What reason could he possibly have to drug me and manipulate me? It's not like he's some cult leader or something." *Shit. Had she already said that, or just thought it?*

Ash shook his head and sighed.

"I'm tired," she said. "I think I'll go rest for a while."

This time, it was much longer before she fell asleep.

When Ash was certain that Jillian was sound asleep, he took the phone into the kitchen, sat at the table, and called Lieutenant Sam Peterson at home.

Speaking quietly, he said, "Sam, old man, I'm sure sorry to bother you at home, but I've got an emergency situation going down here and I need some help. I also need some discretion. I'm not ready to bring in the whole task force just yet."

"Speak, kimosabe."

In as abbreviated a form as possible, Ash brought
Peterson up-to-date.

Peterson let out a low whistle. "Jesus, Ash. If I
hadn't been kind of in on this from the beginning, I'd
think you were nuts."

"That's why I don't want to involve the whole task
force. I've got to accumulate more evidence against
Sloane. And I need a couple of days, probably Monday and Tuesday, to stay with Jillian and make absolutely sure she's all right."

"What about her therapy sessions? *Damn!* I can't
believe this!"

"I know. You and me both. But we caught a lucky
break there. She had a message on her answering machine that the good doctor is canceling all sessions this
week. Naturally, that makes me nervous on another
count. I can't tie up the whole task force doing surveil-
lance, though, not yet, and I can't ask for it from the
PD until I've built a stronger case against Sloane."

"Gotcha. Whatd'ya want me to do?"

"I'd like you to do some background checking on
Sloane. Not just possible criminal record, but I want
to know who his parents were, where he's from, where
he went to school—whatever you can find out."

"I can do some of that right here at home, online."

"Okay. And I need the info as quick as you can get
it, my friend. Every time Jillian takes a dose of those
poison pills, she gets less of the bad stuff. I'll have her
on placebos by tomorrow night. That should mean
that her mind will be back to its old ornery self, and
when I tell her what I know, the shit's going to hit
the fan. I mean, geez, *think* about it. Not only is
Sloane her trusted therapist, but she herself has been
providing him with information that has possibly
caused the deaths of several innocent people. Hell,
she'll probably need more therapy just to deal with
that." He sighed.

"You've really been through it, haven't you?"
asked Peterson.

"You don't know the half of it." He rubbed his eyes. "In the meantime, I want you to tell the task force that I've been called away on a family emergency. Tell them I'm looking at Sloane only because of the connection between the two college kid victims, but that we're nowhere near ready to bring him in for questioning or approach him in any way."

"You got it."

"So just have them work the college angle for now. I just found out that the second summer session is over and most of the professors are out on vacation, so see if they can track them down and find out anything useful on Sloane that we can use. I also want a complete class schedule and office hour schedule for Sloane going back to the spring semester."

"Right."

"Tell them he's on vacation this week and is out of his clinical practice office, so we will postpone looking into that for now. Anyway, that should be enough to keep Kathy and Sal busy for a couple of days until I get back."

"And Washington?"

"Have Washington put together an analysis of all the fires we suspect of being the work of the Firebrand and see if he can make any other connections to Sloane."

"Okay. And me?"

"You I want to stay loose in case I need you. Just keep working on that background check and stay close to the phone."

"Ten-four. That it?"

"For now."

"I don't know about you, but I smell blood," said Peterson with a note of glee in his voice.

Ash grinned. "Don't jinx it," he said.

His mind and heart were calm and steady when he slipped into the house in the usual way, stopping just inside the door to allow his eyes to adjust to the darkness and refamiliarize himself with the layout.

The Beast was in him and would soon come roaring to life.

Moving stealthily, he crept from the back door down the hallway toward the bedroom at the far right. Stopped. Listened to the deep, even breathing. Heard the slow thudding of his own heart.

The heart of the Beast.

A shaft of moonlight shone through a slit in the blinds and outlined her face. She was quite beautiful. For a long moment he stood next to her bed, looking down at her.

Then he lifted the crowbar over his head.

"Mommy?"

He froze.

A child! There wasn't supposed to be a child! Where had the child come from?

He whirled toward the doorway, where a little boy about two or three years of age stood in footed jammies, looking for all the world like a small Ian.

The boy smiled at him.

Behind him, he heard a stirring.

"Tommy? What—oh, my God!"

He fled.

Leapt right over the child and flew out of the house, where he bounded over the back fence and vanished into the night.

The drive home was a nightmarish film noir of neon and traffic lights and panic. He hurried into the house and went around lighting candles with shaking hands. No longer able to stand artificial lighting, he'd stopped using lamps altogether. To cut out the annoying daytime glare of the sun, he'd installed dark window shades in all the rooms and lit candles then, too. Firelight was all he needed or wanted.

With shaking hands, he tried to bring the fire to life in the fireplace, but it was stubbornly resistant, which was its habit whenever he had screwed up.

He had failed the Beast, and now he was being punished!

With a cry of anguish, he curled up in the fetal position on the rug in front of the cold fireplace and shivered, rocking himself.

The deadness spread like a bloody stain, first from a dark secret corner of his mind, growing until he felt almost entirely consumed by it.

He couldn't breathe! He was suffocating!

The blackness was everywhere around him and inside him, and it pressed against the inside of his skin. He could feel it eating him. It was eating his soul and his body, and soon there would be nothing left of him. He would be nothing more than a black gorge in the throat of the deadness.

"I'm sorry!" he wept. "There was a child! There wasn't supposed to be a child! I didn't know what to do! Forgive me!"

Still trembling and weeping, he tossed wads of newspaper into the fireplace and turned on two lighters at once.

Slowly, the corners of the papers caught the flames and curled darkly into themselves.

Sometimes the fire would hide from him, tormenting him, but then it spread, reached the wood chips and the logs, and bellowed to full life, sending dangerous sparks flying around him where he sat, laughing and crying and praying that the whole house would burn down around him and he could become one with the Beast at last, defeating the deadness forevermore.

The Beast spoke.

You must redeem yourself.

"I know, I know," he blubbered. "I will. Anything. I'll do anything."

The girl.

"Which girl?" But he knew.

The girl with the hair of fire.

"Yes. You want me to burn her? I'll burn her."

There is a plan. But first, you must be calm.

"Okay, okay."

Listen to me, and I will command you.

With great effort, he quieted himself. At last he was able to breathe again, and he filled his lungs with great gulps of hot singed air.

And then he awaited instructions from the Beast.

When Monday rolled around, Jillian had lost a day somewhere and believed it was Sunday. She was not surprised when Ash hung around all day. She welcomed his presence, in fact, because he was normally such a workaholic. By Monday afternoon her headache was gone, and she was feeling so much better that they made slow, sweet, passionate, love.

She asked how the investigation was going, but he was noncommittal, which was odd, since he usually discussed it with her at length, hoping the two of them could brainstorm ideas. She missed that. She asked if the *Mirror* article had brought in any promising leads, and he said a few, but that he had not checked them all out.

By Monday evening she was growing restless and annoyed with Ash, and told him so. "What's going on?" she asked.

"C'mere." She followed him into the kitchen. Opening the kitchen cabinet, he took down the bottle of Xonok, shook the rest of the pills into the palm of his hand and said, "Here. Take 'em all."

She stared at him. "Have you lost your mind? I don't want to kill myself."

"My point exactly," he said, and to her horror, he dumped the entire lot into his mouth and swallowed them with a glass of water.

"Oh, God," she screamed. "Ash! What are you doing?"

He smiled. "Nothing. They're placebos."

"Huh?"

"I filled them all myself with baking soda several days ago."

"What?"

"Here. Sit down." He took her by the hand and led her to the kitchen table, where he sat opposite her, still holding her hand.

"Jillian, when I got here Friday night, you were completely drugged. I looked up the medications you were taking, and not only were you on an exceptionally high prescribed dose, but you had been prescribed three drugs that, when combined, could mimic symptoms of acute mental illness."

She stared at him. "I don't believe you."

"I didn't figure you would." He reached behind him and lugged out a *Physician's Desk Reference*. There were three bookmark tabs poking out. He opened to the first one, where he had highlighted the passage under the drug combination whose commercial name was Xonok. "Read it yourself."

Pulling her hand out of his, she read the three passages. Jillian felt a slow throbbing in her throat. Goose bumps crawled over her body. "I don't understand. What have you done?"

"These are powerful narcotics. I couldn't take the chance of sending you into some sort of withdrawal crash, so I cut the dose of the capsules with baking soda. Each day I added more baking soda. That's all they are now."

"But . . . Dr. Sloane . . ."

"Is the Firebrand arsonist, darlin'."

"No." She got to her feet. "You're crazy! Dr. Sloane has been a big help to me! You had no right to interfere—"

"*No right?*" he thundered. "I saved your goddamned life, Jillian! Tell me I had no right to do that!"

"Just because my body reacted badly to these drugs does not mean that Dr. Sloane was trying to hurt me!" she yelled, storming out of the kitchen and into the living room. "I haven't even seen him in . . . a while. How could you possibly accuse him of such a terrible thing!"

Ash ran after her, grabbed her by the arms, and turned her around to face him. *"Think about it, Jilly,"* he said. "You were doing fine. You were even recuperating from the trauma of the riot. And then he prescribed Xonok. After that you started to get confused, didn't you? Brain-fogged. It was hard to work. Your head started hurting. He increased the dosage. You started to slur your speech. Your memory was shot. Then he prescribed this other stuff, and the next thing you knew, you were blitzed out of your mind!"

Stubbornly, she shook her head. It's not that he was not right; it was just that she couldn't bring herself to admit it yet.

"Two of the victims were students, Jillian. Students of Dr. Sloane's."

"What do you mean?" This was too much to handle. She felt herself beginning to tremble.

"He teaches at a small community college. Beginning psych courses. Scott Lancaster, the student I told you about? He had Sloane for a professor. Remember the girl who was bludgeoned in her bed first, and then the fire was set?"

Slowly, disbelievingly, Jillian nodded.

"She went to the same school. Had Sloane for Psych 101."

He squeezed her arms gently. "I even interviewed him, honey. About five-nine or ten, right? Brown hair, brown eyes. Balding. Thin. Stiff handshake."

"Oh, God." Jillian pulled away from Ash and wandered unseeing across her living room. She felt her knees go weak and stumbled to the sofa. Ash sat next to her and pulled her close.

The truth dawned.

She could see everything as clearly as a movie, running in chronological order: Dr. Sloane staring at her, inhumanly still, with reptilian eyes, encouraging her to work on the fire story with Ash. Dr. Sloane asking for details of the investigation. Dr. Sloane discouraging her from publishing the article. Dr. Sloane prescribing the Xonok.

People dying, while she blithely continued to tell Dr. Sloane everything he needed to do to elude discovery by the very arson investigator who was trying to catch him.

She'd told him about crime "signatures," about why some evidence was not burned . . . *specifics* about the investigation into the crimes *he was committing*.

And she, Jillian Ross, had made his job that much easier. Because of her, because of her big mouth and her stupidity . . . innocent people were dead.

"Ash . . ." She pulled away from him and buried her face in the sofa cushions, hot shame washing over her in torrents as the blood drained from her face.

He rubbed her back. "You didn't know, Jilly. He was a master manipulator. He fooled us all—me included."

She couldn't even cry. Couldn't speak. It was too much.

"I screwed up, too, darlin'. I interviewed him. I knew he had the same name as your shrink—I even asked him about it! And when he lied to me, I bought it."

She looked up at him.

"So he fooled me, too. And I had a lot less reason to be fooled than you did."

Gazing across the room, she shook her head. "I can't believe it."

"Look at it this way, babe. Hey, c'mere." He pulled her up and took her into his arms. "If the son of a bitch hadn't gotten carried away in his little mind-control game and drugged you to oblivion, we might never have known. He just drew attention to himself. Now we know who to look at and what to do. We'll catch him."

She shook her head against his chest. Her voice muffled, she said, "No, you won't. I did my homework, Ash. Seven out of ten arson cases never get convic-

tions in a court of law. It's too hard to prove. Unless
you catch him in the act, you will never catch him."

"Sure we will. It's just a matter of time." But she
heard a twinge of doubt in his voice.

The idea, when it came, came with such force of
conviction that the decision came right along with it.
Jillian suddenly pulled away from Ash's chest and
looked deep into his eyes. "I know how we can catch
him," she said.

His eyes narrowed. "What do you mean, *we*?"

"You need me to do it."

"Wait a minute—"

She put her fingers to his lips to silence his protest.
"Listen to me. Sloane still thinks I'm drugged, right?
He has no reason not to."

After a moment Ash nodded.

"Therefore, he thinks I'm still in his control."

She saw the light of recognition come into his eyes.

"So why don't I play him? Like a sting? I go in
for one of my regular sessions, and I slur my speech
and talk gibberish, but somewhere in all that, he
manages to elicit some more information about the
investigation."

"You mean *mis*information," said Ash. "Something planted."

"And using that information, we set him up, and
you really *do* catch him in the act." The more she
thought about it, the more excited she got.

"It's too dangerous," said Ash. "We have no way
of knowing what this guy may do. He's a very clever
and cunning killer, Jillian." He touched her cheek. "I
don't want him to hurt you."

"So wire me," she said. "Do whatever it takes. Wait
outside with the SWAT team, I don't care. You gotta
let me do this, Ash," she pleaded. "It's the only way
I'll ever be able to redeem myself."

Chapter Twenty-Five

Her doors had dead bolts on them.

Even worse, he found that she never left her windows open, not even on the hottest nights. At first he thought he might have gotten a break when he noticed that her place was not centrally air-conditioned. He expected to be able to gain entrance through the windows, which contained air-conditioning window units. But he found to his chagrin that they were sealed up tight. If he entered there, he would make a great deal of noise.

She never left her doors unlocked, not even for a quick trip to the market.

If he didn't know better, he might suspect that she was getting paranoid.

He'd thought the drugs might render her stupid enough to make a careless mistake, but that evil arson investigator kept sniffing around her like a dog in heat.

This was not good.

The guy might start asking questions again.

He itched to burn her, to bring her life to a fiery end. He longed to stand alone in her darkened bedroom and watch her sleep before . . .

But what could he do? He was no lock picker.

He considered surprising her during the day, perhaps sneaking up on her as she was carrying in groceries or laundry, but he was too frightened of witnesses who might spot him, who could then recognize him or help a police artist draw his likeness.

His frustration grew.

The Beast was not happy! The arson investigator was a wicked adversary, and this woman, with her newspaper articles and her sneaky refusal to follow his instructions . . . they needed to be ·stopped!

And then one night, while performing the ritual, the answer came to him, brilliant in its simplicity.

The Beast was perfectly capable of taking care of them both, at the same time!

And *both* Keegans could get clean away with it.

He couldn't wait to get started.

Sam Peterson had good news for Ash.

"Here's the bio as best I can figure it out," he said when they spoke on the phone late that Monday night. Ash could hear him consulting his notebook. "Okay. He came from New York. His dad was a fireman for the Fire Department of New York."

"Perfect," interrupted Ash. "Many arsonists have some background in fire fighting."

"From what I can gather from various sources, his old man let Keegan ride along on the fire truck to some fires. Back then there were a lot of empty-building fires in the Bronx. People trying to trash the building so they could sell it to investors who were willing to pay big bucks just to get the site."

"Right."

"All was hunky-dory until his dad abandoned the family when Keegan was about twelve. He was left with his mom, who was an alcoholic."

Ash whistled. "Where'd you find out all this stuff?"

"Hey, I'm just that good."

Ash grinned.

"He's been like, mediocre his whole life. Attended mid-level universities—nothin' Ivy League or anything. Middle of his class in medical school. I was able to track down some articles he'd done for professional journals, but they were obscure. Didn't make any kind of stir. I read the damn things. Boring as shit."

"Like the man himself, no doubt."

"He's married, got one kid, a boy named Ian who is twelve. And get this—shit—"

Ash heard the clang of a dropped phone.

"Sorry. Okay. His wife is a schoolteacher. Couple of weeks ago, she bailed out. Took the kid and headed for Boston."

"No kidding."

"That's bad, huh."

"Yeah, it's bad." They both knew that a precipitating event such as the walkout of a spouse could often push a violent criminal over the edge and set off an unprecedented act of some kind—murder of the offending relative followed by suicide, or a public shooting. Not good.

"Connections," continued Peterson. "You want connections? How about the fact that the Safeway where Dixie Balboa works is very close to the guy's house?"

"No shit?"

"It gets better. Remember that woman you told me about? The one in the suburb you went to see about, where the investigator figured the cause was spontaneous combustion?"

Ash felt his heart quicken. "Yes."

"Well, she was one of his patients."

"Jesus Christ!" cried Ash. "You gotta be *kidding*!"

Peterson chuckled. "Once the investigator signed off on that bogus cause, nobody looked into her private life."

"Wow." Ash pondered this latest development.

"There's no connection, per se, with Cricket Andrews."

"I hate people who say *per se,"* teased Ash.

"Yeah? Well, screw your vacationing ass."

They laughed. Both men were feeling the tension of a tightening criminal investigation.

"So anyway. The only connection we can see is the one with your girlfriend. At least it's the one I see. I didn't mention her to the ATF guy."

"Thanks."

"Only other connections are the two college kids. There's no connection we can find with either the homeless man or the warehouse security guard or any of the other victims, but we're still digging."

Ash was quiet. "I wish to God I could figure out *why*," he mused.

"Well, gee, boss, that's pretty easy, isn't it? You got yourself one sicko shrink."

"Yeah, true. But there must be some reason he selects each victim. Some are men, some are women, some are young, some older—it doesn't make sense. Most serial killers prefer choosing the same general type of victim."

"But this guy ain't your typical serial killer."

"True." Ash chewed on the inside of his cheek.

"How's Jillian?" asked Peterson. "I been worried about her."

"Oh! Thanks, Sam. She's great, actually. She knows everything now."

"Got the drugs out of her system?"

"Finally, yes. And we've figured out a way we can use her."

"Uh-oh. I don't like the sound of that."

Ash smiled. "Wait until I show up at the task force meeting tomorrow morning. Jillian's coming with me. She'll tell you herself. Then you'll *really* be happy."

Peterson groaned, but as far as Ash could tell, it was a pleased groan. He hung up feeling better than he had in a long time.

Then he felt and heard the explosion.

Jillian was in the kitchen when the explosion hit. It seemed to move the walls, hurling her to the floor while the compression and noise popped her ears.

Windows rattled. Some cracked and broke. Almost immediately, she smelled something burning.

Ash tore into the kitchen and grabbed Jillian. "Get out!" he yelled. "Now!"

"I've got to get my computer disks—"

But he had her by the wrist, dragging her toward the door that led to the garage. He placed his hand on the door. "It's hot," he said. "I thought so. It happened in the garage." Thick black smoke began seeping under the door.

Still holding her arm, Ash raced into the living room and out the front door, speed-dialing 911 on his cell phone as they went. They stood in the front yard. While Ash barked orders into the phone, Jillian could see smoke pouring out of the tiny window on the side of the one-car garage, and as she watched, flames snaked out over the roof.

Everything Jillian owned was in that house, and she suddenly realized she didn't have fire insurance on its contents. Shock and horror rendered her speechless.

"Here, sit down," said Ash, giving her an easy tug. She sank down into the grass, and he knelt next to her, holding her tightly. She clung to him and fought the urge to faint.

The garage was fully engulfed, and the kitchen roof had begun to burn by the time firefighters arrived. They got there very quickly—less than five minutes. Ash led her to the truck, where one of the firefighters sat her down and fitted her with an oxygen mask. Ash showed the captain his badge and immediately took over the scene as an arson investigator, hovering in the background while the firefighters rapidly brought the blaze under control and eventually put it out.

They reported that the explosion appeared to have originated with the car, which was completely totaled, as was the garage. Most of the kitchen damage was due more to smoke and water than from the fire itself, and the rest of the house was mercifully spared. Ash moved in then to ensure that the overhauling operation did not destroy all available evidence. Jillian could hear him talking on the phone to someone named Moses. By this time, the situation had become a blur of unreality to Jillian.

This couldn't be happening, and yet it was. While the firefighters bustled around, tending to their jobs, Jillian sat in a small oasis of disbelief.

What were the odds of surviving a violent riot and an explosion all in one summer? Oh—and a near drug overdose. Were the odds catching up to her? Would her luck finally run out next time?

The what-ifs were terrifying. What if she had been in the garage at the time of the explosion? What if Ash hadn't been with her? Would she have flung open the door leading to the garage and incinerated herself?

What the hell *happened*?

The Saturn had been a perfectly dependable car. Jillian could not imagine why it would have suddenly exploded without so much as a key being turned in the ignition.

Well, she could, actually, but she was not ready to face it.

She found herself shivering in the hot, sweaty August night air.

Ash deposited her in the front seat of his car while he went around to the trunk and withdrew coveralls and heavy boots.

"You're going to start investigating *now*?" she cried. "The fire trucks haven't even left yet!" Fear and shock were making Jillian irritable and jumpy.

"It's the best time to find evidence and discover the point of origin. Moses Washington is on his way to help."

"Who's that?"

"Don't you remember? I told you. He's the ATF specialist who is helping us on the Firebrand Task Force."

"Oh." She did remember now. Whether she'd forgotten because of aftereffects of the drugs or from the stress of the evening, Jillian didn't know. All she wanted to do right now was cry. Take a long hot bath and cry.

"You can go into the house now, ma'am, if you like," said one of the firefighters gently. "The kitchen's a mess, but there's no reason why you can't sleep in your own bed tonight."

"Thank you," she said over the lump in her throat. She struggled to her feet and forced herself to go around and thank them for all they'd done.

"Thank you for saving my house," she said each and every time. The men and women all beamed, clearly pleased, and offered reassuring words to Jillian about the fire damage. They were all very kind, and they all made her want to cry.

Finally, she worked up the courage to enter the house.

Actually, she reflected, it could be a lot worse. Car insurance would replace the automobile, and the building's owner would take care of structural repairs. Her sentimental belongings, clothes, and computer equipment had all been spared. Most of the smoke damage had been confined to the kitchen, so her television and other expensive electronic equipment had also survived.

Still, the house reeked of smoke. It smelled as if the house was still burning.

It was spooky.

The kitchen was flooded with water. Things on the countertops and table had been knocked asunder and broken. Sooty walls and ceiling dripped black, nasty water. She opened the refrigerator door. It was working fine, clean and cool inside.

But the room smelled of fire.

The door leading to the garage yawned open. Finally, Jillian permitted herself to stand in the doorway and gaze upon the holocaust. Her shining green Saturn was a black, gutted, smoking wreck. The charred ceiling had not burned through, but firefighters had chopped through it with axes to make sure no remnants of fire hid in the space between the ceiling and roof. Her boxes of Christmas decorations were burned to a miserable pulp, as was her luggage, a few tools, and some other things she had stored in the small space.

The garage door had been removed and tossed out to one side, and in the glow of bright flashlights, Ash stood in front of the burned car with a handsome black man Jillian did not know. She coughed and then sneezed.

"Yeah, there's no way this could be accidental," Ash was saying. He glanced up. "How ya doin'?" he asked.

"It could be worse," she said with a bravery she didn't yet feel.

He gestured toward his friend. "Jillian, I'd like you to meet Moses Washington, from the ATF. Moses, this is Jillian Ross."

Moses nodded at Jillian. "I'm real sorry about this," he said. "I read your piece on the Firebrand investigation in the *Mirror*." He smiled. "I must say I was pleasantly surprised. You did a real good job."

She returned the smile. "Well, when you're sleeping with the arson investigator . . ."

He threw back his head and guffawed. "Now, I wasn't going to say that!"

"Who did this?" she asked. "What did they do?"

"Well, it's early yet, but from what I can tell so far, it doesn't look like this was a high-yield explosion. Obviously low-yield."

"I'm sorry?"

He gestured with his hands. "If you have some kind of device or, say, dynamite, you get what's called a high-yield explosion. That's the kind that blows out windows, shatters things, see. It may not even produce a fire. The explosion itself does the damage."

"Right."

"But if you have some kind of accelerant and it's

ignited, especially in an enclosed space like a garage, you might have what's called a low-yield explosion. The ignition causes a fireball that might just scorch and char the surroundings, but if there are combustibles nearby—like those boxes over there—then the fireball itself will cause the fire. The more combustibles or accelerants you have nearby, the worse the fire and the faster it spreads. Lucky for you, you kept a neat garage, or the damage to the rest of the house might have been far more extensive."

She nodded.

"Keeping the door closed to the kitchen helped with smoke damage, too, since the fire itself was primarily limited to the garage."

"Right." She glanced at Ash.

"Ash says the windows didn't shatter, but the walls appeared to move. That would also be in keeping with a low-yield explosion."

Moses squatted in front of the wreckage and picked up a piece of brown glass with bubble marks on it. Shining the flashlight on it, he said, "We've got a lot more to do here, and of course lab work, but if you want my best guesstimate, I'd say somebody put a soap cocktail under the car with a detanotor cord leading out of the garage, maybe under the door. The arsonist may have even cut the car's fuel lines to cause a gasoline leak. We'll know more when we've had a chance to examine the vehicle. Anyway, once he had the setup, he got the hell out of the room and lit the det cord. By the time the fireball went up, he was long gone."

Jillian frowned. "What's a soap cocktail?"

"Kind of like a Molotov cocktail, only made with powdered non-detergent soap mixed with gasoline."

"Goddamn it," she said. "Goddamn it all to hell!" Rage, not just at the fire, but at every out-of-control element of her life, swept over her with hot, burning intensity.

She'd never known anything like the emotion that

possessed her at that moment. It was a white-hot heat that encompassed Randi's death, Jillian's mind manipulation and drugging at the hands of a killer, the near-loss of her home, all the senseless deaths at the hands of the Firebrand—it was all there, consuming her as fiercely as the fireball that had destroyed her car.

But she was damned if she was going to let it destroy *her*.

Moses blew out a lungful of air and said nothing.

Heedless of the black, stinking mess, Jillian stepped into the garage.

Ash gestured at her. "I hate to say this, Jilly, but this *is* a crime scene. I can't have you stomping all over it."

She turned a grim face toward the two men and said, "I'm not stomping all over anything, Ash."

"Well . . . what the hell are you doing?"

Placing her hands on her hips, Jillian felt her eyes blazing as she stood tall, lifted her chin, and said, "What do you think I'm doing? The same thing you should be. I'm looking for cinnamon."

Chapter Twenty-Six

They didn't find any cinnamon.

Not that night, and not the next day when Ash and Moses continued to work the investigation, joined by other members of the task force. During a lunch break, they ordered pizza and sat around Jillian's living room while she and Ash and Sam Peterson briefed the task force on Dr. Keegan Sloane.

Everyone's biggest concern was that if the Firebrand had tried to burn down Jillian's house, he had changed his M.O. in a significant way—by using an obvious accelerant readily recognizable to arson investigators. Even worse, he hadn't left his key signature—the cinnamon pile.

Did that mean he knew they were on to the cinnamon and was trying to throw them off the trail? Jillian swore that she had never mentioned the cinnamon in any of her sessions with Dr. Sloane.

Could it mean he had thought of eliminating the cinnamon on his own, knowing it would throw off investigators? How could he possibly know that they had even discovered the spice?

Or could someone else altogether have set the fire, and if so, who and why?

As they brainstormed ideas, the house still smelled of smoke. Not a single member of the arson task force seemed to notice it, but it bothered Jillian a great deal.

At one point she overheard Ash making her a hotel reservation.

"What are you doing?" she asked.

"I'm getting you a room. You'll feel safer and will probably sleep better."

"No."

"Jillian—"

Stubbornly, she shook her head. "I refuse to let this bastard win."

"Jilly, it's not a contest—"

"I don't care. If I let him scare me away from my own home, he wins. And I refuse." The emotion behind the words surprised Jillian. She found herself trembling from head to foot.

Ash's expression softened. He touched her cheek. "Okay, kid," he said.

Ash had been right about one thing, though. She couldn't sleep, and when she did, she had nightmares about being trapped in a burning room. The good news, she thought wryly, was that she no longer had nightmares about Randi.

Ash tried to get her to come and stay with him, but she was still unwilling to leave her home. She had a deep-seated fear that the Firebrand would return in the dark of night and finish the job.

This was no particular comfort to Ash, who certainly didn't want her there alone if the guy *did* come back. Finally, he compromised by moving some of his things into her house. Jillian expected to feel crowded—after all, she'd lived alone for a long time, not counting the brief fiasco with Derek—but she found that it actually felt natural having Ash there. He filled up spaces as only a man could. Jillian decided that was a good thing. She was tired of those spaces feeling so empty.

While workmen rebuilt the garage, Jillian worked vigorously to restore the kitchen. The manual labor was therapeutic and helped her feel more in control, but as night settled over the city, she knew it was only an illusion. As tired as she was, she still had trouble getting to sleep.

She'd stare into the shadows and think about fire.

One night a few days after the explosion, Jillian found herself, as usual, wide awake while Ash slept deeply next to her. After a futile hour or two of tossing and turning, Jillian got out of bed and padded into the living room, turning on only a single lamp so that the light would not disturb Ash. She knew he felt responsible because the Firebrand still danced on hot coals, just out of their reach. The exhaustion and stress were beginning to take their toll.

Jillian sat down at the computer, dialed up the modem, and logged onto the Internet, where she called up one of its largest search engines. She tried several key words, like *cinnamon* and *fire*, but the results were unsatisfactory. The truth of the matter was that a pile of cinnamon left at the site of an arson fire was so incongruous as to make it impossible to find a connection of any kind.

Frustrated, she sat staring blindly at the computer screen and forced herself to slow down, to *think*— even to put herself in the arsonist's shoes. What was he doing? He was murdering people in their own beds and burning their homes down around them.

Burglary had long since been ruled out as a motive, or insurance fraud, or monetary gain, or any of the other reasons some arsonists used as excuses for their destructive behavior. That he was a pyromaniac was a given—

She typed in *pyromaniac*.

The information she turned up was educational and interesting to Jillian, but again, she could find no reference to *cinnamon*.

Okay. *Think*. He built the weird cinnamon piles before he set the fires. It had become a ritual with him. *Ritual*.

She tried that avenue of investigation for a while,

and it gave her some more ideas, until finally it occurred to Jillian to try *mythology.*

And from there . . . *phoenix.*

Bingo.

"Ash!" She leapt to her feet. *"Ash!"* she yelled,
yanking a sheet of information out of the printer and
heading toward the bedroom.

Ash came dodging into the living room wearing
nothing but his underwear and carrying his gun.
They collided.

Jillian took one look at his sleep-interrupted face,
his hair spiking out in all directions. He was practically
naked, brandishing his big gun.

She collapsed onto the floor in a gale of giggles.

"What?" he said sternly. "What the hell is going
on?"

"I just found out something exciting on the Internet
and wanted to show it to you."

"You scared the shit out of me for *that*?" he demanded. "Dammit, Jillian, I ought to shoot *you.*"

"My hero." She laughed out loud.

He made mock motions of beating her, then laid the
gun down carefully and plunked down on the couch,
rubbing his eyes. "So go ahead. Talk. Just wake me
up when you're done." He laid his head on the back
of the sofa and closed his eyes.

"Well, never mind, then. I don't want to deprive
you of badly needed beauty sleep, but I thought you
might want to know why the Firebrand is leaving cinnamon behind when he sets his fires."

He opened one eye. "Ya got me. So talk before I
really *do* beat you."

She grinned and cuddled up next to him. "You're
cute, sitting there in your little panties."

He groaned and closed both eyes again.

"Okay, okay. It has to do with the mythology of
the phoenix."

"The bird that rises from fire."

"Right. But the legend is a bit more detailed, and

there are several versions of it around the world, including the Assyrian." She snuggled closer. "After the bird has lived 500 years, it builds itself a nest, using certain materials. Once these materials are piled up nice and soft, it deposits itself in the nest."

"What kind of materials?" he asked drowsily, his eyes still closed.

"Ancient perfumes, like spikenard . . . and myrrh . . . and *cinnamon.*"

He opened his eyes.

She grinned. "The phoenix does not build this nest until it is dying. While it is breathing its dying breath, it's surrounded by all these sweet, spicy aromas. Then, from the body of the dead parent bird, a young phoenix issues forth."

"So the phoenix gives birth to itself," he guessed.

"In a sort of rebirth, yeah," she said with a nod. "Then, when the bird has gained sufficient strength, it lifts its nest from the tree—the nest, you see, is its own cradle *and* the sepulcher of the dead parent phoenix—and the bird then carries the nest and delivers it to the temple of the sun."

"Wow." Ash was fully awake now.

"Yeah. Wow."

"So the Firebrand pictures himself as a phoenix rising from the ashes?"

"Apparently. With new life."

"He dies in the fire," mused Ash. "And is reborn. Huh."

"But that begs the question . . ."

He quirked an eyebrow at her.

"Why do all these *other* people have to die?"

He could not believe that he had failed *again.*

The Beast could not be fooled. His last few ceremonies had gone badly, and this worried him. He had offended the Beast.

Sitting on the rug in front of the fire, he would beg the Beast's forgiveness for his failure and gaze up at the wall, where the chimera blinked at him in the light of the mantel candles. Something about it looked . . . menacing. Evil.

Of course! That was it!

The Beast knew he had done his best with the explosion, but the Beast had not been pleased by his clumsy attempts to render its likeness. The Beast was not a chimera, after all, because a chimera was a bizarre, two-headed creature, an ugly thing with a lizard's tail.

What had he been *thinking*?

The Beast was beautiful. Glorious. Empowered. Potent. Filled with a sunburst of life.

A phoenix, then, not a dumb chimera.

How stupid he'd been! No wonder his recent attempts to enact the ceremony had failed. What good was a sweet nest of cinnamon for a gargoyle like the chimera?

Dogged by an increasing sense of urgency, he sped to the nearest hardware store, where he bought a couple of gallons of white paint and a roller. They did not match his wall paint exactly, but he couldn't care less. He had to get rid of those ugly creatures right away.

Slopping paint in a frenzy, almost afraid that if he took too long, something awful might happen, he slathered over every one of his chimera paintings. Then, muscles aching, he fell into a deep, trancelike peace for the first time in days. He knew he'd done the right thing.

But there was still so much to be done!

When the paint had dried, he made a quick trip to the college and smuggled home an overhead projector. What an idiot he'd been not to think of that before. Opaque projector, indeed. What an old fart he was getting to be.

Working as rapidly as he could, he hurried to render on his walls a likeness of the most beautiful phoenix he could find in his books. His hands were shaking.

He was so impatient. There was much to be done, and he didn't want to botch the job. Finally, infuriated with his awkward efforts, he shoved the overhead projector out of the way, drove back to the hardware store, and bought up as many colorful cans of spray paint as he could carry.

It was the *power* that counted, not the artistic merit!

This time he used a ladder. Working in a furious fever of bold strokes, he filled the entire wall with a masterwork: the phoenix rising from the fireplace in all its blazing magnificence, backlit by towering flames.

It was resplendent!

He could feel the Beast struggling in its restraints, eager to come to life. But he had to wait a few minutes for the vapors to dissipate. The Beast could be naughty, he knew. It would be too powerful a temptation to resist the easy lure of those flammable vapors.

Soon, he promised. Not yet.

Finally, he was able to close windows and doors, darken the rooms, and light the fire.

It came roaring to instant life without the slightest sputter.

I am well pleased! shouted the Beast. *You will be rewarded with a second chance.*

He knelt before the shrine of the Beast and bowed his head.

Soon. It would happen very soon.

He hoped he would be able to wait that long.

Ash threw Sal Garcia a bone and decided to take him along when he presented the case they'd built so far on Keegan Sloane to Chief Dixon. Guy might be a prick, but that didn't prevent him from being a hell of a good arson investigator, with a better-than-average clearance and conviction rate on his cases.

They laid out all the information they'd gathered so far on Sloane: his boyhood experiences with his firefighting father, his connection to several of the victims, his manipulation of Jillian, the information they'd found on the Internet about the phoenix legend—even a comment from one of his students that he seemed fascinated by fire.

Dixon listened carefully, then said, "So what do you need?"

"I need permission to approach a judge about a search warrant on Sloane. We want to search his house and both of his offices for evidence that might directly connect him with any one of the fires," said Ash. "Also, the case on the explosion at Jillian's home is still open. In spite of the absence of cinnamon, it would fit his M.O. to try something completely different."

Dixon nodded.

"And I want to bring him in for questioning."

Dixon looked dubious. "Have you checked out where he might have been at the times the fires were set?"

"They were all late at night," pointed out Sal. "He'll just say he was home in bed with his wife. And she's in Boston. Unless you want to fly us up there to question her."

"Even if we tracked her down up there," added Ash, "she would probably say the same thing. Guy's too crafty and devious to give any indication to his wife as to his extracurricular nocturnal activities. He probably snuck out of the house after she was already asleep. She probably never knew a thing."

"We'll wait until we're building a case for court," said Dixon, and Ash was hopeful that his deputy chief seemed to think it might go that far.

"What about signs of the fire on his clothes?" asked Dixon.

"Time-delay devices, nearly always," said Ash, beginning to feel queasy. He didn't like the way these questions were leading. "So . . . the search warrant?"

Dixon shook his head. "Too soon, Ash. You can bring him in for questioning if you want, but you won't find a judge anywhere in this city who would sign away a citizen's rights on such flimsy evidence."

"What are you talking about?" cried Ash. "He's connected to so many of the victims—like that woman who was his patient."

"That's not our case. And it's not even our jurisdiction. That fire was ruled accidental. It's got nothing to do with this."

"It's got every damn thing to do with it!" shouted Ash, pounding the chief's desk for emphasis.

"It does not apply here!" yelled the chief, scrambling to his feet to tower over both men. "You know good and goddamned well you've got absolutely *nothing* but a few coincidences! You've got no witnesses, no motive—you don't even have a recognizable M.O. that shows a pattern. *You've got nothing!"*

Ash was not afraid of Dixon, but that made the man no less intimidating when he rose to his full height and expanded his chest like a blowfish. Ash stood his ground, and then from behind him, he heard a weak, "The chief's got a point, man. If we move too soon on Sloane, he could sue the city for millions."

For a long moment Ash said nothing. Then slowly he turned and stared down Garcia like the back-stabbing little prick he was, regretting only that his eyes were not laser beams, capable of burning holes right through the son of a bitch.

Finally, to the chief, he said, "Fine. You need more evidence? I'll get you more evidence."

He turned on his heel and strode out of the office.

They hadn't gotten around to getting Ash his own key yet, so he had developed a secret knock to let Jillian know when it was him at the door. Still, she was surprised when the knock came at the new door leading to the partially repaired garage. When she opened the door, he was standing there in the dark with his back turned to her. With some difficulty, he seemed to be holding something in his arms.

"Well, aren't you going to come in?" she said.

Suddenly, with a sheepish boy-grin on his face, he turned around. In his arms was a brown-eyed, flop-eared, fluff-faced, tail-wagging dog about the size of a Border collie but resembling a German shepherd.

"Oh!" she cried, reaching out instinctively to pet the dog. She knew to let him sniff the back of her hand first, which he immediately licked, and then she was a goner. She fondled his silky ears with delight. "What have you done?"

"Rescued him from the jaws of certain death at the local pound," said Ash. He came into the kitchen and set the dog on the floor, where he wagged his tail so hard it made his butt wiggle.

"He's a mutt, but just look at how smart he is." Ash made a kissing sound to get the dog's attention, then said, "Sit." The dog sat. "Lie down." The dog obeyed. Ash glanced up at her. "That's all he knows for now, but we're working on it." He squatted down, dug a treat from his pocket, which he fed the animal, and stroked the dog's head.

"He's beautiful," said Jillian. "Even if he is a mutt."

"He's got some collie in him, I'd wager," said Ash. "And obviously some shepherd. I can't believe anybody would turn out a dog like this. They said they thought maybe he'd been abused. If you raise your voice to him, he cowers in terror."

She knelt on the other side of the animal. "Do you think he's house trained?"

"We'll soon find out," said Ash with a sideways grin.

She smiled at him. "What on earth possessed you?"

He shrugged. "You needed somebody to keep you company when I wasn't here, and I needed someone to help take care of you when I had to be gone."

"Oh, really? You think I need taking care of?"

"Probably more than he does."

She rolled her eyes. "One wonders how I did manage to survive all those years before you came along."

He held up a finger. "Ah, but see? That's the difference. Before, you were surviving. Now you're living."

She gazed into his eyes for a moment, then impulsively leaned over the dog's head and kissed him. The dog poked his nose in the middle and licked both their chins. They laughed.

And Jillian realized, in that moment, what happiness was.

They continued to sit on the floor for a while, playing with the dog and arguing amiably about names. Ash insisted that when a fire guy got a dog, the dog immediately became a fire dog and therefore needed a name befitting that lofty station in life.

Jillian protested that the dog was a gift to her and therefore should be called something like, "Shakespeare."

Eventually they settled on "Smokey." Jillian had to admit that, grinning up at them with one ear lopped over, he didn't look much like a Shakespeare. And watching Ash with the dog, she had to wonder if he'd really gotten the dog for her.

To her surprise, Ash agreed to use Jillian's help in setting a trap for Sloane, and they spent some time working out the details.

Then they spent a quiet evening listening to music, drinking a bottle of wine, making a simple supper, and discovering Smokey's innate talent for begging. They laughed a lot, in spite of the circumstances, the way they always had, and Jillian felt a comfort in Ash's presence that she had never felt with anyone. He was, after all, her best friend.

She knew, then, that her restless, drifting days were over. He didn't have to propose for her to know that they would be together for the rest of their lives. That knowledge infused her with a strength she'd never known. It was as if she'd been slogging her way through a swamp, struggling not to sink into a bog, and now stood on a rock-solid foundation.

She could run now. Hell, she could fly.

Ash fell asleep on the couch, Smokey curled up at his feet. Jillian sat for a long time, watching them, admiring Ash's careworn face, his strong hands, his lean body. She had known his tenderness and she had known his strength, and she was blessed.

Compelled to get up out of her chair, she crossed to the computer, opened a new document, and began to write. She wrote because writing, to Jillian, was the measure of her life, the rhythmic meter of her existence that made poetry of the events of her days. Some were comic limericks, some dry doggerel, some tragic odes, some heroic epics, some free verse . . . and some even danced across the page like a sonnet.

In recent months, most of those pages had been blank. Her life had been absent the music of language, the structure of form and content. She had stared into those blank pages and seen only emptiness. In her mind, she flipped back through some of the pages of even six months ago, and the verse, in comparison, seemed childish and clumsy.

She began to write:

> *This thing called "life" is funny. Our heart pumps without prompting, sending pulse beats of life blood through our veins; and little chemical reactions in our brains send signals to our lungs to expand and contract. And so we go through our days heedless of our breathing, mindless of the miraculous pulse that keeps us alive. We fill our time with busyness and think we know how to live.*
>
> *We construct an apparatus of life, tacking on material possessions for comfort. We seek love in lust. We take our own measure in the eyes of others.*
>
> *We can fool the others, oh, yes. But we cannot fool ourselves.*
>
> *"Vanity, vanity, all is vanity!" cried the ancient scribe in the book of Ecclesiastes. Even then*

*he somehow knew that life, for so many of us, is
an illusion.*

All vanity.

*Like most of us, I was one of the vain. I never
once gave thought to the breathless magic of
life. I made my own false idols to worship: a fast
car, a rich and handsome boyfriend, a high-
energy, well-paying job, reservations at all the
best restaurants.*

*This is not life. It is only a pale imitation of it.
A counterfeit copy that looks so much like the
real thing that it can fool most everyone. It
fooled me.*

*And then that "life" vanished. I had nothing
but my naked soul, and what a weak, shivering
thing it was.*

*The sweet mystery of life, I found, can be dis-
covered in the pulse beats we so often ignore,
overlook, and forget about. The smile in the eyes
of a cherished friend while she is still alive and
vital and full of laughter on a bright sunny day
in May. The truehearted loyalty of a beloved
who means to stay to the end. The shaft of sunlight through the window in the morning as it
glances off a blue vase filled with yellow flowers.
The wine song of making love at the end of a
very bad day, making everything right and good,
after all.*

*The spirit is the music of life, and we are all
connected, not by its melody or lyrics—for
each of us must write our own—but by the
rhythm that pulses through our hearts each and
every day.*

Jillian glanced at the clock and was surprised to find
that several hours had passed. Ash had rolled over on
his side, and Smokey rested with his chin propped on
Ash's leg. Jillian took an afghan her mother had made
many years before and tucked it around them both.

Smokey glanced up, alert to any hint that he may have displeased in some way, and Jillian patted her reassurance.

She went back to the computer, proofed the piece, and e-mailed it under her "Reflections" column byline to Miles. He'd get it first thing in the morning and would have plenty of time to get it into the *Mirror* by the noon deadline. It would be on the streets by tomorrow night.

Stretching and yawning, Jillian turned off the computer. She was pleasantly tired, pleased with herself for a good piece of work. Leaving Ash asleep where he lay, she shuffled off to bed. She would sleep tonight. Tomorrow she would supervise the repairs on the garage and shop for a new car while she awaited the insurance settlement.

It was the day after that worried her. That was the day of her next appointment with Dr. Sloane. She and Ash had some more preparation to do to get the plan ready, but everything hinged on her.

As Jillian floated off on the gentle swells of sleep, it did not once occur to her that she might have just made a crucial mistake.

Chapter Twenty-Seven

It took a few days for him to get everything in order. First, he had to resign from his position at the college. They would still have time to hire someone else before the fall semester got underway.

Letting his assistant go was tougher. She'd been loyal to him and served him well, and he didn't like the idea of overlooking that. He paid her a generous severance package and wrote a glowing letter of recommendation on letterhead stationary in order to enable her to find another job quickly. He also mentioned her to a couple of colleagues in hopes that she might get an assist in that way. She cried the day she left. Even his wife had not cried.

As for his patients, that was the hardest of all. It would have been monstrous of him to leave it up to his assistant to phone them all. He had to do it. He told them he was being forced into early retirement for health reasons and that he regretted he would no longer be able to see them. He referred each one to colleagues he thought best suited to that person's needs. Most of them, he was gratified to learn, seemed dismayed at having to leave him.

It came as such a pleasant surprise, in fact, that he almost had second thoughts about his plan. Almost.

When everything was in order, there were only two things left to do.

One was to provide a distraction for the arson investigator.

The other was to call Jillian Ross and have her come in immediately rather than at their scheduled four p.m. appointment.

It was important that he be in control of every detail.

The phone call from Dr. Sloane caught Jillian by surprise. The plan had been for Ash to come home for lunch. He would give her the final go-ahead to put their scheme in motion and go over her part one last time.

Now she wasn't sure what to do. Dr. Sloane had said he'd been called out of town on a family emergency and the only time he could see her was right away, as soon as she could get to the office.

Jillian tried to track down Ash. Someone at his office told her he'd been called to another explosion. The entire task force had gone out to the scene. She tried calling him on his car phone but received a message that he was out of the area. Finally, she tried the cell phone, but that, too, seemed jinxed.

They'd already been over what Jillian was supposed to do. Now that the drugs were completely out of her system, she knew she could do it. The main concern had been her personal safety.

What if Dr. Sloane was really leaving town? He might vanish, only to show up in some distant part of the country where he could settle down, hang out his shingle, and go about setting fires again. He might kill people and set fires unimpeded for years.

Jillian was used to taking care of herself. She was tired of being an emotional invalid and determined to stop this killer.

Time was running out.

She pulled on a pair of jeans and a T-shirt with a blazer, then thought better of it and changed into a faded, stretched-out sweatshirt. At Ash's suggestion,

she'd gone without washing her hair that entire week
and now she refrained from brushing it. She even back
combed it some. No makeup, of course.

Finally, she scribbled a note to Ash and left it
propped up on the kitchen table. She ruffled Smokey's
fur, patted him, and left.

When she walked into his office, he hardly recog-
nized her. She looked terrible, and when she said,
"Good morning, Dr. Sloane," it came out slurred:
Shloane.

"How are you feeling?" he asked.

"Everythingsh kinda fuzzshy," she said. "But the
headache'sh gone, thank God."

"Good. I thought the new medications might help.
Have you calmed down somewhat?"

She nodded and blinked. "It'sh jusht . . . I'm kinda
shtoopid-headed." She giggled. "I can't sheem to
think shtraight."

"Well, the purpose of the medication is to take you
somewhere above your problems so that your subconscious can be free to work on some of the more difficult breakthroughs without being absorbed with
insignificant side issues."

"Uh-huh."

"So. How are things going with Ash?"

She waved her hand in the air. "He worksh a lot."

"I'm sure the Firebrand investigation takes up a tremendous amount of his time."

She nodded. "He shaysh that the Firebrand is the
shmartesht, mosht cunning torch he'sh ever sheen."

He smiled, pleased in spite of himself. "Really? And
what, exactly, is a torch? Other than the more obvious
definition, of course."

"It'sh what they call arshon—arsh—people who
set firesh."

"I see."

"It'sh real hard to catch one becaush, um, the evidence burnsh up."

"That so?"

"Yeah. The only way they can catch 'em shome-times ish if shomebody tellsh 'em shomethin'."

"Hmm."

"That'sh why he'sh excshited about thish lady, thish cashier lady? She'sh goin' to help 'em."

"What cashier lady?"

"Oh. She was asha—ash—she was beat up in her bed by thish guy? And he tried to burn her housh down? So . . . so . . . um . . . I forgot what I was shayin'."

He sighed. "The cashier. Someone tried to burn her house down."

"Oh. She got up, and she shaw the guy."

"Really?"

"Only she couldn't remember, sho they're goin' to hypotizshe her tomorrow. They think she can descsh—tell 'em what he looks like and maybe who he ish. They think it might be shomebody who shops at her shtore. So Ash thinksh thish might be the break he'sh been lookin' for. I hope sho, too. I never get to shee him anymore." She pouted, then yawned. "Shorry. Thish shtuff makesh me shleepy." She gave him a drowsy-lidded smile.

"This is all very interesting, Jillian, but I'm afraid it does little to shed light on your own personal problems. I would much rather discuss that with you, but will you excuse me for just a moment? My assistant is on vacation, and I'm afraid I'm having to fend without her. I need to glance out the door and make sure there aren't any other patients in the waiting room. Wouldn't want them to think we'd left or anything!"

"Okay."

He got to his feet, stepped around behind her to reach the door, then suddenly, in one lightning strike, he whirled, yanked a chloroform-soaked rag out of his pocket, and smacked it over her mouth and nose.

He had underestimated the difference between incapacitating someone who was asleep in his or her own bed and doing it to an awake, upright person. Instantly, she arched her back, throwing her head back forcefully into his stomach. The blow knocked him backward, but he did not let go of his iron grip around her head. Consequently, the chair she was sitting in toppled over backward, knocking him flat on his ass and momentarily loosening his hold on her.

But she was weakening. The natural human reaction to fear was rapid breathing, and all it took normally was one or two strong whiffs of the stuff to render a person unconscious. Still, she flailed her arms, reaching up and clawing frantically at his face, which brought forth a bellow of pain from him. He grabbed a handful of her thick hair and slammed her head into the wall.

She went limp in his arms.

Chest heaving, panting raggedly, he leaned his head back against the wall for a moment to catch his breath and regroup after the struggle. Actually, this had been the easy part. Getting her inert form out of the office, in broad daylight, without being observed would be the trick.

Then he had to dispose of her car.

Closing his eyes for a moment, he forced himself to focus. This was too important for him to blow now. The beast was counting on him. After a moment he found himself chuckling softly and shaking his head.

"You stupid little bitch," he said, giving her head a swipe. "Don't you know that shrinks read the *Dallas Mirror*, too?"

The person who took the phone message from Jillian could tell Ash nothing more than that she'd been trying to reach him. He tried calling her at home but got only the machine. Ash figured if it was an emergency, she'd have said so—she'd have tracked him down if she needed to—so he didn't worry about it. He'd see her at lunch.

He had good news for her. The task force had set

up the sting. Jillian already knew the first part of the plan—for her to tell Sloane in her next session that Dixie Balboa had seen the Firebrand and was prepared to undergo hypnosis that would enable her to give an accurate description of him. If he turned out to be one of her customers, then they could do a photo ID and close the noose around the arsonist's neck. Or so Jillian would tell Sloane.

The truth was that poor, brave Dixie had seen nothing that night.

But Sloane didn't know that. Ash was convinced he would return to Dixie's house that night to finish what he had started.

What Jillian didn't know, since Ash had been waiting on authorization, was that they had arranged to put Dixie in protective custody that night. A dummy would be placed in her bed. The task force would be in hiding around and in the house. They would catch the son of a bitch in the act, and if *that* weren't enough evidence for a search warrant, Ash would swallow a fire hose.

He made it to Jillian's house at twelve-thirty in the afternoon. They'd finally had a key made, so he let himself in and was almost knocked flat by an overjoyed Smokey.

There was no sign of Jillian.

Ash was annoyed. She knew they had a lot of stuff to cover before her appointment. She had to familiarize herself with the miniature transmitter he intended to plant on her for her safety, should the good doctor get any crazy ideas.

Ash wandered into the kitchen and stopped cold. It seemed that he had made a crucial error in judgment. He had left the sack of doggie treats sitting on top of the kitchen table, mistakenly thinking that Smokey couldn't reach them there.

He'd forgotten about chairs, and had underestimated the dog's intelligence and determination. Smokey had apparently worked one of the chairs out from under the table and had used it as a booster to jump up and annihilate the sack, tearing it to pieces with his teeth and scattering bits of doggie treats all over the kitchen. Salt and pepper shakers, sugar bowl, and napkins were scattered far and wide.

"Smokey!" cried Ash.

Immediately, the dog cowered at his feet.

With a big sigh, he squatted down and gave the animal a reassuring pat. "Relax. I'm not gonna beat you, buddy, but I can't promise what your mama might do when she sees this mess."

Ash set about cleaning up. He looked around for a note from Jillian, but couldn't find one. Then he made himself a sandwich and paced the house, stuffing down the sandwich and growing increasingly angry when she failed to call and explain why she was running late.

About two o'clock, Ash got a call from Sam Peterson, who was supposed to come by around three to help prepare Jillian.

"Ash, is Jillian there?"

"No, and I'm pissed about it. I don't know where she is. Why?"

"Have you seen the new edition of the *Mirror*?"

"This week's? No." Ash pulled out a kitchen chair with a scrape and sat down. "What about it?"

"I wanted to ask Jillian about this 'Reflections' column."

Ash blinked stupidly. "What column?"

"Don't get me wrong, it's a beautiful piece, very well done. It's just . . . doesn't it kinda defeat the purpose? I mean, Sloane's supposed to think she's zonked out of her mind on drugs, isn't he? If he reads this, man, he's gonna know it's bogus."

"Shit, Sam. Let me call you back." Slamming down the phone, Ash raced around the house, sorting through ever-present piles of newspapers until he finally unearthed the most recent edition of the *Mirror*.

He flipped through impatiently until he came to Jil-

lian's column. Underneath the "Reflections" headline
was a sub-head that read, "The Song of Life."

Ash began to read with growing dismay. On the one
hand, Sam was right. It was a beautiful piece that
showed how Jillian had matured both as a person and
as a writer.

It may have also spelled out her death warrant.

Jillian awoke in hell.

She was securely bound to a hard wooden chair in
the middle of a large living room with high vaulted
ceilings. She was facing a fireplace in which a roaring
blaze sizzled and popped, making the whole room uncomfortably hot—and causing the tape covering her
mouth to feel sticky. She had a throbbing headache,
and her stomach was roiling. It was dark, but there
were dark shades at the windows, so it was impossible
to tell if it was day or night.

Through the flickering shadowy light of the fire and
what looked like hundreds of candles, she saw a horri-
fying apparition. A bizarre bird of some kind, done in
crude spray-paint graffiti, had been scrawled all over
the wall above the fireplace, all the way up to the
peaked ceiling. Gaudy spray-paint flames burst out behind the bird in clashing colors and filled up the rest
of the wall in a lunatic blaze of demented glory.

The colors were crazed, the lines frenzied.

It was the artwork of a madman.

Dr. Sloane walked into her line of vision, and she
jumped.

Speak of the devil.

"Oh! I see you are awake. Good. I timed my injection well." He was carrying a hairbrush. Stepping behind Jillian, he touched her head and she flinched.

"I'm not going to hurt you," he soothed, dragging
the brush through her hair in a gentle, sensual manner
that made her skin crawl. "I'm just preparing you."

He continued to brush her hair, taking care with
the tangles, while her mind worked furiously and her

eyes darted. She couldn't see a clock anywhere, and her hands were tied behind the chair, so she couldn't read her watch, either.

"Your hair. It's magnificent," he said. "Look at how the Beast plays with it in the light—why, it's the very color of flame! Oh! Beautiful! How it blazes across your shoulders. The Beast will be very pleased with my sacrifice."

Jillian's throat constricted, and she gulped air through her nostrils. *Stay cool*, she told herself.

"I'm sorry about the gag," he said, "but I must work in silence."

I guess you're used to corpses, she thought, fighting a sudden, hysterical urge to laugh.

"I thought of undressing you," he said. "I honestly don't know how these sacrifices are made, having never made one myself, but I couldn't bring myself to do that. It seemed so indecent."

Taking my clothes off is indecent, but killing me isn't. Great, Jillian. When it came time for you to pick a shrink, you went with somebody crazier than you.

"You were always one of the live ones." He continued to pull the hairbrush through her hair in a metronomic rhythm. "Even on your saddest days, you could always find a reason to laugh. So vivacious. So vivid, from your fire-red hair to your shining eyes. You overwhelmed me, you know. Just like all the rest of them. You drained the life force from the room and used it all for your own selfish purposes. You're all alike. As long as the spotlight of attention is on you, you don't care about the ones in the audience, the dead ones, the ones fighting for oxygen, struggling to breathe while you suck all the air out of the room!"

He smacked her head, hard, with the hairbrush. The blow brought tears to her eyes, which caused her nose to run, which brought on panic as she desperately breathed in through her stuffy nostrils, trying not to suffocate.

Trying not to die from sheer fear.

"You don't know what it's like to be dead," he continued. "You think you do, but you don't. No one does." The fire, the warmth in the room, the brush strokes against her scalp, and his voice had a mesmerizing effect on Jillian. She wondered what had been in that injection.

"It's a terror beyond imagining, when the deadness encroaches, when it engulfs you, when you feel its cold embrace and nothing, *nothing* can scare it away! Only the Beast. Only the beautiful Beast." He stepped away from her, the brush drooping from his hand, and moved toward the fire, where he stood silhouetted against it.

"What?" He listened, cocking his head toward the fireplace. "Soon. Patience. All must be *perfect*." He reached up to the mantel and withdrew a beautiful wooden box inlaid with brilliant Oriental designs. Turning back toward her, he moved over to stand in front of her. Then he reached his hand into the box, scooped out a brown powder, and sprinkled it over her head.

Cinnamon.

He stepped back toward her and regarded her with cool detachment. "Only from the nest of the Beast," he mused, his voice so quiet she had to strain to hear, "can the dead be reborn."

Determined not to cringe, she stared at him, thinking about the manic bird that seemed to sprout forth from his head. *The phoenix.* Now it was all starting to make sense. Delirious sense, maybe, but sense.

Thud.

It sounded like a car door closing out on the street.

Jillian's whole body came to electrified attention. *Ash!*

Before she could move or think, Sloane slithered back behind her like the snake he was, wrapped surprisingly strong arms around the chair back and her shoulders, lifted the chair and her up into the air, and

deposited them into a closet. Before she could think
how to knock the chair against the door or otherwise
draw attention to herself, he had pressed that foul
chloroform cloth against her nose again and she could
feel the darkness closing in.

When he opened the front door, he was slightly out
of breath. The man standing on the front porch struck
fear in his heart. He knew that man. That man was
the enemy of the Beast.

"Dr. Sloane?"

"Yes?"

"I'm Ash McGraw, an arson investigator for the
Dallas Fire Department. I believe we've met before?"

"Yes, Mr. McGraw. What can I do for you?"

"I'm looking for a friend of mine. I believe she's a
patient of yours. Jillian Ross?"

"Yes, of course. I've been treating Ms. Ross."

"She was supposed to have an appointment with
you at four o'clock today."

He nodded. "Yes, she had an appointment, but I'm
afraid she didn't show up. I waited until four-thirty. I
must say I was a bit miffed. Patients are supposed
to notify me in advance if they are unable to make
appointments. I'm afraid I'm going to have to charge
her for the time."

McGraw frowned. "Mind if I come in and look
around?"

"Yes, as a matter of fact, I do mind. Why do you
need to come in?"

"I'm conducting a criminal investigation, and now
someone associated with that investigation may be
missing. I have reason to believe she may be in your
house."

Standing very still, he put his mouth into a smile.
"In that case, all right. Come in. Look around. And
then please leave. I have nothing further to say to you
without an attorney present."

He stood back and opened the door wide.

McGraw stepped across the threshold.

Ash crossed the entryway, taking care never to turn his back on Sloane. The room was hot, mainly due to the fire the guy had going in the fireplace. Nobody built fires in fireplaces in Dallas in August.

Ash stopped and gawked.

The room was filled with candles, all of them lit, and overhead lights had been turned on to bleach out the effect. But it wasn't the candles that stopped him cold. It was the psychedelic graffiti that had been spray-painted on the man's living room wall.

Sloane came up beside him in a movement Ash found stealthy. He stepped to the side to put distance between them. Sloane seemed not to notice.

"I'm afraid my young son was a troubled boy before his mother left," said Sloane. "You can see what I had to put up with. It's embarrassing to be a psychiatrist who can't keep his own child in line. I wanted to get him some help, but his mother refused." He sighed melodramatically. "I'm afraid I haven't had time to paint over it yet."

Ignoring the comments, Ash began a quick once-over of the house. Without a warrant he was on shaky ground, but he had been given permission to enter the dwelling, so anything he saw in plain sight that could be evidence in a crime could be seized. Any sign of Jillian would be grounds for arrest, to be sorted out later in custody.

Ash was worried half out of his mind. He and the task force had searched for her in vain most of the afternoon, to no avail. When her car turned up at DFW airport, Ash knew they were in terrible trouble. This lunatic had lured her out of the house and into his spider's web.

And I wasn't there when she needed me, Ash agonized.

He'd finally discovered the note Jillian had left,

which had been knocked off the kitchen table by
Smokey and wound up in the slot between the refrigerator and the kitchen cabinet.

He knew there was a good possibility that she was
here. Desperation clawed at Ash. More than anything,
he wanted cops swarming the place, looking for her.

Even so, he didn't have enough to call out the
SWAT team. Not yet. That's what Ash was doing
now. Trying to find some way to prove Jillian was in
this house so they could move in force.

Frustrated, he walked back down the hall and into
the living room, where the asshole bastard stood waiting, standing strangely still, his arms crossed over his
chest, his eyes glittering cold in the hot room.

Ash moved in close to Sloane, deliberately invading
his personal space. When the man flinched back in
surprise, Ash stepped closer. He said, "Sloane, you're
mine. Do you understand that? If you harm one hair
on that beautiful redhead . . ." He left the threat dangling, and in that moment they both heard a *thump*
and a groan from the direction of the closet.

Ash pivoted as if his feet were on springs and
crossed the room in two graceful leaps, flinging back
the door.

"Jillian!" he cried. "Are you all right?"

Before she could nod, two things happened simulta-
neously: one, he realized he'd forgotten never to turn
his back on Sloane, and two, he smelled the overpowering stench of gasoline.

Chapter Twenty-Eight

Jillian managed to fill her lungs with enough air to blow the sweat and saliva-soaked tape off her mouth. Before she could speak, the tableau was frozen before her, Ash standing in front of the closet door, poised to be her savior, and less than ten feet away, Dr. Sloane, with a yellow plastic five-gallon bucket in his hands that, judging from the odor, was filled with gasoline. Next to him, on one of the tables, sat a candle, its flame burning as yellow as the bucket.

The floor was polished hardwood.

Within two seconds the artist who had painted the phoenix on his living room wall in garish, insane colors, could create a conflagration that would kill them all.

Dr. Sloane spoke first. "I'm afraid you can't stop the sacrifice," he said reasonably to Ash. "The Beast would be most displeased. And you know how he can be when he is angry."

After a moment Ash said, "I have great respect for the Beast. We all do, who have ever fought him."

Dr. Sloane inclined his head. "So you understand. This surprises me, though I suppose it shouldn't."

The idea that she might die, might actually *die*, right here and now, began to set in. The bile of sheer terror rose in her throat. *I don't want to die!* her mind screamed. *Not when I just learned how to live!*

She couldn't resist a futile, panicked moment of

straining against her ropes, but they bound her fast to the chair.

Ash stood tall and very still. His courage was contagious, and she felt herself beginning to grow calm. A shred of poetry crept into her mind from some hidden place. *We only love, only suspire, consumed by either fire or fire.*

All these years, she'd thought T.S. Eliot had to have been drunk when he composed those lines, but now she understood.

It was the fire of passion that made life worth living, that gave breath to work and to love and to creativity. Without passion, life could be as barren as the burned-out houses Ash entered each day.

As empty as the soul of Keegan Sloane.

As if reading her mind, Ash reached behind him and brushed her cheek with his fingertips, a butterfly-tap of love.

"Dr. Sloane," she said.

Both men turned to her in sudden surprise that she was capable of speech.

"If I seemed like one of the live ones to you," she said, "it is only because you gave me the tools to live. Don't you remember? After Randi died, I didn't want to live, either. I blamed myself. I hated myself. You taught me to use the gift of life to love again."

He shook his head, and some of the gasoline sloshed onto the floor at his feet.

Jillian saw Ash's entire body tense up.

"But don't you see? We give life to each other."

He shook his head more vigorously, and more gasoline sloshed at his feet. "Only the Beast can give life."

His eyes caught the firelight and shone with that otherworldly glow that she had noticed in his office before. She had not then understood what was clear now: he was insane, and she would never be able to reason with him.

Surreptitiously Ash shifted the weight in his legs. She could see him balance himself—ever so slightly—

on the balls of his feet. She knew he was preparing himself for whatever was going to come next, and she tried to do the same, sitting upright in the chair and trying to place her weight squarely in the middle.

Sloane glanced over at the fireplace. Jillian had been too focused on him and on Ash to realize that the fire was beginning to die. Immediately she sensed that this was a danger to them all. Ash glanced ever so quickly over his shoulder at her, and she knew that he, too, had noticed.

"The Beast is disappointed!" cried Sloane. "We've wasted time! The sacrifice must be made!"

As he raised the bucket to fling its contents toward Ash and Jillian, a rending *crash* sounded at the front door and it splintered open as the house filled with the banshee yells of a SWAT team in full throttle, brandishing mean-looking weapons and followed closely by Sam Peterson and the other Firebrand Task Force members.

She saw Ash waving his arms over his head in an attempt to stop the invasion, and she saw Sloane startle violently and drop the bucket, which gushed waves of gasoline across the floor in all directions. Before anyone could react to that, Sloane lost his balance and the heel of his shoe slid in the slippery fuel, bringing him down on one knee and knocking the candle next to him over onto the floor.

Then the whole world exploded, and Jillian couldn't tell in the chaos and cacophony of flame and fire who was shrieking because her own screams deafened her.

There was a moment, a suspended flash of infinity, in which all he had ever been and all he ever could have been crystallized in his mind's eye. In that moment, the only sadness, the only regret he felt was for his son, Ian.

And then his world exploded into cold, exquisite pain, pain so fine and so complete that his mind was able to separate itself from his body. He was able to think—right in the midst of it all—*At last, I am one with the Beast*.

The fire was all and all was the fire.

The fire was within and without. The fire was Being; the fire was Life.

The fire was . . .

Sloane went up like a torched Christmas tree.

He uttered not a sound.

With knowledge that is without conscious thought, Ash knew the gasoline vapors would burn the most where the vapors were strongest—at least for a microsecond—before the fireball would spread. That gave him a heart-attack second to scoop up Jillian, chair and all, and dive to the side.

It didn't help. He was too slow. His pants legs caught fire first, and he felt his skin beginning to burn. With a last Herculean effort, he flung her chair as far as he could, halfway across the room. She was still shrieking when she smashed against the wall.

He would never forget either sound.

He didn't have time to see if she was all right because he was on fire, and rolling did not help because the gasoline spread all over the floor and all he was doing was soaking his clothing. He heard himself screaming, and he wasn't the only one—several others were on fire as well, and the house was beginning to fill with choking black smoke and the sickening fumes of gasoline.

Suddenly, he felt himself being blasted from head to foot with a stinging so cold it actually burned worse than the gas.

Then he heard Peterson yell, *"A fucking roomful of fire guys and who do you think had the brains to bring a fire extinguisher? The fucking cops!"*

Epilogue

The Firebrand case made nationwide news, and Jillian had to hire an agent to help her field all the offers for her story. She decided to write a book, and the agent had already discussed it with several publishers, who were asking for a brief proposal he could begin circulating. They'd been lukewarm to the idea until they heard that she'd already been offered six figures for the rights to her story by a movie studio. So things were happening fast.

Ash's burns turned out to be mostly first and second degree on his legs. He would need some skin grafts on one leg, but for the most part, he was hobbling around the house with Smokey at his heels, and griping, which Jillian took to be a good sign.

About a month after the flaming death of Dr. Keegan Sloane and the resolution of the Firebrand case—which had, of course, completely exonerated Derek Thorsen of his ex-partner's death—Jillian had a dream.

She and Ash were getting married, but instead of her walking down the aisle in a white dress while he waited at the altar in a tuxedo, they were walking down the aisle together, hand in hand. Somehow, it seemed right. The church was packed with their family and friends. To Jillian's surprise, Randi's sister was there, holding Toby.

And then, sitting in a pew all by herself, was Randi.

Oddly enough again, it seemed right that Randi was not with Toby.

As Jillian and Ash drew parallel to Randi's seat, she turned and smiled at Jillian. It was the sweetest smile.

There was so much Jillian wanted to say! So much she wanted to ask Randi! But she couldn't, because it was her wedding day and she was about to say her vows.

Still, she couldn't take her eyes off Randi, and as she passed the church pew, Randi smiled again and gave Jillian and Ash a thumbs-up sign.

When Jillian and Ash reached the altar, she glanced over her shoulder to see Randi again, but the pew where she had just been sitting was empty.

Jillian woke up, and for the first time since the riot, she was smiling when she opened her eyes. Her first thought was, *When we get married, I think we'll walk down the aisle together.* Her second thought was, *My mind is finally at peace.*

Dr. Sloane might have turned out to be crazy, but that didn't mean he had not been able to help her. Even so, it was Ash who had done the most to restore balance to Jillian's life—or maybe, to put the balance there in the first place. And it was Ash who had said that when Randi was ready to say something to Jillian, she would.

And so she had.

Later that same day, the Dallas Cowboys were playing football. Ash alternately drowsed and lazily watched the game. Sitting at her desk, she watched him. It seemed that she couldn't get enough of simply watching him.

He opened both eyes and mock-glared at her. "What're you lookin' at?"

"You." She smiled.

He winked at her and held her gaze for a long moment.

Smokey, curled up at her feet, thumped his tail on

the floor. She snuggled her toes against him, turned back to the computer keyboard, and began to write:

In the end, all we have is today. Yesterday is gone and tomorrow may never come. We have today, this moment, this fine fiery breath of life with which to fill our lungs. There is no more.

And in the end, it is enough.

Author's Note

While researching this book, I had access to a great deal of information not readily available to the general public. I was entrusted with this information by fire investigation professionals who believed I would be responsible with it. Therefore, I chose never to show the arsonist actually setting the fires. It was not my intention to provide a blueprint to anyone reading this story who might hold a fire setter's fascination with the Beast.

Deanie Francis Mills
November 5, 1998

Acknowledgments

As usual, I owe a debt of gratitude to some very fine professionals for giving so generously of their time and trouble and expertise to help me get the details right. I could not do what I do without them.

This book would not have been written without the assistance of my friend Fred Goethel of Lafeyette, Indiana, who offered not only many years in the field as a volunteer firefighter and fire protection engineer, but who sent me a college degree's worth of books on the subject. Sometimes authors say things like, "This book could not have been written without the assistance of . . . ," but man, I really mean it!

(One more note to Fred: DAFFY LIVES!)

The same credit must go to my brother-in-law and friend Doug Hale, Deputy Fire Marshal for the Richardson Fire Department in Richardson, Texas. It was Doug who encouraged me to go into the mouth of the Beast, so to speak, by visiting a fire-fighting school, Doug who loaned me his turn-out gear and helmet, and Doug who handed over his books on arson investigation that proved absolutely invaluable to me. He did it because he's that kind of person, but being family helps.

I also want to thank the late, great Chief Terry Don McDowell of the Snyder, Texas, Fire Department, who made it possible for me to hang out with the guys at the Abilene, Texas, "Abilene Area Fire Control

Conference" and training exercises at the Abilene Fire Department training facilities.

Because of Chief McDowell, they put me on the nozzle and gave me the adventure of a lifetime. I want to thank this fine man, who died way, way too soon, and all the great guys of Snyder and Abilene who welcomed me with open arms and even managed to scare up some gloves in size "small."

Chief McDowell—we miss you.

Deputy Chief Tom Oney of the Dallas Fire Department could not have been more helpful. He not only answered all my questions in detail, but he didn't even mind when I told him I was going to invent a crazy guy setting fire to his city. I'm very grateful for his input.

During the writing of this book, I had not only superb input on the underpinnings of the emotionally dead from a fine professional in the field of psychology—Dr. Judith Schlesinger of Dobbs Ferry, New York, who teaches at Pace University—but I had terrific moral support and some great laughs from my sistuh-girlfriend, Judith. Someday we're going to get together and paint the town fuschia.

I was also very honored to accompany one of the finest journalists it has been my pleasure to meet, the award-winning Laura Miller, who took me all around the offices of the *Dallas Observer* and helped me see into the eyes of one who lives and breathes newsprint. Laura is an investigative journalist of the highest creed. So devoted was she to making a difference with her life that she resigned her position with the paper and, at this writing, has actually decided to run for city council herself. You go, girl.

All the guys at the *Observer* offices in downtown Dallas were great, especially editor Julie Lyons. Thank you all, and keep up the good work.

I also want to thank my good friend Ray McPhee, who kept me going at a very difficult time in my life and made me laugh when all I wanted to do was cry.

If all writers had friends like Ray, there wouldn't be any such thing as "writer's block."

And as always, to the love of my life, Kent, and my two beautiful college-kid children, Dustin and Jessica, my ongoing gratitude, fierce love, joyous pride, and admiration. Onward and upward, guys.

PENGUIN PUTNAM INC.
Online

Your Internet gateway to a virtual environment with
hundreds of entertaining and enlightening books from
Penguin Putnam Inc.

*While you're there, get the latest buzz on
the best authors and books around—*

Tom Clancy, Patricia Cornwell, W.E.B. Griffin,
Nora Roberts, William Gibson, Robin Cook,
Brian Jacques, Catherine Coulter, Stephen King,
Jacquelyn Mitchard, and many more!

Penguin Putnam Online is located at
http://www.penguinputnam.com

PENGUIN PUTNAM NEWS

Every month you'll get an inside look at our upcoming
books and new features on our site. This is an ongoing
effort to provide you with the most up-to-date
information about our books and authors.

Subscribe to Penguin Putnam News at
http://www.penguinputnam.com/ClubPPI